HOME ON THE RANCH:
A MONTANA HERO

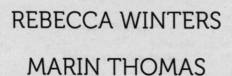

REBECCA WINTERS

MARIN THOMAS

Previously published as *In a Cowboy's Arms* and
Beau: Cowboy Protector

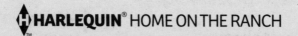

HARLEQUIN® HOME ON THE RANCH

ISBN-13: 978-1-335-50717-4

Home on the Ranch: A Montana Hero
Copyright © 2018 by Harlequin Books S.A.

First published as In a Cowboy's Arms by
Harlequin Books in 2014 and
Beau: Cowboy Protector by Harlequin Books
in 2012.

The publisher acknowledges the copyright
holders of the individual works as follows:

In a Cowboy's Arms
Copyright © 2014 by Rebecca Winters

Beau: Cowboy Protector
Copyright © 2012 by Brenda Smith-Beagley

Recycling programs
for this product may
not exist in your area.

Printed in U.S.A.

HHARLEQUIN®
™www.Harlequin.com

CONTENTS

Rebecca Winters, whose family of four children has now swelled to include five beautiful grandchildren, lives in Salt Lake City, Utah, in the land of the Rocky Mountains. Living near canyons and high alpine meadows full of wildflowers, she never runs out of places to explore. They, plus her favorite vacation spots in Europe, often end up as backgrounds for her romance novels, because writing is her passion, along with her family and church.

Rebecca loves to hear from readers. If you wish to email her, please visit her website, cleanromances.net.

Books by Rebecca Winters

Harlequin Western Romance

Wind River Cowboys

The Right Cowboy

Sapphire Mountain Cowboys

A Valentine for the Cowboy
Made for the Rancher
Cowboy Doctor
Roping Her Christmas Cowboy

Lone Star Lawmen

The Texas Ranger's Bride
The Texas Ranger's Nanny
The Texas Ranger's Family
Her Texas Ranger Hero

Visit the Author Profile page at Harlequin.com for more titles.

IN A COWBOY'S ARMS

REBECCA WINTERS

To Dr. Shane Doyle of the Crow Nation in Montana for his assistance with some aspects of the culture you can't find in a book.

Chapter 1

"Zane? I'm glad you called me back!"

Zane Lawson was the brother-in-law of Sadie Corkin's late mother, Eileen, and uncle of Sadie's half brother. The recently retired navy SEAL had just gone through a painful divorce, yet Sadie could always count on him.

"You sound upset," Zane said. "What's wrong?"

She picked up the Vienna sausage two-year-old Ryan had thrown to the floor and put it in the sink. Her half brother, who had clear blue eyes like his mother, thought he was a big boy and didn't like sitting in the high chair, but today she hadn't given him a choice.

"I got a call from the ranch a little while ago. My father died at the hospital in White Lodge earlier this morning."

Quiet followed for a moment while he digested the news. "His liver?"

"Yes."

"I thought he had years left."

"I did, too. But Millie said the way he drank, it was a miracle that diseased organ of his held up this long." Daniel Corkin's alcohol addiction had caught up with him at a young age, but the impact of the news was still catching up to Sadie. It had been eight years since she'd last seen him. She felt numb inside.

"With news like this, you shouldn't be alone. I'll drive right over."

"What would I do without you?"

"That goes both ways. Have you made any plans yet?"

She'd already talked to Mac and Millie Henson, the foreman and housekeeper on the Montana ranch who'd virtually raised Sadie after her parents' bitter divorce.

"We've decided to hold the graveside service at the Corkin family plot on Saturday. That's as far as I've gotten." She had a lot of decisions to make in the next five days. "I'll have to fly there on Friday."

"Rest assured I'll go to Montana with you so I can help take care of Ryan. See you in a couple of minutes."

"Thank you. Just let yourself in," she said before hanging up. No two-year-old could have a more devoted uncle than Zane.

Ryan had never got to meet his father, Tim Lawson. Tim had owned the software store where Sadie had been hired after she'd moved to San Francisco to be with her mother, Eileen, eight years ago.

Sometimes her mom dropped by the store to go to

lunch with her and that's how Eileen had met Tim. It must have been fate because the two had fallen in love and married soon after. But Tim had died in a car accident while Sadie's mother was still expecting their baby. Tragically, Eileen had passed away during the delivery from cardiac arrest brought on by arrhythmia. Age and stress had been a factor.

Sadie suffered from the same condition as her mother. In fact, just before she'd left the ranch, she'd been advised to give up barrel racing and had been put on medication. If she ever married, getting pregnant would be a huge consideration no matter the efficacy of today's drugs.

Sadie had continued to work in sales for Tim's store even after new management had taken over. Since Eileen's death, however, and taking on fulltime duties as a mother to Ryan, she worked for the store from home.

Tim's younger brother, Zane, had been a tower of strength, and the two of them had bonded in their grief over Tim and Eileen's deaths.

Zane knew the whole painful history of the Corkin family, starting with Sadie's great-grandfather Peter Corkin from Farfields, England. Due to depressed times in his own country, he'd traveled to Montana in 1920 to raise Herefords on a ranch he'd named after the town he'd left behind. When he'd discovered that Rufus Bannock, a Scot on the neighboring ranch who ran Angus cattle, had found oil, the Corkins' own lust for oil kicked into gear, but nothing had turned up so far.

Sadie's father, Daniel Corkin, had been convinced there was oil to be found somewhere on his eighty-five-acre ranch. His raging obsession and jealousy of

the Bannock luck, coupled with his drinking and suspicions about his wife's infidelity, which were totally
unfounded, had driven Eileen away. When she'd filed
for divorce, he said he'd give her one, but she would
have to leave eight-year-old Sadie with him.

Terrified that if she stayed in the marriage he'd kill
her as he'd sworn to do, Eileen had given up custody of
their daughter, forcing Millie Henson, the Corkin housekeeper, to raise Sadie along with her own child, Liz.

Zane also knew Mac and Millie Henson were saints
as far as Sadie was concerned, and she felt she could
never repay their goodness and devotion.

It was their love that had sheltered her and seen her
through those unhappy childhood years with an angry,
inebriated father who'd lost the ability to love. The Hensons had done everything possible to provide a loving
family atmosphere, but Sadie had suffered from acute
loneliness.

Once, when she was fifteen, there'd been a mother-
daughter event at the school. Never really understanding
how her mother could have abandoned her, Sadie had
been in too much pain to tell Millie about the school
function and had taken off on her horse, Candy, not
caring where she was going.

Eventually stopping somewhere on the range, Sadie,
thinking she was alone, had slumped forward in the
saddle, heaving great, uncontrollable sobs. With only
her horse to hear, she'd given way to her grief, wondering if she might die of it....

"What's so terrible on a day like this?"
Sadie knew that deep voice. *Jarod Bannock.*

She lifted her head and stared through tear-drenched eyes at the striking, dark-haired eighteen-year-old. She knew two things about Jarod Bannock. One, his mother had been an Apsáalooke Indian. Two, every girl in the county knocked themselves out for his attention. If any of them had succeeded, she didn't know about it—although he was a neighbor, her family never spoke of him. Her father, whose hatred knew no bounds, held an irrational predjudice against Jarod because of his heritage.

"I miss my mother."

Jarod smiled at her, compassion in his eyes. "When I miss mine, I ride out here, too. This is where the First Maker hovers as he watches his creation. He says, 'If you need to contact me, you will find me along the backbone of the earth where I travel as I guard my possessions.' He knows your sadness, Sadie, and has provided you a horse to be your comfort."

His words sent shivers up her spine. She felt a compelling spirituality in them, different from anything she'd experienced at church with Millie.

"Do you want to see some special horses?" he asked her. "They're hard to find unless you know where to look for them."

"You mean, the feral horses Mac sometimes talks about?"

"Yes. I'll take you to them."

Having lost both parents himself, Jarod understood what was going on inside her better than anyone else. Wordlessly he led her up the canyon, through the twists and turns of rock formations she'd never seen before.

They rode for a good five minutes before he reined

to a stop and put a finger to his lips. She pulled back on Candy's reins and waited until she heard the pounding of hooves. Soon a band of six horses streaked through the gulch behind a large, grayish tan stallion with black legs and mane. The power of the animals mesmerized her.

"You see that grullo in the lead? The one with the grayish hairs on his body?"

"Yes," she whispered breathlessly.

"That's his harem."

"What's a harem?"

"The mares he mates with and controls. Keep watching and you'll see some bachelor stallions following them."

Sure enough a band of eight horses came flying through after the first group. "Why aren't they all together?"

"They want control of Chief's herd so they can mate with his mares, but he's not going to give it to them."

She darted him a puzzled glance. "How do you know his name is Chief?"

"It came to me in a dream."

Sadie wasn't sure if Jarod was teasing her. "No it didn't." She started laughing.

The corner of his mouth twitched. It changed his whole countenance, captivating her. "He has a majestic bearing," he continued, "like Plenty Coups."

From her Montana history class she knew Chief Plenty Coups was the last great chief of the Crow Nation. "Where do these horses come from?"

"They've lived here for centuries. One day Chief will be mine."

"Is that all right? I mean, isn't it against the law to catch one of them?"

A fierce expression crossed his face. "I don't take what doesn't belong to me. Because he's young, I'll give him another two years to get to know me. He saw me today, and he's seen me before. He'll see me again and again and start to trust me. One day he'll come to me of his own free will and eat oats out of my hand. When he has chosen me for himself, then it will be all right."

Sadie didn't doubt he could make it happen. Jarod had invisible power. A short time ago she'd thought she was going to die of sorrow, but that terrible pain had been lifted because of him.

That was the transcendent moment when Sadie's worship of Jarod Bannock began in earnest and she'd fallen deeply in love.

For the next three years Sadie had spent every moment she could steal out riding where she might run into him. Each meeting became more important to both of them. Once he'd started kissing her, they lived to be together and talked about marriage. Two days before her eighteenth birthday she rode to their favorite spot in a meadow filled with spring flowers—purple lupine and yellow bells. Her heart exploded with excitement the second she galloped over the rise near Crooked Canyon and saw him.

His black hair gleamed in the last rays of the sun. Astride his wild stallion Chief, he was more magnificent than nature itself. The stamp of his Caucasian father and Apsáalooke mother had created a face and body as unique as the two mountain blocks that formed the Pryor Mountains on both sides of the Montana-Wyoming border. Through erosion those mountains had risen from the prairie floor to eight thousand feet, creating a sanctuary for rare flora and fauna; a private refuge for her and Jarod.

She'd become aware of him as a child. As she'd grown older, she'd see him riding in the mountains. He'd always taken the time to talk to her, often going out of his way to answer her questions about his heritage.

His mother's family, the Big Lodge clan, had been part of the Mountain Crow division and raised horses. They were known as *Children of the Large-Beaked Bird*. Sadie never tired of his stories.

He told her about archaeological evidence of his ancestors in the area that dated back more than 10,000 years. The Crow Nation considered the "Arrow Shot Into Rock" Pryor Mountain to be sacred. Jarod had explained that all the mountain ranges in the territory of the Crow were sacred. He'd taught her so many things....

She looked around the meadow now. Two days before her birthday their talk had turned into a physical expression of mutual love. They'd become lovers for the first time under the dark canopy of the sky.

To be that close to another human, the person she adored more than life, filled her with an indescribable joy that was painful in its intensity. They'd become a part of each other, mind, heart and body.

She never wanted to leave him, but he'd forced her to go home, promising to meet again the next night so they could slip away to get married. He intended to be with her forever.

He pulled her against his hard body one more time, covering her face and hair in frenzied kisses. She was so hungry for him she caught his face in her hands and found his mouth.

After a few minutes he grasped her arms and held her from him. "You have to go home now."

"Not yet—" She fought to move closer to him, but he was too powerful for her. "My father will think I'm still at Liz's house studying for finals."

He shook his head. "We can't take any more chances, Sadie. You know as well as I do that with his violent temper your father will shoot me on sight if he finds out where you've been tonight. You need to go home now. Tomorrow night we'll leave for the reservation and be married. From then on you'll be known as Mrs. Jarod Bannock."

"Don't send me away," she begged. "I can't stand to be apart from you."

"Only one more night separates us, Sadie. Meet me here tomorrow at the same time. Bring your driver's license and your birth certificate. We'll ride over to the firebreak road where I'll have the truck and trailer parked. Then we'll leave for White Lodge.

"The next morning you'll be eighteen. We'll stop to get our marriage license. There'll be no waiting period. All you have to do is sign a waiver that you accept full responsibility for any consequences that might arise from failure to obtain a blood test for rubella immunity before marriage. That's it. After that we'll drive to the reservation."

She'd gone to the reservation with him several times

over the years and once with his sister, Avery. Everyone in his Crow family had made her feel welcome.

"Remember—you'll be eighteen. I've made all the preparations for our wedding with my uncle Charlo. As one of the tribal elders, he'll marry us. There'll be at least a hundred of the tribe gathered."

"So many!"

"Yes. Our marriage is a celebration of life. You'll be eighteen and your father will have no rights over you by then."

She stared into his piercing black eyes. "What about your grandparents?" Sadie had loved Ralph and Addie Bannock the moment she'd met them. "How do you think they really feel about us getting married?"

"You have to ask? They're crazy about you. I've already told them our wedding plans. They're helping me any way they can. Earlier today my grandmother told me she can't wait for us to be living under the same roof with them until we can build our own place. Don't forget they loved your mother and like to think of you as the daughter they were never able to have. Surely you know that."

The words warmed her heart. "I love them, too." Sadie shivered with nervous excitement. "You really haven't changed your mind? You want to marry me? The daughter of the man who has hated your family forever?"

"Your father has something wrong in his head, but it has nothing to do with you." His dark brows furrowed, giving him a fierce look. "I made you an oath." He kissed her throat. "I've chosen you for my wife. How could you possibly doubt I want to marry you after what we've shared?"

"I don't doubt it," she said, her voice trembling. "You know I've loved you forever. Having you as my husband is all I've ever dreamed about. Oh, Jarod, I love you so much. I can't wait—"

He caressed her hair, which cascaded to her waist, and then his hands fell away. "Tomorrow night we'll be together forever. But you've got to go while I still have the strength to let you go."

"Why don't we just leave for the reservation now?"

"You know why. You're still seventeen and the risk of getting caught is too great." Jarod reached into his pocket and pulled out a beaded bracelet, which he fastened around her wrist. "This was made by my mother's family. After the ceremony you'll be given the earrings and belt that go with it."

"It's so beautiful!" The intricate geometric designs stood out in blues and pinks.

"Not as beautiful as you are," he said, his voice deep and velvety soft. "Now you have to go." He walked her to her horse. Once she'd mounted, he climbed on his stallion and rode with her to the top of the hill. They leaned toward each other for one last hungry kiss. "Tomorrow night, Sadie."

"Tomorrow night," she whispered against his lips.

Tomorrow night. Tomorrow night. Tomorrow night. Her heart pounded the message all the way home.

Remembering that night now, Sadie felt the tears roll down her face. Their love affair had turned into a disaster, permanently setting daughter and father against each other. She was forced to leave for California and never saw Jarod again. And the Hensons had been left to deal with their drunken boss until the bitter end. Guilt had swamped Sadie, but she'd had no choice except to leave the ranch to prevent her father from carrying out his threat to kill Jarod.

While her mind made a mental list of what to do first before she and Zane left for Montana, she hung up the phone and took a clean cloth to wash Ryan's face and hands. "Come on, sweetheart." She kissed his light brown hair. "Lunch is over. Time for a nap."

While she changed his diaper, she looked out the upstairs window of the house she'd lived in with her mother and Tim on Potrero Hill. The view of San Francisco Bay was spectacular from here.

But much as she loved this city where her mother had been born and raised—where she'd met Daniel when he'd come here on business—Sadie was a Montana girl through and through. With her father's death, her exile was over. *She could go home.*

She longed to be back riding a horse through the pockets of white sweet clover that perfumed the land in the spring. Though she'd made friends in San Francisco and had dated quite a bit, she yearned for her beloved ranch and her oldest friends.

As for Jarod Bannock, eight years of living away from him had given her perspective.

He was a man now, destined to be the head of the Bannock empire one day. According to Liz he had a new love interest. Obviously he hadn't pined for Sadie all these years. And she wasn't a lovesick teenager who'd thought her broken heart would never heal after her father's treachery against Jarod. He'd been the one behind the truck accident that had put Jarod in the hospital. But that was ancient history now. She was a twenty-six-year-old woman who couldn't wait to take her half brother back to Farfields Ranch where they belonged.

Ryan might end up being her only child, which made him doubly precious to her. One day Ryan Corkin Lawson would grow up and become head of the ranch and make it a success. In time he'd learn how to do every chore and manage the accounts. She'd teach him how to tend the calves that needed to be culled from the herd.

That had been Sadie's favorite job as a young girl. The sickly ones were brought to the corral at the side of the ranch house. Sadie had named them after the native flora: yellow bell, pussytoes, snowberry, pearly. Ryan would love it!

Before she left his room, she hugged and kissed the precious little boy. While she waited for Zane, she went into the den and phoned the Methodist Church in White Lodge, where she and her mother had once attended services.

In a few minutes she got hold of Minister Lyman, a man she didn't know. Together they worked out the particulars about the service and burial. The minister would coordinate with the Bitterroot Mortuary, where the hospital would transport her father's body.

To the minister's credit he said nothing negative about her father. He only expressed his condolences and agreed to take care of the service. After thanking him, she rang off and sat at the computer to start writing the obituary. She could do everything online. Within a couple of hours the announcement would come out in the *Billings Gazette* and *Carbon County News.* How should she word it?

On May 6, Daniel Burns Corkin of Farfields Ranch, Montana, passed away from natural causes at the age of fifty-three after being the cruelest man alive.

Too many words? On second thought why not make it simpler and put what the munchkins sang when Dorothy arrived in Oz.

"Ding Dong! The Wicked Witch is dead!"

"Hey, boss."

"Glad you came in the truck, Ben. I need you to get this new calf to one of the hutches before a predator comes after it. She has a broken foot from being stepped on." There was no need to phone Liz Henson, White Lodge's new vet. Jarod's sister, Avery, could splint it. "Would you help me put her in the back?"

"Sure." Together they lifted the calf, careful not to do any more damage, but the mother bellowed in protest.

"I know how you feel," Jarod said over his shoulder. "Your baby will be back soon."

Ben chuckled. "You think she understands you?"

"I guess we'll find out the answer to that imponderable in the great hereafter." Jarod closed the tailgate and then shoved his cowboy hat to the back of his head, shifting his gaze to the new foreman of the Hitting Rocks Ranch. The affable manager showed a real liking for his sister, but so far that interest hadn't been reciprocated. Ben needed to meet someone else. "You were going to tell me something?"

"Avery sent me to find you. I guess your phone's turned off."

"The battery needs recharging. What's up?"

"She wanted you to know Daniel Corkin died at White Lodge Hospital early this morning of acute liver failure."

What?

Jarod staggered in place.

Sadie's monster father had really given up the ghost?

"The Hensons were with him. They got word to Liz and she phoned Avery."

The news he hadn't expected to come for another decade or more sent a great rushing wind through his ears, carrying painful whispers from the past that he'd tried to block out all these years. They came at him from every direction, dredging up bittersweet memories so clear they could have happened yesterday.

But Jarod managed to control his emotions in front of Ben. "Appreciate you telling me." After a pause he said, "If Avery can't tend to the calf, I'll call Liz. You go on. I'll follow on my horse Blackberry."

Ben nodded and took off.

Long after the truck disappeared, Jarod stood in the pasture to gentle the calf's mother, adrenaline gushing through his veins. Sadie would show up long enough to bury her father. Then what?

He threw his head back, taking in the cotton-ball clouds drifting across an early May sky. With Sadie's mother buried in California, it no doubt meant the end of Farfields. Sadie hadn't stepped on Montana soil in eight years. The note he'd received in the hospital after his truck accident when she'd left the ranch had been simple enough.

> *Jarod,*
> *You begged me to consider carefully the decision to marry you. I have thought about it and realize it just won't work. I'm going to live with my mother in California, but I want you to know I'll always treasure our time together.*
> *Sadie.*

For eight years Jarod had done his damnedest to avoid any news of her and for the most part had succeeded. *Until now...*

By the time he rode into the barn, twilight was turning into night. He levered himself off Blackberry and led him into the stall.

"You're kind of late, aren't you?"

Jarod couldn't remember when there wasn't a baiting tone in Ned's voice. Out of the corner of his eye he saw the youngest of his four cousins walking toward him. Ned's three siblings were good friends with Jarod.

He scrutinized Ned, who was a year younger than him. Even that slight age difference upset Ned, but the rancor he felt for Jarod ran much deeper for other reasons. They were both Bannocks and lived in separate houses on the Hitting Rocks Ranch, but the fact that Jarod's mother had been a full Crow Indian was an embarrassment to the bigoted Ned. He liked to pretend Jarod wasn't part of the Bannock family and took great pleasure in treating him like a second-class citizen.

Ned was also still single and had always had a thing for Sadie Corkin, feelings that were never reciprocated. "It took me longer than usual to check out the new calves. How about you? Were you able to get the old bale truck fixed today or do we need to buy a new one?"

"If it comes to that, I'll talk it over with my dad."

Grant Bannock, Jarod's uncle, was a good man. But he had his hands full with Ned, who'd been spoiled most of his life and did his share of drinking. Jarod often had to keep a close eye on him to make certain he got his chores done. Not even Tyson Bannock, Ned's grandfather and Ralph's brother, could control him at times.

Ned had always dreamed of marrying Sadie Corkin and one day being in charge of both ranches. But that dream was in no one's interest but his own. Ralph Bannock, Jarod's grandfather, was the head of the ranch and his closeness to Jarod was like pouring salt on Ned's open wound.

Jarod patted the horse's rump before turning to his cousin. "Was there something else you wanted?"

Ned had looped his thumbs in the pockets of his jeans and stared at Jarod, who at six foot three topped him by two inches. Jarod saw a wild glitter in those hazel eyes that felt like hatred, confirming his suspicions that this encounter had to do with the news Ben had brought him earlier. Now that Sadie would be coming back for the burial, Ned wanted Jarod out of the picture.

"I thought you should know old man Corkin kicked the bucket early this morning."

Jarod didn't bother telling his cousin he was way ahead of him.

"If I were you," Ned warned, "I wouldn't get any ideas about showing my face at the funeral since he hated your guts." Jarod noted the heightened venom in his voice.

There'd been a lot of hate inside Daniel that had nothing to do with Jarod. In that regard Sadie's father and Ned had a lot in common, but no good would come of pointing that out to his cousin.

Jarod's uncle Charlo would describe Ned as an "empty war bonnet." The thought brought a faint smile to his lips. "Thanks for the advice."

Ned smirked. "No problem. Because of you there's been enough tension between the Corkins and the Bannocks. Or maybe you're itching to start another War of the Roses and manipulate your grandfather into buying Farfields for you. To my recollection that battle lasted a hundred years."

"I believe that was the Hundred Years War." Ned's ridiculous plan to acquire Sadie and the Corkin ranch in the hope oil could be found there was pitiable. "The War of the Roses lasted thirty years and the Scots only triumphed for ten of them. If my grandmother were still alive, we could check the facts with her."

Addie Bannock loved her history, and Jarod loved hearing what she could tell him about that part of his ancestry.

Even in the semidarkness of the barn, he detected a ruddy color creeping into Ned's cheeks. For once his cousin didn't seem to have a rebuttal.

"Do you know what's important, Ned? Daniel's death

puts an end to any talk of war between the two families, for which we can all be grateful. I have a feeling this news will bring new life to both our grandfathers. Those two brothers are sick to death of it. Frankly, so am I. Good night."

As he walked out of the barn, Ned's last salvo caught up to him.

"If you think this is over, then you're as *loco* as Charlo." It sounded like a threat.

Jarod kept walking. Daniel Corkin's death had shaken everyone, including his troubled cousin Ned.

Chapter 2

"...And so into Your hands, O merciful God, we commend Your servant Daniel Burns Corkin. Acknowledge, we humbly beseech You, a sheep of Your own fold, a lamb of Your own flock, a sinner of Your own redeeming. Receive Daniel into the arms of Your mercy, into the blessed rest of everlasting peace, and into the glorious company of those who have gone before. Amen."

After the collective "amens," Minister Lyman looked at Sadie before eying the assembled crowd. She hadn't noticed the people who'd attended. In fact, she hadn't talked to anyone yet.

"While they finish the work here, Daniel's daughter, Sadie Corkin, and the Hensons, who've worked for Daniel all these years and are like a second family to

Sadie, invite all of you back to the ranch house for refreshments."

The house, with the extraordinary backdrop of the Pryor Mountains, was only a two-minute walk from the family plot with its smattering of pine trees. Sadie had already ordered a headstone, but it wouldn't be ready for a few weeks.

She felt an arm slip around her shoulders. "Let me take Ryan for you so you can have some time alone."

When she looked up she saw Liz Henson, her dearest, oldest friend. They'd been like sisters growing up. Even while Liz attended vet school at Colorado State, they'd stayed in close touch. "Are you sure?"

"Of course I am." Liz kissed Ryan's cheek. "Since you flew in yesterday, we've been getting to know each other, haven't we?" She plucked him out of Sadie's arms. "Come with me, little baby brother, and I'll get you something to eat."

At first he protested, but eventually his voice grew faint. Liz had a loving way about her. Sadie knew he was in the best of hands.

Zane walked up to her. She saw the compassion in his blue eyes. "It was a lovely service. Your father is being laid to rest with all the dignity he would have wanted."

"He wanted Mother with him, but I'm glad she's buried with Tim. He brought her the joy she deserved in this life."

"You brought her joy the day you were born, and she'd be so proud you're raising Ryan. I plan to help you any way I can. I hope you know that."

"You're a wonderful man, Zane. Ryan is so lucky to have you in his life."

"He's a little Tim."

"I know. Those dimples get to me every time," she told him, smiling.

"Yup. Don't forget he's my life now, too!"

"As if I could forget."

Zane, she knew, had reached an emotional crossroads in his life and was still struggling to find himself. There'd been so many losses in his life, her heart went out to him. Thank heaven they had Ryan to cling to.

The afternoon sun caused Zane to squint. "Everyone's gone inside the house. I'm going to help Liz. If you need us, you know where to find us."

She nodded. The mortuary staff was waiting for her to leave so they could lower the casket and finish their part of the work, but she couldn't seem to get up from the chair they'd brought for her. Since the phone call from Millie five days ago, her life had been a blur. She barely remembered the flight from San Francisco to Billings, let alone the drive in the rental car with Zane and Ryan to the ranch. Someone could use her for a pin cushion and she wouldn't feel a thing.

Sadie counted a dozen large sprays of flowers around the grave site. Such kindness for a man who'd made few friends humbled her. The huge arrangement with the gorgeous purple-and-white flowers kept attracting her attention. For as long as she could remember that color combination had been her favorite.

Needing to know who'd sent the floral offering, she stood and walked around to gather the cards. She recognized every name. So many people who'd touched their lives and had loved her mother were still here offering to help in any way they could. When she pulled out the insert from the purple-and-white flowers, her breath caught.

Sadie,
Your mother and father's greatest blessing. Let this be a time for all hearts to heal.
Love, Ralph Bannock and all the Bannocks—including the good, the bad and the ugly. Hope you haven't forgotten I'm the ugly one.

She could hear Ralph saying it. He could be a great tease and she'd forgotten nothing.

A laugh escaped her lips as she put the cards in the pocket of her suit jacket. How she'd loved and missed him and Addie! Sadie had sent purple-and-white flowers when Addie had passed away, and today he'd reciprocated. She would have come for his wife's funeral if there'd been any way possible, but fear of what her father would do to Jarod if she came back had prevented her from showing up.

There could have been so much loving and happiness in her family, but her father's demons had put them through years of grief that affected the whole community. Suddenly she was sobbing through the laughter.

Needing to hide, Sadie hurried over to the granddaddy pine where she used to build nests of pine needles beneath its branches for the birds. She leaned against the base of the trunk while she wept buckets. How was she going to get through today, let alone tomorrow?

Her father's flawed view of life, his cruelty, had occupied so much of her thinking, she didn't know how to fill that negative space now that he was gone. She felt flung into a void, unable to get her bearings. And then she heard a male voice behind her. A voice like dark velvet. Only one man in this world sounded like that.

"Long ago my uncle Charlo gave me good advice. Walk forward, and when the mountain appears as the obstacle, turn each stone one by one. Don't try to move the mountain. Instead, turn each stone that makes up the mountain."

Jarod...

She hadn't heard that voice since her teens, but she'd recognize it if it had been a hundred years ago. His sister, Avery, had once told Sadie he was known in the tribe as "Sits in the Center" because he was part white and straddled two worlds of knowledge.

Since he'd just picked up on Sadie's tortured thoughts, she couldn't deny he had uncanny abilities. But too many years had passed and they were no longer the same people. The agony of loss she'd once felt had been replaced by a dull pain that had never quite gone away. Wiping the moisture off her cheeks with the backs of her hands, she turned to face him.

He was a twenty-nine-year-old man now, tall and muscled, physical traits he'd inherited from his handsome father, Colin Bannock. But the short hair she remembered was now a shiny mane of midnight-black, caught at the nape with a thong. His complexion was bronzed by the sun and she picked out a scar near the edge of his right eyebrow she hadn't seen before. No doubt he'd received that in the truck accident that left him unconscious.

He wore a dark dress suit with a white shirt, like the other men, but there was something magnificent about his bearing. The powerful combination of his Crow and Bannock heritage meant no man was Jarod's equal in looks or stature.

She sensed a new confidence in him that had come with maturity. The coal-black of his piercing eyes beneath arched brows the same color sent unexpected chills down Sadie's spine.

The whole beautiful look of him caused her to quiver. Once she'd lain in his arms and they'd made glorious love. Did he ever think about that night and their plans to marry the day she turned eighteen?

After she'd fled to California, she'd prayed he would ignore the words in her note and call Millie. Once he'd left the hospital and got her number in California from the housekeeper, she'd expected his call so she could explain about the traumatic episode at the ranch with her father.

But Jarod hadn't called Millie, and there had been no word from him at all. Learning that he was out of the hospital and on his feet again, she'd prayed she would hear from him. But after a month of waiting, she'd decided he really was relieved they hadn't gotten married, so she hadn't tried to reach him.

That's when she'd given him another name: *Born of Flint*. The Crow nation referred to the Pryor Mountains as the Hitting Rock Mountains because of the abundance of flint found there, which they chipped into sharp, bladelike arrowheads. Jarod's silence had been like one of those blades, piercing her heart with deadly accuracy.

"It's good to see you again, Sadie, even if it's under such painful circumstances," he said. "Ned warned me not to show up, but my grandfather's been ill and asked me to represent him."

And if he hadn't asked you, Jarod, would you still have come?

"He's too tired to go out. Do you mind?"

Did she mind that Jarod's unexpected appearance had just turned her life upside down for the second time?

"Of course not. Liz told me Ralph has suffered recurring bouts of pneumonia. I love him. Always have. Please tell him the flowers he sent are breathtaking." She plucked a white-and-purple flower from the arrangement and handed them to him. "These are from me. Tell him I'll come to see him Tuesday evening. By then I'll be more settled."

He grasped the stems. "If I tell him that, then you have to promise you won't disappoint him. He couldn't take it."

She sucked in her breath. *You mean the way you disappointed me after you said you would always love me? Not one word or phone call from you in eight years about my note? Surely you knew there had to be a life and death reason behind it.*

"Sadie?"

Another voice and just in time.

She tore her gaze away from Jarod. Zane was walking toward her, holding a fussy Ryan. "Here she is, sport." The moment he put the little boy in her arms, Ryan calmed down. This child was the sunshine in her life.

Zane smiled at them. "He was good for a while, but with all those unfamiliar faces, he missed you."

Sadie clung to her baby brother, needing a buffer against Jarod, who stood there looking too splendid for words. She finally averted her eyes and kissed Ryan. "I missed you, too." She cleared her throat, realizing she'd forgotten her manners. "Zane Lawson, have you met Jarod Bannock, our neighbor to the east?"

He nodded. "Liz introduced us."

At a loss for words in the brief silence that followed, Sadie shifted Ryan to her other arm. "I'm sorry I left you so long, sweetheart. Come on. There are a lot of people I need to thank for coming."

She glanced one last time at Jarod over Ryan's head. "It's been good to see you, too, Jarod," she lied. Her pain was too great to be near him any longer. "Thanks for the wise counsel from your uncle Charlo. In truth I *have* come back to a mountain. Getting through the rest of this day will be like turning over that first stone."

As Jarod grimaced, Sadie hugged her brother harder. "Please give Uncle Charlo my regards the next time you see him. I always was a little in awe of him."

After eight years Jarod finally had his answer. She'd meant every word in the note she'd sent him. *Not one phone call or letter from her in all that time.* It appeared the sacred vow he'd made to her hadn't touched her soul.

Gutted by feelings he'd never experienced before, he watched the three of them walk back to the house. They looked good together, at ease with each other. Comfortable. Just how comfortable he couldn't tell yet. Was there something in the genes that attracted the Corkin women to the Lawson brothers?

But the girl he remembered with the long silky blond

hair hanging almost to her waist was gone. Except for her eyes—Montana blue like the sky—everything else had changed. Her mouth looked fuller. She'd grown another inch.

Blue jeans and a Western shirt on a coltish figure had been replaced with a sophisticated black suit that outlined the voluptuous curves of her body. The gold tips of her hair, styled into a windblown look, brushed the collar of a lavender blouse. And high heels, not cowboy boots, called his attention to her long, beautiful legs.

There was an earthy element about her not apparent eight years ago. He hadn't been able to identify it until she'd caught the towheaded boy in her arms. Then everything clicked into place. She'd become a mother as surely as if she'd given birth. He'd seen the same thing happen in the Crow clan—they watched out for the adopted ones. The experience defined Sadie in a new way. It explained the hungry look in the uncle's eyes.

Jarod was flooded by jealousy, an emotion so foreign he could scarcely comprehend it, and the flowers meant for his grandfather dropped to the ground. Not wanting to be seen, he stole around the side of the ranch house and had almost reached his truck when Connor caught up to him.

"Jarod? Wait a minute! Where's the fire?"

His head whipped around and he met his younger brother's brown eyes. Connor had been through a painful divorce several years ago, but his many steer wrestling competitions when he wasn't working on the ranch with Jarod had kept him from sinking into a permanent depression. This past week he'd been away at a rodeo in Texas, but after learning about Daniel, he'd come home for the funeral.

"Avery and I looked for you before the service."

"My flight from Dallas was late. I just got here. Come inside with me."

That would be impossible. "I can't, but Avery will be glad to see you got here."

Connor cocked his dark blond head in concern. "Are you all right?"

Jarod's lungs constricted. "Why wouldn't I be?"

"I don't know. You seem…different."

Yes, he was different. The passionate, stars-in-her-eyes woman who'd made him feel immortal had disappeared forever.

"I promised grandfather I wouldn't be long. He wants to hear about the funeral and know who attended. He has great affection for Sadie."

His brother nodded in understanding. "Don't we all."

"How's the best bulldogger in the state after your last event?" The question was automatic, though Jarod's mind was somewhere else, lost in those pain-filled blue eyes that had looked right through him.

"I'm not complaining, but I'll tell you about it later. Listen—as long as you're going back to the house, tell grandfather I'll be home as soon as I've talked to Sadie. How is she? It's been years since I last saw her."

A lifetime, you mean.

"She's busy taking care of her brother, Ryan." That shouldn't have made Jarod feel as if he'd been spirited to a different universe.

Connor shook his head. "It's incredible what happened to that family. Maybe now that Daniel's gone she'll have some peace. Avery told me on the phone she doesn't have a clue what Sadie's going to do now."

"I would imagine she'll go back to San Francisco with Ryan and his uncle."

Connor looked stunned. "Do you think the two of them are…?" He didn't finish what he was going to say.

"I don't know."

"He's old enough to be her father!"

"He certainly doesn't look it, but age doesn't always matter." The way her eyes had softened when she'd looked at Zane Lawson had sent a thunderbolt through Jarod. "Why don't you go inside and make your own judgment. I've got to leave. Grandfather's waiting."

"Okay. See you back at the house."

But once Jarod had driven home, he went straight to his room and changed into jeans and a shirt. Before he talked to his grandfather, who was still asleep according to his caregiver, Martha, Jarod needed to expend a lot of energy.

He'd made tentative plans to have dinner in town with Leslie Weston after the funeral. She was the woman he'd been dating lately, but he couldn't be with her right now, not after seeing Sadie again. He would have to reschedule with her. For the moment the only way to deal with his turmoil was to ride into the mountains. He'd take his new stallion up Lost Canyon. Volan needed the exercise.

Though he started out in that direction, midway there he found himself changing course. After eight years of avoiding the meadow, he galloped toward it as if he were on automatic pilot. When he reached their favorite spot, he dismounted and slumped into the bed of wildflowers. Their intoxicating scent was full of her.

Jarod remembered that last night with her as if it was yesterday. After their time together, he'd followed her to make sure she reached the Corkin ranch safely. He'd felt great pride that she rode like the wind. She and Liz Henson had provided stiff competition for the other barrel racers around the county, until Sadie suddenly quit. When Jarod had asked her about it, she'd said it had taken too much time away from being with him.

When he could no longer see her blond hair whipping around her, he'd set off the long way home, circling her property to avoid being seen. But before he'd reached the barn he'd had the impression he was being followed.

In a lightning move he turned Chief around and bolted toward the clump of pines where he'd detected human motion. As he moved closer he heard a curse before his stalker rode away, but Jarod had the momentum. He knew in his gut it was Ned. In half a minute he'd cut him off, forcing him to stop.

He looked at his cousin. "Where are you going in such an all-fired hurry this time of night?"

"None of your damn business."

"It's a good thing I knew it was you or I might have pulled you off Jasper to find out who's been keeping tabs on me. I would think you'd have better things to do with your time."

"You've been with Sadie." Ned's accusation was riddled with fury.

It was possible Ned had seen him and Sadie together tonight, but he decided to call his bluff, anyway. "If you know that for a fact, then why isn't my grandfather out here looking for me right now, waiting to read me the riot act? Wait, I've got an idea. Why don't you ride over to the Corkin ranch and ask Sadie to go for a midnight ride with you?"

When Ned said nothing, Jarod continued his taunting.

"Oh, I forgot. Her father forbid any Bannock to come near her years ago. Have you forgotten he vowed to fill us full of buckshot if he ever caught one of us on his property? Of course, if you can figure out a way to get past Daniel, you can see what kind of reception you'll receive from her."

"Damn you to hell," Ned snarled as Jarod headed for the barn in the distance.

Grandfather would be furious with him for baiting Ned. It was a mistake he shouldn't have made this close to leaving with Sadie, but his cousin had chosen the wrong moment to confront Jarod, who was too full of adrenaline not to react.

For two cents he'd felt like knocking him cold. Ned had been asking for it for years, always sneaking around to catch him with Sadie. No doubt he planned to tell Daniel in the hope Sadie's father would finish Jarod off. For his grandparents' sake, Jarod had never stepped on Corkin property and he'd held back his anger at Ned. But Ned's obsession with Sadie seemed to be getting out of control.

Worse, Jarod couldn't get that night years ago out of his mind.

Once he'd removed Chief's saddle and had brushed him down, he entered the ranch house and found his grandparents in the den. That was the place where they always talked business at the end of the day. It was time to put his plans into action.

Addie hugged him. "I'm glad you're home. You missed dinner. Are you all right?"

"Yes. Everything is set for our marriage. Thank you for standing behind me in this."

"If your father were still alive, he'd understand and approve. We know it's the Crow way to marry young. You're a lot like your dad and have always known what you wanted."

"I'm thankful for your understanding and help, but right now my biggest concern is Ned. He must have been following me tonight. In order for him not to find out what's going on, I'm setting up a smoke screen. I'll pretend Chief is favoring his hind leg.

"After chores tomorrow I'll put Chief in the trailer and drive him to the clinic in White Lodge. If Ned finds out I paid a visit to Sam Rafferty for an X-ray, it should throw him off the scent long enough for us to be married."

"That's as good an idea as any," his grandfather said. "We decided not to tell Connor and Avery your plans. It's crucial they know nothing so that Ned doesn't pick up on any change in their behavior. He's a talker when he drinks and it could get back to Daniel."

Jarod nodded. "Where are they?"

Addie smiled. "Connor's in town with friends and Avery is spending the night with Cassie while they study for their finals. They'll be graduating from high school in two weeks."

"Sadie will be getting her diploma right along with them, but by then she'll be my wife. Here's what I'm going to do. After I leave the vet clinic, I'll drive up to the mountains where Sadie and I will meet. From there we'll go to the reservation to be married and spend a couple of days with Uncle Charlo and his family. We'll be home Sunday night in time for her to be back in school."

His grandfather got up from the chair and hugged him. "When you two arrive, we'll all celebrate."

Jarod's heart was full of love for his grandparents, who'd always supported him.

"Tell me what you need me to do before I leave tomorrow afternoon and I'll get it done."

"Why don't we go over the quarterly accounts after breakfast?" Ralph suggested.

"Sounds good."

He hugged his grandmother hard, then left the den and headed down the hall to the kitchen. After filling up on a couple of ham sandwiches and a quart of milk, he took the stairs two at a time to his bedroom at the top.

His watch said twenty after ten. At this time tomorrow night he'd be with Sadie on reservation property. He knew a private spot where they wouldn't be disturbed. They'd stay there until it was time to drive to White Lodge for their marriage license.

You're going to be a married man, Bannock.

If he had one regret it was that his siblings wouldn't be there. But when he brought Sadie home as his wife, they'd understand the measures he'd had to take to protect Sadie from her out-of-control father.

"So, Dr. Rafferty, you don't think there's a need to take an X-ray?" Jarod asked, walking Chief out of the trailer to the paddock behind the clinic with the vet.

"Not that I can see," Sam Rafferty told him.

"His limp does seem to be a lot better. Last night I was really worried about him."

"Horses aren't that different from people. Sometimes we wake up in the morning and everything hurts like hell. But the next day, we feel better."

"Well, I'll take your word for it nothing serious is wrong."

Sam nodded. "Give him a day of rest and see how he does."

"Will do. How much do I owe you?"

"Forget it. I didn't do anything."

"You can't make a living that way." Jarod put a hundred dollar bill in the vet's lab coat pocket. "Thanks, Doc."

"My pleasure." They shook hands before he led Chief back into the trailer and shut the door.

Jarod started the truck and drove his rig away from the clinic. Out of the corner of his eye he saw Ned's Jeep down the street across from the supermarket. That was no coincidence—Ned must still be tailing him.

Twenty after five. The sun would set at nine. Jarod would have driven to the mountains immediately, but he couldn't do that with Ned watching him. It would only take a half hour to reach Sadie. He had three hours to kill. Might as well drive Ned crazy.

After making a U turn, he parked near the supermarket and went in to buy a meal at the deli. Then he took it out to the truck and sat there to eat while he listened to music. Ned had finally disappeared, but Jarod knew he was somewhere nearby watching, hoping to see Sadie show up and join Jarod. The fool could wait till doomsday but he'd never find her here.

The sun sank lower until it dropped below the horizon. It was time to make his move. His heart thudding in anticipation of making love to Sadie for the rest of their lives, Jarod started the truck and turned onto a road that would eventually lead to the fire road. From that crossroads you could either go to the mountains the back way or head the other way for the reservation.

But as he reached the crossroads, from out of nowhere, something rammed him broadside. The last thing he heard was the din of twisting metal before he passed out.

The next day he woke up in the hospital with a serious brain concussion, bruises and a nasty gash near his eye. Frantic, he tried to reach Sadie, but the report from the Hensons came back that she wasn't at home.

When he awoke a second time, the nurse brought him Sadie's note and read it to him. The words ripped him to pieces.

Jarod lay in the clover remembering the pain until Volan nudged him. Feeling as if his heart weighed more than his body, he climbed on the stallion and rode home.

Avery confronted him in the tack room after he returned. Her brunette hair and bright smile reminded him of their father Colin's second wife, Hannah. She'd been a wonderful mother to Jarod, never pushing him. Avery was a little more aggressive in that department.

"When you didn't come in the ranch house with Connor, I knew you'd gone riding. Did it help?" Her hazel eyes studied him anxiously.

She could read most of his moods, but he didn't answer her this time. There was no help for the disease he'd contracted eight years ago.

"Grandfather was hoping to talk to you."

"I know. I'll go see him now."

"He's gone to bed, but don't worry, Connor and I told him all we could. Great Uncle Tyson came to the funeral with his family. It was so strange, all of us together on Corkin land after so many years of being warned off the property. I think it overwhelmed Sadie. She thanked us for coming, but clung to her little brother the whole time."

Jarod's thoughts were black. "Did Ned behave?"

Her mouth tightened. "Does he ever?"

"Tell me what he did."

"He asked a lot of questions in such bad taste it raised the hairs on the back of my neck."

"Like what?"

At his rapid-fire question, his sister looked startled. "I was standing by them when he asked if she and Zane had an interest in each other besides Ryan. He said he hoped not because he was planning to spend a lot of time with her now that she was back."

Jarod bit down so hard he almost broke a tooth.

"It was appalling, but no one else heard him. Sadie didn't answer him, but I was so angry I broke in on their conversation. That angered Ned and caught Uncle Grant's attention. He wasn't thrilled with his son's behavior, either, and got him out of there as fast as he could."

"Ned gave me an ultimatum the other night."

"What kind?"

"Not to show up at the funeral."

"That's no surprise. He was jealous of you from birth. It only grew worse when grandfather gave you more responsibilities for running the ranch. Ned couldn't handle it. But when you and Sadie became friends, that killed him."

"There's a sickness in him."

"I know. Sadie was never interested in any of the guys chasing after her, least of all Ned. He used to wait for her after school and follow her as far as Corkin property. Sadie never paid him one whit of attention because the only guy she could ever see was *you*."

Until Jarod had planned to make her his wife. Then she'd run like the prong-horned antelope, putting fifteen hundred miles between them. Had his accident been the excuse she'd been looking for not to marry him?

"After today she'll like him even less, but I guess it doesn't matter," Avery added.

He closed his eyes tightly. "Why do you say that?"

"The chances of her having to deal with him are pretty remote. She's got a home in California and a little brother to raise."

"With Zane's help?" Jarod didn't want to listen to another word.

"Forget what you're thinking. I asked her outright if she was involved with Zane. She said no and was shocked at the question. I think it actually hurt her."

Jarod's relief had him reeling.

"I have to tell you I'm envious of her. Ryan's such an adorable boy, I wish he were mine."

Those were strong words. Jarod heard wistfulness

in her voice and eyed her with affection. "Your time will come, Avery."

Her eyes darted him a mischievous glance. "Are you trying to make me feel better, or did you have a vision about your only female sibling who's getting older?"

Her teasing never bothered him. He rubbed his lower lip absently. "I don't need a vision to know you're not destined to be alone. Ben's been crazy about you ever since he was hired."

Avery rolled her eyes. "That has to work both ways, big brother. If anyone ought to know about that, it's you. You're pushing thirty and until two months ago you had no prospects despite the fan club you ignore. Am I wrong or at long last has a woman finally gotten under your skin? Leslie's an extraordinary person, the kind I've been hoping you would meet."

"You and grandfather." But Jarod was too conflicted over Sadie to get into a discussion about anything. She'd just inherited Farfields, a place she'd loved heart and soul. Jarod couldn't imagine her leaving the land where she'd been born. But he'd been wrong about her before. Maybe she was involved with another man in California.

When are you going to learn, Bannock?

Chapter 3

It was Tuesday morning. Sadie had slept poorly and got up before Ryan, who was sleeping in the crib Millie had used for Liz. Zane had been installed in the guest bedroom and was still asleep. Though she'd come to the ranch to bury her father and take stock of her new situation, seeing Jarod after all these years had shaken her so badly, she was unnerved and restless. Through her friendship with Liz, she knew he hadn't married yet, though that made no sense when he could have any woman he wanted.

But recently Liz had dropped a little bomb that over the past few months he'd been seeing an archaeologist working in the area named Leslie Weston. Liz seemed to think it was more serious than his other relationships had been.

Her breath caught. *Had they made love? Were they planning to marry?* Sadie couldn't bear thinking about it.

From her bedroom window she watched Liz leave the Hensons' small house adjacent to the ranch house and head for her truck. No doubt she was on her way to work at the Rafferty vet clinic in White Lodge. Pretty soon quiet-spoken Mac followed and started out for the barn to get going on his chores.

With a deep sigh, Sadie turned away and headed for the bathroom. Once she'd showered and washed her hair, she pulled on jeans and a cotton sweater. After blow-drying her hair and applying lipstick, she felt more prepared to face this first day of an altered life and turn the second stone.

To stay busy she fixed breakfast, woke and dressed Ryan for the day and then returned to the kitchen. She piled some cushions on one of the kitchen chairs for Ryan as Zane joined them to eat. Before the day was out, she'd take her dad's pickup and run into White Lodge for a high chair and a new crib.

Though she had everything she needed back in California, it would take time to ship her things here. While she was at it, she'd also buy some cowboy boots and start breaking them in.

Millie appeared at the back door. The housekeeper still had a trim figure and worked as hard as ever to keep the ranch house running smoothly. Her brown eyes widened in surprise when she walked into the kitchen and found the three of them assembled there. "Good morning, Millie. Come on in and eat breakfast with us." It was long past time someone waited on her for a change.

The older woman kissed Ryan's head before sitting next to him. "I think I'm in heaven."

"Good. You deserve to be waited on." Sadie brought a plate of bacon, eggs and hash browns to the table for her.

No sooner had Sadie started to drink her coffee than they heard a knock on the front door. She jumped up from the table. "That'll be Mr. Varney. I'll show him into the living room. He's here to talk about the will."

The attorney from Billings had come to the graveside service and told her he'd be by on Tuesday morning.

"I'll take care of Ryan," Zane offered.

"Thank you." She got up and kissed her little brother's cheek. "I'll be back soon."

She hurried down the hall to the front room of the three-bedroom L-shaped ranch house. The place needed refurbishing. According to Mac, in the last few years her father had been operating Farfields in the red. He'd ended up selling most of the cattle. Toward the end he'd been too ill to take care of things and there'd been little money to pay Millie and Mac. The value of the ranch lay in the land itself.

Reed Varney had put on weight and his hair had thinned since the last time she'd seen him. He must be sixty by now and had handled her father's affairs for years. The man knew all the ugly Corkin secrets, including the particulars of the divorce, which was okay with Sadie since it was past history.

"Come in, Mr. Varney." She showed him into the living room. A couple of the funeral sprays filled the air with a fragrance that was almost cloying. Mac had taken some of the other arrangements to their cabin. "Would you care for some coffee?"

"No thanks." For some odd reason he wouldn't look her in the eye. She had the impression he was nervous.

"Then let's sit to talk." She chose one of the leather chairs opposite the couch where he'd taken a seat. As he opened his briefcase to pull out a thin file she asked, "How soon do you want to schedule the reading of the will?" For all their kindness, Mac and Millie should head the top of the list to receive the house they'd been living in all these years. She couldn't wait to tell them.

He rubbed his hands on top of his thighs, another gesture that indicated he felt uncomfortable. Sadie started to feel uneasy herself.

"Something's wrong. What is it?"

After clearing his throat he finally glanced at her. "The will is short and to the point. You can read it now. The particulars are all there." He handed her the file.

She blinked. Maybe her father had been in more financial trouble than she'd been led to believe. Taking a deep breath, she started to read. After getting past the legal jargon she came to her father's wishes.

Mac and Millie Henson betrayed my trust on my daughter's eighteenth birthday. Therefore they'll receive no inheritance, nor will my daughter, whom I've disowned.

Over the years several people have wanted to buy the ranch, but so far they haven't met the asking price. I have their offers on record. If no one else makes an offer within a month of my death, then the ranch and all its assets including my gun collection will be sold to the highest bidder through Parker Realty in Billings, Montana. My horse, Spook, has been sold.

No furnishings are to be touched. The new

*buyer will either use or dispose of them. Under
no circumstances can the ranch be sold to a Bannock.*

Sadie gasped and jumped up from the chair. Her
father had lived to drink, hunt and hate the Bannocks
with a passion. The meanest man alive didn't begin to
describe him. Forget the fact that he'd disowned her.
When she'd left for San Francisco, she never dreamed
he'd take out his fury on the Hensons like *this*.

"Does this mean he's thrown Mac and Millie out
with nothing?" Her eyes filled with tears. "After all
they've done for him over the years? The care they gave
him toward the last?"

Varney eyed her with grave concern before nodding.
"However, Mr. Bree at the realty firm has asked that the
Hensons stay on to manage things until the new buyer
takes ownership. It's entirely possible Mac Henson will
be asked to continue on as foreman for the new owner."

Daniel had died nine days ago. In less than a month
from now the eighty-five-acre ranch would be sold?
She couldn't take it in. Her father wanted her and the
Hensons off his land as fast as humanly possible. When
he'd told her to get out eight years ago, he'd meant for
it to be permanent. "What is the sale price?"

"Seven hundred thousand. He was in a lot of debt."

Her mind was madly trying to take everything in.

"What about me, Mr. Varney? Am I supposed to
clear out today?"

With a troubled sigh, the older man got to his feet.
"Legally you have no right to be here, but morally this
is your home and you can stay until the new owner takes

up residence. As for your own personal possessions, you're free to take them with you. I'm sorry, Sadie. I wish it could be otherwise. To be honest, I dreaded coming here today. You don't deserve this."

Reeling with pain, she walked him to the door. "It's Mac and Millie I worry about. The ranch is their home, too. I can hardly bear it."

When Jarod hadn't showed up that night eight years ago, the Hensons were the ones who had tried to comfort her. She'd believed he had decided at the last minute that he couldn't go through with their marriage, and she would never have survived if they hadn't been there to help her get through that ghastly night.

Reed Varney shook his head. "When Daniel summoned me to the ranch, I begged him not to do this, but he was beyond reason."

She stared into space. "He's always been beyond reason." This proved more than ever why her mother had been forced to abandon Sadie.

If Eileen had stayed in the marriage, who knew what would have happened during one of his drunken rages when he'd threatened to kill his wife. Eileen's decision to let him keep Sadie had probably saved both their lives.

When Sadie had found out about Jarod's accident, her father had threatened to kill Jarod if she went to the hospital to be with him. He'd made her write a letter telling Jarod she never wanted to see him again and then he'd told her to get out of his house. Millie and Mac were afraid for her life and urged her to leave Montana and go to her mother in California, saving her once more.

"Thank you for coming," she said quietly to the lawyer.

"Of course. The number for Parker Realty is listed on the paper. They've already put an ad in the multiple listings section. Things should be moving quickly. I'll be in touch with you again soon."

The second he left, she grabbed the file and hurried to her bedroom to hide it in the dresser drawer. She never wanted the Hensons to know what he'd put in the will about them. They'd been wonderful surrogate parents to her. Somehow she had to protect them.

With that decision made, she grabbed her purse and left for the kitchen, determined to lie through her teeth if she had to. She found Millie at the sink and gave her a hug. "Hey! I made the mess and planned to clean it up."

"Nonsense. How did everything go?"

"Fine. Tomorrow I'll drive to Billings and meet with him in his office," she lied. "Where's Zane?"

"Outside with Ryan. If Tim Lawson was as terrific as Zane, then your mother was a very lucky woman."

"She was. So was I, to be raised by you and Mac. I love you and Liz dearly. You know that, don't you?"

"The feeling's mutual."

"You're my family now and that's the way it's going to stay." *No matter what she had to do.*

"Nothing would make us happier." They hugged again.

"I'm going to drive into White Lodge. Do you want me to do any shopping for you while I'm there?"

"We stocked up for the funeral so I think we're fine right now."

"Okay. See you later. Just so you know, tonight I'm going to visit Ralph Bannock. Zane will babysit Ryan." She hadn't asked him yet, but knew he'd do it.

Zane's wife had betrayed him with another man

while he'd been in the navy. After he'd left the military, they'd divorced and, not long after, Zane had lost his elder brother, Tim. "Honey, I can do that."

"I know you can, Millie, but you spent enough time raising me. The last thing I want to do is take advantage of you. We'll be back shortly."

Sadie reached for the truck keys on the peg at the back door and hurried outside. She found Zane walking around with Ryan. He made the perfect father. His ex-wife had been the loser in that relationship. Sadie knew how much he'd wanted a family. It broke her heart.

She scooped her little brother from the ground before darting Zane a glance. "Will you drive me to town? We need to talk."

"Sure."

She handed him the keys to her father's Silverado and walked over to get in. They'd brought a car seat from California for Ryan and had already installed it in the backseat. Once he was strapped in securely, she climbed into the front with Zane and they took off.

Zane gave her a sideways glance. "I know that look on your face. You've had bad news."

"Much worse than anything I had imagined, but Mac and Millie don't know a thing yet. The fact is my father disowned me." She ended up telling him everything written in the will. "I've got three weeks from today to come up with a plan. I don't want the Hensons to find out about this."

"Of course not. That monster!" he muttered under his breath, but she heard him. "I'm sorry, Sadie." They followed the dirt road out to the highway.

"Don't be. With him, the shoe fits. The bottom line

is, if I want to make my home on this ranch, I'll have to buy it from the Realtor in Billings. There was no mention in the will that I couldn't. I have some savings after working for your brother, but not nearly enough to make a dent. In the meantime I need to find a job in town and put Ryan in day care."

Zane grimaced. "I could give you some money."

"You're an angel, Zane, but you gave your ex-wife the house you both lived in, so you need to hold on to any money you've saved. I'll have to find another avenue to pay off the debt owing the bank so I can hold on to the ranch, but I've got to hurry."

"I've got an idea how you can do it." She jerked her head toward him, waiting for the miracle answer. "I could sell Tim's house in San Francisco."

Sadie made several sounds of protest. "After your divorce, mother willed it to you before she died because she assumed I'd inherit the ranch one day. She knew Tim would have wanted you to have it."

"You're forgetting she expected you to go on living there with Ryan."

"But it's not mine, and I don't want to live in San Francisco."

"Neither do I. I have no desire to be anywhere near my ex, so I've got another idea."

"What?"

"The house isn't completely paid off, but I could still get a substantial amount if I sell it. With that money, plus any you have, we could move here and become joint owners of the ranch."

Her heart gave a great clap. "You're not serious!"

"Yeah. Actually, I am. I spent a lot of years in the

military and know I won't be happy unless I'm working outdoors in some capacity. So far I haven't found a job that appeals to me. I can help with the ranching for a while until I know what it is I want to do with the rest of my life."

"Zane, you're just saying that because you're at loose ends and are one of the great guys of this world."

"I'm saying it because I have no parents, no brother and I don't want to lose Ryan. I know you have nothing holding you in California. To be honest, I like the idea of being part owner with you. It'll be our investment for Ryan's future."

Her eyes smarted with unshed tears. "If you're really serious…"

"I'm dead serious. Take a look around. With these mountains, this is God's country all right. It's growing on me like crazy. I already like Mac and Millie. And the little guy in back seems perfectly content. Why don't you think about it?"

"I *am* thinking. So hard I'm ready to have a heart attack."

"Don't do that! If you wake up tomorrow and say it's a go, I'll fly back to San Francisco and get the house on the market. While I'm there, I'll put everything from the house and my apartment in storage for us. What do you say?"

She was so full of gratitude, she could hardly talk. "I say I don't need to wait until tomorrow to tell you yes, but I don't want ownership. The ranch should be put in your name for you and Ryan. I'll get a job and do housekeeping to earn my keep. In time we'll build up a new herd of cattle. Anything less and I won't agree."

He flashed her the kind of smile she hadn't seen since before Tim's death. Zane had dimples, too, an irresistible Lawson trait. "You sound just like your mother when she's made up her mind, but you need to think about this. There's a whole life you've left behind in San Francisco. Men you've dated. Friends."

"I know, and I've enjoyed all of it including my job at your brother's store. But with Mother gone, it hasn't been the same. Now that my father has died, I feel the only place I really belong is here."

After a period of quiet he said, "I can tell you this much. I feel this ranch growing on me."

Like Sadie, Zane needed to put the painful past behind him and get on with life.

"Tell you what, Zane. When I drive you to the airport tomorrow, I'll stop by Mr. Varney's office and let him know we have a plan for you to buy the ranch. He can inform the Realtor and we'll go from there."

"Sadie—" There was a solemn tone in his voice. "If things don't work out, we'll find another small ranch for sale around here. Montana is in your blood. We won't let your father win."

She had no words to express the depth of her love for him. Instead, she leaned across the seat and kissed his cheek.

On Tuesday night Jarod had just returned from the upper pasture when he caught sight of Daniel Corkin's Silverado parked in front of the Bannock ranch house. *Sadie was still here.* The blood pounded in his ears as he let himself in the side door of the den on the main floor. His grandfather's room was farther down the hallway of the two-story house.

With Connor headed for another rodeo event in Oklahoma, either Avery or their housekeeper, Jenny, would have let her in. He planted himself in the doorway of the den. When Sadie left, she would have to walk past him to reach the foyer. Since it had grown dark, he didn't imagine he'd have to wait much longer. His grandfather tired easily these days.

As if he'd willed her to appear, he saw light and movement at the end of the hall. She moved quietly in his direction. When she was within a few feet he said hello to her.

"Oh—"

"Forgive me if I startled you, Sadie. How's my grandfather?"

She stepped back, hugging her arms to her waist. He saw no sign of the vivacious Sadie Corkin of eight years ago who'd caused every male heart in Carbon County to race at the sight of her.

When he'd watched her galloping through the meadow, blond hair flying behind her like a pennant in the sunshine, he'd hardly been able to breathe. The moment she'd seen him, she'd dismount and run into his arms, her hair smelling sweet from her peach-scented shampoo.

Without losing a heartbeat, he'd lay her down in the sweet white clover and they would kiss, clinging in a frenzy of need while they'd tried to become one. Just remembering those secret times made his limbs grow heavy with desire.

"He fell asleep while we were talking," she answered

without looking at him directly. "I'm afraid I wore him out."

"That means you made him happy and left him in a peaceful state. When I had breakfast with him this morning, he was excited to think you'd be coming by. He was always partial to you and Liz." He almost said his grandfather had been waiting to welcome her into the Bannock family, but that would be dredging up the past.

"I care for him a lot." She shifted nervously. "I'm afraid I have to get back to Ryan now, so don't let me keep you. Good night." She darted away like a frightened doe spooked by a noise in the underbrush.

He'd promised himself to stay away from her, but the trail of her haunting fragrance drove him to follow her out the front door to the truck. By the time she'd climbed behind the wheel, he'd reached the passenger side. Not considering the wisdom of it, he got in and shut the door.

"What are you doing?" She sounded panicked.

Jarod forced his voice to remain calm. "Isn't it obvious? We have unfinished business, Sadie. While we're alone, now is as good a time as any to talk." He stretched his arm along the back of the seat, fighting the urge to plunge his hand into her silky hair the way he'd done so many times in the past. "To pretend we don't have a history serves no purpose. What I'm interested to know is how you can dismiss it so easily."

"I've dismissed nothing," she said, her voice shaking, "but sometimes it's better to leave certain things alone. In our case it's one stone that shouldn't be turned."

"I disagree. Let's start with that note you had delivered to me at the hospital. That was quite a turnaround from the night before when you'd promised to marry me. Or have you forgotten?"

"Of course not." She stirred restlessly. "I waited for you until dark, but you never came."

"Ned had been stalking me in town."

"Ned?"

He nodded. "I had to wait until I saw his Jeep disappear before I headed out to get you."

She struggled for breath. "I didn't know that. I was afraid to be out any longer in case my father realized I wasn't home or at Liz's, so I headed back. I thought you'd decided not to come, after all," she said in a barely audible voice.

"*Not come?* I was on my way to you when a truck blindsided me. Everything went black. A hiker found me and I didn't wake up until I was taken to the hospital in an ambulance. By then it was afternoon the next day. I couldn't reach you on the phone. Late that night one of the nurses brought me your note."

He felt her shudder.

"What happened, Sadie? For weeks I'd been asking you if you were sure about marrying me. You had every opportunity to turn me down before I went to the trouble of preparing for our wedding. Surely I deserve a better explanation for you not showing up than the pathetic one you sent me."

Her head was still lowered. "I—I'm afraid to tell you for fear you won't believe me," she stammered. "I've kept this a secret for so long, but now that my father is dead, you need to hear the truth."

He gritted his teeth. "Why didn't you tell me before?" he rasped. "It's been eight hellish years, Sadie."

"You think I don't know that?" She whipped her head around to face him. "I didn't hear about the accident until late the next day when Mac told me. The second I found out, I started out the door to go straight to the hospital. But that's when my father stopped. He said if I went near you, he would kill you."

Jarod frowned. "Kill me? He'd been threatening to kill any Bannock that came near you on his property for years, always when he'd had too much to drink. Why did you suddenly believe him?"

"This time was different!"

He blinked. "Start at the beginning and don't leave anything out."

"After Mac told me about your accident, he gave me the keys to his truck so I could drive to the hospital. I left the house, but my father followed me out and forbade me to leave. I told him I was going to see you and he couldn't stop me. I was eighteen and he had no more right to tell me what to do. But before I could climb into the cab, he said something that made my blood run cold."

Jarod waited.

She stared at him in the semidarkness. "He warned me that if I ever went near you again, another accident would happen to you and you wouldn't survive it."

"What?"

Jarod's thoughts reeled.

"I was afraid you wouldn't believe me." She started to open the door to get out, but Jarod was faster and reached across to stop her.

He knew Daniel Corkin was demented when he got too drunk, but— "Are you saying he drove the truck that ran me down the night before?" Jarod caught her shoulder in his grasp, bringing their mouths within inches of each other.

"No." Sadie shook her head, unable to hold back the tears. "But my father had to be behind the accident. Otherwise why would he have said that? He probably paid someone to drive into you, and after all these years, that person is still out there."

Was it true?

He gripped her shoulder tighter. "I *knew* it wasn't a simple accident. When I felt that kind of force on a dirt road with no one else around, I thought it had to be a small plane making a forced landing that ran into me.

"It all happened too fast for me to see anything. The impact caused the truck to roll into the culvert and twisted the horse trailer onto its side. The police said it had to have been a truck, but after an exhaustive investigation, they couldn't find the person responsible."

Sadie moaned. "It was so horrific. I heard that Chief was injured, too."

"Yes, but he survived."

"Thank heaven. I don't know how, but someone knew we were planning to get married and word got back to my father. Maybe someone from the reservation did some talking in town. Oh, Jarod." She broke down, burying her face in her hands. "You could have been killed."

She was right about that.

"I can't bear to think about that night. There was evil in my father. I realized he *would* kill you another time given more provocation. At that point I did the only thing I could do and promised not to see you again. He made me write that note and then he told me to get out of the house and stay out. He obviously assumed I'd run to the Hensons."

Jarod heard her words, but it took time for him to absorb them.

"I was so terrified to learn you were in the hospital, and so terrified of him, I knew I had to get away and stay away. All these years I've wondered who could have done something so sinister to you. My father must have paid that man a lot of money he didn't have."

He sucked in a breath. "Whether your father was bluffing about the accident or not, his objective of separating us was accomplished. You were gone out of my life as if you'd never been there."

"Please listen to me, Jarod. In the note I wrote, those words were only meant to convince my father. How could you have believed them? I was going to be your wife!"

He stared her down, unable to fathom what had happened. Something didn't ring true, but he'd have to think long and hard about it first. He slowly released her arm.

"Just tell me one thing. Why did you go to your mother after she'd abandoned you for all those years? It made no sense. I couldn't come up with any conceivable explanation, so I finally had to conclude you couldn't bring yourself to marry me."

"Jarod," she pleaded, "I don't know how you could think that! When you didn't come and I still knew nothing about your accident, I thought you'd changed your mind about getting married, or maybe your uncle had urged you to put off the marriage for a while longer. I wanted to die when you didn't show up. Mac and Millie came in my room to try to calm me down. You have no idea what was going on inside me that night."

"That made two of us. I lay on that hospital bed incapacitated with no way to talk to you. My grandparents thought we were on the reservation enjoying our honeymoon."

"I didn't know that!" she half cried. "I was so upset Mac and Millie told me a secret they'd been keeping from me because my father had sworn them to secrecy. If they broke that oath, he would have thrown them off the property. Millie said the only reason they hadn't left him was because of me."

He shook his head in disbelief. "What secret?"

"They told me he'd threatened to kill my mother if she tried to take me away from him. Jarod, all those years I thought she didn't love me, but it was just the opposite. She always wanted me, grieved for me. She kept in touch with the Hensons every day to find out how I was. But they had to keep quiet because of my father."

"Is that the truth?"

"Yes, but I didn't know it until that moment."

Jarod rubbed the side of his jaw. "A mother's love," he murmured. "You wanted it more than you wanted me."

"No, Jarod. You have everything wrong."

"I don't think so," he argued. "When you heard about my accident, it was obvious you didn't want to be my wife or you would have found a way to get in touch with me at the hospital. You knew that when I got out,

I'd come for you and we would have gotten away from your father. I wasn't afraid of him."

"But I *was!* He'd just admitted he would make sure you were dead if I so much as looked at you. I couldn't bear that, so I went to my mother. Don't forget he'd threatened her years earlier. My father was capable of anything! With a gun or a rifle in his hand, he was lethal. Since I'd turned eighteen, Mac and Millie urged me to get away from my father and go to her because he was out of control. Mac drove me to Billings."

Jarod felt as though a giant hand had just cut off his breath. "So you let Mac do that instead of driving you to the reservation where my uncle would have taken care of you until I got out of the hospital. You promised to love me forever."

He could barely make out her words she was sobbing so much. "You were my life, Jarod, but when I never heard from you after you recovered, I thought you didn't want me. I thought my life was over. Don't you understand? I was devastated to think you'd decided it wouldn't be wise to marry me because of my father. He hated you—hated all the Bannocks. You have to believe that the only reason I left was so my father wouldn't hurt you again."

A boulder had lodged in his throat. "How could you think that when I was prepared to be your husband and take care of you? I swore I would protect you. Do you honestly think I would have let him or anyone else hurt either one of us?"

"He managed it the first time."

Jarod's features hardened. "Why don't you tell me

the real reason why you ran away from me? I'm warning you. I won't let you go until I get the truth out of you."

Tears rolled down her cheeks. "I *have* told you, but you're so stubborn you refuse to listen."

"You think I haven't listened? Did Ned get to you, after all?"

"No!" She sounded wild with anger. "I couldn't stand Ned. He revolted me."

"But he told you about my father, didn't he?"

She stared at him through the tears. "What are you talking about?"

"After all this time and all we've been through, are you still going to pretend you don't know the truth?"

"What truth?" she cried.

"My mother and father were never married."

Stillness fell around them.

"They weren't? I swear I've never heard any of this. Ned used to call you a bastard and a half-breed under his breath, but I knew he was insanely jealous of you. He had such a foul mouth, my friends and I always ran from him when he followed us around."

Sadie's earnestness shook him.

"Jarod Bannock, are you trying to tell me you think I heard about your parents and was ashamed to become your wife?"

Jarod struggled to hide the guilt rising up in him.

"You *do* think it! I can see it on your face. How dare you think that about me!"

"That's exactly how it was," he returned angrily. "You were playing a game with me—the half Indian. But you were a teenager then, living through a lot of pain and turned to me. I was three years older and should have known better than to believe you and I shared something rare."

"We did," she whispered, her voice throbbing. "Can't you understand that I was convinced my father would kill you?" Even in the semidarkness her face had lost color. "Listen to me, Jarod. I'm going to tell you something right now.

"Even if I knew about your parents, I was ready to live with you no matter what because I *loved* you. *I* was the one who begged you to take me away before I turned eighteen. Remember? I didn't care. I would have hidden out on the reservation with you. That's how deeply in love I was with you. So don't you dare credit feelings and motives to me that were never mine."

Gutted after what he'd heard, Jarod needed to get out of the truck. He started to open the door, but she grabbed his arm. "Oh, no, you don't! We're not through yet. I want to know why you never, ever told me the truth about your parents."

Jarod realized he couldn't avoid this conversation any longer. While he tried to find the words, she launched her own.

"It seems to me your cousin did a lot of damage I didn't know about, otherwise you wouldn't have held anything back from me. What did he tell you? That a white girl would never want you once she knew the truth? He got under your skin, didn't he? Well, we're alone now, so I want to hear the whole truth. You owe me that much before you walk away again."

He deserved that much and closed his eyes tightly before sitting back.

"Dad was twenty when he drove to the reservation

to look at the horses. The Crow loved their animals and knew good horse flesh. My uncle Charlo showed him around. While they were talking, his younger sister Raven came riding up on a palomino. Dad told me she looked like a princess. He was so taken by her, he forgot about the horses. From then on he kept driving over there and finally told Charlo he wanted to marry her.

"My uncle told him she was destined to marry another man in the clan, but by that time Raven was in love with my father. At that point Charlo took him to meet their mother. Her word was law. She said her daughter was old enough to make up her own mind. They spent that night together on the reservation. It meant they were married. There was no ceremony. I was conceived that night."

"Oh, Jarod." She sniffled. "What a beautiful story. Did they live on the reservation?"

"On and off. Dad took her home to meet my grandparents. They loved my father and welcomed Raven. When she discovered she was pregnant, she spent more time with her family. I was born on the reservation. But Addie had prepared a nursery, so I lived in both places.

"That winter my mother caught pneumonia, and though my grandfather paid for the best health care, she died within six weeks of my birth and was buried on the reservation. My father was grief-stricken. It was hard to take me out to the reservation as often after that because of all the reminders.

"My Bannock grandparents helped raise me. Eventually Dad met Hannah at church and they married, then Connor and Avery were born. That's the whole story. Though secretly I knew Great Uncle Tyson's family didn't approve of what my father had done, they were never unkind to him or to me."

"Except for Ned," Sadie muttered. "He's as intolerant as my father. The fact that you're an exceptional man only makes your cousin angrier."

"There's more to it than that, Sadie. After my parents were killed in a freak lightning storm, Ned became more vocal about his hate for me and my background. He constantly tried to show me up. It grew uglier with time. But *you* were the crux of the problem. He wanted to go out with you himself, and I knew it.

"When I used to watch you compete at the rodeo, I knew Ned was in the crowd, wishing you'd go home with him after it was over. I loved knowing you and I had secret plans to meet later. I had too much pride knowing it was I you wanted."

She shifted in the seat. "I lived to be with you. That's why it kills me to think that Ned was able to undermine your faith in me once I left Montana. I had to write what I did in that note to sound believable to my father, but I can't believe you didn't read between the lines. I waited for weeks, months, years, hoping and praying I'd hear from you so I could tell you everything and we could make plans to meet."

"That works both ways, Sadie. I waited weeks for a phone call from you. Maybe now you can understand how devastated I was when you fled to your mother instead of marrying me.

"But after you'd gone to California and time passed, I realized you were right to escape me. Despite the Bannock name, I'll always be treated as a second-class citizen by certain people. If you had married me, you would have been forced to deal with the kind of prejudice Ned dishes out on a daily basis."

They'd reached an impasse. He opened the door. "Eight years have passed. You've suffered some great losses in your life and now have a child to raise. I only wish you the best, Sadie."

Her features hardened. She wiped the moisture off her face. "If you can accuse me of being afraid to be your wife after all we shared, then you never knew me. I gave you a lot more credit than that. Have you forgotten the evening we met in the canyon and I told you about a lesson we'd had on the Plains Indians and the great Sioux Chief Sitting Bull?"

"Vaguely." Jarod knew he'd always been so excited to be with her, he'd barely taken in everything she'd told him.

"That lesson changed my view of life, but it's obvious you need a reminder of how deeply it touched me. Did I tell you our teacher made us memorize part of Sitting Bull's speech before the Dawes Commission in 1877? I still know it by heart and got an A for it."

Jarod had had no idea, but he nodded.

"Sitting Bull said, and I quote, 'if the Great Spirit had desired me to be a white man, he would have made me so in the first place. He put in your heart certain wishes and plans, and in my heart he put other and different desires. It is not necessary for eagles to be crows.

"'I am here by the will of the Great Spirit, and by his will I am chief.

"'In my early days, I was eager to learn and to do things, and therefore I learned quickly.'

"'Each man is good in the sight of the Great Spirit.

Now that we are poor, we are free. No white man controls our footsteps. If we must die, we die defending our rights.

"'What white man can say I ever stole his land or a penny of his money? Yet they say that I am a thief. What white woman, however lonely, was ever captive or insulted by me? Yet they say I am a bad Indian.

"'What white man has ever seen me drunk? Who has ever come to me hungry and left me unfed? Who has seen me beat my wives or abuse my children? What law have I broken?

"'Is it wrong for me to love my own? Is it wicked for me because my skin is red? Because I am Sioux? Because I was born where my father lived? Because I would die for my people and my country? God made me an Indian.'"

When she'd finished, Jarod sat there in absolute wonder, so humbled he couldn't speak.

"You don't know how many times I wanted to face my father and Ned and deliver that speech to them," Sadie told him. "I wanted to yell at them, 'God made you men white and Jarod's mother an Indian. So be thankful you were made at all and learn to live together!

"That speech made me love you all the more, Jarod. I can't believe you didn't know that. But as you said, it's probably that pride of yours. It's turned your heart to flint and stands in the way of reason.

"Do you know I've given you a second Crow name now that you've grown up? It's Born of Flint."

Born of Flint? That's what she thought of him? Everything was over.

"I wish you a safe journey back to California, Sadie."

Chapter 4

When Sadie walked through the back door of the ranch house Tuesday night, Millie was in the kitchen making coffee. She glanced at Sadie and said, "You look as bad as you did that night eight years ago. It can only mean one thing. Sit down and talk to me before you fall down, honey. Ryan's asleep and Zane's in his bedroom doing work on his laptop."

"Oh, Millie…" She ran into those arms that had always been outstretched to her. They hugged for a long time.

"You saw Jarod."

Sadie nodded and eased away. "I don't think it was by accident."

"No. He knew you were going to visit Ralph."

"He followed me to the truck. We talked about that

ghastly night eight years ago. He said he couldn't come to the meadow until after dark because Ned had been stalking him in White Lodge. That's why he was so late."

"That doesn't surprise me one bit. Ned was always up to no good."

"But it was a revelation to me! When he thought it was safe, he started for the mountains but got broadsided by a truck." She told Millie everything they'd talked about.

"Don't tell me you didn't believe him—" The tenderness in her brown eyes defeated Sadie.

"Of course I believed him," she half protested. "But back then I was dying inside. Now it is eight years too late. Millie—" She scrunched her fists in anger. "All these years I've wanted to hate him for not trying to get in touch with me."

Millie's voice was gentle. "You didn't reach out to him, either. It's a tragedy you both lost out on eight years of loving. Ah, honey…you were so young, struggling with too many abandonment issues. When he didn't come for you in California, the pain was too much for you."

"You should have heard him, Millie. He…he thought I left Montana because I didn't want to marry a part Indian. Did you know his parents got married on the reservation? But no one knew about it, certainly not Ned.

"I didn't realize Jarod suffered so much from Ned's taunting. He *had* to know none of that mattered to me. Can you imagine him believing I thought less of him because of his heritage?"

The housekeeper gave her a sad smile. "Yes. Jarod is

a proud man like his uncle Charlo. But at twenty-one, everything was on the line for him. Don't forget your father's hatred of the Bannocks, let alone his hatred of anyone who wasn't of pure English stock.

"Wanting to marry you was a daring dream for any man, but as we both know, Jarod was always his own person. In his fearless way he loved you and reached out for you. But when you left Montana before he got out of the hospital, all those demons planted in his mind by your father and Ned caused his common sense to desert him for a while."

"I see that now," Sadie whispered, grief stricken. "But I was afraid my father would kill him."

"Don't you know about the great wounded warrior inside him? He needed you to believe in him, to believe he would protect you."

"You're right."

"Did you tell him tonight that you'd wanted to marry him more than anything in the world?"

Sadie wiped her eyes with the palms of her hands. "Yes, but he didn't listen. Do you know what he said? In that stoic way of his he wished me a safe journey back to California."

Millie studied her for a moment. "Perhaps he thinks you and Zane are romantically involved. Have you forgotten that fierce Apsáalooke pride so quickly? According to my daughter, Zane Lawson is the most attractive man she's seen around these parts in years."

"No, Millie. I cleared that up with Avery the other day when she asked about Zane. She's close to Jarod and would have told him." But Ned had been brazen enough to ask her about Zane.

Millie shrugged. "Maybe Jarod thinks you're involved with a man in San Francisco and are looking forward to getting back to him."

"It never happened."

"All I can say is, if you're going to be neighbors with the Bannocks again, it wouldn't hurt to mend a fence that doesn't need to stay broken. Don't you agree? After all, Jarod's involved with another woman right now."

Pain pierced her. "I know. Apparently it's more serious than his other relationships."

"That doesn't surprise me. He's not a monk and he *is* getting to the age where a man wants to put down roots with a wife and children. Honey? Since you're not going back to California, perhaps you could tell him there is no other man in your life the next time you see him. If either one of you had done that eight years ago with a phone call or a letter, you might be the mother of one or two little Bannocks by now."

Except at that point in time, Millie hadn't known that Daniel was the person behind Jarod's accident, and still didn't. Sadie's father had talked to her outside where no one else could hear them. The horror of knowing her father would kill Jarod with little provocation was another secret she'd wanted to keep from the Hensons.

But the mention of one or two little Bannocks had Sadie swallowing hard. She'd entertained that vision too many times and suffered the heartache over and over again.

Sadie thanked Millie and said good-night. She tiptoed into the bedroom. Ryan was sound asleep, snuggled beside his blanket.

Good old Millie. Her sage advice nagged at Sadie

as she got ready for bed. To mend that fence by telling Jarod there was no man in her life meant turning over the next stone. If she did tell him, she didn't know if she had enough courage to deal with the rejection of the grown man he'd become.

"Honey?" Millie peeked in her room. "I need to give you something. Now that you know the truth about that night, you should have this back." She handed Sadie the beaded bracelet Jarod had given her the night they'd made love and planned their future.

Sadie stared at the bracelet in disbelief. "I thought I'd lost it. You kept it?"

"Of course. I knew there had to be an explanation why he didn't meet you, but you were too wild with pain to hear me. When you took that bracelet off your wrist and tossed it across the room, I picked it up and put it away for safekeeping.

"Don't you know he would never have given you a gift like that if he hadn't loved you with all his soul? Jarod's a great man, Sadie. After you left, I cried bitter tears for both of you for years."

Sadie stared at the woman who'd been her mother through those difficult years. "What did I ever do to deserve you? I'll love you and Mac forever."

"Ditto. We couldn't have more children. You were a blessing in our lives, a sister for our Liz. We all needed each other."

Yes. Sadie wouldn't have made it without the Hensons.

She pressed the bracelet against her heart and fell asleep reliving that night in the mountains. *Jarod*...

* * *

So she *was* leaving the ranch. The Sadie he'd once known had gone for good.

Jarod stood outside the ranch house for a long time. The sound of Sadie's truck engine echoed in the empty cavern of his heart, the one she'd likened to flint.

When he'd checked on his grandfather and found him asleep, he'd told Jenny he was going to drive out to the reservation to see Uncle Charlo and would be back by tomorrow afternoon. Again it meant putting Leslie off, but it couldn't be helped.

He'd met the good-looking, redheaded archaeologist from Colorado through Avery. The two women worked at the dig site near Absarokee, Montana, run through the University in Billings. They were unearthing evidence of Crow history. Leslie's looks and mind had attracted him enough to start dating her, but seeing Sadie again made it impossible for him to sort out his feelings.

The reservation crossed several county lines with ninety percent of the population being farthest away in Big Horn County at the Crow Agency. However his uncle resided in the small settlement on the Pryor area of the reservation in Carbon County, only an hour's drive from the ranch.

If Martha needed anything, she could call his uncle Grant. But if there was a real emergency, he could come right back.

After spending the night on the reservation, Jarod drove straight to the ranch on Wednesday to look in on his grandfather. Since his hospital stay the month before, Ralph's condition could change on a dime because of the pneumonia plaguing him. Martha had just served him his lunch. She smiled at Jarod as he walked into the bedroom.

"I'll stay with him while he eats," he told her.

"He's in better spirits than I've seen him in a long time."

Jarod figured that might have had something to do with the visit from the gorgeous blonde on the neighboring ranch. Being with her last night had shaken him, though he wasn't sure in such a positive way.

You were my life, Jarod, but I thought you didn't want me. I thought my life was over. I was devastated to think you'd decided it wouldn't be wise to marry the daughter of Daniel Corkin. He hated you.

Even though he'd talked to his uncle, it had taken until early morning before the cloud over Jarod's mind had dispersed and he'd allowed himself to dig deeper for answers. Daniel wasn't the only person who'd hated Jarod enough to cause him injury. He could think of another man who matched that description.

A member of his own family.

Since Sadie's return to Montana, Ned had shot him glances that said he'd like to wipe Jarod off the face of the earth. Ned had always been up to trouble and had taken it upon himself to be chief watch dog of Jarod's activities. Was it possible he'd heard about Jarod's plans to marry Sadie?

Jarod couldn't imagine it, but if that was the case, then he understood the hate that could have driven Ned to prevent the ceremony from taking place. Couple that with his drinking and a scenario began to take form in Jarod's mind.

"I'm glad you're here, son," Ralph Bannock said. "We need to talk."

His grandfather's raspy voice jerked him from his black thoughts to the present. Since Jarod's father's death, his grandfather, whose thinning dark hair was streaked with silver, had started calling Jarod "son." Though he and Jarod were the same height, his grandfather had shrunk some. He was more fragile these days, and there were hollows in his cheeks.

He was propped against a pillow, sipping soup through a straw. Martha kept him shaved and smelling good. Today he had on the new pair of pajamas Connor had brought him.

Jarod spied a newly framed five-by-seven photograph placed on the bedside table. His breath caught when he realized it was a picture of his grandfather and Sadie taken when she couldn't have been more than six or seven. She was a little blond angel back then, sitting on the back of a pony.

His grandfather's eyes misted over when he saw where Jarod was looking. "Sadie gave me that last evening. I remember the day her mother brought her over to see the new pony. Addie took a picture of us and gave it to her. Sadie said that was one of the happiest memories of her life and wanted me to have it…. With that father of hers, she didn't have many good ones. There was always sweetness in that girl."

No one knew that better than Jarod. He'd never forgotten the day they'd rode into the rugged interior of the Pryors to find one of the wild horse herds. They'd come across a mare attending her foal, their shiny black coats standing out against the meadow of purple lupine. He and Sadie had watched for several hours. "I wish that little foal was mine. I never saw anything so beautiful in my life, Jarod."

The scene was almost as beautiful as Sadie herself. That was the day their souls joined.

Jarod knew in his gut Leslie Weston was becoming more serious about him, yet he kept holding back. It wasn't fair to her. She'd invited him to Colorado to meet her family, but he wasn't there yet.

When Sadie left again for California, maybe that would be the spell-breaker for him. So far no other woman had ever gotten past the entrance to that part of him where Sadie lived. She was his dream catcher, trapping the memories that would always haunt his nights.

Last night his uncle had listened to him before giving him a warning. "Consider the wolf that decides it is better to risk death for some chance of finding a mate and a territory than to live safely, but have no chance of reproduction. You don't know how many winters the Great Spirit will grant you, but they will be cold if you continue to torture yourself with insubstantial dreams that give no warmth."

Jarod knew his uncle was right. He could see a marriage working with Leslie. While he ranched, she'd be able to continue with her career. Together they'd raise a family. For a variety of reasons he felt she'd make a good wife. But would he make a good husband? The answer to that question was no. Not if he couldn't tear Sadie out of his heart.

"Son? Did you hear me?"

His head reared. "What was that, grandfather?"

"I said I need you to do me a favor."

"Anything." He sat in the chair next to the bed, emotionally shredded.

"It turns out Daniel is worse in death than he was in life."

Jarod sat forward. After what Sadie had told him about her father, he wasn't surprised. "What do you mean?" Sadie's father had cast a pall over their lives for too many years.

"He cut Sadie and the Hensons out of his will."

The news shocked Jarod. She'd said nothing of this last night. He shot to his feet. "But there's no one else to inherit!"

"That's right. On June third, the ranch is to be sold to the highest bidder. Parker Realty in Billings is handling it."

So soon? That was only two weeks away. Jarod's hands formed fists.

The lunatic was selling the place rather than give it to his own flesh and blood?

"I would buy it," his grandfather continued, "but Daniel thought of that, too. No Bannock will be able to touch it."

"But Sadie loves that ranch. It's her home. If nothing else, she'd want to keep it in her family."

"She told me she plans to buy it so she and the Hensons can live on the property until they die. It would be just like that lowlife Corkin to force her to come up with her own money to buy it back. You and I know her heart has always been here."

Jarod felt his heart skip a beat. Despite what everyone had been thinking, Sadie wasn't going back to California. Even when the circumstances pointed otherwise, deep down *Jarod had known.*

"Does she have the kind of money it will take?"

"She has savings, but Zane is flying back to California to sell the Lawson house. That money combined with hers ought to be enough to pay off the bank loan so they can hold on to it until they come up with more."

"'They'?" His nervous system received another shocking jolt. "What does Zane have to do with her ranch?"

"Everything! Being Ryan's uncle, he has decided to move here with her. Together they're going to do the ranching."

Jarod frowned. "Does he know anything about ranching?"

"She said he's a retired navy SEAL who just got divorced after finding out his wife was unfaithful. If he was courageous enough to defend our country and survive thirteen years in the military, it stands to reason he can learn. Mac will be there to help him."

His grandfather had an amazing way of humbling Jarod.

"One day she wants it to be Ryan's in honor of Eileen. Their mother put her heart and soul into that ranch before Daniel drove her away. What I want you to do is pay a visit to our attorney in Billings. Ned wants that ranch. He wants Sadie, too, but she was never his to have."

Their eyes locked. His grandfather's steel-gray ones stared at him. "If it wasn't for that accident, she would have been your wife!"

As if Jarod needed to be reminded.

"When Ned hears it's on the market, he'll try to fight the will on the grounds that a third-party designee won't stand up in court these days and anyone can buy it. I want you to get to Harlow before Ned does. Inform him of Sadie's desperate plight and make sure no one else gets their hands on her property. Block him with everything you've got." His gray eyebrows lifted. "I mean *everything*."

Jarod got the message. This was a mission he was going to relish. Ralph Bannock of the Hitting Rocks Ranch was a big name in the State of Montana and wielded a certain amount of power among the business community. For once Jarod planned to use that power for leverage.

"Don't worry about Tyson or your Uncle Grant," his grandfather continued, unaware of the tumult inside Jarod. "I'll take care of them. If they decide the blood between them and Ned is thicker than the blood between them and me, then there will be war. We'll have to get there before they do. Time is of the essence. I'll be damned if I'll let Daniel Corkin cheat Sadie out of her rightful inheritance. Addie wouldn't have stood for it."

Jarod remembered Ned's angry warning in the barn two nights ago about the war not being over. Little did his cousin know what he was in for. Though Ralph had always been Jarod's champion, until this moment he hadn't known how much he loved his grandfather. "I'll drive to Billings first thing in the morning."

"We'll keep this under wraps."

"I'm way ahead of you."

Since Thursday was Liz's day off from the clinic and she wanted to tend Ryan, Sadie had to wait till then to drive Zane to Billings to make his flight. Little Ryan cried when they walked out the back door. They both felt the wrench, but Sadie knew he'd be laughing in a few minutes.

After she dropped Zane off at the airport, Sadie met with Mr. Bree at Parker Realty and they talked business. He couldn't tell her about the other bids, but he did give her a price. If she could meet it, he'd be happy to sell the property to Zane.

She explained about the house in San Francisco, advising that Zane's agent would contact Mr. Bree with a notice of intent to use the money from the sale of the house to purchase the ranch. Everything depended on a quick sale. Sadie put down earnest money from her savings account. With that accomplished, she left his office and headed back to the ranch. She had a lot to discuss with Zane when he called her later.

Ryan was taking his afternoon nap when she returned. Now was a good time to get busy cleaning out her father's bedroom. So far she hadn't been able to bring herself to go in it. When she told Liz and Millie of her intentions, they wouldn't hear of it.

"Give it more time, honey," Millie urged her. "While Ryan's still asleep, why not put on those sassy new cowboy boots and take a ride on Sunflower?"

"She's a lot like Brandy once was," Liz commented. "Playful, with plenty of spirit. You'll love her. But Maisy's energetic, too. Go ahead and ride whichever one you want."

"Thank you." Sadie stared out the living room window facing the mountains. "I presume Dad sold my horse after I left."

"Along with half the cattle."

"Did he get rid of my saddle, too?"

"No. It's still waiting for you in the tack room." Millie got up from the couch and put an arm around her. "Don't dwell on the past. I happen to know a girl around here who never let a day go by without going for a ride."

Obviously, Millie knew she was on the verge of breaking down.

"Maybe for a half hour. If you're sure."

"What else have we got to do? Having a child in this house makes me feel useful again."

"It makes me want one of my own," Liz said on a mournful note.

So far every subject they'd touched on was painful one way or the other. "I'll get ready, but I won't take a long ride. If Ryan starts crying for me, call me on my cell."

Millie shook her head. "Whatever did we do before cell phones?"

If Sadie and Jarod could have called each other eight years ago...

But Sadie's father had forbidden her to have a phone. He didn't want guys calling her without him knowing about it. At Christmas, four months before she'd fled to California, Jarod had bought her one and paid for the service, but she'd been too afraid her father would find out. She'd made Jarod take it back.

If they'd been able to talk before his accident, she would have known he hadn't deserted her. They would have communicated while he was in the hospital and their marriage would have taken place the second he got out....

You're a fool to dredge up so much pain, Sadie.

She put the phone she'd bought ages ago in her blouse pocket, then went in the bedroom to change into her cowboy boots. Just a short ride to the bluff overlooking the ranch and back.

After thanking Millie and Liz, she left the house through the back door and walked to the barn, lifting her face to the sun.

The smell of the barn flooded her with bittersweet memories. Horses had been her soul mates, just as Jarod had said. When her mom had left, this was the place where she'd come to cry her heart out and find solace. They's always listened and nudged her as if to say they understood.

Though the fights between her parents had stopped, for a long time the emptiness of no loving parent in the house had swallowed her alive. From her earliest memories, her father had been a gun-toting alcoholic. He'd always been gruff, though her mother had done her best to shield Sadie from him.

But somewhere along the way he'd turned hard and cold. After the divorce he'd just have to look at Sadie and she'd known he was seeing her mother. Sadie had learned to stay out of his way.

A neigh from the horse in the barn startled her, breaking her free of those memories. She discovered her cheeks were damp. After wiping the tears away, she walked over to Maisy's stall. The sorrel stared at her as if surprised to see a stranger.

Sadie moved on to Sunflower's stall. With a yellowish gray coat set off by a black mane and tail, the dun-colored mare was well named. She nickered a greeting.

Sadie rubbed her nose. "Well, aren't you the friendliest horse around here. Want to go for a ride? I know you're one of Liz's horses, but you won't care if I take you out for some exercise, right?" She marveled that her friend, who'd become a vet, was still Montana's champion barrel racer. But as she'd informed Sadie, this would be her last year of competition and she hoped to go to the Pro Rodeo Finals in Las Vegas in December.

The horse nickered again, bringing a smile to Sadie. She could saddle and bridle a horse in her sleep, and before long she had left the barn and was galloping away from the ranch. As the horse responded to her body language, the exhilaration she hadn't felt in years came rushing back. She'd done this before. She'd felt this way before.

Her inner compass told her where to go. She was on one of those rare highs and discovered herself racing toward the rocky formations in the distance where Jarod had first taken her to see the wild horses. Sadie knew he wouldn't be there. She didn't even know if the horses still ran there, but she was back now and this was one pilgrimmage she had to make.

In a few minutes she'd reached the place where her bond with Jarod had been forged. The deserted gulch held no evidence that anything had ever happened here, but cut Sadie open and you'd see his imprint on the organ pumping her life's blood.

Jarod. It was always you. It will always be you.

when Jarod told Harlow's secretary he needed to see his grandfather's attorney ASAP, he figured he might have to wait hours or come back the next day. But the two men were old friends. As soon as she buzzed her boss and told him who was out in reception, she smiled at Jarod.

"He says you can go right in."

"Thanks, Nancy." He walked across the foyer to the double doors and opened them.

Harlow started toward him. Though the older man was in his seventies and had a shock of white hair, he was a wiry, energetic individual. His shrewd blue eyes played over Jarod with genuine pleasure. "Come on in! It's always good to see you."

They shook hands before the lawyer took a seat behind his desk, motioning for Jarod to sit in one of the leather wing-backed chairs in front of it. "Has Ralph taken another turn for the worse?"

"His last bout of pneumonia left him weak, but he's still fighting."

"That's good to hear. And Tyson?"

"His macular degeneration along with ulcers has taken a real toll." The brothers were only two years apart. "I've come on my grandfather's behalf about something vital."

"Ralph appears to be depending on you more and more to run the Hitting Rocks Ranch. He couldn't choose a better man to be following in his footsteps."

Jarod's uncle Grant probably wouldn't like hearing that, but Jarod had always liked Harlow and felt the man's sincerity. "They're big ones."

Harlow chuckled. "Indeed they are." He pushed a stack of legal briefs to the side of his desk and leaned forward. "Tell me what's going on."

It didn't take Jarod long to explain the problem.

The older man touched his fingertips together. "What a tragedy, but there is a very simple way around the problem. If Ralph wants to make certain Sadie Corkin doesn't lose her ranch without her knowing he's behind it, I'll act as a straw buyer and purchase the property."

"It's going for $700,000."

He nodded. "When all the papers are filed and transactions made, Ralph can pay me and the land will be deeded over to Zane Lawson. He can work out the details with Ralph to get him paid back. No laws have been broken, therefore no grounds for a court case. That part of Daniel Corkin's will doesn't hold water. Anyone has the right to buy that ranch including a Bannock."

With those words Jarod felt his chest expand. Only a friendship as strong as the one his grandfather and Harlow had built over the years could have achieved this miracle. "How soon could you act on it?"

"Today if you want." He quirked one white eyebrow. "You're anticipating a bidding war?"

"According to Sadie, who confided in my grandfather, two other people made offers on the property before Daniel died. The place will be sold to one of them if no other offers come in before the deadline. The ranch is already in the multiple listings online. I'm afraid once my cousin sees it, he'll outbid anyone else to make make sure he comes out on top."

"Which cousin is that?"

"Ned."

"Ah, yes. Grant's son, the one who's always been in trouble. Why would he want to buy that ranch?"

"Though close to a century has gone by without any evidence, Ned still believes there's oil on the land. He's determined to get his hands on it." *And on Sadie.*

"Do you know how many gamblers have squandered

their lives going after that same pipe dream around these parts?"

"Ned has never been able to let it go," Jarod said.

"From what Ralph told me," Brigg mentioned, "that cousin of yours has some deep-seated problems. I recall hearing about the time when he and his friend were caught stealing some wild horses on federal land. It cost Grant plenty to keep that hushed up."

Jarod's brow furrowed in surprise. "I didn't know that. What happened?"

"Instead of ending up in jail, they were charged with drunk and disorderly conduct. It took influence with the judge and a lot of money to keep that under wraps. Ralph said Ned's father was continually bailing him out of some pretty nasty scrapes."

This was all news to Jarod. For Ned to have that kind of serious brush with the law underlined his cousin's dark side. Jarod had no idea his grandfather had confided in Harlow to this extent.

He winked at Jarod. "We'll get there before Ned does. I'll phone Mr. Bree at Parker Realty after you leave and set things in motion."

"When my grandfather hears that news, it'll probably add several years to his life."

The lawyer smiled. "I owe him so many favors for sending business my way, I'm delighted to do this."

"We're indebted to you, Harlow. Sadie's been our neighbor since she was born. It's time she had some joy in her life." He stood to shake the lawyer's hand.

Harlow squinted at him. "I'll give you and Ralph a ring as soon as I've spoken with Mr. Bree."

"Good. I'll see myself out."

On the way to the underground car park, Jarod mulled over the new revelation about Ned. It triggered his memory to the time his cousin had accused him of stealing Chief. Though Jarod had gotten legal permission to keep the wild horse once he'd tamed him, Ned had been furious. Having always been in competition with Jarod, Ned might have decided to steal a wild horse to prove he could have one of his own, too.

Since Sadie had come back, his toxic behavior around Jarod had an edge of desperation that bordered on instability.

Ever since his accident, Jarod had wanted to know the identity of the person who'd intentionally tried to take him out. Sadie believed her father had been behind it. So much so that she'd left the state to protect Jarod. But if it had been Daniel, he would have arranged a series of accidents long before that night. Over the years Jarod had occasionally seen Sadie's father out hunting in the mountains. He could have picked Jarod off at any time.

He suspected that Daniel had used the accident as an excuse to frighten his daughter further, knowing how vulnerable she was at that point. The man had been born with few scruples, but he'd stopped short of murder, only threatened it.

When Jarod really thought about it, there was only one person he was aware of who truly hated him for personal reasons. That was his cousin...

The revelation coming from Harlow had made him see things in a different light. More and more he was convinced that his cousin was the guilty party and had gotten away with his crime for years now.

On the night in question, Ned must have arranged for a truck ahead of time, probably from one of the friends he hung around with when they went off to keg parties. After driving his Jeep around town to throw Jarod off the scent, he'd gotten that friend to drive him to the crossroads where he'd ambushed Jarod. Or maybe Ned had borrowed it and was alone when he drove into Jarod.

Needing evidence, Jarod decided to visit some auto paint and body shops while he was still in Billings.

Before Ned had returned the borrowed truck to the owner, he would have gone to a shop for repairs, but not in White Lodge, where the police had already done a search.

When he reached his truck, Jarod bought a hamburger at a drive-through before starting his investigation of the dozens of body and paint shops in Billings. The police had checked a few places here, but they could have missed some. Most places kept invoices, accounts payable/receivable ledgers and expense reports for a minimum of seven years, but generally longer. Sadie's birthday had been May tenth, a Thursday. That narrowed the field as to time.

It was a long shot, but he might come across a business that had done some work for Ned. He would have used an assumed name and paid cash.

One by one he interviewed the service managers, hoping to come up with a lead. No one could give him information on the spot. He left his cell phone number for them to call him and also used his phone to retrieve a photo of Ned from the ranching office information for the managers to download.

Tomorrow morning he'd leave early for Bozeman and go through the same process. It wouldn't take as long to cover since it was a third the size of Billings, a city with a population over 100,000.

On his way home, his cell phone rang. Hoping it was one of the body shops, he clicked on without looking at the Caller ID and said hello.

"Hi!"

His hand tightened on the wheel. It was Leslie. For the life of him he couldn't muster any enthusiasm at hearing her voice. The only emotion at the moment was guilt that he couldn't give her what she wanted. "Hi, yourself."

"Is this a bad time to call?"

"No. I've been going nonstop and am just leaving Billings to drive back to the ranch. How was your day? Any new finds?"

"A hide scraper made out of bottle glass."

Jarod nodded. "Sounds like traditional technology meshed with a modern material."

"Exactly. I'd love you to work with me one of these days. Am I going to see you tonight?"

He'd already put her off once. "Let's do it. I'll meet you at the Moose Creek Barbecue in White Lodge at seven for dinner. You can tell me what else you've found."

"I can't wait to see you."

Jarod didn't feel the same way. "It'll be good to see you, too. I've had a ton of business to do for my grandfather and will enjoy the break."

"Jarod?" she asked tentatively. "Are you all right?"

He took a labored breath. "Why do you ask?"

"I don't know. You sound…detached."

"It's not intentional. I'm afraid it has been a long day. See you tonight."

After he ended the call, he realized he couldn't go on this way. Leslie needed reassurance, but Sadie's unexpected return to Montana had altered the path he'd been plodding since she'd left, throwing him into the greatest turmoil of his life.

What Daniel had told her that night had crystalized certain things for Jarod. If the statute of limitations hadn't run out and he could discover the proof, Ned would be facing felony assault charges for using a borrowed truck as a deadly weapon. Worse, because he'd left the scene of the crime without reporting it or getting help for Jarod, Ned would be looking at prison time.

If he didn't reopen the case, the most Jarod would do was go to Tyson and Grant with any evidence he found and let them deal with Ned in their own way.

His hand tightened around the phone, almost crushing it. What if he did find enough evidence to have the case reopened?

If Jarod's uncle Charlo knew what was going through his nephew's mind right now, he would intimate that the reason Jarod hadn't received his vision yet was because his cry was selfish. Only those who were of exemplary character and well prepared received the truly great visions. With the taste for revenge this strong on Jarod's lips, he was far from that serene place his uncle talked about.

Chapter 5

Saturday morning Sadie got breakfast for her and Ryan and then they went outside to an overcast sky. The small garden plot on the south wall of the house where it received the most sun needed work. While she watched Ryan toddle around with some toys, Sadie prepared the soil, then laid out black plastic to warm it up, a trick she'd learned from Addie Bannock years earlier. In a week she'd plant seeds.

While her mouth salivated at the thought of enjoying sweet juicy melons all summer, her cell phone rang. She wished it were Jarod, yet she knew that was impossible. As Millie had said, Sadie needed to be the one to tell him there was no other man in her life. But that was complicated because he was seeing another woman.

Even if he wanted to call Sadie, which he didn't, he

would have to use the landline because he didn't know her cell phone number. With a troubled sigh she pulled the cell from her pocket and checked the Caller ID. One glance and her spirits lifted.

"Zane! How are things going?"

"Couldn't be better. I've had all our mail forwarded to White Lodge. Right now I'm at the house sorting things. Tomorrow the moving van will come to put everything in storage. When they're through here, they'll load up the things from my apartment. How's Ryan?"

"Missing you. Just a minute. He'll want to talk to you." She walked over to her brother. "Ryan? It's your uncle Zane. Can you say hello?"

After Ryan greeted his uncle and babbled some other words not quite intelligible, she heard Zane chuckle and a conversation ensued with Ryan mentioning the juice he'd had for breakfast and one of the toy cars he held in his hand.

"You have to hang up now," she told the little boy. "Tell Uncle Zane bye-bye."

Ryan liked saying the words over and over, but finally Sadie put the phone back to her ear. "If I do the planting right, we'll have fresh honeydew all summer."

"How about some cantaloupe, too!"

"I'll plant some of those and maybe some green beans."

"Terrific. Have you heard from Mr. Bree yet?"

"No. I don't really expect to until you have a prospective buyer for Tim's house."

"Let's hope it's soon, but at least our Realtor has contacted him and knows we're serious. If all goes well here, I'll have the cleaners come and leave for Billings sometime Sunday in my Volvo. It can hold the main stuff you wanted me to bring along with my own."

"That's great. What about my Toyota?"

"The salesman at the dealership said he'd get a good price for it."

"I hope so. Dad's old truck is on its last legs. I need to buy a used one."

"Understood. Depending on how late I get away, it might be Monday night before I reach the ranch."

"We'll be waiting. Ryan will be thrilled. He keeps looking for you." Right now he was down on his haunches, pushing his little trucks and cars through the grass.

"I can't believe how much I've missed him."

Her throat swelled. "He's adorable."

"Amen."

"Is it going to be difficult to pull up stakes, Zane?"

"No. I'll always have my good memories, but my life isn't here anymore."

"I know what you mean. Much as I love San Francisco, my home is here."

After a silence, Zane told her, "Don't work too hard, Sadie."

"It's saving my life." Along with making a new home for Ryan, she needed to stay too busy to think. She'd tackled cleaning the house, including her father's bedroom. Now the outside needed attention. "Thank you for taking care of everything, Zane. I don't know what I'd do without you."

"We're family. Let's agree we both need each other. Because of you I can feel a whole new life opening up. When everything fell apart, I couldn't imagine putting one foot in front of the other."

She cleared her throat. "I've been there and done that."

"I know you have." He knew the secrets of her heart. "Talk to you soon."

"Drive safely, Zane." Her voice trembled. "If anything happened to you…"

"It won't."

As Sadie hung up, she felt a shadow fall over her. When she lifted her head she discovered Jarod standing there.

"Sorry," he said in his deep voice. "Once again I've startled you. Millie was out on the front porch washing windows and told me to walk around back."

After wishing he'd been the one who'd phoned her, she was so shocked to see him, she couldn't think clearly. Somehow on Jarod a denim shirt and jeans looked spectacular. "No problem. As you can see, I've been getting the ground ready to plant."

"Shades of my grandmother Addie."

She nodded. He remembered everything.

His enigmatic black eyes swept over her. "I drove over here to talk to you about the accident."

Jarod's reason for coming was as unexpected as his presence. Sadie struggled to keep the tremor out of her voice. "Since you didn't believe me about my father, I'm afraid any answers you need are buried with him."

He put his hands on his hips; pulling her attention to his hard-muscled physique. "I've given it a lot of thought and I don't believe your father was the culprit, Sadie. That's why I'm here."

Shock number two. "But he said—"

"What he did was use a scare tactic to frighten you

away from me for good," Jarod cut in on her. "I'm convinced that when he heard I was in the hospital, he realized it was the perfect moment to play on your fears."

Sadie was afraid to believe it. "Then who could have done such an evil thing?" She removed her gardening gloves.

"I've been doing an investigation and hope to figure it out before long. I wanted you to know that no matter how much pain your father caused you, he wasn't responsible for trying to hurt me or he would have done it much earlier. Though he wished I hadn't been in your life, we both know he was a troubled man with a terrible drinking problem. But it didn't go as far as planning to kill me, so you can cross him off your list."

Her lungs had constricted, making it difficult to breathe. "But according to you, someone *did* want you dead."

His eyes narrowed on her features. "The police and I both felt that the accident had to have been premeditated. Someone went to elaborate lengths to set me up. It took someone whose dislike of me turned to hate. I'll give you one guess."

Suddenly she felt sick. *"Ned,"* she whispered.

"I'm afraid so."

"After you told me he'd been stalking you in town, I thought a lot about that myself. But for him to go after you like that…"

"It chills the blood to think he could have done it to his own family, but I can't rule him out as the prime suspect."

"I agree," she whispered. Being a year younger than Jarod, Ned had been a senior when she'd started high school. He'd always chased after her. The more she'd ignored him, the more he'd mocked her friendship with his "half-breed cousin."

"He never hid his dislike of you."

After his graduation Ned had hung out in White Lodge with his friends and followed her around whenever she went into town. His actions were repulsive to her.

"You're the one girl who never gave him the time of day, but he never stopped wanting you. As our love grew, so did his jealousy. It's my belief he'd been following me on those last few nights when we met in the mountains. But I didn't realize it until the night before you and I were going to leave for the reservation. I caught him spying on me as I rode to the barn."

Horrified, Sadie stared at him. "You think he was watching us wh-when—" She couldn't finish.

"That's exactly what I think. But he couldn't go to my grandfather claiming to have seen us when he had no reason to be watching us. That would have opened up a whole new set of problems for him."

"He was sick!"

Jarod nodded. "The next afternoon after I hitched the horse trailer to my truck, he saw me leave with Chief and knew I was getting ready to do something with you. So he set me up, but he needed an accomplice and couldn't use one of our trucks on the ranch."

"Who would help him do anything that hideous?"

"His best friend, Owen."

"Owen Pearson? Cindy's brother?" She was incredulous. "I know they used to drink and mess around like a lot of guys, but I can't imagine him doing anything like that."

"I found out from my grandfather that Ned and Owen committed a crime a few years ago but it was hushed up." Jarod told her what he'd learned from Harlow. "Ned could wheedle money from his father when he wanted. Don't forget he and Owen have been friends for years and got into so much trouble, Ralph claims it turned Grant prematurely gray."

"I didn't realize Ned gave your family that many worries. It's still hard for me to believe Owen would go that far."

"I've been doing my own investigation." Jarod reached in his back pocket and handed her a sheet of paper, which she opened. It was a photocopy of a receipt from a body shop in Bozeman. The repairs listed included grill and front fender work on a 2003 Ford F-150 pickup owned by Kevin Pearson of the Bar-S Ranch, brought in on May 10 and repairs completed May 16 of the year in question.

"Jarod—" She lifted her eyes to him. Streams of unspoken words passed between them.

"The manager of the shop didn't recognize Ned's picture. It's been too many years. But whoever took the truck in paid cash up front. I checked the police report on my truck, which was totaled. Once I contact the department that investigated my case and give them this receipt, then the case will be reopened to see if there's a match between the two vehicles."

"That means they'll be contacting the Pearsons about the truck." Sadie frowned. "What if it has been sold or traded in for another one by now?"

"The police will track it down. Owen will have to fess up to what happened to his father's truck. Unless, of course, it's a huge coincidence and his father's truck was damaged some other way. But if that was the case, why didn't he let the insurance pay for it?

"I'm afraid he has a lot of explaining to do. If he was helping Ned, then he'll have to make the decision if he wants to go to jail for him or not. But I'm not ready to act quite yet."

Sadie's eyes stung with salty tears. "I don't know why you have to wait. This couldn't be a coincidence. Ned could have killed you— All this time I thought it was my father." Her body grew tense. "Your cousin should go to prison for what he did. You were left to die—"

Her raised voice alarmed Ryan, who stood and came running to her with an anxious look on his precious face. She swept him up into her arms and buried her face in his neck.

"But I didn't," Jarod said in a quiet voice, tousling Ryan's hair. "I'm pretty sure he didn't intend to finish me off, just put me out of commission. As for his plan, it backfired because I was back on the ranch three days later and you'd fled to California out of his reach. Your departure put an end to any dreams Ned entertained about the two of you getting together."

"He was delusional."

"I agree. But now that you're back, he's going to make trouble again."

Her stomach muscles clenched. "What do you mean?"

"I know for a fact he hasn't given up on you. Avery told me about the incident at the funeral when Ned approached you. Be careful around him."

That sounded ominous. "What aren't you telling me?"

"I suppose we'll all find out when this new investigation gets under way. I'll leave now so you can give your little brother the attention he's craving. He really looks like his uncle."

"It's the dimples. They run in the Lawson family. Mom fell in love with Tim's. It kills me Ryan has been deprived of both parents."

"He has a wonderful mother in you."

"Thank you. I'm planning to adopt him."

"Then he's a lucky little boy. Take care, Sadie, and remember what I said."

"Jarod? Wait—" she called to him, but he moved too fast on those long, powerful legs. She couldn't very well run after him with Ryan in her arms. Her brother needed lunch and a nap.

Sadie hurried inside, shaken by everything he'd told her and even more shaken by the things he'd only hinted at. Millie stood at the kitchen sink filling another bucket with hot water and vinegar. "Jarod was here a long time. Everything all right?"

"Yes and no." She didn't dare share the evidence Jarod had uncovered until he gave her permission. But one thing had become self-evident. Her longing to be with him was growing unbearable.

Millie started out the back door, then paused. Sadie thought she detected a faint smile on the older woman's lips. "After you've fed Ryan and put him down, come on outside where I'm working. There's something you ought to know."

With one of those cryptic comments Millie was famous for, Sadie hurried to feed Ryan and put him down with a bottle. The cute little guy had tired himself out playing and fell asleep fast.

She found Millie washing the windows at the rear of the house. "I'm back."

The housekeeper looked over her shoulder at Sadie. "When Jarod drove in, he was pulling a horse trailer. After he left, I saw him drive to the barn and pull around it. Kind of made me wonder what he was doing when the road back to his place goes in the other direction. If I were you, I'd walk down there and find out what's going on."

Sadie's heart raced till it hurt. Feeling seventeen again, she flew down the drive past her father's truck to the barn. But when she rounded the corner, Jarod's rig wasn't there and her heart plummeted to her feet.

After hearing her call to him, had he hoped she'd come after him? Until she had answers, she wouldn't be able to breathe. While she stood there in a quandary, she heard Liz's horses whinnying and wondered what was going on.

She opened the barn doors. "Hey, you guys. What's up?" She walked inside to check both stalls. All of a sudden she heard the neigh of another horse. It couldn't be Mac's. He was out working on his horse, Toby.

Sadie spun around. The light from outside illuminated the interior enough for her to see a gleaming black filly in the stall where she'd once kept Brandy. Her body started to tremble as she moved closer to the three-year-old, which looked to be fourteen hands high.

This couldn't be the foal she'd seen in the purple lupine with Jarod when she was seventeen! That wasn't possible, but the filly had those special hooked ears and broad forehead that tapered to the muzzle, just the way Sadie remembered. On further examination she saw the straight head and wide-set eyes of Chief, the wild stallion Jarod had tamed.

"Oh, you gorgeous creature," she whispered shakily. Sadie didn't need to ask where this beauty had come from. "I'll be back, but first I need to know all about you before this goes any further. I promise I won't be long."

Sadie's feet seemed to have wings as she flew up the road to the house. "Millie?"

The housekeeper turned around. "I'm right here!"

"I've got to find Jarod. Do you mind watching Ryan until I get back?"

"Of course not, honey. What's going on?"

Sadie ran in the house to grab the keys off the peg. When she came out she said, "There's a new filly in the barn. I can't keep her. Jarod needs to come back and get it."

Before she reached the truck a voice of irony called out, "Good luck to that."

Five minutes later she drove through the gates of the Bannock Ranch. The spread resembled a small city. She took the road leading to the barn and corrals where Jarod would have parked the horse trailer. Intent on finding him, she wound around the sheds until she saw his rig in the distance. He still hadn't unhitched the trailer.

After pulling up next to it, she jumped down from the truck. As she reached the entrance, the man she'd come to see was just leaving the barn on his horse. Riding bareback, the magnificent sight of him ready to head out took her breath. His long black hair, fastened at the nape, gleamed despite the gathering storm clouds blotting out the sun.

They saw each other at the same time. He was caught off guard for once, and his eyes gleamed black fire as they roved over her, thrilling her to the core of her being. While she stood there out of breath, he brought his horse close before coming to a standstill.

She couldn't swallow. "I have to talk to you, Jarod."

How she envied him sitting there as still as a summer's day. "I'm going to ride to the upper pasture. Come with me."

Before she could respond, he reached down with that swift male grace only he possessed and lifted her so she was seated in front of him. He wrapped his left arm around her waist and tucked her up tight against him. The way his hand splayed over her midriff infused electricity in every cell of her body.

"Reminds me of old times," he murmured against her temple, "except this time I'll be able to see where we're going. Don't get me wrong. I like your new hairstyle, but now I don't have anything to tug."

That rare teasing side of Jarod had come out, the side she adored. Robbed of words, she was helpless to do anything but give in to the euphoria of being this close to him again. Though it had been eight years, their bodies knew each other and settled in as one entity.

Once he urged his horse into a gallop, the layers of pain peeled away, liberating her for a moment out of time. Heedless of the darkening clouds, they were like children who'd been let out of school and were eager to run until they dropped.

She quickly lost track of where they were going. This

was like flying through heaven, achieving heights and distant stars unknown until now. Filled with delight, she heard laughter and realized it was her own. Through it all her body absorbed the fierce pounding of his heart against her back.

At one point it dawned on her he'd brought them to the pine-covered ridge that looked down on their favorite place. He reined his horse to a stop so they could enjoy the meadow with its vista of wildflowers in glorious bloom.

She gripped the hand pinning her against him. *"Jarod..."*

"I haven't heard you say my name like that except in my sleep. Did you ever dream of me?"

This was a time for honesty.

"Yes," she admitted quietly.

"Every night?"

Haunted by the agony she heard in his voice because it matched her own, she said, "Don't ask me that. It's all in the past. I came to find you because—"

"The filly is yours, Sadie." The authority in his voice signaled the end of the discussion. "Now that the war is over, consider it a peace offering."

She was still in shock over his incredible gift, but it was growing darker. "Jarod, we'd better go back before we get caught in the rain."

"It's too late. We'll stay in the shelter of these pines until it passes over. Volan needs a rest."

He slid off his horse in an instant and gripped her waist to help her down. After tying the reins to a tree branch, he walked her over to the fattest tree trunk and sat against it, pulling her onto his lap. By now the wind was gusting, bringing the smell of rain with it.

"This is only a small storm. We'll wait it out." He gathered her to him in a protective gesture. Cocooned in his warmth, she could stay like this forever. "If you're worried about getting wet, I promise I'll protect you."

She relaxed against him. "Tell me about the adorable filly."

"Chief was her sire."

"I *knew* it. She has the shape of his head and eyes."

"It took two tries with the black broodmare I acquired to produce her." She could tell by the softness in his voice that her observation had pleased him. "Her first offspring was a grullo I gave to Uncle Charlo's boy."

"You mean, Squealing Son Who Runs Fast?"

Jarod chuckled. "You remember."

"I remember everything," she confessed in a tremulous voice. "He must be fifteen by now."

"The perfect age to train his own stallion. But that was his childhood name. Now he's known as Runs Over Mountains."

"Sounds like he has some of the same genes that run through his noble cousin Sits in the Center."

He kissed the side of her brow, sending fingers of delight through her nervous system. "What happened to Born of Flint?"

Jarod had forgiven her. "That name belonged to my world when pain was my constant companion. But seriously, Jarod, no gift has ever thrilled me more. I love her already."

"Your filly has been registered as Black Velvet. Until

now, she has lived at the reservation on my uncle's property. I've been getting her used to a saddle, but you'll need to break her in more before you take her riding."

Sadie gripped his hand harder. Velvet was the name she'd given the new foal they'd seen that wonderful day years ago. Now Sadie had her own filly, a horse who'd known nothing but Jarod's love. She had to clear her throat. "Velvet has been trained by the expert. Thank you doesn't begin to cover what I'm feeling, not when I've done nothing to deserve such a present."

"When my grandfather told me you were going to stay in Montana, I realized you would need a horse."

"Your uncle Charlo must be bursting with pride."

"What do you mean?"

"Do you remember the time you took me to meet him and his family? Before we left he took me aside and told me you possessed a very rare trait like your mother. It was the ability to hear the cries of the oppressed, the sick, the weak. He said that you weren't ashamed to help others.

"I didn't understand what he meant at the time, but I do now. After I visited Ralph last week he told you everything about my situation, didn't he?"

Before she heard his answer, the rain descended, first in individual drops, then it poured, yet they stayed dry. She nestled deeper in his arms, finding a comfort she'd never known in her life, except with him. Together they listened to the elements that had always made up their world.

His lips were buried in her hair. "You think I see you as a charity case?"

"I think that's the way you've always seen me. A

cast-off waif you took pity on because it's in your nature. After eight years, you're still coming to my rescue, trying to right wrongs against me by giving me Velvet. I'll be indebted to you all my life for everything you've done for me in the past, but it's time you gave that side of your nature a rest in order to walk your true path."

He lifted his head in surprise. "My true path?"

"Mmm." The downpour was easing in intensity. She moved out of his arms and stood. "The one you used to talk about that will lead to your ultimate destiny."

After a long silence he asked, "What about yours?"

"Mine was revealed when my mother died and left Ryan to my care."

Before she gave in to her longing and begged him to kiss her, she needed answers about the woman who was in his life now. "Tell me about Leslie Weston."

Immediately he got to his feet. "Listening to so many wagging tongues tends to confuse the listener."

"If you're talking about the way you were confused with wagging tongues concerning me and Zane at the funeral, you're right. But please don't be offended. I've heard she's a lovely woman who works with Avery at the dig site. Your grandfather sounded particularly taken with her, which means you're on the right path."

"Grandfathers are prone to dream."

"Liz tells me that not only is Leslie a highly educated archaeologist studying the Crow culture, she's also well-traveled and comes from a good family in Colorado Springs. How important is she to you?"

"Why do you ask?" His tone grated.

Don't tiptoe around this, Sadie. "Because when word

gets out where Velvet came from, I don't want her to misunderstand or be hurt."

After the telltale rise and fall of his chest, he said, "The rain has stopped. We need to get back to the ranch."

Instead of a protestation that the woman he'd been involved with meant nothing to him, he was ready to leave this sacred place. Sadie had her answer. She just hadn't expected it to feel as if one of those wild stallions they used to watch had just kicked her in the chest, knocking the life out of her.

Schooling her features to show no emotion, she turned to him. "This time I'll sit behind you. That way I can tug on *your* hair for a change."

Her teasing produced no softening of his stone-faced expression. As he walked over to Volan, she followed him. "I liked the way you used to wear it, but I'm glad you gave in to the right impulse to let it grow.

"I know you'll hate hearing this because you don't like compliments, but now that I'm grown up, I'm not afraid to say what I think. You're a very beautiful man, Sits in the Center. Leslie Weston would have figured that out the first time she laid eyes on you."

In seconds he'd vaulted onto Volan's back with practiced ease, then held out his hand for Sadie to climb on behind him. She settled herself and slid her arms around his waist. If she couldn't kiss the life out of him because he belonged to someone else, she could at least hold him in her arms for the ride home.

Judging from his reaction to her question about Leslie, this would be the only time she would ever be allowed to get this close to him again. As the rain that had cleared the air, this conversation had cleared away the last piece in the complicated mosaic of their lives. Their love story had come to its final, tragic close.

Chapter 6

Jarod's uncle Charlo knew of his nephew's struggle to let Leslie or any woman into his life while another woman lived in his heart. This Saturday afternoon Sadie's question ended the struggle. He knew what had to be done to end a situation that couldn't go on any longer.

As they rode back to Jarod's ranch in silence, his uncle's analogy about the wolf took on fresh meaning. It *would* be better to risk death for a chance to find a mate and a territory than to live through every winter in agony alone.

Weighed down by his thoughts, he was surprised to hear Sadie's sudden gasp as they approached the barn. He glanced over to see what had caused the reaction. If it wasn't Ned coming out of the barn on foot! Once again it was no accident he'd been hanging around. He must have seen Daniel Corkin's truck and put two and two together. Jarod thought his cousin looked a little green around the edges. Wasn't that jealousy's color?

Sadie's arms tightened around Jarod as he rode his horse straight to her truck. Aware of her fear, he threw his leg over Volan and pulled her off, then opened the driver's door. "In you go," he whispered, shutting it after her.

Their eyes met for a breathless moment before she started the engine and took off. He stood there watching until she'd driven out of sight.

Ned smirked at him. "Leslie's not going to like it when she finds out what you've been doing all afternoon."

Jarod turned to look at his cousin. "I'm afraid there's a lot more you're not going to like when your father hears you've been spending time in town minding other people's business rather than inspecting the machinery."

When Jarod had hired Ben as the new foreman, one of his jobs was to keep a close eye on Ned, who was lax in his responsibilities and played hooky when he thought he could get away with it. Ben reported Ned's activities to Jarod on a daily basis. Ned's assigned job was to keep all the ranch machinery in good condition and operational, but he often failed in that department, which added to Jarod's workload.

"What in the hell are you talking about?"

"The grain-cutting swathers and forage harvesters for one thing. They haven't been oiled or greased on time. That's your department. One of the grain trucks has a broken part that needs replacing. Have you taken a look at the Haybine mowers lately? If I were you, I'd get busy or it could all rebound on you."

Ned's cheeks turned a ruddy color, a sure sign of guilt. "What do you mean?"

"That's for *you* to figure out." From the corner of his eye, he glimpsed Rusty, the stable manager, and signaled to him. "We got caught in the storm, and now I'm in a hurry. Will you take care of Volan for me? He'll need a rubdown."

"Sure, Jarod."

Ignoring Ned, Jarod walked over to his rig to unhitch the trailer. The puddles from the cloudburst were still drifting away. Climbing into his truck, he drove out of the parking area without acknowledging his cousin and headed for White Lodge.

Leslie would be off work by now. He hoped to find her at her apartment. He knew she'd sensed something was wrong on their dinner date Wednesday. It was time they talked. She lived in an eight-plex near the center of town where they usually met before going out for the evening. He'd brought her out to the ranch one time to meet his grandfather, but it was easier for them to get together in White Lodge, the halfway point between her work and the ranch.

Both his grandfather and uncle approved of her. Charlo had been amenable to her interviewing him for a newsletter she contributed to about the Absarokee dig site. There was nothing not to like about Leslie. But she wasn't Sadie.

Pleased to see her Forerunner parked in her stall, he drove to the guest parking and got out of his truck. Taking the stairs two at a time, he reached her apartment and gave a knock she would recognize.

He didn't have to wait long for her to open the door. "Jarod—" She broke into a smile that lit up her brown eyes. "I didn't know you were coming tonight. Why didn't you say something at dinner the other night or phone me?"

"I'm sorry I didn't give you any warning, but this couldn't wait."

When he didn't reach to kiss her, her smile slowly disappeared. "Come in. Is this about your grandfather? Is he worse?"

He walked into her living room. "No. I'm happy to say he's doing better and off his oxygen for the time being."

"That's wonderful! Have you eaten yet? I just made homemade fajitas. Would you like one?"

"They smell good, but I'm not hungry. Go ahead and eat." He took a seat in one of her overstuffed chairs.

She frowned. "I don't think I can till you tell me what's wrong. You're not yourself. In fact, for the past two weeks you haven't been the Jarod I've known."

He shook his head. "I realize that."

Leslie perched on the arm of the sofa, studying him. "You wouldn't have come here out of the blue like this without a good reason. Have you decided you don't want to see me anymore?" He heard the pain in her voice.

Jarod met her searching gaze head-on. "I can't," he answered. She deserved the whole truth no matter how much it hurt. He was glad he hadn't been intimate with her yet.

Her features looked pinched. "Avery hinted that there

was someone in your past. Are you saying you can't get over her?"

He got to his feet. "I thought I'd put her behind me, but her father died and now she's back in Montana for good. I was with her today."

She averted her eyes. "And the old chemistry is still working."

The blood hammered in his ears. "Yes. Don't get me wrong. We're not together. I don't know if we ever will be, but feeling as I do—"

"I get it," she broke in. "Do you mind my asking who she is?"

"Her name is Sadie Corkin. The Corkin ranch borders our property."

Leslie stood. "Childhood sweethearts?"

"Yes."

"That's an obstacle I'm not even going to attempt to hurdle. One of the many things I admire about you, Jarod, is your honesty, even when it's devastating."

"Leslie... I was trying to make it work with us."

She walked over to the door, her curly auburn hair swinging slightly. "I believe you and I give you full marks, but in the end, trying doesn't cut it. That explains why you weren't anxious to sleep with me, or to drive to Colorado with me."

"If she'd never come back, things might have been different."

"No." Leslie shook her head. "If she hadn't come back, our relationship would still have ended because it's evident you're a one-woman man. There aren't very many of those around." She clung to the open door. "I've loved every minute we've spent together."

"So have I."

"Because of who you are, I know you mean that."

"I do."

"But it's just not enough for me or you. Love means sharing a single soul inhabiting two bodies. That definition doesn't apply to you and me. I'm grateful you stopped by, Jarod, but now I need to be alone."

Jarod had no desire to make this any more painful. "Take care, Leslie." He kissed her forehead before leaving the apartment. He wished there was some way he could have spared her this hurt. No one deserved happiness more than she did.

On his drive back to the ranch, her parting comment played over in his mind. He and Sadie *had* shared one soul. That's why no other relationship had worked for him. But he still didn't know about the men she'd been involved with since she'd moved to California.

If there was someone important, she wasn't letting it get in the way of buying the ranch and living here. So many questions still remained unanswered where Sadie was concerned. But saying goodbye to Leslie had been the right thing to do.

When he entered the front door of the ranch house, the housekeeper came running. "I'm glad you're home. Your grandfather is in an agitated state."

He moaned. "I thought the doctor had taken him off the oxygen."

She shook her head. "It's not his health, Jarod. Tyson was here earlier and they quarreled." *Tyson?* "He's terribly upset about something and says he can't discuss it with anyone but you."

Jarod's gut told him this had to be about Ned, especially after their confrontation earlier. "Where's Avery?"

"She's not home yet."

"Thanks, Jenny." He hurried down the hall to his grandfather's bedroom and found him sitting up at his desk near the window in his pajamas and robe. Though he was gratified to see Ralph was well enough to be out of bed, Jenny's mention of Tyson had filled him with concern.

"Grandfather?"

He looked around with a flushed face. "At last."

"What's happened?"

"What hasn't?" he said with uncharacteristic sharpness. "I'm sorry, son. I didn't mean to snap. I'm just glad you're home. Sit down. We have to talk."

Jarod pulled up a chair next to the desk. "I can see you've been going over the accounts."

Ralph's gray eyes flicked to his. "Tyson needed me to help him with the figures. He just left. I'm afraid we had it out. It's been coming on for a long time. After our father died, Addie warned me I should let my brother take his share of the ranch and make it his own place. But he begged me to go into business with him and I didn't have the heart to say no. For the most part we've gotten along. But with time, there've been issues over Ned. He doesn't have your instincts for ranching and never did.

"Your idea of developing two calving seasons a few years ago has brought in unprecedented profits. When Tyson and I went along with your plan, Ned fell apart and has been impossible ever since. Now that Ned has found out the Corkin property is up for sale, he's asked for a loan from Grant to buy it."

Jarod got up from the chair and started pacing. "Let me guess. Grant's money is stretched due to helping his other children, so he's come to Tyson for $700,000 for Ned to buy the place."

Ralph nodded. "Grant's always been afraid of Ned and doesn't know how to say no to him. It's Grant's opinion that if Ned made a break with the family business and had his own spread to manage, his son might turn into a real rancher."

"We know that's never going to happen."

His grandfather shook his head. "I advised Tyson it would be the wrong decision to give money to a grandson who could never make good on such an investment. But just as I feared, he got angry. My brother isn't well and not up for a fight with Grant. He told me he'd be back tomorrow for my consent. If I don't give it, he'll take the money out, anyway. Of course, it's his right as part owner."

They stared at each other before Jarod said, "What do you want to do? Tell Tyson you've already authorized Harlow to buy the ranch for Sadie and Zane?"

"Never. That has to remain a secret."

Jarod didn't need to think about it. "Then don't try to stop him, Grandfather. You love your brother too much, so make your peace with him and let him negotiate with Mr. Bree. When the time is almost up, Harlow will come in with a little higher offer and that will be it.

"In time Tyson and Grant will learn that Zane Lawson bought the ranch and no one will ever know the truth because the money came out of your savings account and mine. Tyson has no access to them."

His grandfather tilted his head back. "What do you mean *your* account?"

"I've been investing my money and plan to contribute. Sadie'd be my wife if things had been different."

"I know." Ralph's eyes dimmed. "When Addie and I heard about your accident, it was one of the worst moments of our lives. We could have lost you." His voice trembled.

Touched by those words, Jarod squeezed his shoulder. "Don't you know I'm tough like you? Now that you're feeling better, I have news. Let me show you what I found after doing some investigating about the accident on my own."

Jarod showed his grandfather the paper from the body shop in Bozeman incriminating Owen Pearson.

Tears rolled down Ralph's cheeks. "Oh, Jarod… All these years I've asked you to be the bigger man, which you always will be. To think Ned could have done such a thing. It explains why his behavior has grown worse over time. You have every right to go to the police with what you've found."

"That's true." For now he was holding off deciding what to do about it. "Did Sadie tell you she's going to adopt Ryan?"

"Yes, bless her heart." His grandfather reached for Jarod's hand. "Now tell me about that lovely woman you brought to the house a while back. When are you going to bring her again?"

"I'm afraid that's not going to happen, Grandfather."

"Why not?"

"I drove to White Lodge earlier this evening and told Leslie the truth. I can't be involved with her while I still have feelings for Sadie."

"You've done the right thing for Leslie and yourself," he murmured with what sounded like satisfaction. "A house divided against itself can't stand."

In spite of his turmoil, Jarod smiled. He bounced between two cultures. Both his mentors offered the same wisdom.

"So." His grandfather sat back in the chair looking relieved. "We'll keep all this to ourselves and wait a few more days before we tell Harlow to make the final move. When everything has been transacted, Harlow can contact Zane and they'll go from there."

Jarod's thoughts shot ahead. "It's good it will be in Zane's name." He gave his grandfather a hug. "I'll tell Martha to come in and help you get ready for bed."

Ralph tugged on his arm. "Do me a favor, son. Watch your back around Ned. I need you."

The feeling was mutual.

Ryan was ecstatic when Zane came into the kitchen on Tuesday morning. He'd arrived late Monday night. While the two of them walked down to the barn to visit the new filly Sadie had told him about, she had hurriedly put the things away that Zane had brought from California. Now Ryan had his toys and pictures, and his room resembled the nursery Eileen had made for him in San Francisco.

After lunch he went down for a nap with his favorite furry rabbit.

Zane was bringing in the last of his own items from

the car when Sadie stepped out onto the front porch dressed in cowboy boots, jeans and a short-sleeved white blouse. She'd tied an old black paisley bandana around her neck for fun.

"You look cute in that."

"Thanks. When I saw it in the sack you brought in, it brought back memories. I thought, why not look the part."

"All you need is a cowboy hat."

She smiled. "I'm afraid my old one got lost years ago. While Ryan's asleep, I'll run into town and pick one up when I get the groceries."

"Take as long as you want. I plan to devote the rest of the day to him once he wakes up."

"He'll love that. We're so glad you're back safely."

"Me, too." His eyes glinted with curiosity. "That horse is a beauty. For Jarod to give you a present like that means he still cares for you a great deal."

She shook her head. "He feels sorry for me."

"Sadie—"

"It's true. He knew Dad sold my old horse. Before you say anything else, you need to know Jarod's involved with another woman and it's serious."

Zane frowned. "Did he tell you that?"

It was more a case of his not answering her question about Leslie Weston when they'd been out riding the other day. "I've heard it from his grandfather and from Liz, who's very close with Avery. Now, I'd better get going. See you later and we'll talk."

They only had two weeks left to work out an arrangement with Mr. Bree. So far she'd been living on some of her savings while they'd pooled their resources.

With the days passing so quickly, Sadie's fear escalated that their best efforts might not be enough. But she refused to think about that yet, or the possibility that Jarod might be getting married in the near future. Millie had sounded as though she thought it could happen.

After loading up on groceries in White Lodge, Sadie put the bags in the truck, then decided to buy herself a treat in the hope it would make her feel better. The Saddle Up Barn was just down the street. She'd drop by there for a cowboy hat.

It didn't take her long to find the one she wanted. Black, like her new filly, like... Jarod's eyes and hair. The band and sides of the brim were covered in a delicate gold floral pattern that picked up the gold-and-silver cowboy concho on the band. She was partial to the pinch-front, teardrop crown that gave it character.

After paying the bill, she walked out of the shop wearing the hat and was met by a barrage of wolf whistles from various guys passing by in their rigs. Their response reminded her of her barrel racing days in her teens. She'd almost forgotten what that experience was like.

Every time she and Liz performed at the county rodeo she'd watch for Jarod, hoping he'd be in the crowd with his family to cheer on Connor, who was a fabulous bulldogger. Being a contestant, she often carried the Montana State flag as they paraded around the arena for the opening ceremony. During those times when she was all decked out in her hat and fancy Western shirt with the fringe, she'd feel Jarod's piercing black eyes staring at her and almost faint with excitement.

The memories swamped her, causing her to forget

she was headed for the post office. She needed to mail the thank-you notes she'd written to all the people who'd sent flowers for the funeral. While she was buying a book of stamps from the machine, she heard her name called out in a familiar voice and turned around.

"Avery!" Her heart raced to see Jarod's sister come up to her, a smile lighting her gray-green eyes. Avery and Jarod shared similar facial features that identified them as Bannocks.

"I've been following you since I saw you walking across the street. Do you know you caused about a dozen accidents out there?" Sadie laughed in embarrassment. "It's true. You used to knock them dead at the rodeo, but your impact is more lethal now."

"It's the new hat."

"That's bull and you know it. In high school the guys voted you Queen of Montana Days your senior year. To get that nomination, let alone win, you had to be able to stop traffic for *all* the right reasons."

"Stop—" She gave her friend a hug. Avery could make her blush.

"I'm glad I ran into you. Since Connor will be home, we're going to throw a surprise family birthday party on Monday the twenty-ninth, for Grandpa, who's going to be eighty-four. He's feeling so well we thought it would be fun to invite a few close friends. Our cousin Cassie will be coming from Great Falls, of course, and can't wait to see you. Naturally everyone on the Farfields Ranch is invited, including the Hensons, Ryan's uncle Zane and that cute little brother of yours."

Sadie could hardly breathe. It would mean facing Jarod, who would be there with Leslie Weston. Maybe they were celebrating more than a birthday. She felt ill at the possibility, but she'd have to go even if it killed her.

"Sadie, don't worry about Ned," Avery added. "Connor has orders to keep him away from you."

"Thanks." But Ned had been the furthest thing from her mind. "We'd love to come." Sadie marveled that she was even able to get the words out. "I'll tell Millie as soon as I get back to the ranch."

"Wonderful. It'll be very low key. Please, no gifts. I'm making his favorite homemade hand-cranked pineapple ice cream, Grandma Myra's recipe. When he sees what I'm doing, he'll want to help me."

"Don't let him do it, Avery!"

She chuckled. "Try telling him that. Come any time after six-thirty. Grandpa gets tired fast and goes to bed early."

"We'll be there. What can I bring?"

"Yourselves!"

Sadie gave her another hug. When Jarod had asked her to marry him, she'd been so thrilled that Avery was going to be her sister-in-law. Instead, Leslie Weston would be the luckiest woman on earth to become a part of that family.

"See you then, Avery." She watched her leave, then put the stamps on the envelopes and mailed them. With her heart dragging on the sidewalk, she headed back to the truck. How in the name of heaven would she get through the party when she knew Jarod would be there?

Maybe at the last minute she could claim Ryan was running a temperature. Zane could go without her. She'd send Ralph her apologies in a written note. Zane would deliver it with her gift and tell him she'd be over when

Ryan was better. She and Ralph would celebrate with a card game.

On impulse she drove to Chapman's Drugstore and bought him two packs of playing cards and a card shuffler with new batteries. She also bought some wrapping paper and a silly birthday card Ralph would understand with his sense of humor. It said, "Grandfather still looks pretty good on his birthday. If it just hadn't been for_____." You could fill the line in with anything you wanted.

Without having to think about it Sadie wrote "the neighbors."

Chapter 7

Avery had coordinated their grandfather's birthday party with Jarod and Connor's help. She'd hired caterers to do the cooking and serving out on the back patio. Jarod couldn't have been happier when he'd learned she'd included Sadie and the Hensons in the guest list.

Because of Ned, Jarod's afternoon ride with Sadie had ended abruptly, leaving things hanging. Since then he'd broken it off with Leslie, but due to the long hours of calving season, this would be Jarod's first opportunity to get Sadie alone and answer the question of Leslie's importance in his life.

The evening of the party, after a shower and shave, he put on a silky black sport shirt and gray trousers. This was a special occasion. Six weeks ago his grandfather had been in the hospital and Jarod had feared he wouldn't come out again. But he'd rallied and in some respects seemed better than he had been in several months. Jarod was convinced Sadie's presence on the Corkin ranch had had a lot to do with the change in him.

Ralph was furious over Daniel's shameless treatment of her. To help her keep the ranch in her family was a gesture that revealed the depth of his affection for her. Like Jarod, he was in this fight to win. The end of the month couldn't come soon enough for either of them. After Harlow bought the ranch, they could all breathe more easily again.

Once he was ready, he went downstairs. "You look distinguished in that new gray suit, Grandfather. It matches your eyes."

Ralph chuckled. "You think?"

"Connor has excellent taste."

"Come to think of it, you and I match," he said with a smile.

Just as he spoke, Connor walked into the bedroom wearing a tan suit. "Come on, you two. Everyone has started congregating out on the patio."

Jarod hoped that meant Sadie had arrived. He needed to tamp down the frantic pounding of his heart. He and his brother both linked arms with their grandfather and walked with him to the back of the house. Before they could see people, Jarod heard voices and smelled steaks cooking on the grill.

As they stepped out onto the patio, everyone clapped and sang "Happy Birthday." Jarod estimated the whole Bannock clan had showed up with at least twenty other family friends. His grandfather looked pleased with the turnout—sixty-odd people including grandchildren,

young and old, sitting at the tables set up for the occasion.

Ralph thanked everyone for coming. "Go ahead and
eat because that's what I intend to do. I'll bore you with
a speech later!" His remarks drew laughter as Jarod
and Connor helped him to his place at the head table.

"I'll get his food," Jarod said to his brother, who
nodded.

He walked around the other side of the smorgasbord
to fix his grandfather a plate. A quick glance at the assembled group revealed the Hensons had come, but to
his disappointment no Corkins or Lawsons yet. His gaze
traveled to Tyson and his wife's table, which included
Grant and Pat. No sign of Ned, either.

Jarod needed to keep the line moving. His grandfather liked his steak medium-rare. After filling the plate,
he carried it to the table and sat with him. Jarod wasn't
hungry and told Connor to go ahead and get his food.
His eyes went to Avery, looking particularly lovely in
a deep red dress. She moved around, setting up a mike
that could be passed around for people to make toasts.

In another five minutes Ned showed up. His father
motioned him over to his table and the two men got into
a lengthy discussion. Clearly, Grant wasn't happy about
something, but that was nothing new.

As Jarod continued to look around, he saw Sadie and
Zane slip in from the side of the house to sit with Mac
and Millie. Zane held Ryan in his arms.

Sadie had dressed in a sophisticated orange, yellow
and white print cocktail dress, an outfit she'd probably
worn to dinner in San Francisco with some lucky man.
The short sleeves and scooped neck exposed the tan

she'd picked up since moving back to the ranch. Her windblown blond hair had the luster of a pearl. Jarod could find no words.

Before long one of the caterers wheeled out a cart carrying a chocolate birthday cake with lighted sparklers. The cake was in the shape of a giant cowboy boot with the word *Ralph* written in red frosting down the side. More of Avery's doing. Jarod gave his sister a silent nod of approval.

Their grandfather did the honors of cutting the cake. To facilitate matters, Connor and Jarod helped pass the dessert. When he neared Sadie's table and she looked up, it struck Jarod how the years had added a womanly beauty to her that he found irresistible. He couldn't take his eyes off her. "Enjoy your meal?"

"It was delicious," she said in a quiet voice, but a glance at her nearly full plate told him she hadn't been hungry, either. "I brought a present for Ralph. Where shall I put it?"

"I'll take it for you and give it to him."

"Thank you." She handed him a gift bag. The touch of her fingers sent a live current through his body. He walked to the head table and put the small bag in front of his grandfather. "It's a gift from Sadie," he whispered, then went back to handing out the cake.

A little while later Avery announced it was time for people to give toasts. Using the mike, everyone got in on the act, telling anecdotes about Jarod's grandfather that brought smiles and laughter. Finally it was Ralph's turn. With their help, he got to his feet.

"What a gratifying sight! If only Addie could be here with me. Thank you all for coming to help me celebrate.

I don't know what I'd do without my three wonderful grandchildren who made this night possible. It's a very special night because one of our long-lost neighbors, Sadie Corkin, has come back to us after an eight-year absence, along with her new little brother, Ryan, and his uncle, Zane Lawson. I look forward to us being neighbors for years to come."

Only Jarod understood the meaning behind his grandfather's words and loved him for it. After Ralph showed Jarod the card she'd given him, emotion swamped him to realize what a burden her father's hatred had been to her.

"Thanks for this, Sadie." Ralph held up the card shuffler. "Sadie used to play canasta with me and Addie. I look forward to another game soon. I taught her how to play, you know." He winked. "Maybe this time I'll slaughter *you* instead of the other way around."

Amid the laughter and cheering, Jarod saw Sadie smile. A few minutes later she got up from the table with Ryan, who'd become restless. Anticipating her departure, he asked Connor to take care of their grandfather, then excused himself to walk through the house and catch up to her out front. No way was she going to get away from him tonight. He'd been living for it. Zane was right behind her.

"Leaving so soon?"

She looked shocked at Jarod's approach. "I'm sorry to just slip out like that, but it's past Ryan's bedtime and he was getting too noisy."

"Understood." He darted the little boy's uncle a glance. "There's no need for you to leave, too, Zane. Stay as long as you want. There's going to be dancing. I know three unattached females at the party who've been dying to get to know you. Since my duties are done for the evening, I'll drive Sadie and Ryan home in my truck."

Zane's brows lifted. "Would that be all right with you, Sadie?"

"What do *you* think? You've done so much baby-tending, it's time you had a night off. Jarod's right about the ladies. What's nice is, they're *all* beautiful."

With a chuckle, Zane kissed Ryan, and after a thank-you to Jarod, he headed around the ranch house to join the party.

Sadie was trembling so hard, she was thankful she had Ryan to cuddle. For some reason Jarod had been alone tonight. She didn't know what that meant, but at the moment she didn't care because he wanted to take her home.

After she was settled, he reached around to fasten the two of them in with the seat belt. His nearness made her feverish. "I don't have a car seat for him, but I think we can manage to get you home without a problem."

"I'm not worried."

"Good." He shut her door and went around to the other side to climb in. "Your gift made Grandfather's night. Especially the card. He laughed till he cried."

"Cried would be the right word. My father pretty well ruined everyone's lives for years."

"Well, you're back where you belong and he couldn't be happier about it."

And you, Jarod? Are you happy about it, too?

Sadie wished she knew what was going on inside him. It wasn't long before they reached the ranch and she hurried inside with Ryan. Jarod followed. He'd never been allowed on Corkin property before, let alone to step across her threshhold. The moment was surreal for her.

"I'm trying to wean him off the bottle, but tonight he needs a little extra comfort after being around so many strange faces."

Jarod plucked him out of her arms. "Come on, Little Wants His Bottle." Sadie broke into laughter. "I'll change him while you get it."

There was no one in the world like Jarod. "I'm afraid he might not let you."

"We'll work it out, won't we," he said to Ryan. "I've changed my fair share of diapers at my uncle's house."

Delighted and intrigued to see him in this role, she left them alone long enough to half fill a bottle with milk. When she returned, she found Ryan ready for bed in a sleeper. There'd been no hystrionics. Jarod was holding him in his strong arms as they examined the animal mobile attached to the end of the crib. She paused in the doorway to listen.

"Dog," he told Ryan as he pointed.

"Dog," Ryan repeated. His blue eyes kept staring in fascination at Jarod.

"Now can you say horse?"

"Horse."

"That's right. One day you'll have a horse of your own."

Her eyes smarted. Jarod had always had a way with animals, but it was evident that the invisible power he possessed extended to little humans, too.

"I hate to break this up, but it's time to go night-night, sweetheart."

After she handed Ryan his bottle, Jarod lowered him

into the crib. She tucked his rabbit next to him and Ryan started sucking on the nipple as he stared up at the two of them. Sadie went through her routine of singing his favorite songs to him. Pretty soon he'd finished most of the bottle and his eyes had fluttered closed.

They tiptoed out into the hall and went down to the living room. She turned to Jarod. "Thank you for helping me with Ryan. You were such a big distraction, he forgot to be upset."

A faint smile lingered at the corner of his compelling mouth. "I'm glad to know I'm useful for something."

She got this suffocating feeling in her chest. "I happen to know your grandfather couldn't get along without you."

They stood in the middle of the room. Jarod's eyes swept over her face and down her body, turning her limbs to water. "Do you realize this is the first time I've ever been inside your house, except at the funeral?"

"I was thinking the same thing, but I try not to let the ugliness of the past intrude. Ryan makes that a little easier."

"He's a sweet boy."

She could feel herself tearing up. "I just hope I'll be the mother he needs. It's a huge responsibility."

"You're a natural with him, Sadie."

"Thanks, but it's early days yet." Clearing her throat she said, "Shouldn't you get back to the party before Ralph is missing you?"

"Connor's with him. I don't need to be anywhere else tonight. What I'd like to do is continue a certain conversation that came to an abrupt end when we discovered Ned waiting for us after the rainstorm. Mind if I stay awhile?"

Jarod...

Sadie was terrified she was going to hear news that would ruin the rest of her life.

"Of course not. Please, sit down."

After all the years her father had spouted his hatred for Jarod, it was nothing if not shocking to see him take a seat on the couch and make himself at home, arms spread across the top of the cushions. She sat rigidly on one of the chairs in front of the coffee table opposite him.

"When you asked me how important Leslie Weston was to me, I had my reasons for not answering you at the time."

Here it comes, Sadie. "I should never have asked you that question."

He leaned forward. "You were right to ask. Leslie wouldn't have understood about Velvet. How is your filly, by the way?"

"Wonderful." She stirred restlessly on the chair. "Jarod...you don't owe me any explanations."

"Then you're not interested to know why Leslie wasn't at tonight's party with me?"

Sadie lowered her head. "It's none of my business."

"Don't play games with me, Sadie. There's too much history between us to behave like we're strangers."

"I agree," she confessed before eyeing him directly. "I thought she would be with you tonight. In fact, I was half expecting Ralph's birthday party would turn into an announcement of your engagement."

"You and a few other people, but it's never going to happen."

The finality of his words shocked her. "Why not?"

"We've stopped seeing each other."

Her heart ran away with her. "But I thought— I mean, I was led to believe your relationship was serious."

"I cared for her a great deal, but she wanted more from me than I could give her."

"You mean marriage."

"Yes. As long as we're being truthful, why don't you tell me how many men have proposed to you since you left Montana?"

There was no point in pretending there hadn't been men in her life after Jarod. "If any of them wanted to get married, I didn't give them a chance to get that close to me."

"Why not?"

She sucked in her breath. "Like you, I could tell they wanted a permanent relationship, but I wasn't ready to make a commitment."

For years she'd been in too much pain to even look at another man. When she finally did break down and start dating, no man came close to affecting her the way Jarod had done. He was an original. "How's that for honesty?"

"It's a start."

"Since we're going to be neighbors, I hope we can still be friends."

His black brows met in that fierce way they sometimes did. "That would be impossible."

His response was like a physical blow. "Why?"

"Because we've been lovers. There's no going back."

Heat suffused her cheeks. She shot to her feet. "That was a long time ago." She didn't want to talk about it.

"Too long. That's why we have to move forward. Marry me and it will be as if we were never apart."

"Jarod—" Maybe she'd just imagined he'd articulated her greatest wish. Sadie thought she might expire on the spot.

"A very wise person said it best when describing you and me. Love means sharing a single soul."

Tremors ran through her. "Sounds like your uncle talking."

"You're wrong. It was Leslie. After being with you the other day, I went to see her and broke it off. In her pain she admitted it was pointless to love someone who couldn't reciprocate that love. I wanted to make it work with her, but it never happened."

Sadie shook her head, so incredulous she couldn't take everything in. "You don't know what you're saying. Too much time has gone by. You can't still be in love with me." She'd hurt him too deeply. He wasn't the same with her. "We're different people now. I have a little boy to raise."

Jarod was on his feet. "Maybe we've both been in love with a memory, nothing more. But the strength of that memory has prevented us from getting past it. You're a liar if you deny you didn't want to make love the other day while we were out riding."

She'd wanted it so badly, he would never know what she'd gone through to control herself.

He moved to the front door and turned to her. "I'm asking you to marry me, Sadie. In church. In front of everyone. We need to do it soon while my grandfather is still alive and able to give you away. Once we're married, we'll have time to fall in love all over again.

If we don't, then we'll just deal with it." He was silent a moment.

"Think about it," he said at last. "Ryan needs a father. I need a wife. I want children. When you're ready to give me your answer, you know where to find me. But keep one thing in mind. I won't ask a third time. This is it."

Jarod was out the door like an escaping gust of wind without giving her a chance to answer him. *Without touching her.*

She stood there long after she'd heard the sound of his truck fade. He'd asked her to marry him for a second time, but he'd meant what he said. If she wanted him, she would have to go after him.

What was it Millie had warned her about a few weeks ago? *Don't you know about the great wounded warrior inside him? He needed you to believe in him.*

Sadie *did* believe in him. She was wildly in love with him. But it was clear he still wasn't sure about her. Not really. Otherwise he wouldn't have left so fast. He wouldn't have mentioned being married in church rather than on the reservation with his uncle Charlo doing the honors. He wasn't behaving like the Jarod she'd fallen in love with years ago.

It was up to her to prove her love for him. In the past they'd come together as equals. There'd been no need to chase because they'd been one. But that was back then. There was only one thing to do because she wanted the Jarod of eight years ago back again. The man who had no doubts about her, the man who'd ignored her father's threats and had come to steal her away to the reservation....

By the time Zane came home an hour later, she was out on the front porch waiting for him. "I'm glad you're back. Did you have a good time?"

"Yes. As a matter of fact I did." She heard a wealth of meaning behind his words that she intended to explore later. Right now she was in a hurry to find Jarod.

Zane studied her for a moment. "I'm surprised you're still up. What are you doing out here?"

"Waiting for you to get home. I need to go out again. Do you mind? Ryan's asleep."

"Of course I don't mind. But it's getting late. I'll worry about you being out alone."

"I'm just going to drive next door."

"Oh. Well, in that case…"

Zane didn't ask the obvious question. That was one of the reasons she loved him so much. "I'll only be as far away as my cell." She grabbed her purse.

With a subtle smile he handed her the keys. Sadie rushed past him to the truck.

When she arrived at the Bannocks and pulled up to the rustic ranch house, there were still half a dozen vehicles parked in front. Her heart raced to see Jarod's among them.

Making a quick decision, she walked around the side of the house, hoping to catch him helping with the cleanup. Instead, she ran into Connor, who was folding the round tables used for the dinner.

His eyes lit up in pleasure. "Hey! What are you doing back here?"

"I'm looking for Jarod."

"He's helping grandfather get to bed. I'll go tell him you're out here, but you're welcome to come inside."

"Thank you. I'll stay here."

He stacked the last table against the wall, then disappeared inside the house. She walked over to the swing and sat to wait. But it had grown cooler, so she got back up to move around.

"You wanted to see me?" Jarod's deep voice resonated inside her.

She swung around on her high heels. "I didn't hear you come out. Forgive me for intruding. Connor told me you were helping your grandfather, so if this isn't a good time, I'll come again."

He eyed her through shuttered lids. "If it was important enough for you to see me tonight, then let's not put it off." His terse comment alarmed her. "The temperature has dropped. Why don't we go back to your truck where you can be warm?"

Her truck wasn't the place she envisioned talking to him, but since he hadn't invited her in the house, it would have to do. She walked ahead of him, but was so nervous she stumbled several times on the rocky pathway. He was there to cup her elbow till they reached the Silverado.

Sadie climbed into the driver's seat. She had to hike up the dress she was wearing, and knew Jarod caught a glimpse of leg before he shut the door. She hoped he didn't think she was being provocative.

After he got in the other side, she said, "Where can we drive so there's no possibility of Ned watching our every move?"

"Is this going to take a while?" He sounded put out, but *was* he? Or could he be covering some hidden emotion? She had to find out.

Emboldened by her desperation to connect with the old Jarod, she turned to him. "Yes."

Something flickered in the recesses of his eyes. "How soon do you have to get back?"

"Zane's home for the night to take care of Ryan."

"Then we'll leave your truck here and take off in mine."

Sadie said a silent prayer of thanksgiving he was willing to listen to her. The next thing she knew he'd helped her down and walked her over to his truck. After opening the door, he gripped her waist without effort and lifted her into the passenger seat.

He drove them two miles up a badly rutted road that zigzagged behind the ranch house. It led to a shelter of pines where they could look down on the whole lay-out of the Hitting Rocks Ranch. Sadie had never been here before.

Jarod shut off the engine and shifted around, extending an arm along the back of the seats. She felt him tease her hair. "Old habits die hard. I have to reach farther to grab hold. Why did you cut your glorious hair?"

Sadie wasn't prepared for such a personal comment. "Off with the old seemed like a good idea after I got to California." She knew better than to ask him why he'd let his grow long. By doing so he'd made a statement that he was proud of his Crow heritage. It told Sadie's father and Ned Bannock to go to hell. She understood his feelings and loved him all the more for them, but she had to tread carefully right now.

He cocked his dark head. "All right. We're alone at last with no chance of being disturbed. Let's get this over with."

She'd been right. He didn't believe she believed in him anymore. "Why did you leave the house so fast? You didn't give me a chance to respond."

His searching gaze appraised her. "After the failure of our first attempt to become man and wife, I wanted to give you some breathing room before you made a decision about trying a second time. But it seems you didn't need it. Otherwise you wouldn't have come right over to the house again. I only need a one-word answer. Since I know what it is, I'll drive us back and send you home before it gets any later."

She moaned inwardly. "You're so sure of my answer?"

He grimaced. "The Sadie I once knew wouldn't have let me walk out of her house tonight."

Sadie took a deep breath. "The Jarod I once knew wouldn't have had to ask me to marry him a second time. He would have drawn me into his arms and told me we were going to get married as soon as it could be arranged."

His jaw hardened. "You spoke the truth earlier. Too much time has passed. We're different people now and can't go back."

"Isn't it sad that although our marriage didn't take place through no fault of our own, the fallout caused us to doubt each other. How does something like that happen?"

"We were young." His voice grated.

"That's not all of it, Jarod. Tell me something. What prompted you to ask me to marry you in a church in front of everyone?"

After a prolonged silence he said, "It's what every woman wants."

"That isn't what you planned for us the first time."

His body tensed. "I railroaded you into doing what I wanted. I thought I owned you. I believed you were mine. But I've since learned a man can no more own a person than he can the earth or the sky or the ocean."

Jarod's honesty touched her to the marrow. "How do you know it wasn't what I wanted, too? I would have given anything to have known your mother. You planned that wedding for us in her honor. It thrilled me. I've felt cheated ever since." Her heart was thudding out of control.

"You were too sweet and trusting, Sadie. I took advantage of you."

"Oh. So when you say we were too young, you really meant that *I* was too young to know my own mind."

"You weren't too young, but I know I influenced you."

"Don't you know you saved my life the day you found me sobbing on my horse? You helped me to know where to go with my sorrow. You comforted me. Every person could use that kind of influence. I was the lucky one to be able to turn to you.

"What saddens me is to realize that my being a Corkin caused you so much grief. To this day I wonder what I ever did for you to want me for your wife."

She had to wait a long time for the answer.

"Chief Plenty Coups taught that woman is your equal. She's a builder, a warrior, a farmer, a healer of the soul. All those qualities I found in you. That's what you were to me. I believed you loved me."

Jarod, Jarod. "Why past tense? I still do," she said. "That's never changed. It couldn't."

He'd turned his head to stare out the window. Sadie opened her purse and pulled out the bracelet he'd given her the night they'd made love.

"Jarod Bannock? Tonight you asked me to marry you. My answer is *yes,* but there's a condition. I want us to have the same ceremony you planned for us eight years ago."

Sadie got on her knees and moved across the seat to lean toward him, getting in his face so he had to look at her. She dangled the beaded bracelet in front of him. "I want Uncle Charlo to marry us on the reservation. I want your family to be there along with the Hensons. In my heart I know your mother and father will be watching and they'll approve because they know how much I've always loved you."

She'd finally caught his attention.

"Before you fasten it around my wrist for a second time to make this official, there's something vital you need to know."

"You're talking about Ryan," he said, reading her mind.

"Yes. He comes with me."

His chest rose and fell. "You're both flesh of your mother's flesh. Do you think I could possibly love him any less?"

"No," she whispered, brushing his mouth with her own. "You have an infinite capacity for loving. I adore you, Jarod."

Chapter 8

Her words trickled through his mind and body like the wild, sweet Montana honey dripping from a honeycomb he'd discovered in a tree at the edge of the meadow years ago.

He studied the oval of her face, the passionate curve of her mouth so close to him he felt her breath on his lips. Moonlight illuminated the inside of the cab. Those solemn blue eyes were once again searching his. That was the way she used to look at him, as if he held all the answers to the universe.

"Aren't you going to put it on me?" He heard the slightest tinge of anxiety in her voice.

The bracelet.

She'd so mesmerized him, Jarod was slow to even breathe. He'd been convinced that when she'd fled to

California, that token of his commitment had been lost or destroyed.

His fingers trembled as he caught the ends of the bracelet and fastened it around her wrist. The satisfying click echoed in his heart.

"Sadie—" Wrapping his arms around her, he lowered his mouth to hers the way he'd done eight years ago; a kiss he'd relived in a thousand dreams. Yet this was no dream. His loving, precious Sadie was back in his arms, alive and welcoming.

For a while those desolate years they'd been apart seemed to fall away while their minds and bodies communicated their need for each other.

"Darling," she murmured over and over again, as if she, too, was overwhelmed by such emotion.

Sometime later he tasted salt on his lips. "Your eyes are wet," he whispered against her lids.

"So are yours. I can't believe we're together again. It's been such a long, long time." Her tear-filled voice reached his soul. They clung to each other, attempting to absorb the quiet sobs of happiness that shook them both. "I'm so thankful we've found each other again. Jarod— You don't know. You just don't know."

"But I do." Jarod kissed the contours of her moist cheeks, then her mouth, never satisfied. She looked and tasted beautiful almost beyond bearing. Their desire for each other had escalated to the point they couldn't do what they wanted in the confined space of the cab.

"I want you, Sadie. I love you. I'm going to drive us back to the ranch. You'll stay with me tonight."

She moaned her assent as he helped her to sit up. "This is going to be a fast trip, so hold on!" Within seconds he started the engine and put the truck in gear to head down the road.

Sadie flashed him one of her disarming smiles. "We don't need to be in a hurry. My father's no longer on the lookout. The situation has changed and we've got the rest of our lives to be together."

He grasped her hand and kissed it. "That's what I thought the night I was coming for you. Never again will I take another moment of loving you for granted."

"Neither will I." Her voice shook. "How soon do you think we can be married? I don't want to wait."

That sounded like the exciting Sadie he'd thought had disappeared forever. "I'll talk to Uncle Charlo in the morning." June third would make the perfect wedding day. By then the deed to the Corkin ranch would be in Zane's hands, but Jarod wouldn't settle on an actual date with his uncle until Zane owned it free and clear.

"The dreams I've dreamed, Sadie. My grandfather's health has to hold out long enough to see our first baby come into the world. I can hardly wait to feel movement inside you."

She nestled closer to him. "Millie told me that if you and I had communicated, we'd probably have one or two little Bannocks by now. It's all I've been able to think of for days now."

"When I saw you at the graveside service holding Ryan, I was imagining you with our child. It shocked me how strong my feelings ran. Watching you with Ryan, I knew you'd be the sweetest mother on earth. The sooner we give him a brother or sister, the better. Connor and Avery kept me from being an only child."

How he'd love it if he and Sadie were the ones to

give his grandfather his first great-grandchild. Ralph would be overjoyed. Tyson already had three. Jarod's uncle Charlo would be overjoyed, too. He'd carried a heavy burden over the years watching after Raven's headstrong son.

She pressed against him to kiss his jaw. "What's putting that secretive smile on your face?"

He squeezed her hand harder. "In January my uncle told me it was time to go on my vision quest at the top of North Pryor Mountain. It had to be in an area with risks like falling and contact with animals. The more rugged and mysterious the better."

"The snow would have been too deep!"

"It nearly was, but he told me I'd be guided. He said I possessed the power to achieve my ultimate destiny by using the senses and powers already given to me. After four days of fasting, I came back down and told him my mind was still clouded."

"Four days?" she cried. "I could never have done that."

"To be honest, nothing was worse than the way I felt when you never got in touch with me." Sadie buried her face against his shoulder. "My uncle told me my quest wasn't in vain. With more time all would be made clear, but I had to develop patience because everything else in my life had come too easily."

She lifted her head. "Too easily? You lost your mother, then your father and stepmother!"

"But I was given an uncle, grandparents and siblings, a home, money, education, good health. Grades came without effort. I had everything I wanted. And when I decided I wanted Sadie Corkin, I went after her. By some miracle I was able to snatch her away from all the other guys who were hot for her."

"Jarod!"

"That's the word for it, and I was the worst. I came up with a secret plan to marry the one girl in the county who was off-limits to me. I would have succeeded, too. But fate stepped in and taught me life's most bitter lesson."

Jarod covered her hand with his own. "When Ben told me your father had died, all I could think about was you rather than your loss. Suddenly my uncle's comment about my quest not having been in vain came into my mind."

She kissed the side of his neck. "There wasn't a day in my life that I didn't yearn to come home and find out why you'd stopped loving me. We've had to endure so much needless pain."

"Not only us. Everyone who loved us was affected, Sadie."

"I know. I'm still having trouble believing we're back together."

They reached the ranch house in record time. He pulled around in front and parked. After shutting off the engine, he reached out to hold her in his arms.

"By morning you'll believe it. Tomorrow when I ask my uncle to help prepare for our wedding, I'll thank him for being a great and wise man who guided me through my trials on the way to finding my ultimate destiny. He'll give me one of those long sober looks, as if he can see into the future, but I know he'll be smiling inside."

"I know the one you mean. That's how he looked at

me the night he praised you. He couldn't love you more if you were his own son."

"That's how I already feel about Ryan," he whispered into her hair. "But right now I want to concentrate on us. I desperately need to love you all night."

She looped her arms around his neck and clung to him. "I've been thinking about that and would rather we went back to my house. Yours is full of family and they don't know about us yet. It might be a shock when Connor and Avery see us walk out of your bedroom in the morning."

"A happy shock because I've been impossible to live with. They'll get down on their knees to you for coming back to me." He bit gently on her earlobe. "Zane could be a different story."

"You're wrong. We have no secrets. Follow me home. Our being together won't shock him since he knows how long I've been ready to walk through fire for you. His one reaction will be relief that we've been able to find each other again after our painful history."

"Then let's not waste another second." He got out of the cab and went around to help her down. Knowing she was all his to love had made him euphoric. Their mouths fused before he swung her around and carried her over to her truck. After putting her inside he shut the door. "I'll be right behind you."

A shadow crossed over her face. "Promise me." She couldn't prevent the tremor in her voice. "If anything happened to you now..." He knew she was thinking of Ned.

"I'll sit on your bumper."

Her expression brightened before she started the engine. He retraced the steps to his truck and they formed a caravan to the Corkin property. Connor knew Jarod was with Sadie. He'd phone if there was an emergency with their grandfather.

Jarod checked his watch. It was ten to one. For the first time in their lives they had nothing to worry about except to love and be loved. As he followed behind her, he anticipated their true wedding night. She'd always been fascinated with the bygone traditions of his mother's people. The vision of disappearing into their own tepee after the ceremony wouldn't leave him alone.

After Sadie had parked in front of her place, she jumped down from the truck and held out her hand to him. When he reached her, she ran toward the porch, pulling him as if she were in the race of her life. They both were.

But she had to get the house key from her purse. When he saw how she was trembling, he reached for it. "Let me." Within seconds he'd found it. After unlocking the door, he opened it and followed her into the living room.

"Sadie?" A light went on and they discovered Zane standing near the the window.

She came to a halt. "Zane. Is something wrong with Ryan?"

That was Jarod's first thought, as well.

"No, but I'm glad you're both here because we need to talk. Mr. Bree emailed me to let me know he has a client coming by tomorrow at 9:00 a.m. to look at the house and property." His gaze flicked to Jarod. "A little while after that your cousin Ned came by. When he found out Sadie wasn't home he left, but I was afraid he'd wait for her outside so I've been keeping watch. I didn't phone because I knew the two of you were together."

She frowned. "What did he want?"

His mouth thinned into a tight line. "*He's* the client planning to buy the ranch and do a walk-through with the Realtor in the morning."

"But he's a Bannock!"

"That part of your father's will won't hold up in court."

"So that *criminal* who came close to murdering Jarod is planning to buy this ranch out from under us?" Her outrage was as real as Jarod's. "Over my dead body! How dare he come by here this late to trample over our lives!"

"My thoughts exactly," Zane muttered. "He claimed he was hoping to talk to you at the party, but he saw you leave with Ryan so he thought he'd still find you up."

Sadie's proud chin lifted. Jarod knew that look. "What did you tell him?"

"That I was buying the ranch and had already put down earnest money. He gave me a superior smile and said that unless I was paying more than $700,000, I didn't have enough money to close the deal."

"Neither does he. I'm not sure he has a dime to his name."

Zane's brows lifted. "That may be true, but I thought I'd better tell you that tonight because June third is only four days away. I think we'd better start looking for another ranch around here within our price range."

The woman at Jarod's side had gone quiet. Much as he didn't want either Sadie or Zane to know what was going on behind the scenes, he needed to say enough to take the shattered looks off their faces. He put an arm around Sadie, pulling her close.

"He was bluffing, Zane. I do the ranching accounts. Sadie's right. Ned doesn't have any savings, and his father can't fund him any more loans. He certainly can't depend on his grandfather. Tyson has helped all his grandchildren to the point he doesn't have that kind of money, either. He's using scare tactics, but it won't work. Your bid is right in the ball park so don't give up."

"We won't!" Sadie declared. "I know it's Mr. Bree's job, but it infuriates me to think he has the right to come here with Ned, who would do anything to hurt me for loving Jarod."

After her revealing explosion, Zane eyed the two of them with interest. "Why do I get the feeling you've got something to tell me?"

Sadie extended her arm. "Jarod put this bracelet back on me tonight. It's the one from his mother's family he gave me eight years ago. We're going to get married right away."

A broad smile lit Zane's face. "That the best news I ever heard." He gave her a loving hug, then shook Jarod's hand. "When's the wedding?"

Jarod stared down at her. "As soon as it can be arranged."

"Good. It needs to happen fast. I have to tell you this girl has been dying for you."

"Zane—" Her blush warmed Jarod's heart. "You're the first person to know."

"When we've picked the date, we'll tell everyone. We

plan to keep it to family only. My uncle will be marrying us out on the reservation."

"That sounds like heaven," Zane said. "Little Ryan's going to have an amazing dad who'll open fascinating new worlds for him."

Jarod picked up a nuance in the other man's tone. In truth Zane had been the only father Ryan had known since he was born. Zane loved his nephew deeply, and was one of the most genuine, likable men Jarod had ever met. But their news had just changed his world again. "I hope one day to live up to the hero uncle Sadie raves about."

"That's nice to hear. Thanks, Jarod. Now that you're both home safely and have heard the bad news, I'll go to bed."

Sadie gave him another hug before he left the living room. When she turned to Jarod he planted his hands on her shoulders. "I'm going to leave."

"No—" She flung herself at him. It reminded him of the night before they were to be married. She'd clung to him then, too, not wanting to be parted from him. "We're not going to let Ned ruin this night for us."

"He doesn't have the power."

"Then is it because of Zane being here?"

"No, Sadie." He kissed away her tears. "But it *does* have to do with him."

She shook her blond head in confusion. "What's changed since we came in the house?"

"He just found out we're getting married right away. In his mind the plans you two had to ranch together have suddenly gone up in smoke. He sees his nephew slipping away from him and fears he might not be able to buy the ranch, after all. You told me he moved here with you to start a new life after his divorce, but tonight we dropped a bomb on him."

"I know," she whispered. "I had no idea he'd still be up and waiting for me to come home. When we told him our news, there was a look in his eyes that haunted me."

"I saw it, too. You need to go to him before he's in bed and reassure him that whatever plans we make, he's included in them in every way. He's going to be a part of our family now, the same way my uncle Charlo and his family are a part of us. But a talk like that could take the rest of the night. Before you know it, Ryan will be awake."

"You're right, but I can't stand to see you walk out the door."

"The last thing I want to do is leave, but you two need your privacy to talk. Before I go, give me your phone so we can program each other's cell numbers."

Once that was accomplished he pulled her into his arms again. "Call me after Ned and the Realtor leave. Knowing Zane is with you, I'm not worried. I'll pick you and Ryan up. We'll drive over to tell grandfather our news."

Sadie clasped her hands on his face. "You're the most wonderful, remarkable man I've ever known. I didn't think I could love you any more before we came in the house. Now I can't find the right words to tell you what you mean to me. This will have to do until tomorrow." She pressed her mouth to his.

Though he wanted to devour her, he couldn't do that while Zane was in the other room. The man was in a state of hell Jarod wouldn't wish on the retired SEAL.

He'd already lived through a war both at home and in Afghanistan, and Sadie was the one person who could make things right for him.

She had no idea she held the hearts of three men in her hands. As she'd told him earlier tonight, Ryan came with her.

"See you in the morning." He kissed her once more, knowing she was in safe hands with Zane until Jarod could take care of her himself.

On the drive home, he decided that tomorrow morning he'd leave early for Billings to do some business at the bank and talk to Harlow Brigg. Jarod wanted the attorney to make his offer to Mr. Bree before the end of the day and get the transaction finalized. Zane and Sadie deserved good news and they were going to get it.

When he got back to the ranch, he set his alarm for six. He wouldn't get the sleep he needed, but it didn't matter. Until this business was over, he didn't have a prayer of relaxing.

The next morning after he'd showered and dressed, he knocked on Connor's door. Their bedrooms were upstairs across the hall from each other. Avery's was at the other end.

"Come on in." To Jarod's relief his brother was up and seated on the side of the bed, putting on his cowboy boots. Connor looked up at him with concern. "Is grandfather all right?"

"As far as I know. This is about something else. I need to talk to my best friend. That's you."

Connor looked taken aback. "You're mine, too."

"I realize I haven't shared some of my personal thoughts with anyone over the years, not even you. It's the way I'm made. But like grandfather and Avery, I've always known you were there for me. You've never pried or overstepped. I could always count on you."

"Ditto. I wouldn't have made it through my divorce without you."

Jarod nodded. "We've been lucky to have each other. That's why I want to confide in you now."

Connor sat forward. "You sound so serious. What's bothering you, bro? After last night I figure this must have to do with Sadie." Connor eyed him with compassion. "Are the rumors true about her and Zane Lawson?"

Jarod caught a leg of the chair with his boot, pulled it forward and sat. "No. Last night I asked her to marry me for the second time and she said yes."

Connor jumped off the bed in shock. "Second time—"

"The first time was eight years ago. We'd planned for Uncle Charlo to marry us on the reservation. The ceremony was all arranged in secret so Daniel wouldn't get wind of it. Grandfather and I wanted to protect you and Avery. I was on my way to pick Sadie up with the horse trailer the night the accident happened."

For the next twenty minutes he filled his brother in on everything, including the tragic misunderstanding that had sent Sadie to her mom's in California.

"All these years Sadie thought her father was behind it, but that wasn't the case."

His brother shook his head in disbelief.

"The person who rammed me in the side of my truck had every intention of putting me out of commission. I didn't know until recently it was a deliberate act and I have what I call partial proof."

"What?"

Jarod reached into his pocket and then handed Connor the sheet of paper from the body shop in Bozeman. "Notice the date. The accident happened the night Sadie turned eighteen."

"Owen Pearson? But he's—"

"Ned's friend?" Jarod supplied.

Connor's expression turned dark. He walked around the room for a minute, rubbing the back of his neck. Then he turned to Jarod.

"I always thought there was something wrong about that day. When the hospital called, the whole family went en masse to visit you. Avery and I were terrified you might die. Both grandfather and your uncle Charlo must have aged ten years. But the only one who didn't show up was Ned.

"I remember Uncle Grant being particularly upset because Ned wasn't anywhere around. He tried to call him all day but Ned didn't answer his mobile phone. None of the hands knew his whereabouts and none of his friends had seen him, not even Owen. He didn't show up at the ranch until late the next night."

By now Jarod was on his feet. "Did the police question him?"

"I don't know, but I heard Uncle Grant say later that he'd had a date with one of the girls who worked at her mom's beauty salon in White Lodge. Rose, or Rosie? I can't remember. That's why he hadn't heard about the accident."

Jarod frowned. "I saw his Jeep in town that evening. It might be worth checking her out to see if she knows anything about that night."

"Do it, Jarod. Too many times I've wanted to strangle Ned with my bare hands for his treatment of you. If we could prove he or Owen was at the wheel of Owen's truck that night…"

"I plan to find out," Jarod's voice was harsh. "Did you know he's trying to buy the Corkin ranch?"

"Say that again?"

"Daniel didn't will it to Sadie. He put it up for sale. Ned's already found out about it."

"Our cousin?" Connor exploded with an angry laugh. "That's not only impossible, it's absurd!"

"He's going over there this morning with Bree from Parker Realty to make the inspection before he puts down the money."

"*What* money?"

"Tyson told Grandfather he's going to take out $700,000 for him. Uncle Grant believes if he has his own place, he'll become responsible and turn into a rancher."

Connor put up his hands. "Wait a minute here. You mean, Grandfather's okay with that?"

"No. He has his own plan working." Once again Connor was a captive audience while Jarod explained about Harlow's part in the private purchase. "We're making sure Zane ends up owning it. I'm going into Billings right now to see him."

Lines marred Connor's features. "Happy as I am to hear that, Ned's not going to take this lying down, especially when he finds out you and Sadie are getting married."

"That's why I've got to nail him for the accident. Once I know the whole truth, I'll confront him and put the fear in him about having to do some serious jail time. Thanks to your recall about the night I was in the hospital, I've got a valuable piece of information that could be the proof I need to implicate him." He hugged his brother. "I owe you."

Three hours later he'd finished his business and finalized the details of the purchase with Harlow Brigg.

On his way back to the ranch, he phoned his uncle and broke the news. Charlo sounded elated, which didn't happen very often. They talked about possible dates for a ceremony and would make a final decision in the next few days.

When Jarod passed through White Lodge, he stopped at the Clip and Curl beauty salon. The sign said they welcomed walk-in traffic. He got out of his truck and entered the shop. The women stared at him as he approached the counter.

His gaze darted to the license on the wall. It belonged to a Sally Paxton. Her name meant nothing to him, but Jarod was determined to get answers. If this lead didn't reveal any new information, he planned to go to the Pearson ranch to confront Owen.

An older beautician washing a client's hair looked up. "Hi! I've never seen you in here before."

"I usually get my hair cut on the reservation. Does someone named Rose work here?"

"If you mean Rosie, that's my daughter over there."

A dark blond woman who looked to be Avery's age was sweeping the floor after the last client. She looked up at him. "You want to see me?"

"I was told you do a great job so I thought I'd come in."

"Who said that?"

"I heard someone telling the new vet over at Rafferty's."

"You mean Liz Henson?" He nodded. "That's nice to hear. We were part of a group of girls who hung out in high school, but she was usually barrel racing."

"I learned she's going to compete at the world championship in Las Vegas."

"Isn't that great? Be with you in a second. Go ahead and sit in the chair."

Jarod did her bidding. "I'm getting married soon and need the ends of my hair trimmed. Just an inch." This would be a new experience for him. Before he'd let his hair grow, he used to ask Pauline, Uncle Charlo's wife, to cut it.

She smiled. "Lucky woman." After fastening the cape around his neck, she undid the thong. "Do you know how many females would kill for gleaming black hair like this?"

"I hope not."

With a chuckle, Rosie washed and combed it before getting out the scissors. He noticed she wore a wedding ring. "You know I always admired Liz."

Glad he didn't have to get her back on the subject, he said, "Why do you say that?"

"She was serious about school and didn't drink like some of the girls."

"You're talking about the famous keg parties. Even though I graduated before your time, I heard they got pretty wild with Owen Pearson and Ned Bannock around."

"Ned was the ultimate party animal."

"Were you two an item?"

"That's a laugh. Do you remember a girl named Sadie Corkin? She barrel raced with Liz. All the guys were nuts about her."

His breath caught. "I remember hearing about her."

"Ned had it bad for her, but she couldn't stand him and every girl knew it. She moved right before graduation. It was weird her going away like that before she got her diploma."

You'll never know, Rosie.

After she'd tied his hair back again, he winked at her. "So you never dated him?"

"Are you kidding? Guys like that are toxic."

So that was another of Ned's lies. Jarod wondered why the police hadn't interrogated Rosie, but he was going to find out.

"You were wise to stay away."

She undid the cape. "My boyfriend made sure of it."

"Good for you." He pulled forty dollars out of his wallet and put it on her table. "You did a great job. When I need another haircut, I'll be back."

"Congratulations on your upcoming wedding."

"Thank you, Rosie."

Chapter 9

Sadie stood by to watch while Ned and Mr. Bree walked through the house inspecting everything. She could only imagine how much Jarod's cousin was enjoying this. The Corkin property had always been off-limits to the Bannocks. Now it was up for sale and Ned was sure he was going to become the new owner of Farfields.

But Jarod had assured her it wouldn't happen. Sadie believed him, which was the only reason she could stomach this vile intrusion into her life. She continued to watch in disgust as he handled her father's firearms. Before the funeral Mac had moved them from Daniel's bedroom to the hall closet, where they'd been locked up for safe keeping. Millie had insisted that with a child in the house, they would keep all the ammunition stored at their place.

"This is a fine collection." He flashed Sadie a strange smile. "Your father really knew his guns. I plan to buy a permanent display case for them."

There's something wrong in his head. That's what Jarod had told her years ago. Ned Bannock *was* mentally ill. A shudder racked her body.

"I believe we're finished here." Mr. Bree spoke up. Sadie immediately locked the closet. "Thank you for allowing us into your home, Ms. Corkin. We'll see ourselves out."

She nodded and followed them. Through the window she watched them drive away in a car with the Parker Realty logo on the side. Without wasting a second she rang Zane, who was on his way back from White Lodge with the Hensons and Ryan.

The Hensons were overjoyed to hear the news about Sadie and Jarod, but they still didn't know about her father's will and Sadie intended things to stay that way. Zane had taken Mac and Millie to breakfast with him and Ryan, not only to get them all away from the ranch while Ned was here, but to offer the Hensons a business proposition since he would be helping Sadie run the ranch.

Jarod had been so right about Zane. Last night she and Zane had talked for several hours until Sadie had convinced him nothing was going to change, only get better.

In a few minutes he came through the back door holding Ryan. Millie followed them inside. When Zane lowered him to the floor, Ryan grabbed him around the leg, wanting to be picked up again. "Hey, sport." Zane lifted him in the air with a happy laugh Sadie hadn't expected to hear again after he'd left her and Jarod last night.

Millie darted Sadie a secret smile. Nothing got past her.

As he poured some juice for Ryan, Millie pulled Sadie into the front room. "When Zane told us the news, Mac and I were so happy, we almost burst!"

"You need to hear the whole story." After Sadie quickly filled her in she said, "I have to tell you, this bracelet worked its magic. Bless you for holding on to it all this time." She hugged Millie hard. "Without it, I don't know how long it would have taken me to break through that stoic barrier he sometimes erects."

"Maybe another ten minutes?" Millie quipped. "I can't wait to tell Liz. She left early to help with a foaling problem on the Drayson ranch."

"I'll phone her after I call Jarod."

"It's going to make her realize that if this can happen to her sister, it will happen to her, too, when the time is right."

"Of course it will. Oh, Millie. I can't believe this day has come. I never dreamed it would."

"Does Ralph know?"

She shook her head. "We're planning to tell him our news as soon as Jarod picks me up."

"Then don't waste another second. If you or Zane need me, just give me a call."

"You've already helped us so much."

"I wish you'd been there for breakfast when Zane asked Mac to teach him how to be a rancher. My husband could hardly talk he was so flattered."

"Zane's going to learn from the best."

"Honey—" She put a hand on her arm. "I'm sorry about your father, but I have to say how happy I am your mom ended up with Tim Lawson. I really like his brother."

"Me, too. Men like him and Jarod don't come along more than once in a century."

"You can say that again."

"And of course, I include Mac in that group."

Millie laughed, but Sadie could tell she was pleased.

While Ryan was still in the kitchen with Zane, Sadie walked in her bedroom to phone Jarod. He picked up on the first ring. "You must be psychic," he said. "I was just going to phone you. I'm one minute away from your door."

"I can't wait! I'll grab Ryan and meet you outside."

After renewing her lipstick and running a brush through her hair, she put on her cowboy hat. Once she'd stowed some diapers and small toys in her purse, she flew through the house to the kitchen. Millie must have gone home.

"Come on, cutie. I hate to tear you away from your uncle, but we're going with Jarod so you can get acquainted with your new grandfather-to-be."

Zane gave him a kiss. "See you later, sport."

Sadie rushed through the house and out the front door with Ryan. She was greeted with one of those ridiculous wolf whistles. Coming from Jarod, it was a total surprise. He was already out of the truck and had opened the rear door. 'You look good enough to eat."

"Jarod…" She moved closer, melting from the look he gave her. "Oh, you got him a car seat!"

"I picked it up in town on the way home." He took

Ryan from her arms and strapped him in. "Hey, little guy. Remember me? We're going for a ride."

Ryan had fastened his attention on Jarod, but he didn't cry. Once they'd closed the door, Sadie and Jarod reached for each other. Jarod pressed her against the side of the truck, causing her hat to fall off. She didn't care. Their emotions were spilling all over the place. It wasn't until Ryan started to get worked up over being ignored that Jarod lifted his hungry mouth from Sadie's, eliciting a protest from her. She was finding it impossible to let him go.

He looked different somehow. "Did you do something to your hair?"

"You noticed. There's a story behind it. I'll tell you about it later." He picked up her hat and helped her into the cab. After talking to Ryan and handing him a toy, Sadie pressed against Jarod for the short drive to the ranch.

"Tell me what went on with Ned."

A shudder ran through Sadie. "When he was handling one of the rifles, I was so sickened by him, I couldn't watch. He acted as if he already owned the place."

"It'll never happen."

"I believe you."

"Thank God." He put his arm around her and stopped long enough to give her a deep kiss before they ended up in front of the ranch house. Once inside, the housekeeper made a fuss over Ryan, who clung to Sadie.

"I'm sorry, Jenny. He's still getting used to people."

"That's natural."

"How's Grandfather?"

"Feeling so spry he gave Martha the day off. He's out on the patio having lunch. I'll bring some for you, too."

"Thanks."

Jarod led Sadie down the hall and out the door to the covered patio where'd they celebrated his birthday. His grandfather's gray eyes brightened when he saw them. "Well, look at the three of you."

"Hi, Ralph. I can tell you're feeling much better." She kissed his cheek. "You saw Ryan before, but now he'd like to meet you."

"You're a good-looking little fella, aren't you?" He rubbed Ryan's head. "Just like your mom and sister. Sit down and join me."

Jarod helped her to get seated at the glass-topped table. She held Ryan on her lap while Jarod took his place next to her. Jenny brought out two more salads and rolls and glasses of iced tea.

"We're glad you're up because we have an announcement to make."

Ralph preempted him. "About time, too! When's the wedding?"

On cue, tears filled her eyes. "You know?"

"I knew the second I saw your faces just now. It's written all over you."

She reached out to squeeze his hand. "Does that mean you're happy about it?"

"Ah, honey, you know Addie and I were always crazy about you. So was my grandson. Otherwise he wouldn't have made preparations for your marriage the first time around."

Sadie lowered her head. "Jarod's accident changed our lives."

"Indeed it did, but that period is over."

They spent much of lunch talking about plans for the ceremony on the reservation. But after two hours Ryan got restless and it was time to take him home. Once Ralph was settled on the swing with his bifocals and the latest ranching magazine, Jarod picked up Ryan and they made their way back out to the truck.

He shot her an all-consuming glance. "I think it's time for everyone to have a good nap."

Her heart did somersaults as they pulled away from the ranch. But when his cell phone rang and he picked up to answer, her excitement was short-lived. A fierce expression crossed his face, the one that caused her legs to shake.

"What's wrong?" she asked as soon as he'd ended the call.

"It's nothing for you to worry about."

She sat straighter. "How would you like it if our positions were reversed and I said the same thing to you?"

He expelled a troubled sigh. "That was Ben. Fire has broken out in one of the sheds on the property. I've got to go, but I'll be back." As soon as they reached the Corkin ranch house, Sadie jumped out to get Ryan with Jarod's help. "We had a good time today, didn't we, little guy?" He lowered the toddler to the ground.

Sadie looked up at Jarod. "Please be careful."

"Always." He gave her a hard kiss before getting back in the truck. As he pulled away, she realized the Silverado was gone. Zane must have gone to town. This would have been the perfect opportunity for her and Jarod to enjoy alone time, but it would have to come later.

Much as she hated to see him go, there was something she needed to do. After she gave Ryan a bath she put him down for his nap, then got on the phone to speak to her heart doctor in California. His nurse said he wouldn't be able to return her call until after five California time. Sadie would have to wait.

Jarod wanted children. So did she. That was why this call was necessary because he didn't know about her arrhythmia.

Sadie was feeding Ryan dinner in his high chair when the phone rang at ten to six. She glanced at the Caller ID and picked up. "Dr. Feldman?"

"Is this Sadie Corkin?"

"Yes. Thank you for returning my call so fast."

"How are you?"

"Wonderful. I haven't had any problems since you put me on this last medication."

"That's excellent."

"The reason I'm calling is that since mother's passing, I've moved back to Montana and now I'm getting married to the man I told you about."

"What a lucky man. That's splendid news!"

"You can't imagine how happy I am, but he wants a baby soon. So do I. What do you think about my getting pregnant? After what happened to mother, I have to admit I'm frightened."

"It goes without saying you have to keep taking your medication and use a reliable form of birth control until you've seen a specialist. Let me assure you there's a whole new type of procedure for your kind of problem that's had a high success rate."

For the next few minutes he went on to describe the benefits and risks. "Where are you in Montana?"

"Near Billings."

"I'll look on my index. Let me give you the name of a specialist there, Dr. George Harvey, who performs procedures for your particular heart condition. I advise you to get an appointment right away. I'll send your medical records."

"Thank you so much, Dr. Feldman."

"You're welcome. I want to hear back and know what's going on with you."

"Of course." She hung up.

A whole new type of procedure?

How would Jarod feel if she had it done before they were married? But what if she went through with it and it didn't work? Haunted by all the what-ifs, she cleaned Ryan's face and hands before taking him outside for a walk.

She hadn't heard from Jarod yet and was starting to get worried. A few minutes later Zane pulled up in front of the ranch house. He got out of the truck and picked up Ryan, who was thrilled to see him.

Sadie smiled at him. "Where have you been?"

"Bozeman."

"How come?"

"I've been looking up job opportunities on the internet and came across an ad put out by the Bureau of Land Management. I decided to go in for an interview."

Sadie had thought he wanted to learn to be a rancher. Her surprise must have shown.

"Hey, don't worry. I'm not planning to go anywhere. I can combine ranching with another job."

"You're going crazy around here already, aren't you?"

"No. I love it here, but I want to find something where I can use some of my skills, too."

"What kind of work was the BLM advertising for?"

"They need uniformed rangers to provide law enforcement support. Because of my military training, I'm a natural for it. At the moment there's an opening in northeastern Montana. Naturally I don't want to go there. But I've learned there may be an opening soon with the national Community Safety Initiative for American Indians in this area so I can stay home on the ranch. On my days off I'll work with Mac."

"What would you do exactly?"

"Work on eradicating drugs, investigate criminal trespassing and theft of government property including archaeological and paleontological resources. When I was talking to Jarod's sister last night, she told me there's a great need for that kind of protection around the archaeological sites. She also told me about one of the rangers up in Glasgow who apprehended a sniper after several people had been killed."

Yup. That sounded like it was right up Zane's alley. Sadie smiled inside. So that was what Zane meant when she'd asked him if he'd had a good time at the birthday party and he'd said yes. He'd been talking to Avery. Had she been the one to spark his interest in a BLM job?

In school Avery had been known as the Ice Queen. Like Jarod, she had a regal aura about her that in her case intimidated guys who'd wanted to ask her out. Not Zane. Sadie bet he'd danced with her as long as he'd felt like it.

"Sounds like an exciting prospect."

"Maybe. I've still got more research to do before I jump in." He flicked her a glance. "Is Jarod coming over?"

"Yes, but there's been a fire on Bannock property and he had to go. I still haven't heard from him. He's got to be all right, Zane."

"Nothing's going to happen to him. Have you fed Ryan?" She nodded. "Good. Why don't I put him to bed and give you a break?"

"Are you sure?"

"Positive."

"Then I'll let you, because I haven't visited Velvet all day." She hugged both of them. "My horse needs a daily walk around the corral and some loving."

His eyes danced. "Don't we all. You're lucky."

She grinned all the way to the barn. It appeared that finding a job that appealed to Zane had changed his whole outlook. After a career as a navy SEAL she'd feared he would never find anything as challenging. But this evening he looked and sounded happier than she'd ever known him to be.

Sadie was so glad for him and so in love with Jarod she thought her heart would burst. It must be a bad fire, otherwise he would never stay away from her this long and torture her. She prayed he wasn't in danger. *Please come home soon, darling.*

Chapter 10

Jarod and Connor, along with Ben, their uncle Grant, two of their cousins plus other ranch workers, stood outside the smoldering heap that had been one of their hay storage sheds until a couple of hours ago. At one point Jarod had gotten out the backhoe to tear down part of the shed so the firefighters could finish extinguishing the flames.

The fire marshall walked over to them.

"It was a set fire."

"Damn," Grant muttered.

That wasn't a surprise to Jarod. There'd been no lightning, no faulty electrical wiring. Just pure arson. Luckily the shed had only been a third full and the fire hadn't spread to the other buildings. A fifty-thousand-dollar loss. Jarod couldn't help think of the senseless waste of man hours and valuable hay for the cattle. A new shed would have to be built.

"Have you got any enemies?"

Jarod could think of one and shared a silent message with Connor.

Their uncle shook his head, not saying a word, but he had to be worried his youngest son hadn't come running when the fire had broken out. Ned, who was supposed to be working in a nearby building, should have been one of the first to see the flames.

But his cousin wasn't anywhere around.

Jarod knew Ned wanted to buy Sadie's ranch, but if he'd found out someone had gotten in ahead of him with more money, he would have had plenty of time to light a fire in retaliation against his father and Tyson.

Connor and Jarod returned to the house, and Connor seemed to have read his brother's mind.

"We need to confront Uncle Grant and Tyson about the fact that Ned was nowhere around. Grandfather will hate it, but this can't wait."

"Agreed," Jarod replied grimly. "Particularly since I visited the beauty shop this morning and learned from Rosie she never dated Ned. He couldn't have been with her the night of my accident. Your tip gave me the proof I needed that his alibi was a lie."

"Do you suppose Ned found out he was outbid?"

"I do. Since our bid came in at $720,000, Bree probably phoned him to give him the bad news as soon as possible and Ned lost it."

"He's probably at the bar in town getting drunk."

"Maybe." But Jarod had a dark feeling and felt a cold

sweat break out. "Let's talk to Uncle Grant right now. We'll go in my truck."

They headed for Tyson's ranch house half a mile away. Grant and his family were on the porch talking as Jarod and Connor got out of the truck and walked toward them.

"Have any of you seen Ned?" Jarod asked the question of all of them, but he was looking at his uncle.

"Not since breakfast."

"We're pretty sure Ned lit that fire," Connor said. "We also know that today he was outbid for the Corkin ranch. Someone else is buying it."

"Who?"

"Zane Lawson—he wants to be around to help raise Sadie's little brother."

"That's as it should be," Tyson murmured. He sounded a lot like Ralph just then.

Jarod nodded. "Ned's rage has been building for a long time, Uncle Grant. I have proof he had something to do with my accident eight years ago."

"What do you mean?"

He pulled the receipt from his wallet and handed it to his uncle. His cousins looked at the paper along with their father. "Notice the date. Call Owen's father and ask him about that Ford truck. The police would be interested to see the vehicle that almost got me killed.

"Ned used to follow me when I rode into the mountains to meet secretly with Sadie. His jealousy crossed the line. I never told you about those times. That was my mistake."

His uncle weaved silently in place.

"Today I learned that the excuse he made up about

being with Rosie from the beauty shop in town that night was a lie. She never dated him. For some reason the police didn't follow up his story with her. You do realize that every time something bad happens, Ned isn't around and can't account for his whereabouts. His drinking problem is another indication that something's off. He needs psychiatric help and has for a long time. You know it, and we know it."

Grant looked shattered.

"You never had control over him. That part I've always been able to handle. But burning down the hay shed has endangered everyone, not to mention the financial loss. Tyson and Ralph are old and failing in health. I don't want them to be hurt by this."

Grant looked at his sons in alarm. "Boys? We've got to find him."

"We'll all help." Connor had fire in his eyes.

"Let's go." Jarod raced for his truck. When Connor joined him he said, "Before we look anywhere, I need to make sure Sadie is all right." His wheels spun as he took off for her ranch.

"If he has gone after her, at least Zane is there," Connor reasoned. "Ned would be no match for a former SEAL."

"You're right." Jarod broke the speed limit getting to Farfields. Relief swamped him when he saw the Silverado parked out front. "I'll be right back."

He jumped out of the truck and knocked on the front door. After a minute Zane answered. He smiled at Jarod. "You look and smell like you've been battling a forest fire, but Sadie will be so happy to see you, she won't care."

"I hope not. Is she inside?"

"No. She went down to the barn about an hour ago to exercise Velvet. You'll find her there or out in the corral. She's crazy about that horse."

"Thanks, Zane."

He ran back to the truck. "Connor? Come with me."

His brother got out. "Where are we going?"

"To the barn. Zane said she's there, but it's getting late. I've got a feeling something's wrong."

They made their way on foot and checked the corral. No sign of her. Putting a finger to his lips, Jarod walked around to the front of the barn. The doors were closed. On a warm evening like this she would have kept them open. Jarod felt the cold prickle of sweat on the back of his neck as the dark feeling returned.

Sadie was ready to leave after walking Velvet back to her stall when she saw Ned standing there, a dangerous glint in his eyes. She'd seen it before and shuddered. There was no reason why he would be here except for a bad one. Aware she was alone, she felt a dual sensation of fear and nausea rise up in her.

"I don't know what you're doing here, but you're not wanted," she said, trying not to show how frightened she was. "Get away from the doors, Ned. I have to get back to Ryan."

Jarod's cousin had a strong physique like his father. She could try to push him away, but she couldn't stand the thought of touching him. He'd been drinking. She could smell it.

"No, you don't. Zane's there. We've got this whole

barn to ourselves." His looks were attractive enough, but the way he leered at her made her cringe.

"Jarod will be here any minute."

"No, he won't." He gave her that insidious smile. "He's putting out a fire."

The mention of it alarmed her. "How do you know about that?"

"I'm a Bannock, remember? Anything that goes on at the ranch I know about. What I'm here to find out is what you know about the buyer who outbid me for your father's ranch."

"What do you mean?"

"Bree called me this afternoon and told me he sold the ranch to someone else for $720,000. That kind of money doesn't grow on trees."

Her heart lurched. Zane's $700,000 bid had never stood a chance.

"I didn't learn the buyer's name, but the only person I know around here who can fork out that much cash is my half-breed cousin. He's a wealthy son of an injun, did you know that?"

"Don't you ever call Jarod that again." She almost spat out the words. "If he is wealthy, it's through hard work, something you don't know anything about."

Ned laughed. "O-oh. You're beautiful when you're angry, you know? But I'll do and say whatever the hell I feel like. Looks like he got what he wanted. There's oil under your land. He knows it, and he's been biding his time, waiting for you to fall into his hand like a ripe plum. Next thing we know he'll be drilling."

Sadie's body went rigid. There was no oil, but he wasn't listening. "What did he ever do to you?"

Ned cocked his head. "He got born."

"Jarod has as much right to life as you."

"Nature made a mistake."

Incredible. "Is that why you decided to drive Owen's truck into Jarod's eight years ago?"

His smirk faded. "What are you talking about?"

"You know exactly. I can see it on your face. You followed him from White Lodge and picked your spot to ram him."

"Yeah. I did a pretty good job if I say so myself. He had it coming. But even if he could prove it, there's nothing he can do about it. The statute of limitations on that hit-and-run case ran out a long time ago."

She shook her head. "You could have killed your own flesh and blood."

"Nah. Don't you know an injun has nine lives like a cat?"

Ned had lost touch with reality.

"The body shop in Bozeman has proof Kevin Pearson's truck was taken in to be repaired the morning after the accident. Jarod showed me a copy of the receipt. You paid cash. With that evidence, I'll go to the police and reopen the case myself!"

His cruel smile sickened her. "Well, then, honey, before you do that, I might as well take what you've been giving to that no good bum."

He lunged for her and dragged her into one of the empty stalls, knocking her down.

Sadie screamed at the top of her lungs, upsetting the horses, who whinnied. He covered her mouth with a hand that smelled faintly of gasoline and climbed on top of her.

"You fight like a she-cat. What does that long-haired cousin have that I don't? Come on, baby." He'd straddled her. "It's time you showed me what you've got. You need to share. I've waited long enough. This is going to be fun."

With her wrists pinned above her head in one hand, he ripped at the front of her blouse with the other, stifling her screams with his mouth.

Using every ounce of strength, she bit him as hard as was humanly possible. Warm salty blood filled her mouth.

"Ack! You little—" But she didn't hear another word because he was silenced by someone bigger and stronger who seemed to have come out of nowhere.

Ned spewed his venom, but it did no good. It was Jarod who had pulled him off her and now had him on the ground facedown in a hammerlock.

Connor was there, too. Together they tied his wrists and ankles with rope. The sheriff walked in on them as Jarod looked up at her. She'd never seen such fear in those black eyes. "Are you all right?"

"Yes." She tried to cover herself with the torn fabric of her shirt. "You got here just in time."

"Thank God." Jarod turned the sheriff. "We're glad you're here."

While Connor guarded Ned, the sheriff took her statement. Jarod led her outside before wrapping her in his arms. His body trembled like hers. "If anything had happened to you…" he murmured into her hair.

"He needs psychiatric help."

"That's what I told Uncle Grant earlier. We all knew who set fire to the hay shed. You're safe now and this whole ugly business is finally over. Come on. Let's get you home so you can shower and get cleaned up."

She buried her face against his chest as they made their way toward the house. "I was so terrified."

"So was I when I heard your scream, but he'd rigged something against the doors from the inside so we had to climb in through the rear window to get to you."

"Oh, Jarod." Sadie broke down sobbing. "How did you know where to find him?"

"A strong hunch. He'd lost everything else. Knowing how his mind works, I suspected he'd come after you. Rest assured he'll never bother you or anyone else again."

An anxious Zane came hurrying down from the porch. "What's happened?" He sounded frantic.

"She's all right, Zane. Ned decided to pay her a visit in the barn, but Connor and I got there in time and now he's tied up. The sheriff's with them."

"Sadie—" The other man gave her forehead a kiss. "I'll go see what I can do to help."

While Zane took off at a run, Jarod entered the house and walked her through to her bedroom. "You've got blood all over you."

"I bit him so hard, I don't know if he has a bottom lip left."

He hugged her to his heart. "You're my warrior woman all right."

She let out a shaky laugh. "He'll need stitches."

"He'll need a lot more than that. My brave Sadie. You had to deal with him all those years."

"You've had to endure much worse, almost losing your life. He admitted to running into you with Owen's truck, but I don't think Owen was with him. He's insane."

"Shh. That's all behind us now." He stopped in front of the bathroom door. She felt his eyes rove over her, searching for marks and bruises. "What can I get for you?"

"Not a thing. My robe is on the door. I'll be out in a minute. Don't go anywhere!"

"As if I would. I'll be in the living room."

She clung to him until he walked away. After a shower and shampoo, followed by a vigorous brushing of teeth, she emerged from the bathroom feeling rejuvenated. No more Ned. That thought was enough to erase the horror of her experience.

Once she'd dressed in a clean pair of jeans and a cotton sweater, she entered the living room, where everyone had gathered, including the sheriff who needed to bag her clothes for the forensics lab. Jarod reached for her and put his arm around her shoulders.

Now that she was no longer terrified, she saw the soot on his arms and face. The shiny black hair she'd noticed earlier no longer gleamed due to the debris from the fire. Both he and Connor smelled of smoke.

The sheriff nodded to her. "Ms. Corkin? We're sorry to hear about the assault, but are thankful to learn you're all right. Mr. Bannock has been taken into custody and his family notified. If you don't mind my asking you some more questions, I'll leave as soon as we're through."

"That's fine." The next few minutes passed in a blur. After statements were taken, the sheriff left.

Sophie's gaze swept over the man she worshipped.

"You and Connor fought a fire today and look absolutely exhausted. This is one time when I want you to go home. You need food and a shower in that order."

All three men chuckled.

Jarod's white smile shone through the grime left by the fire. "You mean you don't like me just the way I am?"

Her eyes smarted. "You know better than to ask me that question, but I'm thinking of your comfort. Please come right back. I'll be counting the seconds."

"Watch me." He gave her a hard kiss without touching her anywhere but on the mouth.

She walked them to the door. "Thank you," she whispered to Connor. "You and Jarod saved my life."

Connor kissed her cheek. "Any time, ma'am."

After they left, she closed the door and turned to Zane with such a heavy heart, she didn't know where to begin.

"There's something I have to tell you."

His mouth tightened. "Did Ned do something you didn't want Jarod to know about?"

"No. I told him everything. But while Ned had me cornered, he blurted that someone else's bid for the ranch came in higher than his." His ludicrous assumption that Jarod was the one who'd bought it revealed Ned's sickness.

Zane jumped to his feet. "Then that means we've lost the ranch."

"I'm afraid so. It's clear the bad news sent Ned's rage over the top, so he came after me." She could see the pain in Zane's eyes. "I know Jarod promised we'd get the ranch, but he's not in control of everything, so I have an idea. After we hear from Mr. Bree in the morning and know the fate of the Hensons, we'll go find us another place."

He shook his dark brown head. "You're getting married. You and Ryan will be living with Jarod. *I'll* find me a piece of property."

"I want to help. Bring your laptop into the kitchen. Let's start looking."

"Not tonight."

"Yes, tonight! It's not time for bed. We have nothing else to do. I'm anxious to see what's for sale around here. Tomorrow we'll make appointments and go check the places out with Ryan. When Jarod comes back, we'll ask him if he knows of an opportunity for us."

She thought a moment. "Keep in mind it could be a month, maybe longer, before the owner wants to move in. That'll give us time to get resettled. If the Hensons no longer have a job, we'll take them with us."

He frowned. "What do you mean *us?* When Jarod gets back, you'll be making plans for your wedding."

"I'm not doing anything until I know there's a satisfactory solution for all of us."

After a meal and a shower, Jarod took off for Sadie's ranch. With the threat of Ned gone for good, he had news for her and Zane they needed to hear. It couldn't wait until tomorrow.

Once he'd parked the truck, he hurried to the front porch and rapped on the door, thankful the last obstacle to their happiness had been removed and they could start planning their wedding.

The second Sadie opened the door, he pulled her

into his arms. "I got here as fast as I could," he whispered against her mouth before devouring it. Her response was everything he could have asked for, but he sensed something was wrong. When he finally lifted his head, he saw a sadness in her eyes that had turned them a darker blue. He intended to remedy that situation right now.

"Where's Zane?"

"In the kitchen."

He brushed his mouth against hers once more. "Lead me to him. I've got news for both of you."

Her eyes misted over. "We already know what it is," she said in a quiet voice.

Surprised, Jarod shook his head. "You couldn't possibly know what I'm about to tell you."

"Ned told me while we were in the barn."

He frowned. "Told you what?"

"That Bree phoned him this afternoon and notified him an unknown buyer had purchased the ranch."

"So that *was* the final blow that sent my cousin on the rampage."

"I'm sure of it."

"Come on." He grasped her hand and walked her through to the kitchen. Zane looked up from the table where he'd set his laptop. Jarod saw the same sadness in his eyes. "Before another minute passes, I have an announcement to make."

Sadie clung to the back of one of the kitchen chairs. He could tell she was fighting not to break down. Jarod had seen that look too many times in their lives. He planned to wipe it away for good.

"The ranch and everything else on the property is yours, Zane."

Sadie looked as if she was going to faint. "Ned said you were the buyer, but I didn't believe him."

A dazed Zane got to his feet. "What's all this about?"

"We're not the buyers, and we aren't out any money. But Ralph and I didn't want Ned to get the ranch, so our attorney acted as the straw buyer to make certain you were able to purchase it before he did. Your offer was accepted, Zane."

"Jarod—" The emotion in that one word caught at his heart.

"Bree will be calling to set up a time for you to drive to Billings and sign everything. He'll give you the deed, and that will be it."

Zane cleared his throat. "I don't know what to say. 'Thank you' could never cover it." He walked over and gave him a long hug.

Jarod was moved by the other man's gratitude. "I'm the one who's in your debt. No amount of money could compensate for what you've done to help take care of Sadie and Ryan. We should have been married eight years ago, but that was not our path until now." He darted Sadie a speaking glance. "There's nothing else to prevent us from planning our future."

Zane's eyes had gone suspiciously bright. "I'm going to leave you two alone to get started on those plans."

"Did you hear all that?" Jarod whispered after Zane disappeared. Sadie was still clinging to the chair. He'd been waiting for her to run to him, but she hadn't moved. He reached for her. "What's wrong?"

Tears welled in her eyes. "How do you thank someone who's just given you the world? Tell me how you do that." Her voice shook. "I love you so desperately, Jarod, you just don't know. That's why I'm so worried to tell you something that has to be said before we talk about the wedding."

"What's happened?" He sounded anxious.

She put her hands on his chest. "This is about the children you want to have with me."

He saw fear in her eyes. "Go on."

"There's no easy way to say this. I have a heart condition you need to know about."

His own heart almost failed him. "Since when?"

"At my last rodeo two weeks before graduation, I developed palpitations. My heartbeat accelerated abnormally during the barrel racing. Mac drove me to White Lodge to see the general practitioner at the hospital. He put me on birth control and a medication that really helped, but I had to stop the barrel racing. Then he advised me to see a cardiac specialist in Billings."

"*That* was the reason I couldn't find you after your performance that night?"

She nodded. Jarod was dumbfounded. "Since we were making plans to get married and I felt all right on the medicine, I decided not to tell you about it until after we were married. But three days later you had your accident."

"Sadie—" Fear caused him to break out in a cold sweat. He gripped her shoulders. "Your mother died of a bad heart having Ryan."

"That's true, but in her case there were extenuating circumstances."

He couldn't throw this off. "How serious is your condition?"

"Don't worry. It's not fatal. As you can see I'm still alive and have been doing just fine on the medication."

"You haven't answered my question. What's wrong with you exactly?"

"Once I arrived in California and told Mother what had happened, she took me to see her heart specialist. I was diagnosed with paroxysmal supraventricular tachycardia."

"Explain that to me."

"It's called PSVT and occurs when any structure above the ventrical produces a regular, rapid electrical impulse resulting in a rapid heartbeat. The technique to fix it has been perfected and involves placing small probes in the heart that can destroy tissue and then are removed once the tissue is altered.

"The procedure is called catheter ablation. The doctor inserts a tube into a blood vessel and it's guided to your heart. A special machine sends energy through the tube. It finds and destroys small areas of heart tissue where abnormal heart rhythms may start. You have to go to the hospital to have it done."

"Did your mother undergo this procedure?"

"Yes, but it didn't work. Sadly, in her case, the arrhythmia brought on cardiac arrest, something very rare. Her older age and stress played a big factor in what happened to her. I'm thinking of having the procedure done before we're married. Otherwise I won't be getting pregnant because the medicine I take can cause a miscarriage. I'll have to stay on birth control and won't be able to give you a baby."

"I don't like it, Sadie. I don't want you to do anything that will put your life in more jeopardy than it already is."

"I'm not in jeopardy. Listen to me, Jarod. Today I talked to my heart doctor in California. He gave me the name of a specialist in Billings named Dr. Harvey who does this kind of procedure. I'm going to call tomorrow for an appointment. We'll go together. If I find out I'm a good candidate, I'd like to have it done right away."

He struggled for breath. "What if it isn't successful?"

"Then my other doctor told me they'd put in a pacemaker. But think how wonderful it would be if I could plan to get pregnant without the fear of something going wrong."

"I'd rather we adopted children."

"If it comes to that, then I'll get my tubes tied and we'll go in that direction. But more than anything in the world I want to try the procedure so I can have your baby and give it a good Crow name."

Jarod wrapped his arms all the way around her and buried his face in her hair. "More than anything in the world, the only thing I want is for you to be in my bed for the rest our lives. We have Ryan. Let's let that be enough for now. Later on we'll consider adoption."

"Will you at least be willing to go to the doctor with me?"

His eyes closed tightly. "You're asking too much. We almost lost each other before. I can't go through that again."

She eased herself away from him. "Do you really mean that?"

"I do. My mother died after she had me. Your mother

died after Ryan was born. Now you're asking me to live through more torture while you undergo some procedure that could go wrong and you'd need a pacemaker to keep you alive?"

Her face was a study in pain, but he couldn't stop.

"What if that fails? Then it would mean another procedure and another until..." He shuddered. "I can't go along with it."

Sadie's complexion lost color. "What if I told you I've always wanted to have your baby and will do anything to make it possible?"

"Even chance death?"

"That won't happen! I want to do this for us. Remember what you told me a few nights ago? You said, '*The dreams I've dreamed, Sadie. My grandfather's health has to hold out long enough to see our first baby come into the world. I can hardly wait to feel movement inside you.*'"

He searched her eyes, gutted by this conversation. "I said that before I knew about your heart problem. Don't put me in this position, Sadie."

She looked at him with a pained expression. "I won't, because I can see your mind is made up." Her chin lifted in that unique way of hers. "You deserve to have your own baby. You'll make the most wonderful father on earth. So I'm going to do you a favor and release you from your commitment to me."

He stared at her, incredulous she would go this far.

"I shouldn't have accepted your proposal without telling you of my condition, but the night we got back together I wasn't thinking about babies. I was very selfish, only thinking about myself and my happiness. But let's be frank. There are many women out there like Leslie Weston who'd give anything to meet a man like you, and they don't have my heart ailment.

"I've always been a problem for you and it hasn't stopped. One day when you have a wife and several children of your own, you'll thank me. I love you, Jarod. I'll love you till my dying breath, but you shouldn't have to sacrifice every part of your life because of me. You did enough of that while my father was alive and it simply isn't fair to you. It's your turn to find happiness."

"You really want us to be over?"

"No. I want us to have our own baby, and the only way we can do that is for me to go to the doctor to see if he can do that procedure on me. If you're too afraid to even accompany me to the appointment to find out my options, then we shouldn't be together because I don't want to put you through that kind of agony. I'm a liability and have always been."

An overwhelming sadness filled her eyes, but Jarod knew she was determined.

"I—I think you should go," she said. "After fighting a fire and subduing Ned, you must be feeling worse than exhausted."

This just couldn't be happening, but it was....

With the blackness descending upon him, Jarod left the kitchen and headed for his truck.

"Sadie Corkin, you've just done the only terrible thing in your whole life."

Shocked at the tone of Zane's voice, she wheeled around white-faced.

"Because your voices carried, I didn't have to eavesdrop. Don't let him go like this or you'll never get him back. You're the woman he's always wanted, but you just threw everything he ever did for you back in his face. Sadie… You don't tell a man it's either my way or nothing. Not a man like Jarod. You're talking about your lives here!

"The poor man hasn't had two seconds to digest all this new information. He's terrified you might die. Forget having a baby right now. Even if you didn't have a heart problem, how do you know you can get pregnant? And Jarod might not be able to give you children. You're only twenty-six. You've got years to worry about that. Jarod wants marriage. He wants to live with you. You've put having a baby before *him!*"

Sadie had never seen Zane so impassioned.

"If your positions were reversed," he went on, "and he'd given you an either/or proposition, I can guarantee you'd be in such horrendous pain I don't even want to think about it. Take my car. It's all gassed up. Go find him!"

Sadie half expected him to point a finger at her. "I don't want to see you walk in that door again without him. Remember, it's my house now. Your place is with your fiancé."

Zane was right. He was right about everything.

She dashed to the bedroom for her purse. He met her at the door with the keys. "Go get him, Sadie. All the man wants is to be loved."

"Thank you," she whispered against his cheek.

Sadie flew to the car with her purse and drove off.

Jarod usually went to the reservation when he was in pain. She knew that about him, but he'd only had a five-minute start. Just to make sure, she drove to the Bannock Ranch to check if he'd stopped there first.

Thank heaven she'd followed her instincts. There was his truck parked in front. She got out of the car and ran to the front door. Afraid to waken Ralph if he was already sleep, she knocked several times instead of using the bell. In a minute Avery opened the door.

"Sadie—"

"Hi," she said, out of breath. "Is Jarod here?"

"Yes. He passed me on the stairs a few minutes ago looking like death. You look the same way."

"I have to talk to him."

"Come on in and go up the stairs. His bedroom is at the end of the hall on the left. I'm glad you've come because you're the only one who can fix what's wrong with him."

Sadie rushed past her and raced up the steps straight into Connor, who steadied her with his hands. Her head flew back as she looked up at him. "I'm sorry, Connor. I didn't see you."

"Jarod had the same problem when he came up a few minutes ago." He grinned. "That's twice I've been run into tonight. Jarod's at the end of the hall on the left."

She nodded. "Avery told me."

"Then don't let me keep you. One piece of advice. Don't knock. Just walk in."

That wisdom from Jarod's brother told her everything. If she knocked and Jarod knew who it was, he'd tell her to go away and never come back.

Taking his advice, she hurried down the hall and started to reach for the handle when the door opened. Jarod appeared, carrying a saddlebag and bedroll. If she hadn't caught up to him in time, he'd be off to the mountains and she would never have found him.

Without hesitation, she threw her arms around his neck and clung to him, forcing him to drop his things. "I'm sorry, darling." She covered his face with kisses. "Forgive me. The second the words came out of my mouth earlier, I wished I hadn't said them."

His body remained rigid. She knew she was in for the fight of her life.

"I want to live with you. You're all I want! We'll worry about children later. I wanted everything to be perfect for us, but as Zane let me know in no uncertain terms, nothing is perfect or set in this life. We need to seize our happiness while we can. There's no life without you. Please say you forgive me."

His grave countenance made him look older. "Only on one condition. That we leave for the reservation and ask Uncle Charlo to marry us tonight."

"Tonight? Isn't it too late?"

"No. I refuse to spend another night alone without you. It's your decision."

Sadie didn't have to think. "My place is with you."

Jarod's black gaze pierced through to her soul before he shut the door behind them. "Did you drive the truck over?"

"No. Zane's car."

"Give me his keys." She followed him to Connor's room. When he appeared with Avery, Jarod said, "We're getting married tonight." He handed him the keys. "Will you two see that Zane's car is returned to him? Tell him we'll be back tomorrow."

"Sure. Can you get a marriage license this late?"

"We'll take care of that later. We don't need one on the reservation."

"In that case, I claim my right to kiss the bride ahead of time." Connor pressed a warm kiss to her lips. "Take care of my big brother," he whispered. "He badly needs to be loved by a woman like you."

Sadie nodded and threw her arms around him. "I love you, Connor."

"Welcome to the family."

"Amen," Avery chimed in from behind them and reached for Sadie. "Grandfather and I have said every known prayer in the universe for this night to happen."

She laughed through the tears. "I love both of you, too, Avery."

They walked her and Jarod out to his truck.

As they drove away, Sadie waved until she couldn't see them any longer. After closing the window, she realized Jarod was on the phone talking to his uncle. Their conversation lasted a while before he rang off.

"I want you near me." He pulled her against him so possessively, it sent a tremor through her body that didn't stop, even after they reached the reservation.

Chapter 11

The Apsáalooke settlement of two thousand looked like a surreal painting in the moonlight. Most every home had a white tepee in its yard.

Though all the signs of modern civilization were there, in her mind's eye Sadie could see the proud, courageous warriors of years ago mounted on horseback in their search for buffalo. In a fanciful moment, she could imagine Jarod riding with them, his long black hair flying in the wind.

His mother came from this wonderful heritage. Tonight Sadie was going to experience a part of it. When they pulled up in front of his uncle's house, she was excited for what was about to happen.

Pauline Black Eagle was a lovely woman who came outside with her pretty eighteen-year-old daughter Mary

Black Eagle and younger son George, otherwise known as Runs Over Mountains. They were all smiling as they greeted Sadie and Jarod.

His uncle stood on the porch steps in his plaid shirt, jeans and cowboy boots. *"Kahe,"* he called to them. Jarod responded and they spoke in Siouan, the language Sadie was determined to learn.

"My uncle just welcomed us. Let's go in."

They entered the house. Once inside the living room Charlo asked them to sit. Only in his fifties, the tribal elder had obtained a *Juris* doctorate from the University of Montana School of Law. He stood in front of them, an attractive male figure with black hair to his shoulders. His dark eyes fastened on Sadie.

"My nephew says he wishes to get married. Is that your wish?"

"Yes."

"I see you wear the bracelet of our clan."

She nodded. "Jarod gave it to me eight years ago."

His eyes glimmered with satisfaction. "I once told Sits in the Center that the wolf must decide it is better to risk death for some chance of finding a mate and a territory than to live safely alone. I am happy to see he took my advice…for a second time," he added, causing her to glance at Jarod, who stared at her with smoldering eyes.

"I'm sorry about the first time and all the preparations you made that had to be canceled," Sadie said.

"It was no trouble. We were sad that Jarod had to suffer from an accident. But tonight there is only happiness because the circle of your lives has brought you together again."

"I'm so happy I could burst."

The women smiled broadly.

"My nephew has told me of your great interest in our culture, so he wishes to recreate his father and mother's wedding night. Pauline has some things for you to wear. If you'll go with her and Mary, George and I will see to Jarod and meet you outside in back. We've invited a few aunts and uncles to celebrate with you."

Jarod squeezed her hand hard before she followed the women through the house to one of the bedrooms. Sadie saw an outfit laid out on the bed.

"When my husband heard you were back from California, our clan made this deerskin dress and moccasins for you."

"But how did you know? I mean— Jarod and I hadn't been together for eight years."

"My husband sees many things."

Sadie shivered. She would always hold him in awe.

Pauline handed her the dress and Sadie looked at it with reverence. "The beading is exquisite. I'll always treasure it. Thank you from the bottom of my heart."

"You're welcome."

"You can change in my bathroom," Mary told her.

Sadie quickly removed her jeans and sweater, and emerged from the bathroom wearing the soft garment and moccasins. While she'd been changing, the other women had also donned deerskin dresses.

Pauline slipped the belt that matched the bracelet around Sadie's waist. *Bless you, Millie,* Sadie thought.

"You will please Jarod very much."

"I'll do everything I can to keep him happy."

"You already have or he wouldn't have asked you to

marry him two times. Many of the women who are not married have given him a new name—*He Who Has No Eyes*. But they didn't know what my husband and I knew."

Sadie felt heat rush to her cheeks. Pauline was wonderful. She used her skills as a nurse at the tribal clinic.

Mary, who was attending college, handed Sadie the beaded earrings, which she put on. Though Sadie knew that with her blond hair she looked a fraud, it was exciting to play a role for a little while. The most important role of her life. *Jarod's bride.*

"Come with us."

She walked with them through the house and out the back door to the yard. A fire had been lit in the fire pit, casting shadows over the tall white tepee in the background. The magical setting sent goose bumps up and down Sadie's arms.

Several dozen extended family members stood in a semicircle. She marveled that Charlo could assemble so many of their loved ones this close to midnight. They nodded to Sadie, who stayed close to Pauline and Mary. Their presence showed how much they revered Jarod.

Another minute and Charlo came out the back door in deerskin pants and shirt, followed by George in a similar outfit. Jarod walked out last. To her surprise he was wearing modern-day jeans and cowboy boots. But he'd dressed in a black ribbon shirt with a V neck and long sleeves ending in cuffs the men wore for special occasions.

She knew black was the sacred color of the Apsáalooke. The ribbons reflected orange, green, blue and yellow, representing the elements. The intricate pattern would have been passed down through the generations and given to him by his uncle.

Jarod had never worn his hair in a braid before, at least not in front of her. She could hardly breathe, he looked so fiercely handsome. Suddenly his gaze fell on her. Time stood still as they communed in silence as she took in the gravity of this moment. A light breeze ruffled the tips of her hair. If there was any sound, it was the thud of her heart in the soft night air.

Charlo motioned for her and Jarod to come closer and face him. A hush fell as he began to speak.

"If Chief Plenty Coups were here, he would say the ground on which we stand is sacred ground. It is the dust and blood of our ancestors. Sadie… Tonight when you enter the tepee on this sacred ground, our First Maker reminds you to remember that a woman's highest calling is to lead a man's soul so as to unite him with his Source."

She wasn't sure how to respond but gave him a solemn nod.

"Jarod? Tonight when you enter the tepee on this sacred ground, our First Maker would have you remember that a man's highest calling is to protect a woman so she is free to walk the earth unharmed."

When he nodded, Sadie wanted to proclaim to everyone that he'd always protected her and had already saved her from Ned earlier in the day.

"The crow reveals the true path to life's mission. It merges both light and dark, inner and outer, and when in the darkness of emotional pain and turmoil, the crow will carry the lost soul into the light.

"Both of you have endured much sorrow over the years. Don't waste today letting too much of yesterday ruin your joy. Before you lie down together, give thanks for blessings already on their way and you will have peace."

What better advice could anyone give?

He lifted his hands. "Go now. May you live in eternal happiness."

They were married?

She asked the question with her eyes. Jarod's mouth broke into such a beautiful smile that her entire being was filled with indescribable love for him. He grasped her hand. Leading her around the fire to the tepee, he moved the buffalo covering aside so she could enter.

The tepee's cone shape was formed with dozens of poles and could hold five to six people. Blankets on top of buffalo skins had been placed on the floor. Nothing else was inside....

Jarod held both her hands. "My mother's culture didn't do marriage ceremonies, but I think my uncle did the perfect job of performing ours."

"So do I," she said softly. There was enough light from the fire outside to see each other. "Do you mind if we kneel right now and do what he said?"

He kissed both her hands before they got down on their knees, facing each other. "You say the prayer."

"Thank you. I want to."

Closing her eyes she said, "Dear God, my heart is full to overflowing for the many blessings Thou has given us. We will strive to live worthily of the blessings Thou has yet to bestow on us. I thank Thee for my husband, a great man and a great warrior. I thank Thee for Jarod's loving family both on the ranch and on the reservation. I thank Thee for my family, for the Hensons. Amen."

Jarod's eyes were fastened on her as she lifted her

head. "Amen," he whispered in a husky voice. "You have no idea how beautiful you are to me, kneeling there in that dress to please me. Though I see a woman, I also see the sweet, vulnerable, lonely girl inside you who stole my heart years ago. I want to fill your loneliness, Sadie."

She cradled his face with her hands. "You already have. Uncle Charlo said not to dwell on the past. Tonight is the beginning of our future. There's something I want to do before we do anything else."

His breathing grew shallow. "What is it?"

"Take off your shirt first."

He looked surprised, but he did as she asked. Her breath caught to see his well-defined chest and shoulders emerge. "Now close your eyes."

As soon as they were closed, she moved around behind him and began unbraiding his fabulous hair. "I've been dying to do this since you came up to me at the funeral." She threaded her fingers through the glossy strands that fell loose and swung around his shoulders and face.

When she was finished she knelt in front of him. "You can open them now." Sadie almost fell back in amazement. "You're the most gorgeous man. I want an oil painting done of you exactly like this, sitting inside this tepee. After it's framed, I'll hang it in the most prominent place in our home with a small brass plate at the bottom that reads '*He Who Sits At My Side.*'"

Jarod's eyes glowed like black fire. He rose to his full height. She noticed the special belt he wore before he pulled her up and turned her around. Her body trembled as he undid the back of her dress, lowering it off her shoulders till it fell to her feet. His mouth found the side of her neck. "Come lie with me, my love."

A cry of longing escaped her lips as he laid her gently on top of the blankets. Looking down at her he said, "No painting of you could do you justice. I love you, Sadie. You're my heart's blood."

After plunging his fingers through her silky hair, he lowered his mouth to hers, giving her the husband's kiss she'd been waiting for since she'd fallen in love with him at fifteen.

Jarod— As their bodies melded, her heart and soul leaped to meet his.

Morning had come to the reservation. Jarod could see light through the tiny opening at the top of the tepee. He eased himself away from his precious wife, who still slept.

Jarod's hunger for her hadn't been appeased, no matter how many times they'd made love during the night. Now that he'd finally allowed her to sleep, he left her tangled in the blanket while he peered outside the entrance. The direction of the sun shining overhead told him it was at least two o'clock in the afternoon. That's why the interior was heating up.

He caught sight of their regular clothes along with a picnic basket of food Pauline had placed against the outside of the tepee. She'd taken care of everything to make their wedding night perfect.

After struggling eight years along a treacherous path, he'd obtained his heart's desire. Sadie was the most unselfish, giving woman he'd ever known.

Jarod breathed in the fresh air, aware that he felt whole at last. The night had been so perfect, he never wanted it to end, but she would awaken soon and want to get back to Ryan. Recognizing his insatiable appetite for her, he decided he'd better get dressed or they'd be here for another twelve hours.

Once he'd pulled on his cowboy boots, he brought everything inside. He found his cell phone and watch among his clothes and checked for messages. Only one from Connor.

Grandfather is ecstatic and can't wait to welcome both of you home. Tyson and Ned's parents are inconsolable. The police need to know if you want to press charges. You have every right, bro.

"Darling?" He glanced over at his wife. The word still thrilled him. What a beautiful sight she made. Unable to resist, he leaned down to kiss her, which was a mistake. He wanted to climb under the covers with her and never come out.

"Why did you let me sleep?"

"Because you needed to after I wore you out." He put the basket in front of them. "Pauline fixed us a picnic."

"She's incredible."

"I agree."

"I saw you checking your messages just now. Anything from Zane about Ryan?"

"No. It was from Connor. Everything's fine. Let's enjoy our first meal together as man and wife."

They ate sandwiches and drank soda. "I'm so excited to be married to you, I can hardly take it in. Last night—"

"Was miraculous," he broke in. "No man ever had a lover like you."

Her blush delighted him. When he'd finished eating, he reached for his thong.

"Don't confine your hair. I love the way it flows."

"I'll wear it loose at night, but during the day it gets in the way."

She eyed him curiously. "Yesterday you were going to tell me why you changed your hair."

He swallowed the rest of his cola. "I paid a trip to the beauty salon in White Lodge to talk to a woman named Rosie."

In another minute she knew the whole story about Ned's fabrication.

"She washed and cut your hair!"

"What's wrong?"

"I want you to know that no other woman will ever be allowed to do that again."

Laughter poured out of Jarod. He pressed her back against the blankets, kissing her long and hard.

"I want your promise, Jarod."

"I swear I'll never go in there again."

"Rosie probably had a cow when she found out she was going to get her hands on the gorgeous Jarod Bannock."

"A cow?" he teased.

"You know what I mean. I bet she can't wait until you go back."

He couldn't stop laughing. "She's married."

"That doesn't matter. For years I've had to put up with the way women look at you. It's been enough to give me a heart attack."

"Don't say that," he begged her, "not even in jest."

"Sorry. Happily, Pauline told me something about you that makes me feel a lot better."

"What's that?"

"The women on the reservation have been calling you He Who Has No Eyes."

More laughter caused him to bury his face in her throat. "That's because only one woman has ever held my heart."

"Have I told you I'm madly in love with you?"

"All night long," he murmured against her lips.

"Darling? What was Connor's message? I know it had to be something important or he wouldn't have sent it."

"Tell you what." He reached for her regular clothes and handed them to her. "After you get dressed, we'll freshen up in the house and then I'll tell you during the drive home. On the way we'll stop in White Lodge for our marriage license."

She smiled. "It's a little late for that, wouldn't you say?"

He didn't say anything, but fell back against the blankets to watch her.

"Close your eyes."

"That's one thing I can't do."

"The trouble with this tepee is that there's nothing to hide behind."

"My Apsáalooke ancestors knew what they were doing," he teased.

"Your *male* ancestors."

He loved it that she tried her hardest to pretend he wasn't there while she put on her clothes. Sadie never did seem to know how beautiful she was. Everything about her made her so desirable to him, and he was terrified of ever losing her. Their argument over her wanting that heart procedure still had a stranglehold on him.

Her blue eyes flashed. "I'm ready now, as if you didn't know."

"You did that far too fast for my liking. Next time things will be different."

"*How* different?"

"For one thing, we won't be in a hurry to go anywhere." His comment put color in her cheeks.

He gathered up their things and they left the tepee. No one was home when they went inside to use the bathroom. Jarod wrote a note and left it on the counter, thanking his aunt and uncle for everything.

We're now one soul in two bodies and have come into the light.

As they drove away from the reservation toward home, Sadie nestled up against him and pressed kisses to his jaw. "Tell me about Connor's message."

"Ned is in huge trouble. But I don't want to talk about him right now."

Sadie looped her arms around his neck. "You're such a noble man, Jarod Bannock." She started kissing him until he could hardly see to drive. "Sorry," she whispered when he had to slow down. "I'll behave myself until we get home."

"That's the next thing I want to talk to you about, *Mrs. Bannock*. I'm planning to build us our own home on the ranch, but until we've decided what kind we want and how big to make it, where is our home going to be for the next few months?"

"Would you mind terribly moving in with me? The nursery's already set up for Ryan, and it's only a few minutes away from your ranch and Ralph."

"Sadie, I'd live anywhere with you and can bring over some of my clothes. In fact, it's the Apsáalooke way for the husband to move in with the wife's family. But you'll need to feel Zane out."

"Honestly, I know he won't care. He's been looking for work."

"What about his plan to become a rancher?"

"With Mac's help, I think he wants to try to do both." For the rest of the drive home, she told him about Zane's interest in working for the BLM as a ranger.

When they arrived at the ranch, Jarod pulled up next to the Volvo. Sadie jumped out and they both hurried in the house.

"Zane?"

"In the kitchen, Sadie."

They found him alone. "Where's Ryan?"

He got up from the table where he'd been working on the laptop. "Millie and Liz wanted to watch him at their house. They're keeping him overnight so you can have some alone time."

"You're kidding—"

His eyes zeroed in on Jarod. "That's an amazing shirt you're wearing."

"It's a ribbon shirt with a design from his clan woven into the strips appliquéd to the fabric. Isn't it beautiful? Jarod wore it for the wedding ceremony."

"Nice." Zane's brows lifted. "What did *you* wear?"

"A beautiful, beaded deerskin dress. It's out in the truck. I'll show it to you."

"What are you doing home already? You're supposed to be on your honeymoon. I hoped you'd enjoy another night on the reservation at least!"

"We couldn't have done that to you. When I left here last night, I didn't even know if Jarod would forgive me. I caught him leaving the bedroom with his bedroll."

He grinned. "Yeah?" His gaze flicked to Jarod. "How long did it take you to decide to get married instead of high-tailing it to the mountains?"

"Not long," Jarod admitted.

"Well, now that you're here, I might as well tell you about the conversation I had with Connor and Avery last night when they brought back my car."

Jarod was all ears.

"They said they didn't know your plans yet, but figured if you two wanted to live here with Ryan for the next few weeks while you figure everything out, it could be like a honeymoon for you. Because of your grandfather, they know you wouldn't want to go away yet.

"In the meantime I'll temporarily move into your room, Jarod. It's only an idea, but let's be honest… You two need some space, and you won't get it at *your* ranch. We'll all split up the babysitting."

"It's a fabulous idea!" Sadie cried.

Jarod could see Connor coming up with that idea, but *his sister?* Avery was such a private person.

"My room's yours, Zane. I'm building Sadie and me a new house, so I don't plan to be in it any longer."

"In that case, why don't you two go see your grandfather? I understand he can't wait to congratulate you.

When you come back, I'll drive over with a few of my things."

Sadie hugged Zane before they went back out to the truck.

"Before we leave, I want another one of these." Jarod gave her a kiss that she returned with such passion, he couldn't wait for night to come.

When he would have let her go, she clung to him. "I think I'm in shock. For almost thirty years this ranch was off-limits to you. Now we're going to live here and we're married, and Zane and Ryan are happy and it's all because of you and—" She couldn't finish what she was trying to say.

Jarod knew she was happy, but not completely. The next step on their path would be the decision about children. When he'd awakened this morning with her lying in his arms, he'd remembered something he'd been taught by his father about fear when they were trying to tame a horse out in the corral. It had been speaking to him all day.

Courage was not the absence of fear, but rather the judgment that something else was more important than fear. Sadie wanted his baby. He wanted to give her his baby. To do that, he had to overcome his fear.

Tonight they'd talk about his going to the doctor with her.

He drove them to the ranch. Ralph was waiting for them in the living room with Jarod's siblings. They'd thrown together a quick celebratory meal with champagne. For the next hour they sat around and talked about the ceremony and the outpouring of love from Charlo's family.

"Thank you for doing this for us. To be here with all of you in the home I've known all of my life, and to be with my wife, whom I've loved for so long, I—" Jarod couldn't go on. His heart was too full.

In his whole life he'd never known such a completeness of joy, but he couldn't forget Connor's text message. There was something important they needed to discuss.

"What's happened to Ned?"

Ralph cleared his throat. "He and Owen have both been taken into custody and will be arraigned before the judge. Naturally his parents are grieving. I told the police you were on your honeymoon. They want to speak to you when you get back and are waiting for you to press charges for the accident."

Jarod clasped Sadie around the shoulders before letting out a deep sigh. "Marrying Sadie has made me so happy, any feelings of revenge I've wrestled with have fled. In their place is a deep sadness."

Sadie nodded. "At this point that's how I feel about my father, too."

He stared at his family. "Ned has been sick for years, but I don't believe he's evil. Perhaps there's still time for him to heal if he gets the kind of intense therapy and counseling he needs. Tomorrow I'll have a talk with Grant. Even if it takes years, I'd rather see Ned go that route than face a felony charge. As for Owen, he was only doing what Ned wanted, but Owen wasn't the one who drove into me. I'd say he needs therapy, too."

"You're a fine man, Jarod," his grandfather told him, trying to hold back the tears. "You make us all proud."

"To finally have peace so we can get on with our lives means the world to us, doesn't it, sweetheart?"

Sadie kissed his cheek. "Jarod and I have loved each other for what has seemed like eternity. It's hard to believe we can actually plan for the future."

"We want a family, but first Sadie has to undergo an operation on her heart to fix the palpitations. I just found out it's the reason she stopped barrel racing."

Sadie's look of joy and gratitude made him realize it was the right decision.

"Once that's behind us, then we'll start to build our own home on the property. With Zane next door to help us raise Ryan, life couldn't get any better. Speaking of Zane, we need to get back to the ranch so he can start to move in here." Jarod got to his feet, pulling Sadie with him.

Sadie moved around the room to hug everyone. "We were given wonderful advice by Jarod's uncle. He said, 'Both of you have endured much sorrow over the years. Don't waste today letting too much of yesterday ruin your joy. Before you lie down together, give thanks for blessings already on their way and you will have peace.'

"Jarod and I are going to take his advice and remember it. We love all of you."

Jarod's throat tightened.

He was going home with his angelic wife. Today was their first step to a shared destiny.

* * * * *

Marin Thomas grew up in the Midwest, then attended college at the U of A in Tucson, Arizona, where she earned a BA in radio-TV and played basketball for the Lady Wildcats. Following graduation, she married her college sweetheart in the historic Little Chapel of the West in Las Vegas, Nevada. Recent empty-nesters, Marin and her husband now live in Texas, where cattle is king, cowboys are plentiful and pickups rule the road. Visit her on the web at marinthomas.com.

Books by Marin Thomas

Harlequin Western Romance

The Cowboys of Stampede, Texas

The Cowboy's Accidental Baby
Twins for the Texas Rancher

Harlequin American Romance

Cowboys of the Rio Grande

A Cowboy's Redemption
The Surgeon's Christmas Baby
A Cowboy's Claim

The Cash Brothers

The Cowboy Next Door
Twins Under the Christmas Tree
Her Secret Cowboy
The Cowboy's Destiny
True Blue Cowboy
A Cowboy of Her Own

Visit the Author Profile page at Harlequin.com for more titles.

BEAU: COWBOY PROTECTOR

MARIN THOMAS

To my grandmother Dorothy West... Grandma, you blazed your own path through life... rather than becoming a hairdresser like your mother and sisters you became a bookkeeper. And you raised several eyebrows when you set your sights on the lead trumpet player in a popular dance band. Socializing was a huge part of your life and I know you're up in heaven dancing your toes off and swigging down Manhattans while listening to Grandpa Bud's band. Thank you for being such a wonderful grandmother to me, Brett and Amy and a patient, loving great-grandmother to Desirée, Thomas, Michael, Tylesha and Marin. You will be forever in our hearts.

Chapter 1

"Where's your better half?" Bull rider Rusty McLean stopped next to Beau Adams in the cowboy-ready area of the Sweetwater Events Complex in Rock Springs. "Duke was makin' a run at the National Finals Rodeo this year, then he slipped off the radar. He get injured?"

Beau wished an injury had sidelined his twin from today's rodeo—he was the only Adams competing this first weekend in October. He'd hauled Thunder Ranch bucking bulls, Bushwhacker and Back Bender, to the competition by himself. Duke, aka deputy sheriff had remained at home protecting the good citizens of Roundup while the Thunder Ranch hands had taken a string of bucking horses to a rodeo in Cody, Wyoming. Beau's father was off doing who knows what with his new lady friend.

"My brother quit," Beau said. In July, Duke had blindsided him when he retired from rodeo, leaving Beau to carry on the Adams' bull-riding legacy. He'd flipped out, angry that his brother had walked away from a possible world title when Beau had sacrificed so much for him. Beau had spent his childhood defending his twin when bullies had teased Duke about his stuttering. Standing up for his brother had carried into their teen years and when they'd reached adulthood, it had become second nature for Beau to make sure that Duke remained in the rodeo limelight.

"You're joking," McLean said. "Duke was ranked in the top ten in the country at the beginning of the summer."

"No joke, McLean. Duke's done with rodeo." Once Beau's anger had cooled, he'd realized Duke had never asked him for any concessions, which made Beau wonder why he'd allowed his brother to beat him in bull riding all these years. He had no one to blame but himself for the tight spot he was in—not enough rodeos left in the season to earn the necessary points to make it to Vegas. Regardless, Beau was determined to salvage what was left of the year by winning a handful of smaller rodeos leading up to the Badlands Bull Bash and Cowboy Stampede in South Dakota the weekend before Thanksgiving. A first-place win would show rodeo fans that Beau Adams was a serious contender for next year's title.

"You're pullin' my leg, Adams." McLean stuffed a pinch of tobacco between his lower lip and gum. "Duke wouldn't throw away his points 'less'n he had a good reason."

The sooner the truth got out, the sooner Beau's competitors would forget his brother and take notice of him. "Duke's been bit by the love bug." At McLean's puzzled expression Beau clarified. "He got married."

"The hell you say. I didn't know he had a girlfriend."

"It happened fast." Crazy fast. So fast Beau's head still spun. Of all women to go and fall in love with, Duke had picked Angie Barrington, a single mom with a grudge against rodeo. She ran an animal rescue ranch outside their hometown of Roundup, Montana, and a few of her boarders happened to include horses injured in rodeos. Much to Beau's chagrin, Duke had traded in a trip to the NFR for a ring and instant fatherhood.

You're jealous. Hell, maybe he was. There must be a bug in the water back home, because Duke and all but one of Beau's cousins had married in whirlwind romances reminiscent of Hollywood movies. It irked him that Duke was all in love and Beau had yet to catch the eye of Sierra Byrne, a woman he'd been flirting with since spring.

"Too bad about Duke. His loss is my gain," McLean said.

"Don't get cocky." Beau grinned. "You gotta beat me to win that buckle." Buckle aside, Beau wanted to take home the prize money—three thousand dollars. Not a fortune by any means, but with the tough economy, the cash would help pay a few ranch bills.

"Adams." McLean snorted. "You ought to know better than anyone that Bushwhacker's the best bull here. All I gotta do is make it to eight on him and the buckle's mine."

The braggart was right—Bushwhacker was the top-rated bull at the rodeo. At five, he was a year older than Back Bender, but both were money bulls. So far this season, Bushwhacker had thrown every cowboy who'd ridden him and only one rider had made it to the buzzer on Back Bender. "The odds aren't in your favor, McLean."

"Ladies and gentlemen." The rodeo announcer put an end to the cowboy banter. "As was broadcast earlier, due to one of our stock contractors encountering a flat tire, the rodeo committee has switched the order of events. Bull riding will take place next, followed by our final event of the day—the bareback competition."

The crowd booed its displeasure, but quieted when the announcer continued his spiel. "You're about to witness some of the toughest and bravest men alive…."

Beau blocked out the booming voice and studied his draw—Gorgeous Gus. His new best friend was a veteran bull with a reputation for charging anything on two legs. Beau adjusted his protective vest and put on his face mask. He hated wearing the gear, but if he intended to win a title he'd sacrifice his vanity to remain healthy and injury-free. He climbed the chute rails and straddled the two-thousand-pound tiger-striped brindle Brahma-Hereford mix.

"Folks, I gotta say this next bull makes me nervous. Gorgeous Gus hails from the Henderson Ranch in Round Rock, Texas. Gus has already put three cowboys out of commission this season."

Music blared from the sound system but Beau kept his gaze averted from the JumboTron. He didn't care to watch as it replayed Jacob Montgomery's attempt to ride Gorgeous Gus in Denver this past July. Gus had thrown Montgomery and then, before the cowboy had gotten to his feet, the bull had gored his leg. A few seconds later the collective gasp that rippled through the stands sent chills down Beau's spine.

"Goin' head-to-horns with Gorgeous Gus is Beau Adams from Roundup, Montana. This is the first matchup between cowboy and bull."

Beau closed his eyes and envisioned Gus's exit out of the chute, but Sierra Byrne popped into his mind, interrupting his concentration.

"You ready, Adams?" the gateman asked.

"Not yet." Beau shook his head in an attempt to dislodge Sierra's blue eyes and flaming red hair from his memory. That he'd allowed the owner of the Number 1 Diner to mess with his focus didn't bode well for the next eight seconds. He flexed his fingers and worked the leather bull rope around his hand, fusing it to Gus's hide.

Breathe…in…out…in…out…. The blood pounded through his veins like roaring river rapids after the spring snowmelt in the Bull Mountains.

I'm the best.

No one can beat me.

Win.

He repeated the new mantra in his head—different from his previous pep talks when he'd taken a backseat to his brother's performances. Since Duke's retirement Beau had won several rodeos, but the bulls hadn't been rank bulls—not like the notorious Gorgeous Gus. A bead of sweat slid down Beau's temple. In a few seconds, he'd know if he'd been blowing hot air when he'd sparred with McLean. Satisfied with his grip, he crouched low and forced the muscles around the base of his spine to relax, then he signaled the gateman.

Gus exploded from the chute, twisting right as he kicked his back legs out. Beau survived the buck and Gus allowed him half a second to regain his balance before a series of kicks thrust Beau forward and he almost kissed the bull's horns. Beau ignored the burning fire spreading through his muscles as he squeezed his thighs against the animal's girth.

The dance went on...*twist, stomp, kick. Twist, stomp, kick.* Gus spun left then right in quick succession, almost ripping Beau's shoulder from its socket. Sheer determination and fear of being trampled kept him from flying off. The buzzer sounded and the bullfighters waved their hands in an attempt to catch Gus's attention.

Taking advantage of the distraction, Beau launched himself into the air. He hit the ground hard, the oxygen in his lungs bursting from his mouth like a six-pack belch. He didn't check on Gus—a one-second glance might mean the difference between making it to the rails...or not.

Ignoring the sharp twinge in his left ankle, Beau rolled to his feet and sprinted for safety. The mask on his helmet obscured the barrier, making it difficult to judge the distance. When his boot hit the bottom rung, a hand crossed his line of vision and a hard yank helped him over the top of the gate just as Gus rammed his head into the rails, the impact rattling the metal.

"Holy smokes! What a ride by Beau Adams!"

Applause thundered through the arena, and the ear-piercing racket of boots stomping on metal bleachers brought a smile to Beau's face as he removed his mask.

"Eighty-six is the score to beat!" The JumboTron replayed the bull ride.

"Congratulations, Beau."

Beau spun at the sound of the familiar voice. His cousin, Tuf Hart, stood a foot away, the corner of his mouth lifting in a cautious smile. "Tuf!" Beau clasped his cousin's hand and pulled him close for a chest bump and a stiff one-armed hug.

Tuf looked tired. Worn out. Maybe even a little beaten down. He'd left the Marines and returned to the States almost two years ago but had kept his distance from the family. Beau knew for a fact that his cousins Ace and Colt were upset with their baby brother for not returning to the ranch. Beau snagged Tuf's shirtsleeve and pulled him away from the chutes.

"Do you know how worried the family is about you?"

His cousin's gaze dropped to the tips of his boots.

"Fine. I won't pry. Just tell me you're okay."

"I'm getting there."

What the hell kind of answer was that? "Where've you been all this time?"

"I'd rather not say."

The youngest Hart had missed all the family weddings and good news. He bet Tuf hadn't heard that Ace and Flynn's first child was due around Thanksgiving or that Tuf's sister, Dinah, had married Austin Wright and they were expecting a baby next summer.

"Man, you gotta know your mom misses you."

Tuf removed his hat and shoved his fingers through his short brown hair. "I'll be in touch soon."

The twenty-eight-year-old standing before Beau was

a stranger, not the cousin he remembered. "You don't know, do you?"

"Know what?"

"Aunt Sarah—"

"I can't talk right now." Tuf made a move to pass, but Beau blocked his path.

Didn't Tuf care that his mother had suffered an angina attack this past May and that the ranch had hit upon tough times? As a member of the family, Tuf should have known his mother had been forced to take Thunder Ranch in a new direction. Aunt Sarah had sold off most of the cattle, leased a sizable chunk of grazing land and had secured a hefty bank loan that Ace had cosigned.

"Call your mom and let her hear your voice."

The muscle along Tuf's jaw pulsed but he held his tongue.

Had something happened to his cousin in Afghanistan? The Tuf Beau had grown up with would never have shut out his family.

"Tell my mom I'm in Maryland and that I'm okay." His cousin walked off and joined the other bareback riders preparing for their event.

What was so important in Maryland that it prevented his cousin from returning to Thunder Ranch? Beau figured if Tuf had traveled this far west to compete in a rodeo he must be homesick. Hopefully, Tuf would come to his senses soon and haul his backside to Montana before Aunt Sarah dragged him home by his ear. Forgetting about his cousin, Beau focused on the Thunder Ranch bulls, eager to view their performances and he didn't want to miss Bushwhacker tossing McLean on his head.

"Next up is Pete Davis from Simpleton, North Dakota, riding Back Bender from the Thunder Ranch outside Roundup, Montana." The crowd applauded. "Back Bender's a young bull but he's got energy and lots of gas. This bull goes all-out for eight seconds and then some."

The announcer summed up Back Bender pretty well. The bull never ran out of kick—it was as if electricity flowed through the animal's veins instead of blood. When the gate opened, Back Bender erupted from the chute with a fierce kick before turning into a tight spin, then coming out of it with a double kick, which sent Davis flying at the three-second mark.

The bullfighters rushed in, but Back Bender continued to kick and the fans cheered in appreciation. Beau shook his head in wonder. The dang animal loved to buck.

"Like I said, folks, Back Bender's tough to ride and his brother, Bushwhacker is nastier. Turn your attention to chute number three for the final bull ride of the day."

Beau scaled the rails for a better view of the brown-and-red bull. Bushwhacker kicked the chute, warning those around him that he meant business.

"Bushwhacker also hails from Thunder Ranch and this bull loves to ambush cowboys. He lulls a rider into thinking he'll make it to eight then tosses him into the dirt. Bushwhacker is undefeated this season. Let's see if Rusty McLean from Spokane, Washington, can outsmart this bull."

McLean adjusted the bull rope, his movements jerky and uneven. The boastful cowboy was nervous—he should be. He had a fifty-fifty chance of being the star of the day or going home the biggest loser.

C'mon, Bushwhacker. Show everyone why you're the best.

McLean signaled the gateman and Bushwhacker exploded into the arena. The bull's first buck was brutal—his signature move. He kicked both back legs out while twisting his hindquarters. Too bad for McLean. Bushwhacker's raw power unseated him, and the cowboy catapulted over the bull's head. McLean stumbled to his feet as the bullfighters intercepted Bushwhacker and escorted him from the arena. Staggering into the cowboy-ready area, McLean flung his bull rope and cussed.

"Better luck next time," Beau taunted.

The cowboy spit at the ground and stomped off.

"Beau Adams from Roundup, Montana, is the winner of today's bull-riding competition. Congratulations, Adams!"

Excited he'd taken first place, Beau collected his gear and the winning check, then found a seat in the stands to watch Tuf compete.

"Ladies and gentlemen, our final event of the day is the bareback competition. Those of you who don't know…a bareback horse is leaner, quicker and more agile than a saddle bronc. Bareback riding is rough, explosive, and the cowboys will tell ya that this event is the most physically demanding in rodeo." The crowd heckled the announcer, several fans shouting that bull riders were the toughest cowboys in the sport.

"Sit tight folks, you'll see what I'm talkin' about."

The announcer was right—a bareback cowboy's arm,

neck and spine took a brutal beating and Beau worried about Tuf. If his cousin was just returning to competition, then he might not be in the best physical shape and the ride could end in disaster.

"First out of the gate is Tuf Hart, another cowboy from Roundup, Montana."

While Tuf settled onto the bronc and fiddled with his grip, the announcer continued. "Hart's gonna try to tame Cool Moon, a three-year-old gelding from the Circle T Ranch in New Mexico. Cool Moon is a spinner, folks."

Seconds later, the chute opened and Cool Moon went to work. The bronc twirled in tight, quick circles while bucking his back legs almost past vertical, the movement defying logic.

Hold on, Tuf. Hold on.

The moment Beau voiced the thought in his head, Tuf flew off Cool Moon. As soon as he hit the dirt, he got to his feet quickly. Beau watched him shuffle to the rails—no limp. His cousin hadn't won but more importantly he'd escaped injury.

After the final bareback rider competed, Beau made his way to the stock pens. Bushwhacker and Back Bender had rested for over an hour and it was time to load them into the trailer. First, he wanted to wish his cousin well and tell him to hurry home. He weaved through the maze of cowboys and rodeo fans, stopping once to autograph a program for a kid. Finally, he made it to the cowboy-ready area. "Hey, McLean," Beau called.

"Don't rub it in, Adams."

No need. Bushwhacker had had the final word. "Have you seen my cousin?"

"He left after his ride."

Miffed that Tuf hadn't cared enough to say goodbye, Beau sprinted to the parking lot then stopped. He didn't even know what vehicle Tuf drove. Disgusted, he retrieved the Thunder Ranch truck and livestock trailer.

With the help of two rodeo workers, Beau loaded Bushwhacker and Back Bender into the trailer. When he pulled out of the Sweetwater Events Complex, he drove north, intent on arriving home by the ten-thirty news. He made a pit stop for gas outside Rock Springs then purchased a large coffee and a Big Mac from the McDonald's restaurant inside the station. Back in his truck he popped three ibuprofen tablets to help with the swelling in his ankle—already his boot felt tight.

Once he merged onto the highway, he found a country-western station on the radio and settled in for the long drive. Less than five minutes passed before his thoughts turned to Sierra Byrne.

Physically, she was the opposite of the women he'd dated in the past. In heels, Sierra might reach five-seven. Full-figured—not slim or willowy—and red hair. He usually went for blondes.

Ah, but her eyes... Sierra's eyes had stopped Beau in his tracks the first time he'd gotten up the nerve to begin a conversation with her. Bright blue with a paler blue ring near the pupil. He'd locked gazes with her, mesmerized by the way the blue had brightened when she'd smiled.

And her hair... Sierra wore her hair in a springy bob that ended an inch below her jaw, and her bangs skimmed the corner of her right eye, lending her a playful, sexy look.

Her cuteness aside, there was something stirring… vulnerable in Sierra's gaze that tugged at him. If only he could get her to agree to a date with him. He'd first asked her out this past June…then in July…then in August… September. Each time she'd made up a lame excuse about the diner keeping her too busy.

She was proving to be a challenge, but Beau wasn't one to back down when the going got tough. Sierra might have rebuffed his advances, but she wasn't as clever at hiding her attraction to him. A few weeks ago, she'd run into the edge of a table at the diner and he'd rescued a plate of food from her hand. Their bodies had collided, her lush breasts bumping his arm. Everyone in the booth had heard her quiet gasp, but only Beau's ears had caught the sexy purr that had followed.

Worrying about his love life wouldn't get him home any faster. He switched the radio station to a sports talk show and forgot about his crush on Sierra.

Five hours later, as Beau approached Roundup, he noticed a vehicle parked on the side of the road. His truck's headlights shone through the car's rear window, illuminating a silhouette in the driver's seat. He turned on the truck's flashers then pulled onto the shoulder behind the car. When he approached the vehicle, the driver's side window lowered several inches.

What the hell?

"Hello, Beau," Sierra said.

Well…well…well… This surely was his lucky day.

Chapter 2

Drat!

Sierra had the worst luck—go figure Beau Adams would end up rescuing her from her own stupidity.

Beau had set his sights on her early this spring when he'd begun eating at the diner on a regular basis. She found the handsome bull rider's attention flattering and would have jumped at the chance to date him, but circumstances beyond her control had forced her to keep him at arm's length.

"Engine trouble?" Beau's gaze drifted to her lips. The man had the most annoying habit of watching her mouth when they engaged in conversation.

"I'm not sure what the problem is," she said, ignoring her rising body temperature. There wasn't a thing wrong with her RAV4, except for the dent in the rear fender from a run-in with a minivan in the parking lot of the diner.

Sierra's sight had left her marooned on the side of the road.

He swept his hat from his head and ran his fingers through his hair. Beau's brown locks always looked in need of a trim, but it was his dark brown eyes and chiseled jaw that made her heart pound a little faster.

"I bet I can figure out what's wrong," he said.

Typical cowboy—believing he could repair anything and everything. Too bad Beau couldn't fix her eyes.

"How long have you been sitting here?"

Hours. "A short while." No way was she confessing that she couldn't see well enough to drive at night.

If not for a freeway wreck on the outskirts of Billings, she would have made it home, but ten miles from town dusk had turned to darkness. With few vehicles traveling the road, Sierra had decreased her speed and continued driving, but her confidence had been shattered when she'd crossed the center line and almost collided with another car. The near miss scared years off her life and she'd pulled onto the shoulder, resigned to wait until daybreak to drive into Roundup.

She'd phoned her aunt, who'd been visiting her since July, and had informed her that she planned to spend the night with a friend. Silence had followed Sierra's announcement. Everyone in town was aware of Beau's frequent visits to the diner and Jordan probably wondered if Sierra's *friend* happened to be Beau.

She appreciated that her aunt hadn't pried—after all, Sierra was thirty-one, old enough to have a sleepover with a man. In truth, she'd love to get to know Beau better, but life wasn't fair. Too bad he'd happened along tonight. She'd been certain she'd get out of this mess without anyone the wiser.

"Pop the hood," he said.

"There's no need. I called Davidson Towing. Stan is out on another call but should be here in a little while." Maybe if she distracted Beau, he'd forget about checking the engine. "Returning from a rodeo?"

"Yep. Hauled a couple of Thunder Ranch bulls down to Rock Springs, Wyoming."

"Did you compete?"

He rested an arm along the top of the car. "Sure did, and I won." His cocky grin warmed her better than her down parka.

"Congratulations." The diner's patrons kept Sierra up to date on their hometown cowboys' accomplishments. Since she'd moved to Roundup five years ago, most of the gossip about the Adams twins focused on Duke's rodeo successes. Lately, Beau was getting his turn in the spotlight.

"Wanna see my buckle?"

She swallowed a laugh. "Sure." He removed the piece of silver from his coat pocket and passed it through the open window. "It's beautiful."

"There's no need for you to freeze. Stan'll tow your car to his garage and square the bill with you in the morning." Beau reached for the door handle.

"No!" Sierra cringed. She hadn't meant to shout. For a girl who'd lived most of her life in Chicago, small towns were both a blessing and a curse. She handed Beau the buckle. "I appreciate the offer, but I'd prefer to wait with my car."

Instead of backing away he poked his head through the window, his hair brushing the side of her face. A whiff of faded cologne—sandalwood and musk—swirled beneath her nose. "Just checking to make sure there's no serial killer in the backseat holding you hostage."

Oh, brother.

"If you're determined to wait for Stan, then sit in my truck. I've got the heat going and I'll share the coffee I bought at the rest stop."

"Thanks, but you should get your bulls back to the ranch." *C'mon, Beau. Give up and go home.*

"I don't like the idea of you waiting out here all alone."

"This is Roundup, Montana. Nothing's going to happen to me."

"You're forgetting the break-ins this past summer. This area is no Mayberry, U.S.A."

Sierra regretted her flippant remark. Although Roundup had been and would continue to be a safe place to live and raise a family, a rash of thefts in the ranching community had put people on edge for a while. Even Beau had been victimized when one of his custom-made saddles had been stolen and sold at a truck stop miles away.

"I'll be fine. Besides, your cousin caught those thieves." She switched on the interior light and pointed to her winter coat. "And I'm plenty warm." A flat tire during her first winter in Big Sky country had taught Sierra to keep a heavy jacket in her vehicle year-round. Unlike Chicago, car trouble in rural Montana could mean waiting an entire day for help to arrive and the state's weather was anything but predictable—sixty degrees one hour, a blizzard the next.

"How long did you say you've been waiting for Stan?"

"Twenty minutes maybe." When had she become such an accomplished liar?

Beau walked to the front of the car and placed his hand on the hood.

Busted. She'd been parked for over three hours—surely the engine was stone cold. "Thanks again for stopping to check on me," she called out the window, hoping he'd take the hint and leave.

"You're sure you don't want a ride to the diner?"

"Positive."

"Okay. Take care." He retreated to his truck where he took his dang tootin' time pulling back onto the road. As soon as the livestock trailer disappeared around the bend in the road, Sierra breathed a sigh of relief.

Then the tears fell.

Ah, Beau. Darn the man for being...nice. Handsome. Sexy.

Over a year ago, Sierra had become aware of the subtle changes in her eyesight, but she'd steadfastly ignored the signs and had gone about life as usual. Her resolve to pretend her vision was fine had grown stronger after each encounter with Beau. Then her aunt had arrived unannounced—thanks to the busybodies who'd informed her of Sierra's recent mishaps around town—determined to persuade Sierra to schedule an appointment with an ophthalmologist. Sadly, she didn't need an examination to tell her that she'd inherited the gene for the eye disease that had led to her aunt's blindness.

Why couldn't Beau have paid attention to her when she'd first arrived in Roundup years ago? Darn life for being unfair. Sierra rested her head on the back of the seat. Maybe she'd see—*ha, ha, ha*—things in a different light come morning.

Morning arrived at 6:25 a.m., when a semi truck whizzed by her car and woke her. She wiggled her cold toes and fingers until the feeling returned to the numb digits. If she hurried, she'd have time to mix a batch of biscuits before the diner doors opened for breakfast at seven.

She snapped on her seat belt then checked the rearview mirror. *Oh. My. God.* Beau's pickup, minus the livestock trailer, sat a hundred yards behind her. Embarrassed and humiliated that he'd caught her red-handed in a lie, she shoved the key into the ignition and the SUV engine fired to life. After checking for cars in both directions she hit the gas. The back tires spewed gravel as she pulled onto the highway. Keeping a death grip on the steering wheel she glanced at the side mirror—Beau remained fast asleep, slouched against the driver's-side window.

Don't you dare cry.

Her eyesight was blurry in the mornings, and if she gave into the tears that threatened to fall she'd be forced to pull off the road again—and then what excuse would she give Beau?

Beau woke in time to catch the taillights of Sierra's SUV driving off. The least she could have done was thank him for watching over her through the night.

Sierra mystified him. After finding her stranded on

the side of the road he'd been puzzled by her insistence that he not wait with her for a tow. Then, when he'd placed his hand on the hood of the car and discovered the engine was cold, his suspicions had grown. For the life of him he couldn't figure out what she'd been up to, but she'd made it clear she didn't want his help, so he'd moseyed along. When he'd reached Roundup, he'd driven past Davidson Towing. Stan's tow truck had sat parked in the lot, the lights turned off in the service garage.

For a split second, Beau had wondered if Sierra had intended to rendezvous with a man, but he'd nixed that idea. Before he'd begun his campaign to convince her to go out on a date with him he'd asked his cousin Dinah, the town's sheriff, to find out if Sierra was involved with another man. According to Dinah's sources Sierra wasn't. Boyfriend or not, Beau hadn't been about to leave Sierra alone in the dark.

He'd delivered Bushwhacker and Back Bender to Thunder Ranch, then had hollered at his father through the door that he was meeting up with friends at the Open Range Saloon. Alibi taken care of, he'd high-tailed it back to the highway.

When he'd passed her SUV, the truck's headlights had shown her asleep in the front seat. Alone. Relieved he'd been wrong about a clandestine meeting, he'd parked behind the car, resigned to wait until morning for answers. Those answers were right now fleeing down the highway.

Although tempted to stalk Sierra until she offered an explanation for the crazy stunt she'd pulled last night, he started his truck and turned onto the county road that bypassed Roundup and brought him to the back side of Thunder Ranch, where the Adams men were in charge of the bucking bulls and the cattle that grazed this section of the property. He pulled up to the small house his father had raised him and his brother in after their mother had died in a car accident thirty years ago. He shut off the engine then tapped a finger against the steering wheel. Was he coming on too strong with Sierra?

When he'd first begun pursuing her, his brother had pointed out that folks might mistake his actions as those of a man on the rebound. He'd discarded Duke's words. Beau and his former girlfriend Melanie had given their long-distance relationship a shot but they'd grown apart months before their official breakup last December. Now that Duke and all their cousins, except Tuf, had married, Beau was feeling left out of the holy-matrimony club. He wanted for himself the same happiness his brother and cousins had found with their significant others, and something about Sierra made Beau believe she could be the one.

He hopped out of the truck and used the side door to enter the house. He found his father sitting at the kitchen table, eating donuts—usually by this time in the morning he was checking the water tanks and feed bins in the bull pasture. Beau hung his sheepskin jacket on the hook by the door. "Skipping your oatmeal and English muffin today?"

"Jordan sent the donuts home with me last night. Leftovers from the diner."

Jordan Peterson was Sierra's aunt and his father's… friend…girlfriend? The moment Jordan had stepped off the bus with her seeing-eye dog in July, his father had been hot on her heels. Beau had no idea where the older couple's relationship was headed, but he was ticked off that his father spent most of his time with Jordan and neglected his responsibilities around the ranch.

"When did you get in last night?" Had his father been home when Beau had dropped off the bulls?

"'Round midnight."

Guess not.

"Since we're keeping tabs on each other's where-abouts…." His father nodded at Beau's jacket. "Where'd you hang your hat last night?"

Admitting that he'd slept in the cab of his truck would raise more questions than Beau cared to answer. Besides, he doubted Sierra wanted her aunt or the good folks of Roundup to learn she'd spent the night on the side of the road.

Rather than lie, Beau changed the subject. "Did you eat supper at the Number 1 yesterday?"

"Only an emergency would keep me from missing the Saturday special."

Beef potpie baked in a homemade crust. Beau had memorized the daily specials when he'd begun his campaign to woo Sierra.

His father carried his coffee cup to the sink. "Sierra phoned Jordan and said she wouldn't be back in town until morning, so I helped close up the diner last night."

Sierra had covered all her bases—clever girl—but why?

"Speaking of Sierra… Jordan tells me that you've been dropping by the diner every day."

Beau never talked about his personal life with his

father and didn't feel comfortable now. "Do you have a problem with that?"

"As a matter of fact, I do. I want you to keep away from Sierra."

Beau's hackles rose. He and his father had never been close, and up until now his dad had kept his nose out of Beau's affairs. Why all of a sudden did he care if Beau had his sights set on Sierra? "I'm a grown man. I don't need your permission to date a woman."

"You don't have time for a relationship right now."

"And you do?" Beau asked.

"What's that supposed to mean?"

"You and Jordan are becoming awfully tight." Beau and his father exchanged glowers.

"Instead of chasing after Sierra, you should focus on mending fences with your brother. There's a lot of work around here and if you're squabbling with each other things don't get done."

Afraid he'd say something he shouldn't, Beau helped himself to the last donut on the plate and poured a cup of coffee.

"You talk to your brother lately?" his father asked.

"No. Why?"

"Duke said you've been giving him the cold shoulder since he quit rodeo."

Not exactly true. Beau was still talking to Duke—he just didn't go out of his way to do so. After their blow-up this past summer, he'd had a few superficial conversations with his brother, but they'd steered clear of discussing rodeo. Beau accepted most of the blame for having kept his distance from Duke—he needed time to come to grips with all the changes in his brother's life.

"You hurt Duke's pride when you told him you'd never given your best effort in the arena all these years."

Where did his father get off lecturing Beau? If the old man had shown a scrap of concern or compassion over Duke's childhood stuttering, or defended Duke from bullies, Beau wouldn't have felt compelled to do the job, which had naturally led Beau to allowing Duke the limelight to build his self-esteem.

"I never told you that you had to be second best," his father said.

"No, but you were oblivious to Duke's struggles. Someone had to encourage him."

"I wasn't oblivious." His father's gaze shifted to the wall. "Figured if I ignored his stuttering, Duke would grow out of it faster."

Part of Beau felt sorry for his father—raising twin boys without a wife would be a challenge for any man. Even so, had his father shown any compassion for Duke, Beau might not have overstepped his bounds with his brother.

"The only reason you want me to make nice with Duke is because you've been shirking your duties around here and you need your sons to pick up the slack."

His father's steely-eyed glare warned Beau he was treading on thin ice—time to change the subject. "A while back Duke said you were thinking about retiring." He hoped the news wasn't true.

"Been tossing around the idea."

The timing couldn't be worse—Beau adding rodeos to his schedule and Duke trying to balance family and his job as deputy sheriff. Then again, his father only considered what was best for him—never mind the rest of the family. "Why retire?"

"What do you mean, why? That's what men do when they get old—they quit working."

Joshua Adams was fifty-eight years old and although ranching took a toll on a man's body, his father didn't look or act as if he was ready to spend the rest of his life twiddling his thumbs.

"Does this urge for less work and more free time have anything to do with Earl McKinley leasing his land and moving to Billings?" Joshua Adams had punched cows for Earl's father until Beau's mother had died, then Aunt Sarah had talked her brother into moving closer to family and working for her husband at Thunder Ranch.

"I don't care what Earl does," his father said.

"Ever since Jordan arrived in town you haven't cared about anything but spending time with her."

"You got a problem with that?"

Maybe. "Aunt Sarah isn't sure if she's going to keep Midnight. If she sells the stallion then we may have to invest more in our bucking bulls and Asteroid needs a lot of attention." Beau didn't have time to deal with the young bull, but his father did.

"Midnight and Asteroid will be fine. You worry too much."

And the old man didn't worry enough.

"Whatever you decide about retirement, I hope you put it off another year."

"Why's that?"

"I'm making a run at an NFR title next year. I'll be on the road a lot."

"You think you can win that many rodeos?"

"I don't think—I know I can."

A horn blast sent Beau to the back door. "It's Colt." His cousin's truck and horse trailer barreled up the drive. "Aunt Sarah's with him." Beau snatched his jacket from the hook and his father followed him outside.

"It's Midnight," Colt said as he rounded the hood of his Dodge.

The newest addition to the bucking-stock operation, The Midnight Express, was wreaking havoc at Thunder Ranch.

"Something the matter with Midnight, Sarah?" Beau's father asked.

"He's run off again. Gracie thinks one of her boys accidentally left the latch on the stall door unhooked when they were helping her in the barn this morning." Gracie was Midnight's primary caretaker and no doubt in a state of panic over the valuable horse.

This past summer, Midnight had suffered a flesh wound from a run-in with barbed wire after he'd escaped his stall and had gone missing for over a month. Although the horse was fully healed, Ace had kept Midnight's physical activity to a minimum, which didn't include a ten-mile sprint across the ranch.

Beau's father put his arm around his sister's shoulder. "Don't get yourself worked up. The stress isn't good for your heart."

"What about the paddocks?" Beau asked. "Maybe Midnight jumped a fence to get to one of the mares."

"We checked. He's running free somewhere on the property," Colt said.

Beau shielded his eyes against the bright sunlight and searched the horizon.

"Help Colt look for Midnight, Beau. He can't have gone far." Joshua motioned toward the house. "There's hot coffee in the kitchen, Sarah. I'll be in after I check on the bulls."

Once his father was out of earshot, Beau asked, "Does Ace know Midnight's on the run?"

"Not yet. I was hoping to put the horse back in his stall before my brother got wind of it," Colt said.

"We'll find him."

"You head north on the four-wheeler and I'll meet you there with the trailer." Colt handed Beau a walkie-talkie then hopped into his truck and took off.

Before Beau forgot, he fished his wallet from his back pocket and removed the cashier's check for three thousand dollars. "I won yesterday." He held the draft out to his aunt.

She didn't take the money. "Congratulations."

"C'mon, Aunt Sarah." He waved the check. "It'll help pay for some of the expense that went into searching for Midnight over the summer."

The Midnight Express had cost Thunder Ranch a hefty $38,000, and when the stallion had gone AWOL the family had shelled out big bucks—money they could ill afford in this bad economy—to locate the horse. In the end, the dang stallion had been right under their noses at Buddy Wright's neighboring ranch.

Reluctantly his aunt accepted the check. "Thank you, Beau." She sighed. "I'm worried I made a mistake in believing Midnight could bring Thunder Ranch back from the brink."

"Midnight's not just any horse, Aunt Sarah. He'll come through for us." Midnight's pedigree had been traced back to the infamous bucking horse, Five Minutes to Midnight, who lay buried at the National Cowboy Hall of Fame. If given half a chance, Beau believed the stallion could win another NFR title.

Beau opened his mouth to tell his aunt he'd run into Tuf at the rodeo but changed his mind. She was already upset over Midnight; mentioning Tuf might cause her heart to act up. "Keep the coffee hot, Aunt Sarah." Beau kissed her cheek then jogged to the equipment shed where the ATVs were stored.

A minute later, he took off, the cold wind whipping his face as he wove through two miles of pine trees. When he cleared the forest, he spotted Midnight drinking at the stock pond. Beau stopped the four-wheeler and pulled out the walkie-talkie. "Midnight's at the pond."

"Be right there."

The ATV's rumbling engine caught Midnight's attention. The coal-black stallion pawed the ground. In that moment, Beau felt he and Midnight were kindred spirits—both needed to prove they were the best, yet neither had competed in enough rodeos this season to make it to Vegas and show the world they were number one.

Colt arrived, leaving the truck parked several yards away. He grabbed a rope and joined Beau. "Is he spooked?"

"Nope." Midnight was the cockiest horse Beau had ever been around.

"Since he came back from Buddy's he's been more difficult to handle," Colt said.

"I've got an opinion, if you care to hear it."

"Speak your mind."

"Midnight's jaunt across the ranch is his way of letting us know he's feeling penned in and he's ready for a challenge."

"By challenge, you mean rodeo."

"Midnight's a competitor. Bucking's in his blood. He's not happy unless he's throwing cowboys off his back."

"You might be right. He's probably feeling restless now that Fancy Gal's expecting and wants nothing to do with him."

No wonder the stallion was acting out of sorts—his companion mare was snubbing her nose at him. "Enter Midnight in the Badlands Bull Bash." The one-day event had a purse of fifty thousand dollars.

"Ace would have my head if I took that horse anywhere without telling him," Colt said. "A win, though, will increase Midnight's stud fees."

"Sure would."

"I'll talk to Ace." Colt pointed to the stallion. "You ready?"

"Nothing I like better than a good chase."

"Keep him penned in until I get close enough to throw a rope over his head."

Midnight allowed Colt to get within fifty feet of him, then when Colt raised his roping arm, the stallion took off. Beau followed on the ATV, cutting Midnight off at the pass. The horse spun, then galloped in the opposite direction. Beau turned Midnight back toward Colt. The game went on for several minutes. Finally, Midnight exhausted himself and Colt threw the rope over the horse's head.

"Nice work," Colt said after Beau shut off the four-wheeler.

"Midnight could have escaped if he'd wanted to."

"Yeah, I know." Colt tugged on the rope and led the stallion to the truck, Midnight snorting hot steam into the brisk air.

Beau followed the pair and opened the trailer doors, then lowered the ramp. Midnight tossed his head and reared. Colt gave him plenty of rope, then waved his hand in front of the stallion's nose. Midnight clomped up the ramp and into the trailer.

"Why are you the only one who can get that horse to load?"

Colt opened his fist to reveal a peppermint candy. "Don't tell Ace my secret." Midnight poked his head out the trailer window, and Colt gave the stallion his reward then latched the door. "Thanks for your help, Beau. I promised Leah we'd take the kids to an early-bird matinee. Now we won't be late."

Colt had seamlessly adjusted to married life and fatherhood, but Beau was curious. "When's the family going to meet your son?" His cousin had confessed to the family that he'd fathered a child twelve years ago but had only recently made contact with the boy. Colt was also stepdad to Leah's son and daughter.

"I'm not sure. I invited Evan to spend Thanksgiving at the ranch but I'm leaving it up to him to decide when he's ready to meet the family."

Speaking of family... "Hey, Colt."

"Yeah?"

"I ran into Tuf in Rock Springs."

"You didn't tell my mom, did you?"

"No. I thought you and Ace should be the ones to tell her if you think she should know. I was worried the news might upset her."

"Is he okay?"

"Hard to say. I asked when he was coming home, but he didn't know."

Colt stubbed the ground with the toe of his boot.

"I suggested he call your mom, but—" Beau shrugged.

"I'm not one to judge. I didn't always uphold my share of responsibility around the ranch through the years, but I kept in touch with my mother. The least Tuf can do is call home once in a while." Colt hopped into the front seat of the truck. "Thanks again for your help."

"Sure thing. Enjoy the movies."

After Colt departed, Beau stood in the cold, staring into the distance. Today was Sunday and he had a hankering for beef sirloin tip roast—Sunday special at the Number 1. He'd return to the house and help his father with ranch chores, then shower and head into town to do some more chasing…of the two-legged variety.

Chapter 3

Sierra climbed the steps of the hidden staircase inside the diner's pantry and entered her living room. There were only two ways into the upstairs apartment—the staircase and the fire escape behind the building.

"It's me, Aunt Jordan. I brought you a late lunch—baked potato soup and a roll." She set the food on the kitchen table.

Her aunt's seeing-eye dog, Molly, ventured from the guest bedroom first, followed by her owner. Sierra was amazed at how quickly Jordan had learned the layout of the apartment and could navigate the space without bumping into any furniture.

"Have you been a good girl, Molly?" Sierra scratched the yellow lab behind the ears. Jordan washed her hands at the sink then sat at the table and confidently familiarized herself with the items before her—take-out soup container, wheat roll inside a paper towel, butter dish, knife and spoon.

"This was nice of you, dear." Her aunt buttered the roll. "What time did you get in this morning? I didn't hear you."

"Early." Sierra disliked being evasive but she'd been on pins and needles, worried Beau would drop by the diner and demand an explanation for her bizarre behavior last night. She owed him the truth, but facing reality took more courage than she possessed at the moment.

Hoping to dissuade her aunt from prying into her whereabouts, Sierra asked, "What did you do last night?" Several of Jordan's friends from high school lived in the area and often invited her out to eat or shop.

"Joshua helped Irene close the diner, then we watched a movie up here."

"Watched…?" Her aunt possessed a wicked sense of humor regarding her blindness, but Sierra didn't see a darn thing funny about having to live in the dark.

"Joshua watched. I listened."

Since returning to Montana, Jordan had been spending a lot of time with her old boyfriend, which Sierra couldn't be more pleased about. She'd love for her aunt to sell her condo in Florida and relocate to Roundup.

"This tastes similar to your mother's recipe, but there's something different…"

"Rosemary. I used it a lot in cooking school." Sierra poured two glasses of iced tea and joined her aunt at the table.

"Your mother was so proud when you graduated from that famous Cordon Bleu program," Aunt Jordan said.

"Mom always envied your talent for dancing."

Jordan reached across the table and Sierra clasped her hand. "I wish your mother were still with us."

"Me, too." Sierra's parents had died in a plane crash five years ago. A former Air Force pilot and captain for United Airlines, her father had survived near misses and engine malfunctions, yet it had been a summer thunderstorm that had brought down her parents' twin-engine Cessna while flying to their cabin along Mus-selshell River.

"Do you have any regrets, moving from Chicago to Roundup?" Jordan asked.

"None." After her parents' funeral, Sierra had decided to use her inheritance to renovate the old news-paper building in town and turn it into a diner where she could put her catering recipes to good use.

"Your mother would have loved helping you run the diner."

Sierra was sad that she hadn't been able to share her business venture with her parents, but at least they'd been spared the agony of watching their only child face monumental, life-altering changes. Then again, Sierra would have appreciated their support when the going got tough...tougher...toughest. At least her aunt was by her side, and Sierra hoped she would remain so for a long time to come.

"Don't feel you have to keep me company," Jordan said. "I imagine it's busy downstairs."

"Irene has everything under control." Sierra's sec-ond in command ran the diner like a military mess hall. Even the two high school students Sierra employed toed the line when they worked with Irene. "Mind if I ask you a personal question, Aunt Jordan?"

"Not at all." Her aunt's smile erased ten years from her age.

"How serious were you and Joshua when you dated in high school?"

A wistful expression settled over her aunt's face. "We were very much in love."

"What happened?"

"I wanted to go to college and see the world, and Joshua was content to remain in Roundup."

"Mom said she never regretted leaving town, but I think that's because she and Dad spent their summers at the cabin. Do you wish you would have stayed closer to home?"

"No. I needed to spread my wings. I knew if I wanted a dancing career that I'd have to move to California."

"Then you met Uncle Bob in Sacramento."

"And Bob showed me the world through the military."

Did her aunt realized how fortunate she'd been to be able to *see* all her dreams come true before her eye disease had caused her to go blind?

You've seen your dreams come true.

She'd become a chef and had opened her own business, honoring her great-grandfather who'd died in a flood at the Number 1 Mine outside Roundup. But what about her wanting to marry and have children? The odds of that wish coming true were a long shot.

"What happened to your dance career after you married Uncle Bob?"

"I cut back on my performances, then eventually quit when we decided to have children. I knew I'd have to put on weight before I became pregnant." She paused. "In the end, my weight didn't matter. I couldn't get pregnant."

"I'm sorry, Aunt Jordan."

"I had just talked your uncle into agreeing to try in vitro fertilization when I noticed something wasn't right with my eyes."

"How old were you?" Sierra asked.

"Thirty-three." Jordan sighed. "After the doctor confirmed that I'd eventually go blind, Bob insisted we stop trying to have children." Her aunt waved a hand before her face. "Life goes on. Speaking of which, you need to make an appointment with an ophthalmologist."

"I've got time." Sierra wasn't ready for an official diagnosis.

"Sandra—" Aunt Jordan's high school friend "—was in the diner last week and said you walked right by her without saying hello."

Since Jordan helped in the diner once in a while, the place had become a coffee klatch for her gossipy friends. "I wasn't rude on purpose."

"I didn't think you were."

"I'm sure I was distracted." Sierra would rather believe that than admit she had trouble with her peripheral vision.

"You don't have to be afraid."

"I'm not afraid." Sierra was scared—bone-chillingly terrified of going blind. "Are you sure you won't miss spending the holidays with your friends in St. Petersburg?" Her aunt had rented her condo to a businessman until the end of the year.

"Is that a polite way of telling me I'm cramping your style?"

"Not at all." It was Sierra's way of conveying that she didn't want her aunt to leave Roundup. *Ever.* Jordan had leaned on her husband as her eyesight had worsened through the years, but Sierra had no one to guide her down the frightening road ahead. "It's just that Montana winters are long and cold."

"I remember them, dear. I'm looking forward to snow for the holidays."

"I'm sure it will be nice to spend Christmas with Joshua." If her aunt and former boyfriend really hit it off, Jordan would have another reason to remain in Roundup.

"Thank you for reminding me that I need to make a Christmas list. I have no idea what Joshua would like."

Sierra took her glass to the sink. "I'm sure he'll be pleased with whatever you choose for him." It was obvious that Joshua was crazy for Jordan—not a day went by that he didn't visit her or call.

"I think I'll read this afternoon," Jordan said.

As much as Sierra loved her aunt and needed her encouragement, there were times when she grew weary of being impressed by the woman. Jordan had taught herself to read braille before she'd completely lost her eyesight. "Would Molly like a walk before I leave?"

"I'm sure she would, but she'll have to wait until three."

"I forgot about her schedule." Molly was on a set timetable for eating, walks and bedtime. "Holler if you need anything, Aunt Jordan."

"I won't, dear."

That was the truth. No one had been more surprised than Sierra when her aunt and Molly had ridden a Greyhound bus clear across the country by themselves. From the very first day in town, her aunt had demonstrated her independence. It didn't take long to learn Jordan became perturbed when people did things for her without asking if she needed their help. Sierra was counting on her aunt to teach her how to be just as gutsy and courageous.

Sierra took the back stairs down to the diner. Sunday was her favorite day of the week. Roundup's spiritual citizens attended morning church services at the various places of worship, and afterward many of them stopped by the diner for lunch. Folks were usually in a congenial mood after listening to God's word, and her employees swore tips were better on Sundays than any other day of the week.

When Sierra entered the kitchen she found her waitresses sharing a piece of peach cobbler. "Taking a break?"

"Yeah. Mr. Humphrey finally left," Amy said. "The old fart drives me crazy." The teen snorted. "Who leaves a tip in nickels?"

That her waitress found Mr. Humphrey an odd duck amused Sierra. Amy possessed her share of interesting traits, such as short, dark hair with hot-pink bangs. Tattoos covered Amy's right arm from wrist to shoulder, and she wore numerous silver rings in her ears and fake diamond studs pierced her nose and eyebrows.

"Mr. Humphrey is one of my faithful customers. Please be nice to him," Sierra said.

"I always am," Amy grumbled.

Amy was a nice girl, but she ran with a rough crowd

and had gotten caught shoplifting twice this year. Dinah Hart-Wright, Roundup's sheriff, had asked Sierra if she'd give Amy a job to help keep her out of trouble. The teen's first few weeks at the diner had been a challenge, but Susie, an honor student at the high school and one year younger than Amy, had befriended the delinquent teen and shown her the ropes.

"When you girls finish your dessert, please clean off the mustard and ketchup bottles, then fill the salt and pepper shakers on the tables."

"Sure. But Sierra," Susie said. "I checked the storeroom this morning and we're out of salt."

"Okay, thanks for letting me know." Sierra had taken inventory a week ago and hadn't noticed they were low on salt. Had it been an oversight on her part or had she not *seen* that the salt canister had been missing from the shelf?

"Did you enjoy your visit with your friend?" Irene asked when Sierra joined her behind the lunch counter.

"What frien—" Sierra caught herself. "Um, yes. Thanks for closing up last night. I'm sorry it was such short notice."

Irene waved her off. "We all need a little downtime. Speaking of which, Karla agreed to work the rest of my shift this afternoon."

"Aren't you feeling well?" Because Irene's husband was a long-haul truck driver, she often worked more than an eight-hour day so she didn't have to sit at home alone. Maybe the long hours were catching up with the fifty-year-old.

"Ed called. His run to Boise got canceled. He's coming home tonight."

"That's great news. Be sure to fix a plate of food for each of you before clocking out."

"Thanks, Sierra. The less time I spend in the kitchen the more time Ed and I can spend in the bedroom." Irene winked. "I'll finish getting the potatoes ready and put the pans of sirloin into the oven before I leave." Irene returned to the kitchen, leaving Sierra alone in the diner.

The rumble of a truck engine caught her attention and she glanced out the front window. Beau's red Dodge pulled into a parking spot across the street in front of Wright's Western Wear and Tack. He got out of the truck and glanced over his shoulder. Sierra ducked behind the counter, hoping he hadn't caught her spying. After counting to five, she stood. Beau strolled along the sidewalk, his cocky swagger tugging a quiet sigh from her. She loved the way he filled out his Wranglers.

Go talk to him.

She owed Beau an apology and a plausible explanation for why she'd spent the night in her car—as soon as she got up the courage.

"HEY, AUSTIN," BEAU called out a greeting when he entered Wright's. He'd driven into town to speak with Sierra but at the last minute had decided to check on his saddles.

"Heard you took first place in the bull-riding competition yesterday." Boot heels clunked against the wood floor as Austin wove through the racks of clothing.

Beau shook hands with his cousin's husband. "Word gets around quick in this town." How long would it take for people to gossip about him and Sierra if he persuaded her to go on a date with him?

"Colt phoned Dinah a while ago. Good thing you two caught Midnight before he escaped the boundaries of the ranch." Austin shook his head. "My wife doesn't need the aggravation of working a second missing-horse case on that stallion."

"Is Dinah's pregnancy making her moody?"

"No comment." Austin grinned. "Hey, before I forget." He reached into his shirt pocket and removed a business card. "This guy's interested in having you make him a saddle."

"He didn't like either of those?" Beau glanced at the saddles in the front window.

"He wants a cutting saddle with a shallower seat and a higher horn." Austin motioned to the business card in Beau's hand. "Jim Phillips is the new foreman at the Casey Beef Ranch south of Billings."

"Did you give Phillips one of my cards?" Beau asked.

"Sure did. He said he'd call in a few days."

Beau shoved Phillips's contact information into the back pocket of his jeans. "How's married life?" Heavy footfalls sounded overhead and both men looked up at the decorative tin ceiling.

"Married life is good. Real good."

The bell on the door clanged and Ace Hart entered the store, wearing a scowl. Beau attempted to humor his cousin. "For a man who's about to become a father, you don't look too happy." When the teasing remark failed to lighten Ace's somber expression, Beau said, "Flynn's feeling okay, isn't she?"

"Aside from swollen ankles she's fine, thanks for asking."

"What's the matter? You look pissed," Austin said.

Ace stared pointedly at Beau. "Colt said you suggested Midnight compete in South Dakota next month."

"A win there would increase his breeding value," Beau said.

"I know better than anyone when Midnight's fit to compete again." Ace rubbed his brow.

Beau sympathized with the tough position his older cousin was in. Ace was under a lot of pressure to insure the family's investment paid off. If the stallion got injured, had to be put down, or for some reason could not be bred, Ace could lose his livelihood. With a baby on the way, his cousin had to protect his interests.

"Are you saying Midnight can't compete next month?" Beau asked.

"I haven't made up my mind," Ace said. "By the way, congrats on your win."

Austin slapped Beau on the back. "You sure are lighting up the circuit since Duke quit."

"Mind if I have a minute alone with Beau?" Ace asked.

"No problem. I'll be in the storeroom."

After Austin walked out of earshot, Ace spoke. "Colt mentioned you ran into Tuf in Wyoming." The lines bracketing Ace's mouth deepened. "Did he seem okay?"

"He said he's working through some stuff."

"Tuf needs to come home."

For as long as Beau remembered, Ace had been the strong, confident one in the family. At times his cousin could be too rigid, too controlling, but there was no hiding the concern in the man's eyes for his little brother. Ace cared deeply about his family and wanted Tuf home where he could be looked after.

The bell on the door clanged a second time. *Sierra.*

"Let me know if you run into Tuf again."

"I will."

Ace left, tipping his hat to Sierra on the way out.

Once the door shut behind Beau's cousin, Sierra's smile wilted.

"I was planning to stop by the diner after I talked with Austin," Beau said, closing the gap between them.

"I'm sorry, I didn't mean to interrupt." She grappled for the door handle.

"Wait." Beau pried Sierra's fingers from the knob but didn't release her hand. "I finished my business with Austin. Walk with me?"

"Sure."

He ushered Sierra outside then led her around the corner. Single-story homes lined the street and a small park sat in the middle of the block. "If you're cold we can talk in the diner," he said. The afternoon temperature was in the low forties, but there wasn't a cloud in the sky.

"I'm fine. The sun feels good on my face."

They strolled in silence, Beau holding Sierra's hand. That she didn't pull away stroked his ego. When they reached the park, he guided her to the lone bench near the swing set. "You don't have to worry," he said. "I won't pressure you for an explanation about last night."

"That's generous, but..." She twirled a button on her coat then noticed her action and shoved her hand into a pocket. "How do you feel about your dad and my aunt dating?" she asked.

Amused by the delay tactic, he chuckled. Heck, no one was more surprised than Beau that his father was goo-goo eyes over Jordan Peterson.

"I'm serious, Beau. Are you okay with their relationship? Because I believe my aunt really cares for your father."

He'd be a lot happier about the matchup if Jordan didn't distract his father from his ranch chores, but Beau didn't want to discuss the older couple. "They're both adults. They don't need anyone's permission to date." He opened his mouth to change the subject when a shout down the block drew his attention.

"Z-Zorro!" Duke's stepson, Luke, chased Duke's German shepherd. The dog sprinted, the leash flying in the air behind him. The seven-year-old was no match for Zorro and Beau made a dash for the sidewalk.

"Zorro, heel!" Beau extended his arm and the dog skidded to a stop, his legs becoming entangled with his leash. Luke caught up, his little chest heaving.

"Th-thanks, Uncle Beau." Luke took the leash. "B-bad dog, Zorro."

"Where's your mom?" Normally Angie didn't let her son out of her sight.

"T-talking with Dad in the jail. I was t-taking Zorro for a w-walk but—" Luke sucked in several breaths.

Pitying the kid's miniature lungs Beau said, "Come with me. There's someone who'd like to meet Zorro." Beau steered Luke and the dog toward the park bench.

"Hi, Luke," Sierra said. "I guess Zorro wanted a run, not a walk."

Luke smiled. "He went after M-Molly."

Sierra spoke to Beau. "My aunt takes her seeing-eye dog for a stroll around town in the afternoons." She switched her attention to Luke. "Is Molly still with my aunt?"

"Yeah. M-Molly never runs off."

Sierra rubbed Zorro's head. "Poor boy…chasing after a lady who doesn't want you."

Beau cringed. He hoped Sierra's comment hadn't been meant for him.

"Luke! Luke, where are you?"

"Here!" Beau waved at his brother and Duke jogged toward the group.

"What happened?" Duke asked.

"Z-Zorro s-saw—"

"Slow down." Duke laid a hand on the boy's shoulder.

"Zorro saw Molly and ran away." Duke had a calming effect on his stepson and Luke stopped stuttering.

"Good thing Uncle Beau was here." Duke glanced at Sierra and switched the subject. "Did you have car trouble yesterday?"

Face flushing Sierra mumbled, "Ahh…"

"Clive Benson thought he saw your car parked on the shoulder of the road outside town around eleven."

"No," Sierra answered, casting a quick glance at Beau.

He wasn't spilling the beans about last night.

"Clive must have been seeing things, or had one too many beers at the Open Range Saloon," Duke said.

The dog tugged on his leash. "Zorro wants to walk, Dad."

Beau had yet to wrap his mind around his twin becoming a father and got a kick out of watching the father-son duo.

"See you later." Duke walked off holding Luke's hand and the dog leash.

"About last night—"

"Forget last night." Suddenly Beau didn't want to know the truth. "Will you have dinner with me tonight?"

"I have to close the diner."

"We can eat a late meal. I'll take you to Maria's Mexican Café."

Sierra wrinkled her nose. "Maria's isn't even authentic Mexican food." She stood and Beau scrambled to his feet. "Come to the diner around eight-thirty. The least I can do is feed you a meal for the trouble I caused."

"It's not much of a date if only one person eats."

"I'll have dinner, too."

"Okay, then, I'll be there at eight-thirty."

"If you run late—"

"I won't."

Sierra spun and walked briskly down the block. When she reached the corner she looked both ways then stepped onto the street. Car brakes squealed and for a split second Beau's heart jumped into his throat. The driver lowered his window and shouted at Sierra before driving off, then she hurried across the street and disappeared into the diner.

Beau's heart slid back into his chest. Dang, that woman had better pay attention to where she was going or she'd find herself in a world of hurt.

Maybe you distract Sierra.

Wouldn't that be something.

Chapter 4

"There's someone at the door, dear." Jordan's voice carried through the apartment.

Sierra glanced at her watch. Eight o'clock—Beau was on time. "I'll be right out." She'd snuck up to the apartment to change clothes for her date and had been studying her reflection in the bedroom mirror for the past five minutes. The black, short-sleeved knee-length dress flattered her full figure. The tight-fitting bosom showed off her feminine curves while the pleated skirt hid the extra few pounds she needed to lose.

Guilt pricked her for wearing a cocktail dress. She hoped to impress Beau but didn't want him believing she was interested in dating, because anything long term with the handsome cowboy was out of the question. Keeping that in mind, Sierra intended to savor every moment of the evening.

After spritzing on perfume, she left the bedroom and waltzed past her aunt, who sat on the couch reading. Molly rested dutifully at her feet. When Sierra opened the door off the kitchen...*wow*.

Beau stood on the fire escape, holding a bouquet of daisies. He wore slacks and casual shoes—she couldn't remember ever seeing him in anything but jeans and boots. Her gaze inched higher, taking in his button-down shirt and brown bomber jacket. Even in dress clothes, Beau's chiseled looks screamed *cowboy*.

He held out the flowers. "The color reminds me of your eyes."

The reference to her eyes triggered a mini heart-ache, but she ignored the pain and accepted the bouquet. "They're lovely." She waved Beau into the apartment, then searched through the cupboards for a vase.

"Who's here, dear?"

"Sorry, Aunt Jordan. It's Beau."

"Hello, Mrs. Peterson."

While Sierra arranged the flowers in a vase, Beau crossed the room and patted Molly on the head. "Heard my dad gave you a tour of the ranch a few days ago."

"Driving around with Joshua brought back fond memories. Seems like only yesterday that your father and I snuck off to the fishing hole on the McKinley property."

"I guess you've heard Earl McKinley leased his land to the Missoula Cattle Company."

"Joshua mentioned that was the same corporation leasing acreage from Thunder Ranch."

Her aunt's knowledge of the Adams and Hart family business pleased Sierra. She doubted that Joshua would have shared the information if he hadn't felt he could trust Jordan. For her aunt's sake and Sierra's, too, she hoped Joshua's intentions were honorable. She worried that he might be caught up in reliving the past, then once the excitement wore off and he realized his former high school sweetheart was still blind, he'd end the relationship, leaving Jordan with a broken heart and a desire to return to Florida.

"I was wondering, Mrs. Peterson—"

"Call me Jordan, Beau."

"Jordan. How far back do you and my dad go?"

"Your father pulled my pigtails in fifth grade, and from then on I was smitten."

"So you two have known each other most of your lives," Beau said.

"We went steady all through high school."

"Why'd you break up?" Beau asked.

"I went off to college."

Beau's questions sounded more like an interrogation than benign chitchat and Sierra wondered if he had reservations about his father dating her aunt. Feeling the need to intervene, she said, "Aunt Jordan, Beau and I are having dinner downstairs."

"That's fine, dear, but I need to talk to you before you turn in for the night."

"What about?"

"Scheduling an appointment with the ophthalmologist."

Since her aunt's arrival in town, not a day had passed that she hadn't hounded Sierra about seeing an eye doctor. After a few weeks the nagging had gone in one ear and out the other. Sierra would make an appointment when she was good and ready and not a minute sooner.

In any event, she had no intention of discussing the private matter in front of Beau. "I'll handle it, Aunt Jordan." She walked through the living room and stopped in front of a door that looked suspiciously like a closet. "We'll use the back staircase."

"Didn't know this building had a secret passageway," Beau said.

Sierra opened the door and switched on the sconces in the stairwell. Beau followed her, closing the door behind him. Before she'd descended two steps, he clutched her arm.

"You look...hot." His gaze traveled the length of her body.

The compliment sent a rush of pleasure through her. "Thank you."

"You know what that dress says, don't you?"

Sierra couldn't think straight—not with the heady scent of Beau's cologne swirling around her head. "Wh...what does it say?"

"Kiss me," he whispered.

They hadn't sat down to eat and already Beau was making a move on her.

Go ahead. Sierra had fantasized about kissing Beau for months. Did it matter if he kissed her at the beginning of the date instead of at the end? Sierra made a feeble attempt to take the high road. "My aunt's sitting a few feet behind the door."

Beau's gaze zeroed in on Sierra's mouth. "I'm a quiet kisser."

Short of breath, she whispered, "Prove it."

His lips covered hers, then his hand settled on her hip, pulling her closer until her breasts bumped his leather jacket. Lord, the man could kiss. She followed Beau's lead, relaxing in his arms, opening her mouth to his tongue. The kiss grew more urgent, his callused hand caressing her neck...his fingers sifting through her hair.

Sierra couldn't recall the last time she'd been so thoroughly kissed and she gave herself over to the magic of the moment, memorizing Beau's scent...his taste...the scratchy feel of his beard stubble...the intimate rumble reverberating through his chest.

The kiss ended abruptly, Beau resting his forehead against hers. "You have no idea how long I've wanted to do that."

Me, too. "I think we should get off the stairs before one of us tumbles to the bottom."

"Sorry." Beau nuzzled her cheek then smoothed a hand over her hair. "I didn't mean to come on so strong."

Blushing, she descended the steps, which opened into the large pantry connected to the kitchen. When she entered the dark room Beau stopped her.

"Hold up."

With only the swath of light streaking across the floor from the passageway, Sierra was unable to see much except the shadowy outline of Beau's jaw. She waited for him to speak.

"I can't help myself." He clasped her face and his mouth inched forward.

Sierra raised her arms, intending to wrap them around his neck when the door on the other side of the pantry opened.

"Oops, sorry. Didn't mean to interrupt." Karla Dickson, the waitress who'd taken over for Irene this evening, smiled sheepishly.

"Hi, Karla." As if Beau hadn't been caught red-handed with his fingers in the cookie jar, he released Sierra and stepped into the kitchen.

Karla turned away, leaving Sierra all but forgotten in the pantry. "Duke stopped in a few minutes ago looking for you."

"I'll call him later. How about those Panthers? Your husband's team has a chance of winning the conference title this year."

"Please, no football talk." Karla groaned. "I hear enough about it at home."

Sierra shut the pantry door and faced her employee. "Any problems after I left?"

"Not a one. The tables are cleaned off and supplies restocked. If you want, I'll run the dishwasher and prepare the coffee machines for tomorrow."

"No, thanks. I'll take care of that after Beau and I have dinner. Thanks for finishing Irene's shift today." Sierra walked Karla out of the kitchen to the front door. By tomorrow morning, the Roundup grapevine would be buzzing with rumors of Beau and Sierra kissing in the pantry.

"I'll see you on Tuesday for my regular shift," Karla said.

"'Night." Sierra locked up, then switched off the neon sign outside and returned to the kitchen where she found Beau at the stove with his finger in the gravy pot. "I'm the chef and I don't stick my fingers in the food."

"Your sirloin is one of my favorites."

She fetched two plates and dished out one small serving and one cowboy-sized serving of food. "There's wine in the pantry." The diner didn't have a liquor license, because Sierra didn't want her patrons driving home inebriated, especially when many of them lived outside the town limits. However, she kept the pantry stocked with several bottles of wine for her recipes.

Beau returned with a merlot from Napa Valley—interesting that he'd selected her favorite. She covered the bistro table in the corner with a red-and-white-checked cloth, then added two wineglasses and silverware.

A second later a pop echoed through the kitchen when Beau opened the wine bottle. He filled the glasses, then held out Sierra's chair after she brought their plates to the table. "Shall we dim the lights?" he asked.

As much as she yearned for a romantic atmosphere, Sierra worried she'd make a fool of herself if she could see only a few inches in front of her nose. "I'd prefer to keep the lights on. I like to see what I'm eating."

"Must be a chef thing." Beau sat down and raised his wineglass. "A toast."

"To what?"

"To beautiful women who can cook." He touched the rim of her glass with his own.

Sierra enjoyed watching Beau wolf down his food. He mumbled praise between bites while she contemplated how best to explain her odd behavior yesterday. As much as she wished for her life to go on as if everything were normal, she could no longer pretend her vision problems would disappear.

"What's the matter?" Beau clasped her hand, preventing the fork from swirling her mashed potatoes.

"I'm a little distracted."

"Ouch."

Sierra hadn't meant to offend him, but before she

expressed her regret, he released her hand and patted his stomach. "That was the best meal I've eaten—" he grinned "—since my last visit to the diner."

"You haven't been in the past few days." Who cared if he guessed she'd kept track of his visits?

"It's not because I haven't wanted to. I added extra rodeos to my schedule."

"How long do you plan to compete?"

He pointed his fork at her. "I know what you're thinking—I can't rodeo forever. I guess thirty-two is old for a bull rider."

"You're in great shape for thirty-two." Her eyes twinkled.

Glad Sierra approved of him, Beau said, "I'd like to make it to the NFR before I hang up my rope."

"Will you get there this year?"

He shook his head. "Don't have enough points." If Duke had quit rodeo in the spring instead of in July, Beau might have been able to win enough rodeos to make the cut.

Sierra wiggled in her chair. She hadn't stopped fidgeting since they'd sat down to eat. Was she upset about the kiss? *No.* She'd participated fully and would have allowed him to kiss her again if Karla hadn't interrupted them.

"I—"

"Before you say anything," Beau said. "Are you involved with another man?"

Her eyes widened. "I wouldn't have kissed you if I was."

"Last night... I thought...well, it crossed my mind

that maybe you were waiting in your car to meet with a lover."

"Why would I wait alone on a deserted road after dark?"

"Roundup's a small town. People gossip. If you wanted to keep a relationship private…" The more Beau talked, the dumber he sounded.

"Sorry to disappoint you, but the reason I was stranded had nothing to do with a lover's rendezvous."

Feeling foolish for jumping to conclusions, he chugged the remainder of his wine.

After a stilted silence Sierra set her fork aside. "Have you paid any attention to the rumors about me?"

"I didn't know you were a hot topic of conversation." He grinned. "Not that a beautiful woman like you shouldn't be talked about." His comment failed to make her smile. "I've been too busy with rodeo to listen to gossip."

Twice Sierra opened her mouth to speak but stopped.

"Whatever it is, it can't be that bad."

"I'm sorry. It's difficult to talk about."

He held her hand, encouraged when she didn't pull away.

"The reason Aunt Jordan showed up unexpectedly this summer and moved in with me is because several of her old friends told her that I've been acting…weird."

"Weird?"

"I'm having trouble with my eyesight."

"You need glasses but you don't want to wear them," Beau said.

"I already wear contacts."

"Oh." Did she mean her vision problems were more serious than needing a new prescription?

"I don't see well in the dark."

Ahh...now he understood her wanting to leave the kitchen lights on.

"And my peripheral vision isn't so good, either."

Beau recalled eating at the diner and attempting to flirt with Sierra a couple of months ago, but she'd marched past his booth as if she hadn't seen him—evidently she hadn't.

"Is that why you spent the night in your car, because you couldn't see well enough to drive home in the dark?"

"Yes."

Beau was baffled that she hadn't been truthful with him. "I offered to give you a lift into town."

"In retrospect I should have accepted your help, but I didn't want to trouble you."

"It's not like the diner was out of my way." There was more to this than Sierra not wanting to inconvenience him, but Beau didn't want to ruin the mood by pushing the subject.

"I'm sorry I lied last night. You've probably figured out I'm a little stubborn."

"A little?"

Sierra lowered her gaze to her lap. "It was nice of you to return and wait with me until morning."

"Would have been more fun if you'd joined me in my truck."

A blush spread across her cheeks. "I'd appreciate it if you didn't tell anyone about this."

He wondered why she was so bashful about her eyesight failing. "We're a close-knit community. Some of your customers would be upset if they knew you needed help but didn't ask for it."

"Please, Beau." She shook her head. "I don't like sharing my private business."

"I understand...you being a flatlander and all."

"Hey, I spent summers in Roundup when I was a kid. That makes me a semi-native."

"I'll give you that." Discussing her eyesight obviously made Sierra nervous, so Beau changed the subject. "Are we having dessert?"

"Of course." She opened the commercial refrigerator. "Peach cobbler or German chocolate cake?"

"I'll have the cobbler," he said. Sierra dished out a heaping serving for Beau and a stingy one for herself.

"Don't tell me you're one of those women who's on a diet all of the time." He liked—*really* liked—Sierra's curves.

"I have a habit of sampling the food when I cook, which makes maintaining my target weight virtually impossible."

"You look great."

Sierra laughed.

"I'm serious. You're perfect."

"You always acted a little shy when you came into the diner." She smiled. "I didn't expect you to be so forthright." Her gaze clashed with Beau's and he felt a connection to Sierra that went deeper than physical attraction. He hoped she felt it, too, because he definitely wanted to get to know her better. On the other hand, she appeared eager to end the evening when she checked her watch for the fifth time.

"I'll help you clean up." Beau didn't want to leave, but he also didn't want to overstay his welcome.

"Guests don't wash dishes."

"Sierra?"

"Yes."

"Go out with me again."

"I can't."

There hadn't been a moment's hesitation in her answer and Beau's gut twisted. "Is it because of the kiss?" His plan to move slowly with Sierra had been blown to smithereens on the back staircase. "Did I come on too strong?"

"No, I enjoyed your kiss."

The knot in his stomach loosened but not much.

Sierra collected the dirty dishes and placed them in the sink. "My life is hectic, Beau. Running the diner seven days a week takes a lot of time and then with my aunt visiting…"

Her voice trailed off and Beau had a hunch she was trying to persuade herself that she wasn't interested in dating. "We don't have to rush things." When she remained quiet, he said, "You're a beautiful woman, Sierra, and I've been trying to catch your attention for months." He tipped her chin, forcing her to make eye contact. "The money I've spent on meals at the diner could have paid for an Alaskan cruise."

Instead of making her smile, his comment drew a deep sigh from her. "You should have picked the cruise, Beau."

He tucked a strand of red hair behind her ear. "Why?"

"I'm not looking to get involved with anyone."

When she didn't elaborate, he backed off, but not all the way. "You're busy, but so am I. If I'm not riding in rodeos, I'm helping with the cattle and bulls at Thunder

Ranch." He paused, waiting for her to look at him. "I'd like to spend time with you whenever we're both free."

"You mean we'd see each other as friends?"

Friendship was a good place to start. "Yeah. Friends."

"Okay. I'd like to be friends with you, Beau."

Feeling the need to leave before he said or did something to make her change her mind—like kiss her—he grabbed his jacket from the chair.

Sierra followed him out of the kitchen. He stopped at the lunch counter and pulled two napkins from the holder. "Got a pen?"

"Sure." She handed him the pen from next to the cash register.

He wrote his cell number on one napkin. "What's your number?" She recited it. Beau wanted a good-night kiss so bad his mouth watered. "Sierra?"

"Yes."

Before he lost his senses, he asked, "You ever been to a rodeo?"

"When I was a little girl my parents took me to one."

"Would you like to see me ride?"

"I'd love to go to a rodeo with you. When?"

"I'll check my schedule and call you."

She brushed at an imaginary speck on her dress. "Okay."

Leave. Before she changes her mind. Beau stepped outside into the chilly night air. "I had a really nice time."

"Me, too. And Beau…"

"Yeah?"

"Can we keep last night just between us?"

Beau dropped his voice to a whisper. "We can keep anything you like between us."

Chapter 5

"Hey, Beau!"

Beau stopped next to his truck parked outside the Number 1 and glanced up. Duke waited for a car to pass, then jogged across the street.

"How's—"

"I wanted—"

"Go ahead," Beau said.

"Thanks again for catching Zorro this afternoon."

"Happy to help." The awkward silence that followed the exchange bothered Beau. Things just weren't the same between them since Duke had quit rodeo and married.

"I stopped in the diner earlier."

"Karla said you wanted to talk to me. I was upstairs with Sierra."

The comment tugged a smile from his brother. "Did you finally convince Sierra to go with you?"

"We had dinner together."

"Congratulations."

Beau wasn't sure congratulations were in order after Sierra had proposed a friends-only relationship.

"Heard you won in Rock Springs," Duke said.

"McLean misses you."

"McLean's an ass. I'm glad you beat him." Duke scuffed the toe of his boot against the sidewalk.

"I entered the Badlands Bull Bash next month."

"I heard. Dad got a call from Nelson Tyler Rodeos this afternoon."

Nelson Tyler Rodeos had a reputation of running top-notch events. "What did they want?"

"One of their stock contractors had to withdraw his bulls because of a fever in the herd. They asked Dad to bring Bushwhacker and Back Bender to the Bash."

Their father and aunt must be ecstatic over the news. "If Bushwhacker has a good showing he might get an invite to the NFR." Beau wished he and not a bull would represent Thunder Ranch in Vegas at the end of the year, but Bushwhacker's value would greatly increase with NFR experience and that meant more money for the ranch. "I guess I'll be helping Dad haul the bulls to South Dakota unless you plan to ride along." Beau had been doing most of the livestock hauling since Duke had gotten married and his father had begun chasing after Jordan Peterson.

"I'll check my work schedule, then I'll see if Angie has any plans that weekend."

"Since your wife thinks so highly of rodeo, I'm sure she'll find something to keep you at home."

Duke curled his fingers into fists. "Watch what you say about Angie."

Ah, hell. What was the matter with him—provoking his brother? Beau's emotions were tied in knots over Sierra's insistence that they remain friends and he was taking his frustration out on his brother. "Sorry. I was out of line."

Duke, always quick to forgive, didn't make an issue of Beau's wisecrack. "Dad said you're serious about making a run for the NFR next year."

"I am."

"If you don't let anything get in your way—" Beau assumed *anything* meant Sierra "—then you've got a good chance of going to Vegas." His brother spoke from experience; when Angie came along, Duke had lost his interest in rodeo.

"I'd be away from the ranch more often," Beau warned.

"I'll do what I can to help Dad with the cattle and bulls."

Duke had extended an olive branch—why was it so dang hard to accept it? "I won't be making a run for anything if Dad decides to retire."

"Did he bring up the subject with you?"

"I mentioned it."

"What'd he say?"

"He said he'd be happy sitting on his keister all day."

"It's her fault." Duke pointed to the apartment window above the diner.

"What's Sierra got to do with Dad retiring?"

"Not Sierra, her aunt. Jordan's got Dad acting like a lovesick fool."

"I guess you'd know all about that lovesickness stuff." Beau flashed a crooked grin. Heck, if he played his cards right, he might have a chance to make a fool out of himself over Sierra.

"This isn't funny, Beau."

"Funny or not, I know why Dad's smitten."

"Why?"

"Jordan and Dad were high school sweethearts."

"How long has it been since Jordan lost her husband?" Duke asked.

"Not sure. A few years, I'd guess."

"Then why did she wait this long before returning to Roundup?"

"Jordan didn't come back to see Dad. She's here to spend time with Sierra." Beau rubbed his cold hands together.

"I couldn't care less who Dad dates, but he called me this afternoon while I was on duty and wanted me to contact Ace and ask him to check on one of the bulls."

"He could have called Ace himself," Beau said.

"Of course he could have, but he said he needed a haircut before he stopped in to visit Jordan and he didn't want to get stuck on the phone chatting with Ace about ranch problems." Duke shoved a hand through his hair. "I'm getting tired of Dad expecting us to pick up the slack every time he runs off to be with his lady love."

"Yeah, well, be prepared for Dad handing off more responsibility the deeper he becomes involved with Jordan."

"We already do our fair share—more so you than me—but I've got a family to look after now," Duke said.

"Maybe we're worrying for nothing. One of these days, Dad's true colors will shine through and Jordan will see he doesn't know the meaning of the word *compassion*."

"Since you're chasing after Sierra, keep your eyes and ears open around Jordan."

"For what?"

"If you hear about either of them talking marriage, let me know. I need to prepare myself and Angie for the possibility of having to spend every day off at the ranch."

"If it comes to that, we'll ask Aunt Sarah to hire another ranch hand," Beau said. "She can pay the cowboy out of Dad's retirement."

Duke chuckled then his face sobered. "You'd better watch yourself with Sierra."

Beau's hackles rose. "Why's that?"

"If you hurt Sierra, you'll not only have to answer to her aunt but Dad, too."

"No one's going to hurt anyone." Not if Beau had his way.

Duke's cell phone beeped and he checked the text message. "Duty calls. Talk to you later." He headed across the street to the jailhouse.

Beau hopped into his truck and started the engine. While he waited for the heater to warm the cab he identified the nagging twinge that always gripped his stomach when he talked with Duke. *Jealousy*. His brother appeared happier than ever in his roles as deputy sheriff, husband and father. Beau closed his eyes and envisioned him and Sierra married with kids of their own.

Be careful what you wish for...

It would be so easy to lose himself in Sierra, then end up like his brother—allowing a woman to stand in the way of winning an NFR title. Beau refused to let that happen. He was determined to focus on finishing out the year on a high note both in rodeo and his personal life. He'd win at the Bash and he'd win Sierra.

Laughter filled the diner and Sierra cringed at the happy sound. It was Wednesday afternoon and expectant mothers Dinah Wright and Flynn Hart had come in to appease their cravings for sweets. A few minutes later Leah Hart, Angie Adams and Cheyenne Sundell with her twin daughters had arrived and joined the group.

Steeling herself, Sierra carried a tray of water glasses to their table. "You all appear to be in good spirits," she said.

Flynn rubbed her large belly. "I'm hoping your carrot cake will take my mind off how fat I'm feeling."

"You don't know what fat is until you've carried twins," Cheyenne said as she brushed a strand of hair from her daughter Sadie's face. The little girl jerked her head away, but her sister Sammie refused to sit anywhere but in Cheyenne's lap.

"Carrying a baby is the easy part," Leah said. "Giving birth...now that's when things get tricky."

"After helping mares birth their foals, I think we have it easier in the delivery room," Angie said.

Dinah grimaced. "Please, no childbirth stories. I just

want to eat my dessert so I'll be in a better mood. Austin says I'm grumpy all the time."

Sierra steadfastly ignored the ache in her heart as she waited for the chitchat to die down. "Okay, Flynn's having a slice of carrot cake, what would everyone else like?"

"I'll take the apple pie," Dinah said.

"Make that two slices of apple pie," Leah added.

"I'll have a blueberry muffin." Cheyenne glanced at her daughters. "The girls will share a piece of chocolate cake."

"Oh, what the heck. I'll have the carrot cake," Angie said.

"Coming right up." Sierra smiled then hurried away. After passing along the dessert orders to Karla, Sierra stepped into the kitchen to check on the beef Stroganoff. "Irene, when you finish unloading the dishwasher, would you please set the water to boil for the noodles?"

"Sure."

"I'm going to check on my aunt." Instead of taking the back stairs, Sierra left through the delivery door, which opened to the parking lot behind the diner. A cold gust of wind slapped her in the face. Yesterday, the temperature had hit fifty degrees—darn near springlike. This morning she'd woken to plenty of sunshine but she doubted the temperature had made it out of the low forties yet.

She lifted her face to the sun and breathed in deeply, hoping the crisp air would freeze out the anxiety she'd felt the past few days. Three days had passed—almost passed—and Beau had yet to contact her about going to a rodeo with him. She'd give anything to watch him ride, but she didn't dare drive too far—Saturday night's fiasco had proven the boundaries of her world were shrinking with each passing day.

Maybe Beau changed his mind about being your friend.

Sierra should have told Beau the whole truth about her eyesight and not just that she had trouble seeing at night. Pride and vanity had coaxed her to fudge about the seriousness of the disease. She'd wanted Beau to view her as a healthy, young woman—not a woman doomed to a life of darkness.

"Where's your jacket?" Beau came around the corner of the building. His grin rivaled the sun, chasing away Sierra's melancholy. "Irene said you'd gone upstairs to check on your aunt."

"I was on my way," Sierra said.

"I dropped by to ask you to a rodeo this Saturday."

He hadn't forgotten. "Where?"

"Billings."

"I'll check with Irene to see if she's willing to handle the diner."

"I don't compete until the afternoon, and there's no snow in the forecast this weekend so we could leave as late as ten o'clock in the morning."

"Wait right here." Sierra ducked her head inside the door and asked Irene if she'd work from ten to close on Saturday. Irene was more than happy to work the entire day.

Sierra shut the door and faced Beau. "I'd love to go."

"Good. It'll be nice to have company on the drive." He touched a finger to the brim of his hat and walked off.

Where was the amorous cowboy who'd kissed her a few nights ago?

Friends, remember? Sierra had set the terms of their relationship, but a part of her yearned to throw caution to the wind just to see what might happen between her and Beau. Ah, well, a girl could dream.

"Sierra?" Jordan stood on the fire escape above Sierra's head.

"I was coming up to check on you." She climbed the steps to the apartment.

"I don't need checking on, dear. Was that Beau's voice I heard a moment ago?"

Aunt Jordan had bat ears. "Beau asked me to go with him to a rodeo on Saturday. I hope you don't mind, but I said yes." Sierra opened the apartment door and ushered her aunt inside.

"What about your eye-doctor appointment?" Jordan pulled out a kitchen chair and sat.

"What appointment?" Sierra hadn't called the eye doctor.

"I took the liberty of scheduling you an appointment in Billings with Dr. Ryder. I thought we'd stop for lunch on the way home."

Sierra counted to five as she fought her rising anger. "Aunt Jordan, I'm capable of making my own appointments."

"Are you?"

"What's that supposed to mean?"

"You keep telling me you'll see a doctor but—"

"When I'm good and ready."

"Time isn't on your side."

"What difference does it make if I learn this Saturday or three months from now that I'm going to be blind one day?" The last thing Sierra wanted to focus on was her failing eyesight.

"What about Beau?"

The quiet question bounced off the kitchen walls, smacking Sierra on all sides. "Beau is a friend."

"A friend for now, but maybe that will change."

"My love life isn't any of your business, Aunt Jordan."

"Beau should know—"

"Beau doesn't need to know anything."

"Even if he remains just a friend, dear, he deserves to be told the truth."

A dull throb pulsed behind Sierra's eyes and she rubbed her brow. How could she make her aunt understand that she yearned for a little time to enjoy being with Beau without her vision problems standing between them? Once the doctor gave her the official diagnosis, reality would come crashing down around her and Beau would move on to another woman—one who wasn't going blind.

"Do you want me to cancel the—"

"I'll take care of it." Sierra would attend the rodeo with Beau and enjoy every second of his company. If he asked her out again, she'd make up an excuse and keeping making excuses until he got the message that friends were all they'd ever be. Needing to escape, Sierra made a dash for the door. "I'll bring up supper later."

"Don't bother, dear. I'm going out with Joshua tonight."

At least her aunt's love life appeared promising. "Have a good time." Sierra closed the door behind her and descended the fire escape, wondering if Beau was anything like his father. Would he care that she was going blind? She'd never know the truth because she wouldn't be with Beau when the day of reckoning arrived.

"Ladies and gents, before we kick off our men's bull-riding event here in the Rimrock Auto Arena at the MetraPark, we've got a special treat for you."

Sierra touched Beau's thigh to catch his attention. "Don't you have to prepare for your ride?" She pointed to the cowboys standing behind the bull chutes. Beau had sat with her through several rodeo events explaining the rules and answering her questions.

"I have plenty of time. I'm riding last this afternoon."

"Today we're honored to have Shannon Douglas here with us. A native of Stagecoach, Arizona, Shannon and Wrangler Jeans have teamed up together to promote women's rough-stock events." The crowd applauded and several cowboys let loose wolf whistles.

"I didn't know women rode bulls," Sierra said.

"Not many do, but rumor has it this Shannon Douglas is one of the more talented athletes on the women's circuit."

Sierra studied the female bull rider. Even though she wore a protective vest and the customary headgear with a face mask, Shannon appeared small and vulnerable on the back of a huge bull.

"Shannon's riding Black Beauty from the Spur Ranch near Luckenbach, Texas," the announcer said. "Here's hoping Shannon makes it to eight."

The gate opened and Black Beauty burst from the

chute, almost unseating Shannon. Sierra held her breath as the bull flung the cowgirl around like a rag doll. Amazingly, Shannon hung on and when the buzzer sounded she launched herself off the bull. She landed on her shoulder but quickly got to her feet and ran for the rails.

"Shannon Douglas scored an eighty-two, folks! Not bad for a girl!" Once the crowd quieted, the announcer added, "Shannon will be available for autographs in front of the VIP section after the men's bull-riding event. If you stop by and see Shannon, she'll enter your name into the Wrangler drawing for free merchandise."

"I'd better go," Beau said. He smiled at Sierra, his brown eyes warming when his gaze dropped to her mouth. "How 'bout a good luck kiss?"

Friends...remember? The warning went unheeded, and she leaned forward, pressing her mouth to Beau's, the contact sending a bolt of heat through her body. His tongue slid sensuously across her lower lip, but the instant she relaxed her mouth he pulled away.

"I should warn you that the congratulatory kiss after I win is a whole lot hotter."

"I can handle the heat, cowboy..." she teased. "If you win."

"Oh, I'm gonna win." He tapped his finger against the brim of his hat then took off for the cowboy-ready area.

Sierra pressed her tingling lips together as the loud music and raucous fan noise faded into the background. She was amazed at how easily Beau had slipped through her defenses. They were playing with fire, and the pesky voice inside her head dared Sierra to inch as close as possible to the flames without getting burned.

Relaxing in her seat, she enjoyed the rodeo until Beau's name was announced, then she gripped the armrests and sent up a silent prayer to the rodeo gods to keep the cowboy safe.

"Turn your attention to gate four. Beau Adams is the final ride of the day and he's coming out on Warrior, a descendant of the famed Houdini from the Circle T Ranch in Oklahoma. Folks this bull spins right out of the gate. Adams is in for a jolt!"

Sierra's gaze latched on to Beau as he wrapped the bull rope around his hand. She was relieved to see he'd worn the protective gear he professed to hate. Without warning, the gate opened and Warrior charged into the arena, his powerful kicks attempting to unseat Beau. Sierra gasped when the bull came dangerously close to the rails, but Beau clung to the animal.

The bull ride played out in slow motion…as if Beau and the bull were partners in a cowboy ballet of wild bucks, tight spins and wicked twists. Sierra was awed by the sheer power and beauty of Beau's body as bull and man became one violent burst of energy.

The buzzer sounded and Sierra held her breath, waiting for Beau's dismount. He dove for the ground, landing on his belly in the dirt. He lay still for an agonizingly long moment before struggling to his feet. The bullfighters distracted Warrior and Beau jogged to the rails.

"Folks, that's only the second time this season Warrior has been ridden to eight! What do the judges think of Adams's ride?"

The fans gaped at the JumboTron waiting for the score to flash across the screen, but Sierra's attention remained riveted on Beau. Several cowboys slapped his back and shook his hand. When he removed his face mask, he glanced toward the stands. She waved her arms wildly and he grinned the moment he caught sight of her.

"Eighty-seven! Beau Adams beat Pete Monroe by one point! Congratulations, Adams!"

Sierra joined the fans in honoring Beau with a resounding round of applause. Proud of his accomplishment, she made her way out of the stands and down to the cowboy-ready area, where she promptly put the brakes on when she witnessed a blonde woman throw her arms around Beau's neck.

Friends…remember?

To heck with that. Sierra marched toward the pair. Beau might not be her cowboy forever, but he was darn sure her cowboy for today.

Chapter 6

"For a minute, I thought Duke was riding that bull." Melanie Kimball released Beau from her hug. "You must be a late bloomer."

"Looks that way." Beau studied his pretty former girlfriend, relieved he felt no twinges or surges of attraction to her. "How've you been?"

"Good." She stuck out her lower lip in a playful pout. "Maybe a little lonely."

Still no twinge...yeah, he was definitely over Melanie.

A cough caught his attention. "Sierra." Beau didn't have a chance to introduce the women before Melanie spoke.

"You must be the reason Beau's winning." Melanie offered her hand and Sierra hesitated before shaking it. "I'm Melanie Kimball, Beau's ex-girlfriend."

"Sierra Byrne."

"Nice to meet you, Sierra."

"Sierra owns the Number 1 Diner in Roundup," Beau said.

"That was quite a ride your cowboy gave today," Melanie said.

Sierra's gaze glanced off Beau's face before returning to Melanie. "This is my first time watching Beau compete."

"Really? Boy, could I tell you stories about him and his brother." Melanie frowned. "Speaking of Duke, why isn't he here?"

"Duke retired from rodeo." When Melanie's mouth hung open, Beau explained. "He's married now and spends his time apprehending bad guys and raising his seven-year-old stepson."

"I never pictured Duke the marrying kind." Melanie's mouth twitched. "You on the other hand..." A rowdy group of cowboys caught her attention. "Gotta go," she said. "Nice meeting you, Sierra."

Beau escorted Sierra through a maze of fans to the rodeo secretary's office where he collected his winnings. Since their run-in with Melanie, Sierra had remained quiet. Before they left the arena, he pulled her aside. "I'm sorry."

"For what?"

"If Melanie made you feel uncomfortable."

"She didn't." Sierra's blue eyes shone with sincerity.

Relieved, he asked, "Would you like to browse the vendors before we leave?"

"That's okay. I've seen enough."

Before they exited the MetraPark, Beau bought coffees for the road. Once they left the parking lot, Sierra spoke. "Mind if I ask you a personal question?"

Fearing she wanted to discuss Melanie, Beau attempted to distract her. "I bet you want to know how many buckles I've won." Her answering smile was weak at best, and Beau's stomach clenched.

"Melanie seems like a nice girl. Why did the two of you break up?"

"She's from northern Montana. The long-distance relationship took a toll on us and we grew apart."

Beau glanced across the seat and caught Sierra watching him. God, he loved her eyes…so big and round and blue. He wondered how many other men had fallen into their warm depths and drowned.

"Why didn't one of you move closer to the other?" Sierra's question snapped Beau out of his trance. He'd better focus on his driving or he'd run them off the road. "We're both from ranching families. When we're not on the rodeo circuit, we're herding cattle, hauling bulls or cutting hay."

Expecting a follow-up question, Beau remained silent. When none came, he asked, "Were you involved with anyone when you lived in Chicago?"

"Ted and I dated almost two years before my parents died and I moved to Montana."

When Sierra didn't elaborate, Beau pushed for details. "Did you and Ted try a long-distance relationship?"

"We did. Ted thought after spending a winter in Montana I'd pack my bags and return to the Windy City."

"Chicago winters are nothing to brag about."

"True, but spring and summers along Lake Michigan are warmer than here."

"What happened when spring arrived and you didn't leave Roundup?" he asked.

"Ted stopped calling."

Teddy-boy's loss. "I'm sorry." He wasn't, really, but it seemed like the right thing to say.

"In the end, everything worked out for the best. Ted's law practice and family are in Chicago. He's happy there and I'm happy here." Sierra's attention shifted to the milling cattle in the distance.

"That's the fall calf crop." Beau slowed as he approached a line of cattle trucks parked on the shoulder. Portable pens had been set up to contain the young cows.

"Are the animals on their way to the slaughter house?"

"No, the calves are being shipped south to feedlots for the winter. Once they fatten up they'll land on someone's dinner table."

"I cook meat all the time, but I prefer not to think about how it arrives at the diner."

Beau didn't mind talking beef, but he'd rather learn more about Sierra. "I heard you went to a famous cooking school in Chicago." He hadn't heard—he'd asked Irene where Sierra had learned to cook so well and the waitress had shared everything she knew about Sierra's catering business in Chicago, including where Sierra had gotten her education.

"I studied at the CHIC. The school was part of the Le Cordon Bleu program in France. I credit my mother with nurturing my interest in cooking. She taught me the basics at a young age."

"You must miss your parents," he said.

"Very much."

"I remember the afternoon their plane crashed. Half the town rushed up to Twin Peaks to search for them, but…" He silently cursed. Why the hell had he brought up the deaths of her parents?

"It's okay, Beau." Sierra touched his arm. "I find it comforting to know so many people cared about my parents."

Roundup was a tight-knit community and those who'd searched for her parents had also eaten at Sierra's diner once it opened, ensuring her business thrived.

"I for one am glad you took those fancy food classes," he said. "Growing up without a mother was tough enough, let alone Duke and I having to eat our father's cooking. His specialty was anything that could be made in the microwave."

"Then I'm glad I helped expand your palate."

"Whoever puts a ring on your finger is going to be one lucky, well-fed man."

Sierra's smile disappeared and Beau wondered at her reaction. Was marriage a sensitive topic with Sierra? He checked the dashboard clock—six-thirty. They'd eaten a hot dog at the rodeo but that was five hours ago. "There's a burger joint about fifteen miles up the road that serves great onion rings."

"I'm not really hungry. If you don't mind, I'd rather head home and check on the diner."

"Sure." Beau swallowed a curse. He'd been hoping to spend more time with Sierra—that she wanted to cut their day short was a huge disappointment. A few minutes before eight o'clock he pulled into the parking lot behind the diner. Before he'd shifted the truck into Park and unsnapped his belt, Sierra had opened her door and hopped out. Sticking her head into the cab she said, "Thanks for the lovely day. And congratulations on winning first place."

Panicking, he said, "Wait. I'll walk you to—"

"No need. I'm going straight to the kitchen to get a jump start on tomorrow's menu." The door shut in Beau's face. Stunned, he stared out the windshield at Sierra's retreating figure. When the back door of the diner closed behind her, Beau shook himself out of his stupor. Sierra owed him a victory kiss and he wasn't leaving until she gave him one.

He rapped his knuckles on the back door of the diner, and a moment later Irene's face appeared. "Hello, Beau."

Right then Sierra walked into the kitchen, carrying a plastic tub of dirty dishes. She froze. "Did you forget something?"

Beau stepped into the kitchen, aware that Irene eavesdropped as she pretended to search the refrigerator. "No, you forgot something," he said.

"I did?"

"You forgot to give me my victory kiss."

The fridge door closed and Irene made a hasty exit from the kitchen.

Beau moved across the room, took the tub of dishes from Sierra and set it on the counter, then cupped her face with both hands and locked gazes with her. "I warned you earlier that a victory kiss is a whole lot hotter than a good luck kiss." He rubbed the pad of his thumb across the fleshy part of her lower lip. Did she want his kiss as badly as he wanted to give it to her? He got his answer when she swayed forward, her breasts bumping his chest.

He pressed his lips to hers, building steam slowly. When he slid his tongue inside her mouth she trembled and he crushed her to him. Their breathing grew hot and heavy, and somewhere in the midst of all the noise they made, Beau felt Sierra purr. Emboldened by her response, he cupped her breast, his thumb caressing her nipple, before freeing the button on her blouse. The loud gasp that followed startled Beau and they broke apart. What the hell was he doing—trying to undress Sierra in the middle of the kitchen where her employee could walk in on them?

Sierra stood in stunned silence, her eyes wide, her breathing ragged. She looked so pretty with her hair mussed, her cheeks flushed and her lips swollen. Feeling as if he was on the verge of losing control again, Beau backed toward the door. "Better fix your lipstick." He stepped outside and filled his lungs with cold, crisp air, which did nothing to calm his aroused state.

The apartment door above his head opened and Jordan Peterson stepped outside with Molly.

"Hello, Mrs. Peterson. It's Beau, ma'am."

She descended the steps with the dog. "I thought I told you to call me Jordan?"

"Yes, ma'am… Jordan." Beau waited at the bottom of the stairs, wanting to make sure the older woman didn't slip.

When she reached the pavement, she said, "I'm glad I ran into you."

"Why's that?"

"Join me while I walk Molly."

"Sure."

"I need you to do a favor for me," Jordan said.

"Okay."

"Are you free next Wednesday?"

"I'm not competing in a rodeo if that's what you're asking."

"Would you be able to drive Sierra into Billings to see her eye doctor?"

Beau recalled Sierra's explanation for why she'd spent the night on the road and assumed visiting the ophthalmologist had to do with her not seeing well in the dark. "What time is the appointment?"

"Ten in the morning."

An early appointment would allow Sierra to make the drive back to Roundup before dusk fell. Maybe Jordan was matchmaking, in which case Beau would gladly cooperate.

"Tell Sierra I'll pick her up at eight-thirty."

Molly found a place to do her business and Jordan pulled a plastic grocery bag from her pocket and handed it to Beau.

"I get to do the honors, huh?" After he picked up the mess, he asked, "Where do you want me to toss this?"

"I'll throw it away." She took the bag from Beau and they walked back to the parking lot.

"Beau?"

"Yes?"

"Did Sierra have a nice time today?"

His lips still warm from Sierra's kiss he said, "Yes, she did."

"Good. She needs to get out and do things like that more often."

They stopped at the garbage bin and Beau lifted the lid. After Jordan threw the bag inside, he said, "I'd better head back to the ranch."

"Your father left a few minutes ago. You might catch up with him on the road."

Great. Beau wondered what chores had been neglected while his father had hung out with his girlfriend. "Have a nice evening, Jordan."

The drive to Thunder Ranch wasn't nearly long enough to figure out what was going on with Sierra, Jordan and the infamous eye appointment he'd been dragged into. Instead of heading home, Beau turned onto Thunder Road and drove to the main house. He'd drop off his winnings and ask his aunt if she believed his father was going through a phase or if his intentions toward Jordan were serious, and the family had to reconfigure the work load to make up for his father's slacking off. Beau parked in the ranch yard then took the front porch steps two at a time. He knocked once before letting himself into the house.

"Aunt Sarah? You home?"

"In the kitchen, Beau."

"Something smells good." He waltzed into the room and gave his aunt a kiss on the cheek.

"Butterscotch cookies. Suddenly I have all these grandchildren, and I can't keep up with my baking."

Even though his father insisted Aunt Sarah was wearing herself out catering to all the rug rats in the family, Beau figured the kids took his aunt's mind off the ranch's financial situation and her worry over Tuf. He reached for a cookie, but she swatted his knuckles.

"They haven't cooled."

"I won in Billings today." Beau set the check on the counter and his aunt peered at the amount.

"Good gracious. You keep this up, and we'll be debt-free in no time," she teased.

"Speaking of Midnight—"

"Don't you start in on me, young man."

"Start what?"

"Pleading for Midnight to return to rodeo. Colt's pestering is driving Ace crazy and it's not difficult these days to set Ace off with Flynn's due date approaching."

"Is he worried about Flynn's health?"

"Like all expectant fathers Ace hopes she has an easy delivery, but he's also nervous about becoming a father."

"Why? He filled Uncle John's shoes without missing a beat. Unless he's worried about being too over-protective." Beau's father sure hadn't been. He'd subscribed to the parenting philosophy of sink-or-swim.

"Nothing wrong with taking care of your own, and Ace certainly does that job well."

"No argument there." Beau moved aside when his aunt slid a cookie sheet into the oven. "Some horses shouldn't be held back and Midnight's one of them."

She snorted.

"C'mon, Aunt Sarah. You've seen that horse in action. He lives for rodeo."

"I won't argue that Midnight loves competition, but we can't afford for him to get injured."

"Back Bender and Bushwhacker have had a heck of a season on the bull circuit and they haven't even peaked. Another year of competition and I bet they both make it to the NFR and bring us top dollar in breeding fees."

"God forbid, but if anything happens to Midnight

and we can no longer breed him, we're going to need those bulls to cover his loss."

"We're taking Back Bender and Bushwhacker to compete in South Dakota next month. Why not enter Midnight into the competition?"

"Midnight's been out of rodeo for a long time." Aunt Sarah handed Beau a cooled cookie. "Who's going to work with him? Ace is busy with his vet practice. Colt and Duke have kids and families to look after." His aunt had intentionally left out Tuf.

"What about me? I'll go a few rounds in the ring with Midnight."

"And if you get hurt, then you've ruined your chances of winning at the Bash."

"No worries. It's just a couple go-rounds in the corral. If Midnight looks like he's not a hundred percent ready to compete, then we don't take him to South Dakota."

His aunt's gaze dropped to the check on the counter. "Okay, but no one is to know you're practicing with Midnight."

"My lips are sealed."

His aunt playfully shoved a whole cookie between Beau's lips. "You be sure to keep that mouth of yours full and don't let our secret leak out."

Beau grinned, chewed twice then swallowed. "I might need a few more cookies for the road just so I'm not tempted...."

She stuffed cookies into a Baggie then handed it to Beau. "Aunt Sarah, what do you know about Jordan Peterson and my dad?"

"Mostly what everyone else in town knows...that

they dated in high school and broke up because Jordan left for college."

"Dad keeps his feelings close to the vest, but do you think he was really shaken up over their split years ago?"

"I don't know, honey. I was five years younger and wrapped up in my own life. Why?"

"Did you know Dad's been seeing a lot of Jordan lately?"

"How much is a lot?"

"Every day."

His aunt's eyes rounded. "I had no idea things had gotten that serious between them."

"We might need to think about hiring another ranch hand."

"Why?"

"Dad's been passing off his chores to me and Duke, and we're having a tough time handling our own responsibilities and covering for Dad, too."

"I'm glad your father's found someone he cares for," his aunt said. "I'll speak with Royce and Harlan. Maybe they can pick up some of the slack."

Royce and Harlan already did the work of four men and it was hardly fair to ask more of them without offering a pay raise. Beau doubted his father considered how his actions affected others.

Aunt Sarah nudged his side. "Speaking of old and new flames…"

No way was Beau sticking around for an inquisition about his relationship with Sierra. "Gotta run. Thanks for the cookies."

"Chicken!" The accusation chased Beau through the house and out the front door.

"Sierra, may I speak with you for a moment?"

Most days, her aunt waited until ten before making an appearance in the diner, but the clock on the wall read eight-thirty. Sierra didn't mind the interruption, but this morning the diner was busier than usual because members of the high school booster club were conducting their monthly meeting over breakfast. She ushered her aunt behind the register. "What is it?"

"Please don't be mad at me, but I took the liberty of scheduling you an eye appointment with Dr. Ryder for 10:00 a.m. today."

Shocked, Sierra said, "I can't leave in the middle of all this—" she spread her arms wide "—craziness."

"I asked Karla to cover for you and I'll do my best to help."

As if on cue, the diner door opened and Karla waltzed in. She smiled at Sierra then disappeared into the kitchen. "You shouldn't have called Dr. Ryder's office and—"

"If I had left it up to you, you'd have never made the appointment."

Lest she become the subject of gossip for the remainder of the day, Sierra lowered her voice. "I'm not going."

"You have to."

Embarrassed by her childish behavior, yet too scared to care what her aunt thought of her, she whispered, "You can't make me." She wasn't ready to face reality.

"Beau's waiting outside for you."

She spun toward the window. Beau leaned a sexy hip

against the grille of his truck and waved. "How could you, Aunt Jordan?"

"How could I what, dear?"

"Ask Beau to drive me?" He was the last person she wanted with her when the doctor conveyed the bad news.

"I thought you two were friends."

"We are, but he doesn't have time for this kind of thing."

"Friends make time for each other. If he hadn't been able to accompany you today I'm sure he would have said so."

Sierra glanced at Beau and automatically her fingers pressed against her mouth as she recalled the victory kiss he'd claimed after the rodeo last weekend. She'd gone to bed every night since dreaming about that kiss. "Fine. I'll go."

She escaped upstairs to the apartment. After powdering her nose and applying lipstick, she collected her coat and purse and marched through the diner and out the front door.

"I'm sorry my aunt put you on the spot and asked you to drive me into Billings. I'm capable of getting there and back on my own."

"I know that."

"Then why did you—"

"Because I'll take any excuse to be with you." Beau's slow, easy smile warmed her blood even as she thought his words weren't something a *friend* would say.

What did it matter? After today, Beau would no longer be interested in friendship much less anything else.

Chapter 7

What was taking so long?

Almost two hours had passed since Beau sat down in Dr. Ryder's waiting room and Sierra had been whisked away by a nurse. In that entire time, no other patients had arrived or left the office. Aside from the receptionist at the check-in desk and the nurse who'd escorted Sierra to the exam room, the clinic remained eerily quiet.

What kind of eye appointment took two hours? Had the doctor performed some kind of procedure on Sierra's eyes? Beau rose from his chair and paced the professionally decorated room, stopping to stare at the wilderness painting hanging on the wall. The grizzly bear in the picture made him guess the location was northwest Montana or Glacier National Park. Beau had been to the famous park once with his brother and father, but a spring snowstorm had forced them out after only a few days in the area.

Beau's stomach growled and he continued pacing. He was on his third lap around the room when voices drifted down the hallway. A moment later Sierra appeared in the doorway. Her eyes were puffy—had she been crying? He moved closer and brushed the pad of his thumb against her cheek. "Those beautiful baby blues are okay, aren't they?"

Tears pooled in her eyes and Beau panicked. "We're out of here." He escorted her from the office and straight into the elevator across the hall. They rode in silence to the lobby then stepped outside into the chilly air and bright sunlight. Whatever had taken place inside the exam room hadn't been good and Beau floundered, wondering what to do first—ask questions or give Sierra time to pull herself together? He voted for the second option.

"Let's grab a bite to eat." He helped her into the truck then drove to a Mexican restaurant called the Cantina, which looked like a dive but had excellent food and a cozy, dark atmosphere that allowed for plenty of privacy. Beau glanced at Sierra, but she sat in stony silence. Feeling helpless, he reached across the seat and took her hand. She surprised him when she threaded her fingers through his and squeezed.

The strong urge to protect Sierra proved to Beau that his feelings for her were deepening quickly and he told himself to proceed with caution. He was under a lot of pressure—granted it was self-imposed—but he had to remain focused on his goal to win the Bash if he intended to begin next year's bull-riding season on a positive note.

When they entered the restaurant, he asked the hostess to seat them at a table in the corner. A waitress delivered tortilla chips and salsa then took their drink orders, promising to return in five minutes.

"The chicken enchiladas and pork tamales are good," Beau said.

Sierra didn't open her menu. "You pick for me."

The waitress set their drinks on the table then tapped a pen against her order pad. Beau chose the enchilada dinners for both of them. Left alone while they waited for their food, he hoped Sierra would tell him what the doctor said, and her continued silence tied his gut in knots. She looked devastated and he wanted to hug her. Had her vision deteriorated to the point where she could no longer drive? Or had the doctor told her that contacts weren't an option anymore and she had to wear glasses from now on?

"You don't have to talk about it, but I'm a good listener," he said.

"I'm ashamed to admit I'd hoped if I ignored the symptoms, the disease would go away."

"What disease?"

"Fuchs Endothelial Dystrophy. The cornea swells, which causes problems like tunnel vision, glaring, sometimes a halo effect and blurriness." She sighed. "I just didn't want to believe I'd inherited the same disease as my aunt."

Beau's lungs tightened. "Jordan's...blind."

"Blindness is the final stage of the disease."

Stunned, Beau asked, "There's no cure?"

"A corneal transplant might be an option down the road."

The band squeezing his chest loosened. There was hope. "Are there medications that slow the progression?"

"No. As the disease worsens the doctor prescribes medicated drops and ointments to ease the pain."

Their meals arrived and they ate in silence, Beau barely tasting the food. He wanted to slay Sierra's dragon, battle the disease for her, but he couldn't. The powerlessness he felt at not being able to protect someone he cared about was new to Beau and he didn't like it. Not one frickin' bit.

He opened his mouth to tell Sierra there were worse things in the world than going blind but reconsidered. He'd tried that speech when bullies had teased Duke because of his stuttering, and all he'd gotten for his effort had been a punch in the gut from his brother.

Wanting to cheer her up, Beau suggested, "Why don't we stay in Billings and shop for Christmas gifts."

"I'm not in the mood." Sierra understood exactly what Beau was trying to do—take her mind off the doctor's diagnosis. She'd known for a while now what the official verdict would be, but she'd clung to a smidgeon of hope that maybe…just maybe her vision problems had been the result of some other issue that was curable. Fear suddenly gave way to anger—a deep, burning rage that made her want to raise her fists toward the heavens and scream at the unfairness of life.

"Have you been to the movies lately?"

As Sierra stared at Beau's mouth, the raw fury that had control of her body melted into a yearning urgency that left her breathless. Images of her and Beau making love spun through her mind, feeding an overpowering desire to live in the moment and forget about tomorrow. Embracing the newfound feeling of recklessness, Sierra vowed to live life to the fullest while she still had her sight—starting today.

There were so many things she'd dreamed of doing but the clock was ticking on her eyesight. Right then she decided to create her own personal bucket list, and who better than Beau to help her kick off her pledge to live in the moment? She reached beneath the table and caressed his thigh.

"There is something I'd like to do." She leaned close, her breast bumping his arm. "Let's get a motel room."

Beau stared, dumbstruck, and Sierra suppressed a giggle. The thought of making love with Beau felt right and good, and Sierra refused to consider the consequences. She wanted to lose herself in Beau and live as if there were no tomorrow...no next week...no next month. No next year. Before Beau had a chance to respond to her suggestion, the waitress arrived with their check. He paid cash for their meal, then escorted her outside and straight to his truck. His silence continued as he gripped the steering wheel so tightly his knuckles whitened.

She shifted closer and played with a strand of his hair. "Please, Beau."

"We shouldn't."

"We should." The longing in his gaze made her tremble. Why was he fighting his feelings? She nuzzled his neck, flicking her tongue against his warm flesh. He smelled like sandalwood and musk. Sierra's excitement fizzled when Beau started the truck and headed north on the highway.

The trip to Roundup was the longest of her life. Beau pulled into the parking lot behind the diner shortly after 9:00 p.m. and insisted on escorting her up to the apartment. Sierra wasn't raising the white flag yet. She veered away from the fire escape and entered the diner through the delivery door. Standing on the threshold she faced Beau.

Ever the gentleman, he leaned in to kiss her cheek, but Sierra turned her face and their mouths bumped. Flinging her arms around his neck, she kissed Beau as if she were marching off to war. She slipped her thigh between his legs and pressed herself against him, rejoicing in the hardness that nudged her hip. She knew the moment she'd won—he grasped her face and thrust his tongue inside her mouth. While tongues dueled, Beau cupped her breasts, squeezing softly.

Please, Beau…for tonight be the bright light in my life.

He inched her farther into the kitchen then shut the door, the quiet click of the lock echoing through the room. The soft glow of the security lights in the dining room spilled beneath the kitchen door, outlining Beau's body. The thrill of a secret encounter surged through Sierra, feeding the reckless frenzy inside her. Beau removed her coat, tossing it to the floor. Sierra kicked off her shoes and helped Beau out of his jacket. Shirts followed.

"This is crazy." His fingers released the hook on her bra, then his hand cupped her bare breast and brought it to his mouth.

"Don't stop."

Beau tugged Sierra's slacks off and lifted her onto the stainless-steel countertop. "Are you protected?" he asked.

"No," she huffed in his ear. "Please tell me you have a condom."

"My wallet." While Beau kissed a path down her neck, Sierra reached behind him and pulled the wallet from his pants pocket.

There was no turning back now.

Crap. Had they really made love on the countertop in the diner's kitchen? Even as Beau struggled to comprehend what had just transpired between him and Sierra, he couldn't resist nibbling her ear. When he pulled back and gazed at her face, her mouth widened in a satisfied smile then she playfully pushed him away and buttoned her blouse before grabbing her slacks from the floor. Jeans bunched around his ankles he turned his back and straightened his own clothes. He'd never done anything like this before and didn't know what the heck to say.

Sierra, I'm sorry I let things get out of hand? Or what he really wanted to say… *Sierra, let's do that again.*

Shoot, she was the one who engineered this…this… tryst. He'd tried to be noble and resist her advances, but he was just a guy—a guy who'd been fantasizing about making love to Sierra for months.

She cleared her throat and he faced her, relieved she smiled. "We should talk about this," he said.

"No worries, Beau. I don't expect things to change between us."

She didn't? Why the hell not? "I don't understand."

"People have sex all the time. It doesn't have to mean anything."

A queasy feeling settled in the bottom of his gut. He hadn't a clue what was going through Sierra's mind. Maybe he should leave. They both needed time to absorb what had happened between them.

"You're okay?" he asked.

"I'm fine." She unlocked the door and stood back.

He slipped on his coat. "You're sure—"

"Positive." She held out his wallet.

When his boots hit the pavement, she said, "Good night" and shut the door in his face.

What the hell? Beau had the weirdest feeling Sierra had just used him for sex.

After Beau left, Sierra washed up at the kitchen sink, wiped off the counter with disinfectant spray—twice—then made her way up the back staircase to the apartment. When she opened the door she was caught by surprise—her aunt and Beau's father were locked in a passionate embrace. "Oops." Sierra retreated into the stairwell. "I didn't mean to interrupt."

"I should be going," Joshua said.

After a few seconds, Sierra entered the apartment. She offered an apologetic smile but Joshua's gaze skirted her face. "There's a quarantined bull at the ranch I need to check on."

Jordan grasped Joshua's hand and she followed him into the kitchen. Sierra thought it was sweet that the older couple always held hands. After Joshua shrugged on his coat, her aunt lifted her face and there wasn't a moment's hesitation before Joshua kissed her.

"Good night, Sierra," he said.

"'Night, Joshua."

After another quick kiss, Joshua left and Aunt Jordan closed the door. "Sierra?"

"In the living room."

Jordan sat down on the sofa.

Sierra would have preferred to put off this conversation until tomorrow and retreat to her bedroom where her memory could relive her passionate lovemaking with Beau, but her aunt had waited all day to hear the doctor's diagnosis.

"You were right," Sierra said.

"How far has the disease progressed?"

"Far enough that I've been warned never to drive at night." As if she didn't already know that.

"Did Dr. Ryder give you any idea when you'll…"

Sierra said the word *blind* in her head but still refused to accept the offensive word. "Dr. Ryder said there was no way to determine when I'd lose my sight." But he had predicted that it wouldn't be for many years and Sierra was grateful for that small blessing. "There's a chance that I might be a candidate for a cornea transplant."

"Then there's hope."

Yes, but Sierra wasn't wasting another day waiting around for hope. From now on, she intended to live each day to the fullest.

"Now that you have an official diagnosis, you can prepare yourself."

How did anyone map out a life in the dark? "I don't care to think about that right now, Aunt Jordan."

"You need to plan for the future, dear. There are ways you can make the transition easier."

Sierra appreciated her aunt's advice, and in due time she'd devise a battle strategy, but not now. "Forget about me, let's talk about you," Sierra said. "How's your love life?"

A soft smile flirted with the corner of her aunt's mouth. "Joshua and I realized that neither of us has ever stopped caring for each other."

"But you married Uncle Bob."

"Yes, and I loved Bob, but when I went off to college I left a piece of my heart with Joshua. Every now and then through the years I thought of him and wondered what would have happened if I'd remained in Roundup and married him."

"You wouldn't have become a dancer or earned a college degree or traveled the world with Uncle Bob."

"That's true. And I credit your uncle with helping me conquer my fear of going blind. With his guidance, I remained independent despite the loss of my eyesight."

"How did he help you?"

"Because of your uncle's military background, he viewed my eventual blindness as a war—one he determined I'd win. If not for his insistence that I learn to fend for myself and do everyday tasks without his help, I wouldn't be able to get around on my own as much as I do."

"You don't believe that if you'd married Joshua he'd have helped you live a fulfilling life?"

"Joshua would have become impatient with me and stepped in to help when he shouldn't have. I'd have become too dependent on him." Jordan sighed. "Your uncle was a soldier. Not even my tears or pleading for help swayed him to give in to me."

"Sounds like Uncle Bob used the tough-love approach."

"Because of Bob's determination, I've enjoyed a rich, full life since I lost my sight."

"How is Joshua handling your blindness?"

"Better than I expected, but he's changed since we dated."

"Changed how?"

"He's quieter." Her aunt laughed. "He was such a prankster when we went steady. Playing tricks on me, then when I'd become frustrated with his jokes, he'd surprise me with a poem or a bouquet of wildflowers." Jordan's smile weakened. "I think his wife's death deeply affected him."

Selfishly, Sierra hoped Joshua had gotten over the death of his wife and was ready and willing to commit to Jordan. "How did his wife die?"

"Her car careened off the road during a snowstorm. The twins were only two at the time, but thank goodness they weren't in the car with her. Frankly, I'm surprised Joshua never remarried. Raising his sons alone must have been trying at times."

"Does Joshua ask about your life with Uncle Bob?"

"No. That's why I've been hesitant to bring up his wife."

Testing the waters Sierra said, "I guess it doesn't matter if you're just friends."

"We're more than friends, Sierra."

"So…you might be willing to relocate permanently to Roundup?" Sierra crossed her fingers.

"It's a definite possibility. Life goes by fast. I don't want to regret not reaching for happiness when it's within my grasp." Her aunt tapped a finger against the couch cushion. "Speaking of men who make us happy… how do you feel about Beau?"

If what had transpired between herself and Beau a few minutes ago was any indication, then Sierra definitely had the hots for the cowboy. "Beau's a nice man—" and sexy as heck "—but all we're ever going to be is friends." No way would Sierra allow her feelings for Beau to deepen, knowing in the end that there was no future for them.

Sierra faked a yawn then said, "I'm going to turn in early."

"But we should discuss setting goals for—"

"Not right now, Aunt Jordan. Sweet dreams." Sierra slipped into her room and shut the door. She sat on the bed and tears flooded her eyes. Making love with Beau had been both a thrill and a curse. A thrill in that he'd made her feel things she'd never thought she'd feel with a man, and a curse because now she knew she'd never have what she yearned for—a husband and children of her own.

Still in a state of shock over what had transpired between him and Sierra, Beau parked outside the barn and went into his workshop. He might as well get started on the saddle for Jim Phillips. Keeping his hands busy would calm his jumbled thoughts. He hung his coat over the stool next to the workbench then selected a medium-sized fiberglass frame from his stockpile and placed it on the wooden saddletree. For extra reinforcement he attached a steel plate from the pommel to the cantle beneath the tree.

Next, he added the stirrup bars—three-inch wide brackets with a movable catch set into the bar. While he hammered the bar into the proper shape, his memory replayed the scene at the ophthalmologist's office.

He didn't want to admit that learning Sierra might one day go blind had shaken him to the core. He couldn't imagine those beautiful blue eyes of hers left in the dark. He stopped pounding the bar and closed his eyes.

What would it be like if one day he woke up and the sights that had been familiar to him all his life…saddles…cattle…the mountains…bulls went dark? Beau wasn't sure he could handle that. How would he cope if he couldn't make his saddles? His chest physically hurt when he thought of Sierra's love of cooking and the possibility that one day she might have to give it up.

If Beau were to lose his sight, activities he'd taken for granted—walking to the barn, showering or answering the door—would become potential hazards. He sifted through his stash of leather stirrups until he found a pair he liked, then sat on the stool and stared into space. How had he allowed things between him and Sierra to get out of hand—sex in the diner kitchen? What if someone had walked in on them? The idea of getting caught stirred Beau and he squelched the X-rated images that popped into his mind. Sierra gave no sign that what they'd shared had meant anything to her except sex, and no reason to believe their lovemaking had changed their relationship.

What the heck was their relationship anyway? He'd thought they'd started dating then all of a sudden they'd skipped getting-to-know-you and had gone straight to doing the down-and-dirty.

In retrospect, he wondered if Sierra's actions were a direct result of the eye doctor's diagnosis. He'd heard stories of people who reacted to bad news in bizarre ways and he had no intention of holding Sierra's actions against her. To Beau's way of thinking, the best thing for them to do as a couple was take it one day at a time. He liked Sierra a lot—no sense worrying about the future when there was nothing he could do to change the course of her eye disease.

Chapter 8

Friday afternoon Beau left the equipment barn and spotted his brother's blue Ford barreling up the drive. Almost an entire week had passed since Beau and Sierra's sexy interlude in the diner kitchen. He hadn't phoned Sierra or dropped by the diner in five days, believing they needed a cooling-off period. Boy, had he been wrong. Keeping his distance from Sierra had only fueled his erotic dreams.

"Aren't you supposed to be at work?" he asked when Duke stepped from the truck.

"Dinah said I deserved a day off, so I thought I'd see if you or Dad needed my help."

Beau continued walking to the barn, Duke falling in step alongside him. "You should have asked Dinah if you could have tomorrow off, instead."

"Why's that?" Duke stopped short when Beau put on the brakes and faced him.

"I could use an extra hand hauling the bulls to Three Forks."

"Bushwhacker and Back Bender are old pros. They won't give you any trouble."

"Asteroid's going, too. He's competing in his first rodeo and there's no telling how he'll behave."

"Sorry. Dinah's driving into Billings with Aunt Sarah on Saturday to shop for baby furniture."

"Guess Royce or Harlan will have to help out." The ranch hands wouldn't mind. They enjoyed meeting up with old acquaintances at the rodeos.

"Why isn't Dad going?" Duke asked when they entered the barn.

"He's taking Jordan to a ballet in Bozeman."

"Ballet?" Duke frowned.

"Yeah, that was my reaction, too."

"Jordan's blind. Why would they—"

"I guess she performed with a dance company in California years ago."

"The two of us need to talk to Dad. He can't keep throwing extra responsibilities at us," Duke said.

"I'll leave you to do the talking," Beau said, even though he knew his brother wouldn't confront their father. Duke was the peacemaker in the family so it would be left up to Beau to square off with the old man if push came to shove. "Dad's ticked off at me for seeing Sierra."

"I don't understand."

"He warned me away from getting involved with her," Beau said.

"Seriously?"

"He's worried I'll do something that will sabotage his relationship with Jordan."

Duke shook his head. "He's gone off the deep end."

Beau entered the room at the back of the barn where a twenty-five-year-old bucking machine was stored and flipped the light switch.

"I still don't get what Jordan sees in Dad. He's not exactly the kind of guy who sticks by your side through thick and thin," Duke said.

"Maybe Jordan's softened him up."

"I guess Dad's finally gotten over Mom."

"Looks that way." Beau believed their father had been so heartbroken over the death of his first wife that he hadn't been able keep any photographs of her around the house. The few times Beau had asked about his mother, his father had changed the subject. Beau straightened the mats beneath the bucking machine—mats that had been worn thin by years of use.

Duke laughed.

"What's so funny?"

"Remember the night we snuck out here to try the machine after Dad warned us to keep away from it?"

"We were seven at the time, weren't we?" Beau wiped his dusty hands on his jeans.

"Dad woke up and discovered our beds empty—"

"—and Uncle John was so pissed at him for not checking the barn before he roused the whole ranch to search for us." Beau chuckled.

"I have a confession to make," Duke said.

Before their falling-out over the summer, Beau and his brother used to discuss everything and anything.

Missing that connection with his twin, Beau said, "You know I can keep a secret."

Duke stared longingly at the bucking machine. "I miss riding bulls."

Since when? Duke had been one hundred percent certain that he was finished with rodeo when he'd married Angie.

"Don't get me wrong. Angie and Luke are the best things that ever happened to me and I don't regret walking away from rodeo."

"Then what is it you miss about riding?"

"The adrenaline rush."

"Don't you still get that feeling when you see Angie in her birthday suit?"

Duke shoved Beau playfully. "Brothers aren't supposed to talk about their sisters-in-law that way."

"Says who?" Beau teased.

"I see I'm gonna have to teach you a lesson in respect." Duke narrowed his eyes.

"You and what army?"

Duke lunged at Beau, wrapping him in a bear hug. He lifted his brother off his feet then tossed him to the mats. Beau seized Duke's ankle and down his twin went, Beau rolling out of the way before Duke crashed on top of him. The brothers grunted, groaned and laughed as they wrestled. Several minutes later, and out of breath, Beau hollered, "Stop!"

"Giving up already?"

"Hell, no. There's a better way to settle this." Beau hopped to his feet. "We'll have ourselves a ride-off."

"You're on." Duke started the machine, the old motor

groaning and squeaking. "It's been a while, so I get a warm-up ride."

"Real cowboys don't need practice runs," Beau taunted.

Duke hopped onto the machine and after catching his rhythm, he said, "Turn it up a notch."

Arm high above his head, Duke's body swayed with the machine. Duke was all about finesse while Beau's performances were choppy. There were pros and cons to both ways of riding, but Beau conceded that his brother *looked* better busting bulls than he did. Beau flipped the machine to High without warning and the sudden jolt sent Duke to the mats.

"Cheater."

"Watch how the professionals do it." Beau slowed the machine, hopped on and waited for Duke to saunter over to the wall and switch gears. Duke flipped the machine to High and Beau flopped around like a fish on dry land. He relished the fight—even if it was with a machine. Duke cheered him on, reminding Beau of days gone by when they'd traveled the circuit together.

When Beau remained on the bull a full minute, Duke shut off the machine. "You're ready to compete tomorrow."

"We should do this more often. Bring Luke next time, and we'll teach him how to ride."

"I just got married. I'm not looking to give Angie a reason to divorce me."

While the brothers threw the tarp over the machine, Beau's cell phone chimed with a text message. "It's Aunt Sarah. She wants us up at the main house."

"Anything wrong?" Duke asked.

"She didn't say. You go ahead. I'll lock up here."

After the rash of robberies over the summer, Beau and his father no longer left the property unsecured when they weren't close by. Beau made sure all doors were bolted then hopped into his truck and headed to his aunt's. When he arrived, the driveway was filled with trucks. Then he spotted the patrol car and decided it must be serious if Dinah had driven out to the ranch while on duty. Beau entered through the back door and stepped into a kitchen full of arguing people.

Aunt Sarah noticed him first and offered a nervous smile. "Beau's here." The announcement quieted the group. "Royce and Harlan went out to check on the pregnant mares a short time ago and discovered Miss Kitty miscarried," his aunt said.

No wonder the family was upset—Miss Kitty, a former bucking bronc, was a proven breeder and had been carrying Midnight's foal. Ace paced the tile floor. "I checked Miss Kitty two days ago and she showed no signs of being in distress."

"This isn't your fault." Aunt Sarah patted her eldest son's arm. "Mother Nature works in her own mysterious way."

Beau felt bad for Ace. His cousin looked miserable. No one worked harder than Ace to keep Thunder Ranch afloat and its animals healthy.

"Midnight hasn't settled down since he returned from Buddy Wright's ranch this past summer. Maybe it's time we discuss our options," Aunt Sarah said.

Ace spoke first. "One option is that we sell Midnight and cut our losses."

"Midnight stays." Colt's chin jutted. "I'll put more hours in working with him."

"You've busted your backside on that stallion for months, and he still won't have anything to do with a dummy mount," Ace argued.

"He'll come around," Colt said.

"Even if you work with Midnight 24/7 all through the winter, there's no guarantee he'll relax enough that we can trust him again with the mares next spring," Ace said. "By then, we'll have invested money we can't afford to lose in his care and upkeep. And we don't know if any of the other mares we put him with will miscarry in the coming months."

"Let Midnight earn his keep." All eyes shifted to Beau. "If Midnight's allowed to rodeo, he'll bring in enough money to pay for his feed while Colt continues to work with him."

"Beau's right," Colt said. "Midnight's a competitor. He'll settle down if he has a chance to get rid of his excess energy."

"I'm more worried about Mom than Midnight." Dinah hugged her mother. "No horse is worth the trouble if the stress affects your health."

"My heart is fine, sweetie." Aunt Sarah spoke to the group. "We were all hoping Midnight would be our lucky charm, but we have to do what's best for the ranch and for Midnight."

"I'm with Ace on this one," Duke said. "Midnight's had his chance and he's not living up to our expectations."

"Joshua." Aunt Sarah studied her brother. "You've been awfully quiet. What do you think?"

"I'd like to see Midnight go for broke," he said. Beau

wondered if his father wasn't also referring to his relationship with Jordan Peterson.

"What do you want to do, Mom?" Colt asked.

Aunt Sarah straightened her shoulders. "Before we put Midnight on the auction block, he deserves another chance." The room erupted into arguing. Aunt Sarah opened the utensil drawer, removed a spatula and smacked it against the counter until everyone was silent. "We keep Midnight until next spring. If he's still unpredictable and difficult to control at that time, then he goes."

The kitchen cleared out quickly, leaving Beau alone with his aunt. "Does this mean Midnight can definitely compete in the Badlands Bull Bash?"

"Yes."

"When are you going to tell Ace?"

"I'm not."

Beau's eyes widened.

"I'll leave that up to you."

"Do you want me to sneak Midnight off the property to practice?"

"Not unless you want the others to alert Dinah or Duke and begin another statewide search for the stallion."

"I'd planned to ride Midnight this Sunday after I return from Three Forks."

"That's fine." She tugged his shirtsleeve. "Be careful, Beau. I don't want either of you hurt."

"Wait and see, Aunt Sarah. Midnight will be a different horse once he's in the arena bucking off cowboys."

"I pray you're right. We could use the money and a little hope around here."

Beau wondered if the *hope* his aunt referred to had more to do with his cousin Tuf's estrangement from the family than a spirited horse with a stubborn streak.

Sierra was down on her knees, stocking paper goods behind the lunch counter when the sleigh bells on the diner door jingled. She glanced at her watch—7:45. Go figure—a late customer would happen along right before closing time. "Be with you in a moment!" She set aside the bundle of napkins and climbed to her feet, then sucked in a surprised gasp. Beau sat at the end of the lunch counter.

He hadn't called her since they'd returned from Billings a week ago and…and…she slammed the door on the image of her and Beau having sex on the kitchen counter. Good grief, not an hour in the day passed in which she didn't recall the steamy scene.

"Got a minute?" he asked.

Relieved that the last patron had left a few minutes ago, Sierra moved from behind the counter and flipped the Open sign to Closed. When she turned away from the window, she bumped into Beau and automatically pressed her palm to his chest to regain her balance. The heavy thump of his heart beneath her fingertips made her pulse race. Beau placed his hand over hers, pinning her fingers to his shirt.

She couldn't think straight, standing this close to him.

"I'm riding in Three Forks tomorrow. Come with me."

"I can't. Irene's husband is sick and she's staying home to take care of him."

"I'll help out." Karla emerged from the kitchen,

flashing a mischievous smile. Had she been eavesdropping behind the door?

Beau grinned. "Karla's willing to cover for you."

"Aunt Jordan—"

"Your aunt is going to a ballet in Bozeman with my father."

"That's right. I forgot." Sierra's face heated.

"I can run the diner," Karla said. "You've already prepared tomorrow's special. It's just a matter of heating the food."

Before Sierra could come up with a plausible excuse to skip the rodeo, Beau kissed her. A slow and steady I'm-in-no-rush kiss—right in front of her employee.

"When should I be ready?" The question slipped from her mouth in a satisfied sigh.

"Six-thirty." Beau nodded to Karla then left the diner.

"Things are moving right along between you and Beau," Karla said.

Oh, joy. With Karla in charge of the diner tomorrow, Sierra and Beau would be the topic of conversation among the Roundup regulars.

"You sure you don't want something to eat or drink?" Beau asked.

"No, thanks. I'm fine." If he bugged her about food one more time Sierra would smack him. She and Beau sat in the stands at the Three Forks Rodeo, watching the barrel-racing event. At least his former girlfriend wasn't competing—that took some of the sting out of Beau's hovering.

Was it her imagination or had he morphed into a cowboy hen? All day he'd stood too close or gripped her elbow at the oddest times as if expecting her to suddenly walk into a wall. As she'd feared, learning about her eye disease had made Beau more vigilant around her. The last thing she wanted was to be smothered.

"Isn't it time for you to ride?" Bull riding was the final event of the rodeo—thank God, because she needed a little breathing room before they drove back to Roundup.

He leaned close and whispered, "Can't leave without my good luck kiss."

As if she could stop herself... Sierra brushed her lips across his. "Good luck." *And please don't get hurt.*

Her gaze followed Beau out of the stands. There was a huge part of her that yearned to latch on to him as if she hadn't a care in the world, but she doubted he'd be willing to live in the moment with her as she tackled the items on her bucket list. As much as she wanted to be with Beau, he was a take-charge kind of guy who'd only get in the way of her goals.

"Ladies and gents, it's time to kick off America's most extreme sport—bull ridin'!"

The raucous noise that followed the announcer's spiel drowned out Sierra's introspection and she turned her attention to the JumboTron. Images of past bull rides flashed across the screen while the Garth Brooks song about the sport of rodeo blasted through the arena.

"This afternoon we've got eight foolhardy cowboys ready to do battle with the meanest critters on God's green earth."

The fans stomped their boots on the metal bleachers, tugging a smile from Sierra—she enjoyed watching the crowd as much as she did the actual events. Switching her attention to the cowboy-ready area, she searched for Beau—not an easy task for her eyes when all the cowboys wore colored shirts that blurred together in a kaleidoscope of bright hues. She'd asked Beau why none of the men wore yellow and he'd told her that yellow was the color of cowards. Cowboys and their kooky superstitions.

When Sierra noticed Beau climbing onto the back of a bull, she edged forward in her seat and sent up a silent prayer for his safety.

"Turn your attention to gate six and Beau Adams from Roundup, Montana. After a slow start earlier in the year, this cowboy's had a steady run of good luck the past few months. We'll see if Adams has what it takes to tame a bull called Tankulicious. Tank hails from the Norton Palmer Ranch in Nebraska."

Beau slipped in his mouth guard. His teeth clanked together more times in eight seconds than a hockey player's did during an entire game and if he intended to kiss Sierra again, he didn't want to damage his pucker. Next, he adjusted his Kevlar vest then shoved his hat down on his head. A cowboy hat might not look like much protection but a good quality hat could mean the difference between a bruise and a gash.

Closing his eyes, Beau emptied his mind of all thoughts except Tank. Bull riding was twenty percent talent and eighty percent mental toughness. Ready as he'd ever be, he leaned over the bull's right shoulder, lifted his arm in the air and braced for combat.

The chute door opened and Tank barreled into the arena like a derailed freight train. Beau was prepared for the first buck, lunging forward over the bull's shoulders.

Focusing on Tank's momentum, Beau allowed the bull to guide him into the next kick. Like a ballroom dance, Tank led and Beau followed. Neither beast nor man raised the white flag as seconds ticked off the clock. When Beau heard the buzzer, his mind switched gears and he waited for an opening to dismount.

Tank continued to buck and spin, but Beau hung on, praying the bull wouldn't yank his arm from the socket. Finally, Tank's engine sputtered and Beau took advantage of the bull's letdown. Releasing his hold on the rope, he used Tank as a springboard and launched himself through the air. He hit the ground on all fours and his hat popped off his head.

The bullfighters moved in, escorting Tank from the arena. Beau grabbed his hat and saluted the cheering crowd then blew a kiss toward the stands where Sierra sat. The camera replayed his actions on the JumboTron before turning the lens on the blushing redhead.

"There you have it, folks!" the announcer shouted. "Beau Adams becomes the first cowboy this season to ride Tankulicious to eight!"

"Don't get a big head, Adams." Royce slapped Beau's back. The ranch hand had driven the stock trailer to the rodeo, and Beau and Sierra had followed in Beau's truck.

"I ripped that ride, didn't I?" The more wins Beau tucked under his belt before the Bash in November, the more confident he'd feel going into the event. He stuffed his gear into his bag and handed it to Royce. "Will you keep an eye on this for me? I'm going into the stands to get Sierra."

"Sure."

Beau tipped his hat to the fans who acknowledged his performance as he worked his way through the rows to Sierra's seat. When he reached her, he whispered, "Come with me." Taking her by the hand Beau walked out to the concourse, then pulled Sierra aside and kissed her.

Mmm...she tasted like honey. He backed her into a dark corner that afforded them more privacy. Even though the shadows hid them from rodeo fans he kept the kiss PG-rated—until Sierra melted against him and he captured her moan in his mouth. Her eagerness sucked him in and he deepened their embrace. Someone whistled and Sierra ended the kiss, burying her face against his neck.

Her lips nuzzled his skin, and Beau imagined waking each morning with her cuddled in his arms, limbs entwined, their quiet breathing filling the room. Eventually, they'd have to start their day and open their eyes—one pair seeing...the other pair left in the dark.

The abrupt thought startled Beau and he stepped back. Cheers from the fans and the announcer's voice faded into the background as Sierra threaded her fingers through his hair, coaxing him to push aside thoughts of the future and focus on the here and now.

"That was some congratulatory kiss," he murmured.

"Better than others you've received, I hope?"

"What others?"

She playfully punched his arm.

"How would you like to watch the last few bull rides down by the chutes?"

"I'd love to see the action up close," she said.

Holding Sierra's hand, Beau led her through the

throng of competitors in the cowboy-ready area. He tightened his grip, guiding her around a maze of cowboy gear bags and saddles on the ground. When they reached Bushwhacker, he kept Sierra close at his side.

"Beau," she whispered. "You're squeezing too hard."

"Sorry." He relaxed his arm around her. "Sometimes Bushwhacker kicks out in the chute." Instead of appreciating his concern, Sierra moved away from him.

Beau didn't have time to figure out what he'd done to deserve her cold shoulder when the chute door opened and Bushwhacker exploded into the arena. Just as in the previous rodeo, the bull gave his best effort and the cowboy went airborne at the three-second mark. Two rides later, Back Bender had the same success in the arena. Now it was time to see what Asteroid would do in his first rodeo.

Asteroid left the chute running. *Buck, Asteroid, buck.* The bull ducked to the right so suddenly that the cowboy landed on his rump in the dirt.

"Crap," Beau grumbled.

"What happened?" Sierra stood on tiptoe to gain a better view of the arena.

"Asteroid was a dink."

"What's that?"

"A dink is a bull that doesn't buck."

Royce approached Beau. "Looks like we've got our work cut out for us with Asteroid."

"Dad won't be happy when he hears about his performance." Beau turned to Sierra. "I need to help Royce load the bulls once they settle down."

"That's fine. I don't mind waiting."

Cowboys gathered up their gear while rodeo workers began to tear down the chutes and makeshift holding pens. Fifty yards away, a shoving match between two cowboys drew the attention of rodeo officials who broke up the fight. The cowboy-ready area was no place for a lady. "You'd better wait in the stands."

Sierra scowled.

Okay, so she didn't care to be told what to do. "Things get crazy down here after the rodeo, and I don't want you to get caught in the cross fire."

Her blue eyes turned icy. "See you later then."

Before Beau had a chance to escort her back to her seat, she stomped off. He watched her retreat, wincing when her foot tangled with the handle of an equipment bag. Thanks to the quick reflexes of a nearby cowboy who steadied Sierra, she was spared a possible injury from an embarrassing fall.

Stubborn woman.

Chapter 9

Beau slowed the truck as he drove down Main Street in Roundup. He pulled into the lot behind the diner then turned off the engine. "Thanks for coming along today." He stared longingly at the back door of the building, hoping Sierra would invite him inside for a late-night coffee.

She grappled for the door handle. "Congratulations on winning another buckle."

He didn't care about the buckle. Why was Sierra suddenly eager to end their day? Was she still upset with him for asking her to sit in the stands while he loaded the bulls? He hopped out of the truck, rounded the hood and opened the passenger door. He offered his hand but she ignored his help and walked toward the fire escape. Damn. He didn't want to end the day on a sour note.

He trailed her up the stairs and waited as she opened the apartment door, then stepped inside and gasped.

Beau's first thought was that a burglar had broken in. Bracing for a confrontation, he pushed past Sierra. The intruder turned out to be his father—locked in a passionate embrace with Sierra's aunt. "Sorry for interrupting." Beau wondered whose face was redder— his or his father's? Despite everyone's embarrassment, Beau found his father's predicament amusing. He'd never seen the old man with his shirttail hanging out and his hair mussed.

"Sierra's home." Beau's father attempted to straighten his clothes then gave up, scowling at Beau as he retrieved his coat from the back of the chair.

"I thought you'd be gone longer, Sierra." Jordan smoothed a hand down her slacks.

"I'm tired," Sierra said. "I enjoyed the rodeo, Beau, thanks for taking me." She waltzed into her bedroom and shut the door.

So much for ending the date on a positive note. "How was the ballet?" Beau asked.

"Wonderful," Jordan said.

"Bushwhacker and Back Bender both came out on top." When his father didn't inquire about Beau's ride, he said, "I won, too."

"Doesn't surprise me."

The backhanded compliment startled Beau. His father rarely praised his twins.

"Good night, Jordan." Beau waited outside on the fire escape while the older couple said goodbye. When his father stepped onto the landing, Beau grinned.

"Don't say a word."

They walked in silence to their trucks, then Beau followed his father back to the ranch. When they entered the kitchen, his dad said, "We need to talk." He filled the coffeemaker with water, flipped the switch and sat across the table from Beau.

"This is about Jordan, isn't it? You've got serious feelings for her," Beau said.

"No, this is about you and Sierra."

"What about us?"

"I thought I told you to keep your distance from her."

Swallowing an angry retort, Beau said, "What happens between Sierra and me isn't any of your business."

"Well, I'm making it mine because Jordan means..." His father's voice trailed off. He left the table and fetched a beer from the fridge.

"You just put a pot of coffee on."

"I need something stronger." His father twisted off the cap and took a long swallow.

"Jordan means what?" Beau asked.

"She means the world to me. If you hurt Sierra—"

"Last time I spoke with Jordan I got the impression she approved of me and Sierra dating." Beau struggled to understand his father's objections to his relationship with Sierra. Did a couple of dates and hot sex on a kitchen counter even constitute a relationship? "Sierra and I are grown adults capable of making our own decisions."

"Watch it, young man. You're treading on thin ice."

After the way the day with Sierra had ended, Beau was itching for a fight and his father appeared determined to oblige him. "You've got a lot of nerve assuming you know what's best for everyone when you were such a crappy dad." He expected his father to explode—when he didn't, Beau mumbled, "Sorry. I shouldn't have said that."

"No, you're right. I wasn't a good father."

Shocked his dad had owned up to the charge, the anger fizzled out of Beau. "Was it because of Mom's death?"

"I loved your mother." Then his father dropped a bombshell. "But I've always loved Jordan more."

"So you settled for Mom when Jordan left Roundup after high school."

"I held out for a while believing Jordan would come home, but she didn't."

"Did Mom know you felt this way about another woman?"

"Not in the beginning."

Oh, man, this didn't sound good. "When did Mom figure out you were still in love with Jordan?"

"Right after your second birthday."

"How?"

"She found a box of old love letters between Jordan and me, and guessed that I'd only proposed to her after I learned that Jordan had become engaged to another man."

"What did Mom do?"

"We argued and she left the house."

Beau felt light-headed. He'd heard many accounts of his mother's death from various people and family members, and all the stories had involved his mother driving in bad weather and her car sliding off the road and hitting a tree head-on.

"The fight happened the afternoon Mom died, didn't it?"

His father rested his face in his hands. "I can't tell you how many times a day I think about that moment and regret not stopping your mother from going out in that storm."

Wait until Duke heard the truth. "Did you tell Jordan?"

"No. And I'm not going to. It wasn't her fault, Beau. It was mine. I'm the one who couldn't let Jordan go all these years." The lines bracketing his father's mouth deepened and he looked every one of his fifty-eight years. "If I'd burned those letters...who knows, maybe your mother and I would still be married today."

His father had kept this secret to himself all these years and Beau couldn't imagine carrying around such a heavy burden.

"I take full blame for you and Duke having to grow up without a mother, and for that I am deeply sorry." The misery in his father's eyes conveyed his sincerity.

So many pieces of the puzzle finally fit together. Maybe later Beau would process his father's confession. "Jordan's not the same person you dated in high school. How can you be sure she's what you want this time around?"

"Jordan is the same spirited girl I fell head over heels for. The only difference is that she's blind. I'm the one who changed, and I'm humbled that Jordan still sees something worthwhile in me."

"Have you asked her to marry you?"

"No, but I've dropped several hints."

"And...?"

"She changes the subject."

"Why?"

"Jordan hasn't said as much, but I believe she's too worried about Sierra to think of herself right now." Beau remained silent and his father continued, "Promise me you'll stop leading Sierra on."

"How am I leading her on? I've taken her to a couple of rodeos. That's it." *And you've had sex with her. That's a lot.*

"Sierra's not the kind of girl you have a fling with, son."

"Whoa, hold on a minute. Who said anything about flings?" Had Sierra told her aunt they'd slept together?

"Just keep your pants zipped."

"Why should things be any different for Sierra and me? You're dating a woman who's already blind."

"That's right. I know what I'm getting into. You don't. There's no telling how long it will take for Sierra to lose her sight completely—could be a few years or three decades."

"So?"

"So…that means Sierra will be riding an emotional roller coaster for years, and that kind of stress can ruin a relationship."

"I get it now. You want me to quit dating Sierra so you can move forward with your plans for you and Jordan."

"You're making me sound selfish."

"If the shoe fits." Beau shoved his chair back and stormed out of the house. As much as his father's advice offended him, he conceded the old man was right about one thing—Beau had to decide where he stood with Sierra. He couldn't continue to ask her out on dates, flirt with her and maybe have sex with her again unless he was willing to stand by her through good, bad and blindness.

At half-past one in the morning, Beau's cell phone went off. He'd thrown himself into working on the Phillips' saddle, the task taking his mind off the conversation with his father, and he'd lost track of time. He checked the number. *Duke*.

"What's wrong?" Beau asked when he answered the call.

"It's Sierra."

The blood drained from Beau's face. He'd dropped her off at her apartment a few hours ago—what could have happened between then and now that would involve a deputy sheriff? "Is she okay?"

"She's more than fine at the moment, but I doubt she'll be feeling too chipper in the morning."

"Hell, Duke, Sierra's either okay or she's not. What's going on?"

"I got a call from Ted Malone over at the Open Range Saloon. Sierra's tearing up the dance floor."

Beau had never run into Sierra at the Open Range, or any other bar in Roundup. "Are you sure it's Sierra?"

"Oh, I'm sure. I'm at the bar right now watching her line dance by herself." Duke sounded worried. "She's had an awful lot to drink, Beau. She shouldn't drive home."

Sierra had driven her car after dark? Why would she do something so reckless—even though the bar wasn't far from the diner? "I'm on my way."

"You might want to hurry."

"Why's that?"

"Some cowboy's hitting on her and it looks like she might leave the bar with him."

"Arrest her if you have to, but don't let Sierra out of your sight." Beau disconnected the call and raced from the barn. The drive to the Open Range took twenty minutes going ten miles over the speed limit and he pulled into the lot behind the bar right at closing time. Two trucks, Duke's patrol car and Sierra's SUV, sat parked near the back entrance.

Having no idea what to expect, Beau braced himself when he entered the bar. As his eyes adjusted to the dim interior, he scanned the room. Only die-hard boozers closed a bar down, but the few patrons sucking on last-call drinks appeared harmless. Then Beau's gaze shifted across the room and he spotted Sierra's image in the wall-length mirror behind the mahogany bar. She was draped like a tablecloth over a cowboy who didn't look familiar to Beau. He took a step in their direction but Duke cut him off. "Ted said Sierra's snockered."

"What's she been drinking?"

Duke grinned. "You sure you want to know?"

"Tell me."

"Let's see—" Duke counted off his fingers "—she's had a Sex on the Beach, a Between the Sheets, a French Kiss and a Screaming Orgasm. Followed by a Slippery Nipple. The drink in her hands right now is a Slow Screw." Duke checked his watch. "All since eleven-thirty when she walked into the place."

Holy crap. Sierra had gone off the deep end. Beau walked toward the couple, his boot heels sticking to the hardwood floor. He tapped the cowboy on the shoulder. "Excuse me. That's my girl you're holding."

The cowboy's glazed eyes told Beau he'd already passed his booze limit.

"Hey." The cowboy shook Sierra's shoulder. "This your guy?"

Sierra lifted her head and smiled. "Beau?"

"In the flesh."

She shook her head, then rested her forehead on the cowboy's shoulder and muttered, "I'm not his girl."

"She says she's not your girl. That makes her my girl." The cowboy tipped Sierra's chin and stared her in the eye. "You wanna go back to my place, sugar?"

The endearment grated on Beau's nerves. Aware of Duke standing by ready to intervene, he said, "She's not going anywhere with you, buddy. You're both drunk."

"Party pooper," Sierra said. She crawled out of the guy's lap and took Beau's hand. "I wanna show you something." She led him to the empty dance floor, but stopped when she noticed Duke. "When did you get here?" she asked.

"Almost an hour ago."

"Oh. You wanna dance with us?"

"I'm not really into threesomes."

Beau jabbed his elbow into his brother's gut.

"I'm going to teach Beau how to line dance." She tugged him to the center of the floor. "It's called the Tush Push." She swayed and Beau's hand shot out to steady her. She rubbed her head and looked disoriented.

"Get ready, she's going down," Duke warned.

"First, you step like this." Sierra moved left, then right, then spun and fainted dead away in Beau's arms.

"Need help?" Duke asked.

"Nope." Beau swung Sierra over his shoulder in a fireman's carry. With her fanny sticking high in the air, he marched toward the exit.

"Don't forget her purse," Ted hollered from behind the bar.

Beau switched directions and returned to the bar where the saloon owner held out the black clutch.

"Arlene coaxed Sierra to let her keep it after her third drink."

"Thanks." At least Ted's wife had looked out for Sierra tonight. Any crazy fool could have stolen her purse and she'd never have known it. Duke held the door open for Beau and followed him to his truck. Beau set Sierra in the front seat and snapped the belt around her, then shut the door.

"Appreciate you telling me what was going on with Sierra," Beau said.

"If you want, I can lock you two up for the night in one of the jail cells."

That wasn't a bad idea. If the good folks of Roundup learned Sierra had gotten hammered and spent the night in lockup she'd be less inclined to tie one on again. "Thanks, but I'll sit with her in the diner tonight in case she gets sick."

"Good luck." Duke got into his patrol car and drove off.

Soft snores filled the cab as Beau drove down Main Street. When he parked behind the diner, he searched through Sierra's purse for her keys then turned off the truck. He stared at the fire escape, wondering if he should wake Jordan and ask her to keep an eye on Si-

erra. No. Beau wanted to remain at Sierra's side through
the night—for his own peace of mind.

Once he'd carried her into the diner, Beau set her in
a booth. She slumped over and his quick reflexes caught
her right before she banged her forehead on the table-
top. He propped her against the wall next to the booth
then tucked her legs beneath her before retrieving one
of the plastic tubs used for bussing tables. He placed
the tub in front of Sierra then put on a pot of coffee and
sat in the booth with her.

The wait began. At three o'clock Sierra sat up straight
and slapped a hand over her mouth. Beau moved the
dishpan closer and they were off—round one of a tri-
ple-header. The next few hours were spent rinsing out
the dishpan and mopping Sierra's forehead with a cool
cloth. Around five in the morning he offered her a soda
cracker, but she refused.

Noise woke Beau at 6:00 a.m. He shifted in the
booth, the left side of his body numb where Sierra was
draped across him. Her hair was a tangled rat's nest,
her mascara smudged and her lips pale. She looked terrible but Beau's heart swelled with emotion. He set her
aside and slid from the booth.

"Morning, Irene," Beau said when he stepped into
the kitchen.

"She get plowed last night?" Irene's eyes twinkled.

"I guess you could say she had a little too much fun."

"Heard she was dancing up a storm at the Open
Range."

By noon the entire town would know about Sierra's
drinking binge.

"You take Sierra upstairs and put her to bed. I can manage the morning shift."

"You sure, Irene?"

"Positive. That girl works way too hard. I'm glad she's letting her hair down and enjoying herself for a change."

Enjoying herself? Sierra's reckless behavior worried Beau. What if Duke hadn't been called to the bar to check on her—would she have gone home with a stranger? The thought of Sierra waking up in another man's bed sent a surge of anger through Beau. He might not have any legitimate claim on Sierra but they'd made love, and in his mind that gave him at least a right to some answers.

Beau parked his pickup in front of his aunt's house Sunday morning at 7:30 a.m. Even though he was dead tired after watching over Sierra, he looked forward to riding Midnight. Hopefully the stallion would take Beau's mind off the crazy stunt Sierra had pulled last night.

"You ready to rock-n-roll, Midnight?" Beau stood outside the horse's stall. All was quiet in the barn— Gracie and her boys were still at church.

The stallion eyed him warily but didn't object to being led into the adjoining corral. The moment Beau released him, the horse circled the enclosure, snorting clouds of white steam into the cold morning air.

After retrieving the bareback rigging and flank strap he'd brought in his truck, Beau returned to the corral and allowed Midnight to sniff the gear. The stallion threw his head back then raced to the opposite end of the enclosure.

The next fifteen minutes were spent rearranging the fencing panels until Beau had constructed a makeshift chute. Since he didn't have a helper, he didn't bother with a gate. The only problem with his plan was that he'd have to back Midnight into the chute; the horse might balk at the unfamiliar routine.

"Ready, boy?"

Midnight took off, bucking. His high-arching kicks would make any seasoned rodeo cowboy nervous. Once he calmed, Beau approached with the gear then walked backward toward the chute. Midnight followed him.

The sweet purr of a diesel engine met Beau's ears. Colt parked his truck in the drive. "Are you doing what I think you're doing?" he asked in a hushed whisper as he approached the corral.

"Yep."

Colt grinned when he noticed Beau's predicament. "Need a little help?"

"Looks that way."

"Got any ideas on how you're going to get that horse to back himself up?"

"Nope. You?"

"Maybe." Colt walked Midnight forward then stopped him when the stallion's back end aligned with the opening. He then placed his palm on the horse's chest and pushed firmly. Midnight didn't budge. When Colt removed his hand, the stallion backed himself slowly into the enclosure, stopping when his rump nudged the rails.

"I'll be damned," Beau said. "Think Ace'll believe this when we tell him?"

"I doubt it." Colt glanced at Beau. "Does my mom know you're working with Midnight?"

"Yep."

"She always let you and Duke get away with the same shit she raked me and Ace over the coals for."

Beau chuckled. "That's because we didn't have a mom."

"Better quit yammering and ride. Midnight won't stay in there forever."

Once they secured the flank strap and rigging around the stallion, Beau climbed the rails and settled onto Midnight's back. Satisfied with his grip, he said, "I'm ready."

Midnight didn't flinch, so Beau pressed his knees against the stallion's sides. Nothing. "What's he waiting for?"

Colt backed up slowly. "I've got an idea. Hold tight." He hurried into the barn then returned with a pitchfork.

"You planning to jab him in the butt to get him to move?"

"Ready?" Colt lifted the rake toward the top rail of the pen and clanged it against the metal.

Midnight bolted at the sound, vaulting from the chute and almost unseating Beau. He didn't have time to think about anything but hanging on for dear life. As soon as he got a little cocky, believing he might outlast Midnight, the horse went into a spin that sent Beau flying. He landed hard, but rolled to his feet, grinning. "Whew! Did you see that, Colt?"

"Don't get a big head, hoss. That was far from Midnight's best effort." Colt patted his cousin on the back. "My turn."

When the men glanced across the corral, Midnight was already standing near the chute. "He's a competitor, that's for sure," Beau said.

"He needs practice with a real chute. Next time we'll rig up something better."

"As long as Ace doesn't find out," Beau reminded his cousin.

"Don't worry, he won't."

Beau wasn't as confident that they could keep their secret from Ace. His older cousin had a sixth sense about things and eyes in the back of his head. Beau just hoped that when Ace did find out, he wouldn't blow a gasket.

Chapter 10

By Wednesday afternoon Sierra had survived the worst of the inquiries about her excursion to the Open Range Saloon. Of course people would speculate that she'd gone off the deep end when she rarely visited the bars. Gossip aside, what bothered Sierra most about her night on the town was the fact that Beau had whisked her out of the bar as if he'd been her keeper.

Okay, so she'd found out from Irene, who'd been told by Dinah, who'd spoken to Ted the bartender, that Sierra had passed out in Beau's arms on the dance floor. And maybe she should appreciate that Beau had taken her back to the diner and sat with her through the wee morning hours while she'd tossed her cookies, but Sierra hadn't asked for Beau's help and she resented his interference.

Just because they'd had sex didn't mean they were a

couple. Beau had no right to decide what was best for her. Besides, it wasn't like she was going to make a habit of partying at the bars. Her night at the Open Range had been a one-time thing—a chance to let her hair down and release the stress that had been building inside her for months. She'd already moved on from that night, making plans to tackle the first item on her bucket list.

The diner door opened and the thorn in her side waltzed in. Beau's gaze clashed with hers and she felt her face warm—not from embarrassment but because the man was too darn sexy for his own good. She hadn't phoned Beau after she'd recovered from her hangover, because he'd been the last person she'd wanted to explain her actions to.

Regardless, she owed Beau an obligatory *thank you* even if she hadn't asked for his assistance. He took a seat at the lunch counter and she grabbed a white mug and the coffeepot. She poured his coffee then choked the words out. "Thank you for taking care of me Saturday night."

"I was surprised when Duke said you were having a rip-roaring time at the bar."

Sierra didn't care to discuss her private business in front of customers so she changed the subject. "Are you eating?"

"No. I just stopped by to see you." His mouth curved in a smile.

Even as her heart sighed, Sierra straightened her shoulders and jutted her chin. She couldn't allow Beau to sneak past her defenses because she knew there was no future for them.

"I also wanted to invite you to a rodeo this coming

Saturday. It's a small event in Bridger. I won't be haul-ing any Thunder Ranch bulls, so I thought we'd stop for dinner afterward."

No more rodeos. The last thing she wanted was more of Beau's hovering. Besides, she already had plans for Saturday afternoon. "I'm sorry. I can't."

The sparkle in Beau's eyes dimmed. "I'll bring you straight home after I compete."

"I appreciate the offer, but—"

"I'll help Irene, Sierra." Her aunt stood by the kitchen door, wearing yellow latex gloves covered in soap suds.

Sierra held her tongue and counted to ten for fear she'd shout at everyone to back off and give her a little breath-ing room. "Thanks, Aunt Jordan, but no." Good grief, she'd spent all Sunday in bed with the dry heaves. She couldn't afford to play hooky for an entire day, but unbe-knownst to her aunt, Sierra was taking the afternoon off.

Beau's big brown eyes studied Sierra and she almost changed her mind. The memory of their lovemaking still haunted her when she crawled into bed. Reliving the inti-mate moments they'd shared made her yearn for a future with Beau, but common sense intervened. She'd stick with her own plans—much safer for her heart. Sierra mo-tioned to the menu lodged between the condiment bottles. "Let me know if you change your mind about eating." Steeling herself against the hurt look on his face, she re-treated to the kitchen where she remained until Beau left.

"Got a minute?" Beau poked his head inside the door of the sheriff's department and waited for Duke to glance up from the file in front of him.

"Sure." Duke set aside the paperwork and walked over to the watercooler. "Thirsty?"

"No, thanks." Beau slouched in the chair facing his brother's desk. His ego had taken a beating after Sierra's brush-off a few minutes ago and he was too agitated to drive home. He motioned to the file his brother had been reading. "What's the latest report on crime in the area?"

"Investigating a broken window out at widow Haney's house. Dinah believes the widow slammed her storm door too hard and it cracked the glass. Mrs. Haney claims she's been targeted by Roundup's hooligans."

"Mrs. Haney likes to stir up trouble because she's bored and doesn't have anyone to henpeck since her husband died," Beau said.

"You're right, but Dinah's got a soft heart. She'll jump through hoops for Mrs. Haney and talk to the schoolkids."

"Speaking of broken windows...remember those slingshots Dad made for us when we kids?" Beau said.

"Aunt Sarah was so pissed after we broke her kitchen window."

"And she really got riled when we told her we'd been aiming for the bird on the ledge."

"Boy, did Dad get a dressing-down from his sister."

"Joshua, if you let those boys attack innocent birds they'll be aiming at people before you know it." Beau mimicked their aunt's voice. "Who knew Aunt Sarah had a soft spot for yellow-bellied sapsuckers?"

"I don't think I said two words to Aunt Sarah for a month after Dad hid the slingshots," Duke said.

A stilted silence followed and Beau squirmed in his seat.

"Trouble in paradise?" Duke quirked an eyebrow. "If you need any advice—"

Beau scoffed. "Just because you found your better half and settled down doesn't mean you're an expert on male-female relationships." The urge to unload on Duke was tempting, but Beau wasn't used to seeking his brother's counsel. Most of their lives Beau had been the one to defend and protect Duke's feelings. Beau changed the subject to one Duke was always eager to discuss—their father. "Had a long chat with Dad the other night."

"That so?"

"I guess it was more of an argument than a discussion."

"What happened?"

"Sierra and I walked in on him and Jordan kissing." Beau grinned. "Dad's shirt was untucked."

"I've never seen Dad so preoccupied. It's like he's someone else, not the man who raised us." Duke rested his feet on the corner of the desk and leaned back in his chair. "What did the two of you bicker over?"

Beau left out the part about being warned way from Sierra—he hated to believe his own father would put his happiness ahead of his son's. Heck, it might not even matter anymore… Beau had a feeling Sierra was pulling away from him and he felt powerless to prevent it from happening. "We talked about Mom."

Duke's eyes rounded.

"Dad confessed that he never loved Mom the way he loves Jordan. He said he proposed to Mom after he heard that Jordan had gotten engaged to another man."

"Jeez. Poor Mom. Good thing she had no idea Dad had betrayed her."

"She knew."

Duke sat up straight, his boots hitting the floor with a thud. "What?"

"Mom found Dad's love letters to Jordan and figured it out on her own."

"How did Mom react?"

Beau stared at his brother for several seconds, communicating without words.

"The car accident," Duke whispered.

"They got into an argument over the letters and Mom stormed out of the house."

"Dad didn't try to stop her?"

"No."

"Unbelievable." Duke sprang from his chair and paced across the room.

"Dad feels pretty bad about what happened and he blames himself for us growing up without a mother."

"No wonder he's always been a curmudgeon. Must have been hell living with all that guilt," Duke said. "Do you think they would have stayed married if Mom hadn't died?"

"Who knows? In any event, Dad's determined not to waste his second chance with Jordan."

"Did he say they're getting married?" Duke asked.

"No, but I think it's only a matter of time before he proposes to her. I figure Dad's slacking off is going to be the norm from now on."

"I never pictured the old man marrying again, did you?"

"No." Beau hesitated, feeling awkward, then asked, "Was it tough for you to give up rodeo for Angie?"

"Not as much as I'd believed it would be. I was used to being on the road a lot and I worried I'd miss all the excitement if I stayed in one place."

"What changed your mind?"

Duke smiled. "When you love a woman with all your heart you realize pretty quick you don't want to be away from her for very long."

"And fatherhood? You were thrown into that role and didn't have much time to get used to the idea."

"I love Luke. We're kindred spirits. He's a lot like me when I was younger."

"Do you and Angie want more kids?"

"Why all the questions?" Duke asked. "You didn't get Sierra pregnant, did you?"

"Hell, no!" A flashback of Sierra's sexy sprawl on the stainless-steel counter shot through Beau's brain and he swallowed hard. They'd used a condom… He shook his head. Sierra wouldn't have gone on a drinking binge if there had been a chance she was pregnant.

"My turn to be nosey," Duke said. "Did Sierra ever tell you what Saturday night was all about?"

Embarrassed and hurt that Sierra had shut him out after they'd made love, he said, "I don't have any claim on Sierra. She's free to party and have a good time if she wants."

"For someone who's laid back about your relationship you sure rushed to her rescue at the bar."

"I care about Sierra and wanted to make sure she got home safe." And Beau hadn't been about to let her go home with another man.

"It isn't any of my business what's going on between

you and your lady love," Duke said, "but I'm going to speak my mind."

Turnabout was fair play. Beau had blistered Duke's ears earlier in the summer when his brother had quit rodeo. "I'm listening."

"Angie's a strong, independent, stubborn woman."

"So is Sierra," Beau said.

"Then beware. Don't let a woman's strength fool you into believing her heart can't be broken. The last thing Sierra needs is a man to bail on her when the going gets tough."

And the going would get tough…a little more each and every day. "Warning received." Beau headed for the door and Duke followed him outside.

"Are you riding anywhere this weekend?"

"Bridger."

"Is Dad going?"

"What do you think?"

"He's spending time with Jordan."

Beau nodded.

"He'd better not call me for help. Angie's got a fix-it list a mile long waiting for me to tackle."

"Good luck with that." Beau moseyed down the block to his parked truck. He glanced across the street as he passed the diner and watched Sierra move about the tables, talking to her customers. Maybe she needed time to come to terms with the doctor's diagnosis.

He'd give her space, but that didn't mean he had to like it.

Sierra's bucket list rested on the passenger seat of the car as she drove through Billings early Saturday afternoon. According to the GPS she was within a mile of the Yellowstone Drag Strip. She was nervous yet excited about her first time drag racing. Yellowstone Drag Strip advertised weekend specials, which included a half-hour instruction class, three practice runs in a race car with an instructor, then two drag races against an opponent. The package cost Sierra $350 but she didn't bat an eyelash at the amount. She spent little money on clothes and she rarely treated herself to manicures or pedicures, so she had plenty of money in her savings to finance her bucket list.

Ever since her father had taken her to a real drag-racing event when she'd been a little girl, the sport had fascinated Sierra. She remembered loving the loud rumble of the powerful car engines and the incredible speed at which the cars traveled. One day in the not-too-distant future she'd have to give up her driver's license, but today she intended to race the wind.

The building came into view and the GPS directed Sierra to turn onto a frontage road, which emptied into a crowded parking lot. After finding a parking spot she entered the building and filled out a packet of forms. She fudged on the health questions—who needed perfect eyesight to steer a car in a straight line? Once she paid her fee, she was loaned a driver's suit and helmet then introduced to her instructor—a woman named Mandy. Mandy asked about Sierra's driving experience and she confessed that she'd never driven a vehicle with a larger motor than a six-cylinder engine. Mandy escorted Sierra and three others to a small classroom where they watched a video on racing safety then stowed their belongings in lockers, put on their driving suits and walked out to the racetrack behind the building.

Heart pounding with excitement, Sierra wished Beau wasn't so overprotective. She would have loved to have invited him along today so they could have raced each other on the track.

Beau had just entered Billings when flurries hit the windshield. He fumbled with the radio until he found a weather report—sleet changing to snow with a possible two-inch accumulation—nothing unusual for late October in Montana. What *was* unusual was that the TV weatherman the previous evening had forecast clear skies with clouds rolling in after midnight and a slight chance of flurries by morning. Must be nice to have a job where you got paid whether you were right or wrong.

His cell phone rang and Beau recognized his father's number. Now what? The old man never called to ask how Beau did in his rodeos. "What's up, Dad?"

"Where are you?"

"Just entered Billings, why?"

"It's Sierra."

Beau's stomach dropped. He changed lanes then turned into a business and shifted into Park. "What's going on?"

"Jordan's worried about Sierra. She left this afternoon to go into Billings but said she'd be back by five."

Beau glanced at the dashboard clock—five-thirty. Why was Sierra in Billings? He'd thought she'd had to work in the diner all day. "Did Jordan try Sierra's cell phone?"

"Of course she did. Sierra's not answering."

Anger competed with worry. "What do you want me to do, Dad?"

"Sierra scribbled an address on a piece of paper that Irene found. Plug it into your GPS and see if she's there."

This coming from the man who'd told him to keep his distance from Sierra? Beau grabbed a pen from the glove box and used the back of a fast-food bag to write down the address his father recited. "I'll let you know what I find out." He disconnected the call, entered the information into his GPS, then left the parking lot and merged with traffic. Ten minutes later he pulled into the Yellowstone Drag Strip, figuring his father had transposed the numbers in the address.

When he stepped into the building and asked if a Sierra Byrne had been there, a young kid pointed to the exit that led outside to the track. "She's got one more race. She had trouble with her car and it put her behind schedule."

When Beau left the building, a blast of cold air hit him in the face. The snow was falling harder and the wind gusts were stronger—not the safest racing conditions. Beau searched for Sierra, but the pit area was empty. Then he heard the sound of revving engines and jogged around the side of the building where two race cars—one red and one black—gunned their engines. A woman stood on the side of the track holding a flag. God help him—was Sierra driving one of the cars?

Before Beau came to grips with the possibility, the woman waved the flag and race-car wheels spun against the slick pavement before lurching forward onto the straightaway. The black car edged out the red one as they neared the finish line, then the red car put the brakes on too hard and fishtailed. The driver over-corrected, sending the car careening into a blockade. Rubber tires spewed into the air then rained down on the car. The flag woman hurried toward the wreck.

Beau's boots remained rooted to the cement and his heart pounded so hard it hurt. Eyes glued to the red car, he held his breath as he waited for the driver's door to open. The driver emerged from the car and removed his—her helmet. *Sierra*. Beau was too far away to hear the conversation between the drivers and the instructor, but the smile on Sierra's face assured Beau that she hadn't been injured. When her gaze landed on Beau, the smile vanished and her solemn stare punched him in the gut. He retreated inside the building to wait for Sierra and for his heart to stop pounding like a jackhammer.

"What are you doing here?" Sierra asked Beau when she emerged from the locker room twenty minutes later.

Acting as if finding Sierra drag racing was an everyday occurrence took more effort than Beau imagined. He kept his distance from her, fearing if he got too close he'd hug her so hard she'd suffocate. As far as he could tell there wasn't a scratch on her, so why the heck did he feel light-headed?

"My father called when I was on my way home from the rodeo in Bridger. Your aunt was worried when you didn't answer your cell phone. Jordan wanted to warn you about the storm heading this way."

"So you had to run to my rescue?"

Rescue was a bit harsh. "Your aunt was worried."

"I don't need your help, Beau."

Okay, now he was angry. "It's dark outside and the

snow's falling harder. How did you plan to get back to Roundup tonight when you're not allowed to drive in the dark?"

"I listened to the weather forecast yesterday and the snow was supposed to hold off until late tonight." She motioned to the exit that led to the track. "I didn't count on there being a problem with the race car. That delayed my start time or else I would have been on my way home well before now."

Beau was ticked that Sierra was acting as if her decision to drag race wasn't a big deal when in his mind it was a *very* big deal. She had no business engaging in activities that put her in danger. "What's your game plan now?"

"I guess I'll find a motel room." She narrowed her eyes.

"Who's going to drive you to the motel from here and bring you back in the morning to get your car?"

Her chin rose higher. "I'll take a cab," she said, then retrieved her cell phone from her purse.

"C'mon." He clutched her arm. "Let's get out of here." All he wanted was to keep Sierra safe and sound with him. He helped her into his truck then drove through Billings. The snow flurries turned to sleet, freezing on the pavement. Traffic slowed to a crawl and Beau realized there was no way he could make the drive to Roundup safely tonight. He was stuck in Billings, too.

Suddenly the driver in front of him slammed on the brakes and spun into the fast lane. Sierra gasped and Beau white-knuckled the steering wheel as he watched the driver narrowly escaped a collision. Before Beau's heartbeat returned to normal, a second car hit a patch of black ice and slid through a red light. That driver wasn't as fortunate. A pickup slammed into the passenger-side door.

"That's it," Beau said when he noticed the motel across the street. He signaled and switched lanes then pulled into the parking lot. "We're both getting a motel room for the night."

Chapter 11

"Will you call your aunt and let her know we're staying in Billings tonight?" Beau pulled behind a line of cars checking into the Holiday Inn Express. The place was filling up fast and he worried they wouldn't get a room.

Sierra pressed the speed-dial number on her phone. "Aunt Jordan, it's Sierra." Pause. "I'm fine. Beau and I are waiting out the storm in Billings."

Beau noticed Sierra neglected to tell her aunt that they were getting a motel room or that she'd been drag racing this afternoon.

"I'll be back first thing in the morning," she said.

Now that Sierra was cooperating with his plan, the anxiety in Beau's gut eased. He'd never forget the sickly feeling he'd gotten when her race car had careened into the pile of tires. At least tonight he'd have peace of mind knowing she was safe with him and not out somewhere pulling another daredevil stunt.

"Please see if Karla or Irene will open the diner tomorrow," Sierra said. "I promise. Love you, too. Bye."

"Promise what?" Beau asked after she disconnected the call.

"Aunt Jordan said to thank you for helping me—her words, not mine."

Jordan might be grateful to Beau for rescuing her niece, but Sierra sure wasn't appreciative. Beau didn't understand this new pattern of risky behavior Sierra was engaging in, and he was clueless as to how to help her through this tough time. The one thing he knew for sure was that if she continued pulling these stunts his hair would turn gray before his next birthday. A guest exited the motel, and as soon as he drove off Beau took his parking spot.

"How did you do at the rodeo?" Sierra asked.

"Not good. Monstrosity kicked my butt." Once Beau had been thrown, the bull had continued to buck and his hoof had caught Beau on the hip. The force of the blow had sent him flying through the air a second time.

"I'm sorry."

"You should be. It was your fault I got thrown in the first place," he said.

"Me? How did I cause you to fall off the bull?"

"Cowboys don't fall off bulls...they get bucked off."

"Whatever." She waved a hand. "Why is it my fault that you lost?"

Tell her the truth. "I was preoccupied before, during and after my ride."

"By what?"

Not what—who. "I couldn't stop thinking about you."

Sierra dropped her gaze to her lap.

"If you'd agreed to go with me to the rodeo, I wouldn't have had trouble concentrating." Because he would have known Sierra was sitting in the stands while he'd been in the cowboy-ready area. Instead, he'd thought about her recent excursion to the Open Range and had worried about her change in behavior. After seeing what she was up to today he had a right to be concerned.

"Beau…"

"What?"

"Just because we…slept together doesn't mean you have a say in what I do with my life."

Her words shouldn't have hurt, but they did. He was looking out for Sierra's best interests, but anything he said right now would only upset her. He reached for the door handle. "Wait here while I check on availability."

When the truck door shut, Sierra breathed a sigh of relief. Her knight in shining armor had rescued her again and she didn't like it, not one darn bit. Her thrilling afternoon had ended on a sour note—being stuck in a motel room with Beau interrogating her wasn't on her bucket list.

Fifteen minutes later, receipt in hand, Beau drove to the lot behind the motel and parked.

"I guess they had rooms left," she said.

"Room. We got the last one."

"Double beds?"

"One king-size." He turned off the engine. "And I'm warning you right now, I starfish in bed."

"What do you mean, you starfish?" she asked when he opened her door.

"I sleep with my arms and legs spread apart."

Their room was located next to the exit on the first floor. Beau inserted the key card into the lock, opened the door and flipped on the lights. Ever the gentleman, he allowed Sierra to enter first.

"I'll call the front desk for a roll-away," she said.

"Already asked." Beau shut the door and secured the locks. "All the cots are taken." He walked farther into the room and adjusted the heater. "The desk clerk recommended the burger joint across the street. I'll head over and get us dinner."

She wasn't hungry but the scowl on Beau's face warned her not to be difficult. "I'll have a cheeseburger, small fries and a diet cola."

"Lock up after me."

Sierra shut the door and slid the safety chain into place, then hurried into the bathroom and washed her delicates in the sink with the motel shampoo. Afterward, she spread them to dry on the heater then returned to the bathroom to shower. She raised her face to the hot spray and closed her eyes.

If anyone had told her how this day would end—her and Beau sharing a motel room and a king-size bed—she would have insisted they were crazy. As much as Beau's overprotectiveness annoyed her, she still found him sexy as sin. Thank goodness she was still upset with Beau—at least she didn't have to worry about jumping the cowboy's bones.

Sex would only complicate their relationship. Sex led to expectations. Commitment. Taking the other person into account when making decisions. Right now Sierra only wanted to worry about herself.

She finished her shower and wrapped herself in a towel. Once her skivvies dried, she'd slip on her street clothes again. Sleeping in jeans and an itchy turtleneck wouldn't be comfortable, but there was a price to pay for having too much fun. Tightening the towel she slid beneath the bed covers and turned on the TV. In a matter of minutes, she became engrossed in a cooking show and lost track of time.

A knock on the door startled her. "Just a minute!" She crawled from the bed, adjusted the towel then checked the peephole. The image in the hallway was bleary. "Beau, is that you?"

"Yeah, it's me."

Keeping the safety latch secured she peeked through the open door. The two-inch gap provided enough light for her to make out Beau's features.

She opened the door and he stepped into the room and secured the locks. When he turned around, his eyes widened. Sierra backpedaled until her legs bumped the mattress, then she tugged self-consciously at the edge of the towel.

"I don't have a change of clothes with me," she mumbled. Beau attempted to look away, but his gaze strayed to her and Sierra silently cursed the tingle that raced through her.

"I asked the front-desk clerk for toothbrushes and toothpaste." He moved closer, tossing the travel-sized toiletries on the bed along with his duffel, then he set the fast-food bag on the table in the corner. "I carry a change of clothes with me when I rodeo in case—"

"You end up stranded in a motel room with a woman?"

"Something like that." He removed a pearl-snapped

dress shirt from the leather bag and held it out to her. "This might be more comfortable to sleep in."

She clutched the material to her chest. "Thank you."

His mouth curved in a lopsided grin. "The shirt will look better on you than it does on me."

Sierra slipped into the bathroom, buried her nose in the cotton material and inhaled. The garment smelled like detergent and a little like Beau's sandalwood cologne. The shirttail ended an inch above her knees and covered all the important body parts. When she stepped from the bathroom she caught Beau in front of the heater, her pink panties dangling from his finger.

"Forget something?" he asked.

She snatched the silk from him and returned to the bathroom. A moment later she joined him at the table where he'd set out their food. "Thank you for picking up dinner."

They ate in silence, Sierra amused by Beau's intense interest in the cooking show. "You can change the channel, if you'd like."

"Doesn't matter to me." He crushed his hamburger wrapper into a tiny ball and tossed it inside the food bag before digging into his fries.

Finished with her meal, Sierra escaped to the bathroom to brush her teeth. When she came out, Beau was sitting on the end of the bed. "My turn?" he asked.

"It's all yours."

After the bathroom door shut, Sierra climbed into bed and turned down the volume on the TV, preferring to listen to the sound of the shower and fantasize about Beau's naked, wet body. For someone who wasn't planning on any hanky-panky tonight she was torturing herself with X-rated images. She pulled the blanket higher as if it would smother the smoldering desire building in her body. To make love with Beau or not... Sierra was debating the issue when he stepped from the bathroom wearing a skimpy towel around his waist.

"You okay?" He stopped next to the bed. "You're turning blue."

Sierra gasped, unaware she'd been holding her breath. Good Lord, Beau's naked chest was all muscle that rippled when he moved his arms. Her gaze followed the line of hair that ran down the middle of his chest and disappeared beneath the edge of the terry cloth. Her eyes drifted lower, skimming over the body part she knew from experience was as impressive as his chest.

Then he turned away and she hissed when she noticed the red-and-purple welt above his hip. "What happened?" She gently brushed her fingers over the swollen mark.

"The bull's hoof caught me."

"Shouldn't you see a doctor?"

"It's just a bruise."

His answer rubbed her the wrong way. "So you can tell me what I should and shouldn't do, but when someone gives you advice you discount it and do what you want?"

He frowned.

Sierra got to her knees on the bed and pointed her finger. "You might as well get it off your chest."

"I don't know what you're talking about."

"You disapproved of me drag racing today."

The muscle along his jaw bunched but Beau held his

tongue and that ignited Sierra's anger. "You think you know what's best for everyone but—"

"I don't take stupid chances."

"I wasn't taking a stupid chance. People drag race all the time and I had an instructor. I followed the rules and—"

"Ran the damned car off the track." He shoved a hand through his hair. "You could have been seriously injured."

She scoffed. "I hit a pile of rubber, and I wore a helmet and a safety harness."

"The car could have flipped over."

She sprang from the bed and paced across the carpet. "You're making a big deal out of it."

"And you're not making a big enough deal out of nothing."

A glare-down ensued. "You make me so mad I want to pull my hair out," she said.

"You make me so mad I want to kiss you."

They shouldn't. Not when they were angry. Not ever. Beau's towel slipped lower on his hips and Sierra sucked in a quiet breath.

Make love with Beau. She winced at the voice in her head. *You both want it.*

There was no mistaking the desire flashing in Beau's eyes.

It doesn't have to mean anything.

Her frustration with Beau taunted her to see how far she could push him, as if the exercise was sensual foreplay. "You owe me an apology," she said.

He crowded her space, his clean scent going to her

head. "If anyone should apologize, it's you for making people worry."

"I didn't ask you to worry about me."

"Too bad. I can't help it."

They stood toe-to-toe, his hot stare breaking through her defenses. "And I can't help this." She curled her hand around his neck and brought his mouth to hers. The kiss was hot and wet and wild. Her fingers dipped beneath the edge of the terry cloth and gently caressed his injured hip. She thought she heard Beau groan as she loosened the knot at the front of the towel. Bingo! The covering fell to the floor.

No turning back now.

"You look damned sexy in my shirt." He nibbled her neck.

"And you," she whispered. "Look sexy wearing nothing."

He released the top snap of the shirt and kissed her exposed flesh...popped open the next snap...another kiss...on and on until he set her whole body on fire.

"Leave the light on, Beau." This would be the final time they made love and Sierra wanted to experience every detail. One day she wouldn't be able to see Beau at all, so tonight she'd use all her other senses to commit him to memory. His taste...texture...scent...the sound of his breathing...then, when her eyes saw nothing but darkness, she'd recall this moment with Beau and remember it in vivid color.

Beau didn't care if they made love in the dark or bright sunlight. He didn't need to see Sierra's face to know she yearned for his touch. Her short gasp when he cupped her breast told him that she loved his hands on her. She curled a leg over the back of his thigh, aligning their bodies intimately and he groaned in her ear then sifted his fingers through her hair, messing the silky strands. He buried his nose in the scented cloud and walked her backward to the bed. "You smell incredible."

Her nails scraped his thigh, the tickling sensation intensifying his arousal. Her touch electrified his skin and he burned for her. Forget slow and easy.

They tumbled to the bed in a no-holds-barred race to the finish line.

The repetitive clicking sound coming from the room heater pushed its way into Beau's subconscious and he slowly awakened. His arms automatically tightened around the warm, naked body snuggled against his side. *Sierra.*

He smiled in the darkness. He and Sierra should argue more often if their spats ended in lovemaking. He found it incredibly sexy that she was a hellion in the bedroom and prim and proper in public—every man's fantasy wife.

Wife.

Wife meant marriage. Marriage meant a lifetime commitment.

He cared for Sierra a great deal and admitted his heart was heading full-steam ahead toward a deeper, lasting emotion. There was much he admired about her—the strength and courage she'd shown in the face of her parents' deaths. Moving her life to Roundup and starting a business. And what man wouldn't admire a woman with phenomenal cooking skills?

Beau even admitted—reluctantly—that he respected

Sierra's stubborn pride. Yet, if he was honest with himself, he'd admit that being with Sierra scared him. Pressure built inside his chest, making it difficult to draw a deep breath. He didn't want to have this conversation with himself, but the voice in his head insisted.

Sierra's going blind.

That didn't change the way he felt about her.

How will you feel ten or twenty years from now, when Sierra needs a seeing-eye dog and she can no longer drive or manage the diner?

Beau yearned to believe he'd adjust to her needs as the eye disease progressed.

What if you don't?

His chest ached when he considered how worried he'd been after his father had informed him that Jordan had been unable to contact Sierra. If he thought she was vulnerable now... Beau pressed his lips together, picturing a future with him hovering and Sierra frustrated by the boundaries he'd insist on setting for her—for his own sanity. And what about the times he couldn't be with her...couldn't warn her of impending danger?

He thought about his goal to win an NFR title. How would he handle being on the road and not knowing what Sierra was doing or if she'd gotten herself into a situation where she needed help? Rodeo took every ounce of concentration he possessed. Would concern about Sierra's safety lurk in the far reaches of his mind each time he climbed onto the back of a bull?

Would his constant worry wear them down and ruin their relationship? He didn't want Sierra waking up one morning and resenting him and the stranglehold he had on her.

Don't forget children.

What about his desire to be a father? Did Sierra want children, knowing she'd be blind one day? Beau thought of his brother, Duke, and his cousins who were starting families of their own. He didn't want to be left out of the experience. If he persuaded Sierra to have children, was *he* up to the challenge of taking on the child-rearing responsibilities she couldn't manage on her own?

He pondered the amount of time and energy parents invested in caring for their children. How would he manage if he had to help out more than most fathers?

"Beau...?" Sierra's lips brushed against his neck and he shivered.

"Shh..." He didn't know who he'd shushed—the pessimistic voice in his head or Sierra.

"You're squeezing me too hard."

"Sorry." Beau relaxed his hold.

Like a gentle breeze, her sigh floated past his ear, the sound blowing away his negative thoughts, leaving only a raw desire to make love to her again. He rolled Sierra beneath him and kissed her, not caring if she tasted his desperation. He lost himself in her scent, feel and taste, each kiss and caress marking her as his, as he sought reassurance where there was none.

In the aftermath of their lovemaking, Sierra listened to Beau's breathing transition from ragged to even and knew the moment he'd fallen asleep—the heavy weight of his arm relaxed across her chest, constricting her breathing. Carefully she moved his arm aside, slipped from the bed and retreated to the bathroom. After wrapping a towel around herself she sat on the edge of the tub and rested her face in her hands.

Was she crazy?

Don't answer that.

Why couldn't she have been stronger and resisted Beau? Now he was likely to believe he'd earned the right to tell her what to do and interfere in her life.

There would never be a better time in her life for exploring the things she'd always dreamed of doing, but Beau was like a big, tall boulder standing in her way.

As far as morning-afters went, Sierra and Beau's wasn't a big deal—at least that's the attitude *she* tried to convey. Sierra used the bathroom first, then watched the local news while Beau finished dressing. When he emerged from the bathroom, she said, "Sunny skies for the next few days and the roads are clear." She checked the time on her cell phone. "If we hurry, I can make it back to Roundup by nine."

"While you were in the bathroom earlier, my father called and invited us out to the ranch for brunch," Beau said.

"That was nice of him, but I have to get to the diner." Sierra didn't care to explain to anyone her spur-of-the-moment decision to drag race.

"Jordan made arrangements for Irene to work the whole day." Beau brushed a strand of hair from Sierra's cheek, his finger lingering against her skin, stirring her arousal. "We can spend the afternoon together," he said.

Sierra didn't want to take advantage of Irene, especially when she'd need her employee's loyalty in the future when Sierra's vision worsened. She cringed as she pictured herself struggling to find her way around the kitchen, experiment with new recipes and keep tabs on the diner's finances.

"I can't take the day off, Beau. I'll phone my aunt on the way to Roundup and let her know I won't be coming." The disappointment on Beau's face almost made Sierra change her mind.

He caressed her cheek, tilting her chin upward, then he kissed the sensitive patch of skin below her ear.

Knowing it wouldn't take much effort on his part to make her change her mind, Sierra said, "Beau, stop." She moved out of reach. "We can't… I'm not going to let… It's just that…" The emotions she'd tried to ignore when she'd woken this morning got the best of her and tears blurred her vision.

"What's wrong, honey?" He squeezed her shoulders.

"I can't think with you touching me." Sierra retreated to the other side of the room.

"That's a good thing, isn't it?" Beau's mouth curved in a sexy grin.

She didn't know where to begin, but she'd better figure it out quick or things would get out of hand and they'd end up back in bed. "We can't keep doing this."

"Doing what?"

"Having sex. We're just friends, remember?"

"I think we're more than friends, Sierra."

"No, last night was a mistake."

He jerked as if she'd slapped him. *Blast it.* This wasn't going well.

"What we shared was special."

"Be that as it may, my future is already mapped out for me, Beau."

"You enjoy being with me."

"Of course I've enjoyed your company." And making love…that had been off-the-charts enjoyable.

In two strides he gathered her in his arms. "What's got you running scared?"

It would be so easy to take a chance on Beau, but for her own survival she had to face the future alone. "In case you've forgotten, I'm going blind."

"Not for a long time."

She pressed her hands against Beau's chest, forcing a little space between them. Was he being obtuse on purpose or did he really view the two of them riding into the sunset together and living happily ever after? If so, then she had to protect him as well as herself.

"You're going to run away from what we have—could have—because you're afraid," Beau said.

"If you aren't afraid of a future with me then you sure as heck should be." She grabbed her coat and purse and fled the room.

The ride back to the Yellowstone Drag Strip was made in stony silence and not until Sierra got into her own car did she breathe a sigh of relief. Of course, for the entire drive to Roundup the headlights of Beau's truck shone in the rearview mirror.

When they reached the outskirts of town, Beau took the turnoff to Thunder Ranch. Sierra drove the rest of the way to the diner, ignoring the pain in her heart as she contemplated what next to tackle on her bucket list.

Chapter 12

Beau parked in front of his father's house and a moment later the front door opened. Joshua Adams stepped outside, Jordan right behind him.

"You made good time." Joshua stared at Beau's truck.

"Sierra's not coming," Beau said.

Jordan frowned. "Where is she?"

Sierra hadn't phoned her aunt? "Sierra said she needed to get back to the diner."

"But I phoned Irene and she—"

"I told Sierra, but she didn't want to impose on Irene." Beau silently cursed. Why was he making excuses for Sierra?

"Would you mind if I have a word with Beau, Jordan?"

"Of course not." Jordan went inside the house and shut the door.

Beau wasn't in the mood for a lecture and the look on his father's face warned he was in for one.

"What happened between you and Sierra that made her not want to be here this morning?"

"Do we have to get into this right now?" Beau was tired and frustrated. Sierra had put him through the ringer the past eighteen hours.

"You better not have crossed the line in that motel room last night."

That's it. Beau had had enough. "And what if I did?"

His father's face reddened. "I warned you—"

"Lay off, Dad. You were a crappy father to Duke and me when we were kids. You haven't earned the right to tell me what to do with my personal life. And just because you have feelings for Jordan doesn't mean your relationship with her is more important than mine with Sierra. It's your problem if you can't live with that." Beau walked off to the barn.

"Where are you going? Your brother and Angie will be here any minute."

"I'm not hungry. Eat without me." Beau went straight into his workshop. He had a few finishing touches to put on the Phillips saddle. Depending on how long he remained angry with his father, Phillips might get some fancy stitching in the leather that he hadn't asked for.

Less than an hour had passed when Duke appeared in the doorway. "I suppose Dad sent you out here," Beau said.

His brother didn't deny the charge. Duke nodded to the saddle stand in the corner. "Is that one finished?"

"Almost. I'm working on the toe fenders." Beau motioned to the bench where various strips of leather lay.

Duke examined the intricate stitching along the seat. "Pretty fancy for a work saddle."

"You didn't come out here to discuss my leather-working skills, did you?"

His even-tempered twin didn't rise to the bait. "I remember the belts and wrist bands you made in middle school. You've come a long way from those days."

"I have you to thank for telling me I was nuts not to make money off my hobby."

"You repaid me when you made a saddle for my eighteenth birthday," Duke said.

"Keeping that a secret was tough."

"Is that why you put a lock on your workshop door?" Duke asked.

"Heck, yes." Beau dabbed a cloth in linseed oil then polished a toe fender.

"You used to come out here when Dad was in a bad mood," Duke said.

"And you'd lock yourself in your bedroom and watch Westerns." Beau set the cloth aside.

"Is everything okay between you and Sierra?" Duke had finally stopped beating around the bush.

"We're fine." They weren't, but damned if Beau would discuss his troubled love life with his brother.

"Dad wants you to back off for a while and allow Sierra a chance to come to grips with the reality of her situation," Duke said.

The last thing Sierra needed was to be left alone. Look at the trouble she'd already gotten into—drinking too much and drag racing. The risks she'd taken sent his blood pressure skyrocketing.

"Angie and Jordan put a plate of leftovers in the

fridge for you." Duke checked his watch. "I'm on duty this afternoon." He paused at the door. "Just a heads-up... Dad and Jordan are going to the movies later and he wants you to move the bulls to the north pasture."

"Figures."

"I could call Dinah. Maybe she can cover for me while I help you," Duke said.

"I'll be fine. Thanks, though."

After Duke left, Beau flung the oil rag across the room. He didn't want to give Sierra more space, but he didn't have much of a choice.

Space or no space, he and Sierra weren't through yet.

Sierra waited until the last possible moment before turning out the diner lights and heading up to her apartment. She'd managed to avoid her aunt all day but knew an inquisition awaited her. "It's just me," she said when she entered the living room. Her voice woke Jordan who'd fallen asleep on the couch with a book in her hands.

"What time is it?"

"Ten-thirty," Sierra answered.

"You're closing up awfully late tonight."

"I did a little extra cleaning."

"Sit down." Jordan patted the sofa cushion next to her.

Sierra obeyed. "How are things between you and Joshua?"

Her aunt's cheeks turned pink. "I stayed the night at the ranch with him."

She and Beau had been...while Jordan and Joshua

had been… *Don't go there.* "I'm happy you and Joshua are getting along so well."

"It's deeper than that, dear."

"You mean you might move here permanently?" That would be one worry off Sierra's mind, knowing her aunt was close by to help her through the tough times ahead.

"I'm fifty-eight years old and I'm not getting any younger. I want a second chance with Joshua, but first I need to make sure you're okay."

"What do you mean? I'm fine."

"I have no doubt you will be fine, but right now you're running scared."

Sierra opened her mouth to protest but nothing came out. Okay, so she was frightened of going blind. Most people would be, but that didn't mean she was running from anything.

"You didn't tell anyone where you were went yesterday."

Guilty.

"Beau said I should ask you what you were doing in Billings."

"I'm an adult, Aunt Jordan. I didn't think I had to check in with you or my employees."

"That may be, but it was inconsiderate not to inform someone of your whereabouts. What if I'd gotten ill? Joshua wouldn't have been able to reach you."

Guilt pricked Sierra. "Just because my eyesight isn't the greatest doesn't mean I have to give up my privacy and let everyone know my business."

"I understand how you're feeling right now. You want to believe the test results were wrong and you're praying the disease will somehow cure itself."

Yes, Sierra was struggling to accept her fate but deep down she felt time was running out and every minute that passed was a minute she couldn't gain back before she went blind. No one was going to stop her from living each day to the fullest. "Aunt Jordan…"

"Yes, dear."

"What did you do after the doctor told you that you'd eventually lose your sight?"

"I cried for twenty-four hours straight. Poor Bob didn't know what to do with me."

"After the tears…what then?"

"A sense of urgency took over inside me. The first week I remained awake almost twenty-four hours a day, worried I'd miss something exciting if I went to sleep."

Bingo! That's exactly how Sierra felt. "Did that feeling pass?"

"Eventually. Your uncle insisted I needed something to focus on other than my deteriorating eyesight so he told me to get a job."

"A job?" That wasn't the answer Sierra had expected.

"Bob said I had to be able to take care of myself as I grew older, especially if I outlived him, which happened to be the case. And he was protecting his own interests."

"How so?"

"He didn't want my blindness to prevent him from doing the things he'd always enjoyed in life, like taking a yearly fishing trip to Canada with his buddies. He knew he couldn't travel if he had to worry about leaving me alone at home."

"You make adjusting to your blindness sound easy."

"Easy?" Jordan laughed. "I was terrified. And the worst part was that I couldn't show Bob how scared I was or he'd have slacked off on his tough love, and the progress I'd made would have been for nothing." Jordan reached for Sierra's hand. "I wish I'd had someone to confide in. Someone who'd gone through what I was going through. Someone to tell me that it would be okay. That I'd be okay."

Sierra wished she could ask Beau to stand by her side and help her, but she refused to be a burden to him. "I don't know what I'm going to do if I have to sell the diner," Sierra whispered. Cooking was her life's blood. If she was forced to give up her sight so be it, but not being able to cook...that would be devastating.

"Why would you have to sell the diner?" her aunt asked.

"How would I know if one of the employees took money from the cash register? Or stole food from the pantry? They could rob me blind—no pun intended—and I wouldn't know."

"Then don't allow yourself to be taken advantage of. Memorize every inch of your kitchen and pantry and rely on your friends to help watch over your employees."

"It seems...overwhelming."

"Running the diner will allow you to lead a fulfilling life. Even when you can't see the food you prepare, you'll be able to taste it. You'll find that when you lose your sight, your sense of smell and taste will improve and that might even make you a better chef."

Sierra drew strength from her aunt's reassurances. Nothing would weaken the blow of living in darkness, but working in the diner would give her a sense of purpose and a place to be every day—better to fumble around the kitchen than to sit in her apartment and feel sorry for herself. "I'm going to miss seeing the golden color of a perfectly baked pie crust and the soft pink tinge of my almond-raspberry frosting."

And Beau's beautiful brown eyes.

"Never underestimate the power of your memory. Your mind will recall all your favorite things in brilliant color."

As her aunt's words soaked in, Sierra decided that once she tackled her bucket list she'd settle down and plan for her future. With her aunt's help she was determined to keep the Number 1 Diner the most popular restaurant in town.

Wednesday morning Sierra entered the diner kitchen and set her backpack by the door. Before she'd taken a step toward the coffeepot, her cell phone went off. She checked the number. Beau. *Again.*

Since she and Beau had returned from Billings on Sunday, he'd left her numerous voice mail messages. He claimed he was calling to make sure she was okay. Okay from what? Their lovemaking? The drag race? Their argument before leaving the motel? She understood her actions worried Beau and that he wanted her promise she wouldn't go off and do something crazy, but right now the only person she was making promises to was herself. As a matter of fact, Beau's overprotectiveness had pushed Sierra to schedule her next adventure sooner rather than later, before he or anyone else changed her mind.

Sierra filled her thermos with coffee, grabbed her backpack and almost made it out the door before Irene waltzed into the kitchen. Darn. Sierra had been hoping to escape the diner without having to answer any questions.

"Will you be back before eight or should I close up tonight?" Irene asked.

"I'll be back." If she wasn't, that meant she was stuck sleeping in her car in the mountains.

"Have fun...wherever you're off to."

"Thanks, Irene." Sierra slipped outside, got into her car and drove toward the Bull Mountains where she planned to meet up with a bungee-jumping group and take her first and only leap off the railroad trestle bridge that spanned Sweetwater Canyon. The drive would take a half hour, and then the group would hike another twenty minutes to the bridge. Sierra's blood pumped faster as she imagined free-falling three-hundred feet— the length of a football field.

After today's jump, the remaining items on her bucket list weren't as exciting—a cruise, a shopping spree along Rodeo Drive, a Broadway play, a trip to Europe, and she wanted to visit Egypt.

When Sierra parked at the ranger's station she searched her backpack for her bucket list so she could cross off bungee jumping, but it was nowhere to be found. She must have left it in the pocket of her other coat—the one she'd worn Sunday to the racetrack. Backpack in hand, Sierra introduced herself to the other jumpers.

By the time the group reached the trestle bridge, Sierra was huffing and puffing. Their leader, Scott, attached the gear to the bridge then checked the safety equipment. Sierra chatted with Lisa, a twenty-two-year-old graduate student from Montana State University

who was visiting family in the area. She and her boyfriend, Alan, had planned this jump to celebrate their
recent engagement. Sierra would have loved to invite
Beau along today, but he'd have insisted the jump was
too risky.

Once the equipment was ready, Scott asked if Sierra would like to jump first and she agreed. He helped
her into the body harness, which served as a backup
to the ankle attachment, then he checked the length of
the braided shock cord, explaining that it needed to be
significantly shorter than the three-hundred-foot drop
to allow the elastic to stretch. Once Sierra was ready,
Scott assisted her over the bridge rail to a small plat-
form that extended away from the structure. Sierra refused to glance down, instead she looked straight ahead
at the beautiful pine-covered butte at the far end of the
canyon.

"Whenever you're ready, Sierra," Scott said.

"I'll take plenty of pictures." Alan's hobby was pho-
tography and he'd offered to snap photos of Sierra's
jump.

One...two...three! Sierra launched herself into the
air. The rush of the cold wind hitting her face snatched
her breath as everything around became a blur. She'd
been falling forever when the rope snapped her backward toward the top of the bridge—the going up almost
as much fun as the going down.

When Sierra's rebound leveled off, she felt a hard
jerk and the body harness tightened around her chest
with crushing force. For a few terrifying seconds she
twirled in a circle, then hung suspended over the dry
riverbed filled with large boulders and jagged rocks.

Her heart pounded with fear and her mind raced with horrifying images of the rope snapping sending her spiraling to her death. She resisted glancing over her shoulder, fearing any unnecessary movement might sever the cord.

"Don't move, Sierra! Help is on the way!"

Her fate in the hands of others, Sierra dangled over the bridge, wishing she'd told Beau that, even though they couldn't be together, she loved him.

"You sitting down?" Duke asked when Beau answered his cell phone.

Beau had just finished loading hay onto the flatbed and was heading out to fill the bale feeders in the pasture. "Sitting down—fat chance." He wiped his sweaty brow with the sleeve of his flannel shirt. "I'm working my ass off. Dad's at home showering for his date with Jordan tonight. What's going on?"

"It's Sierra."

Beau's heart gave a tiny lurch. Sierra had ignored his phone calls the past few days and although he didn't want to admit it, he was hurt. "What's she gone and done now?"

"I'm on my way up to the Bull Mountains. We got an emergency call from the park ranger. A bungee jumper got their gear caught on the old Johnston Railroad Trestle Bridge."

Beau swallowed hard as he walked quickly to his truck. He knew in gut without even asking. "It's Sierra."

"'Fraid so. You heading up there?"

"I'm on my way." Cussing up a storm, Beau peeled out of the driveway. Once he turned onto the highway he dialed his father's cell and left a message. He tried hard not to think about Sierra hanging precariously off a bridge. What the hell was she thinking—bungee jumping? She wasn't a daredevil. She was a woman who spent her days cooking in the kitchen.

By the time he arrived in the parking area at the head of the trail leading to the bridge, his muscles were tied in knots. He spotted Sierra's car and several other vehicles, as well as Duke's patrol unit. It was the fire-and-rescue truck that sent a cold chill down his spine. Making sure he had his phone, Beau entered the path. He'd never walked so fast in his life, and when he arrived on the scene he almost had a heart attack. Sierra dangled at least two hundred feet over the side of the bridge. Her head drooped forward and Beau feared she'd passed out. As he approached the group, he listened to the forest ranger speak.

"We're going to drop another rope down to Sierra and she's got to attach it to the harness. There's a small metal ring on the front where the clip can be secured."

The forest ranger pulled out a bullhorn and shouted instructions to Sierra, asking her to raise her hand if she understood him. Sierra lifted her arm only a few inches. Beau prayed to God she didn't pass out before she attached the rescue rope to the body harness.

The forest ranger tossed the rope over the bridge away from Sierra, then guided the rope closer until it bumped her body. No one said a word as they watched and waited for Sierra to grasp the rope. After two attempts she held the end.

"What's wrong?" Beau asked the park ranger when Sierra fumbled with the self-locking hook.

"She might be having trouble finding the ring. It's small." The ranger shouted encouragement but just when she located the ring, the safety rope slipped from her hand.

Beau was sweating profusely as Duke stood at his side. The park ranger once again wiggled the rope close to Sierra and this time she succeeded in attaching the clip to the ring. The forest ranger and the bungee-jumping instructor slowly hoisted her up—the longest minute of Beau's life. When they lifted her over the rail he rushed forward but was blocked by the paramedics who began taking Sierra's vitals.

Duke clamped a hand around Beau's arm and he was grateful for the bruising hold. He'd rather square off with a bull any day than suffer the overwhelming helplessness he felt right now as he watched the paramedics work on Sierra.

"Is she going to be okay?" he asked. No one answered. Unable to stand back and watch any longer he broke free of Duke's hold and squeezed between the two paramedics. "Sierra, its Beau." He knelt by her head. "Can you hear me, honey?" When her eyes remained closed, he leaned down and whispered, "You're going to be okay. Hang in there." She had to be fine—he refused to believe anything else.

The hike down the mountain with Sierra on a stretcher was long and arduous. When they reached the trailhead, Duke spoke to the paramedics. "I'll give you guys an escort." Before Duke climbed into his patrol car, he said, "I'll call Dad and let him know where they're taking Sierra. Meet you at the hospital." Duke flipped on the emergency lights and led the way out of the park. After the rescue truck left, the park ranger packed up his gear and drove off. The bungee-jumping instructor looked like he needed a drink and offered to buy the young couple a round at the Open Range Saloon. Beau imagined news of Sierra's mishap would spread like wildfire if it hadn't already.

Once the parking lot cleared and Beau was left alone, he walked into the bushes and heaved until his stomach was empty. Feeling shaky, he took a bottle of water from the cooler he kept in the backseat. Sticking out from beneath the cooler on the floor was a sheet of notebook paper that didn't belong to him. He tugged the paper free.

Sierra's Bucket List had been printed across the top. Beau read the items listed on the paper.

#1 Drag Race

#2 Bungee Jumping

#3 Vacation in Egypt

#4 Shop on Rodeo Drive

Beau skimmed the rest of the items, ticked off that *he* wasn't on the list. If Sierra was taking risks, why wasn't she willing to trust him and give their relationship a chance? He crumpled the paper in his fist. Sierra could have died today—all because of a stupid bucket list. He shoved the wad of paper into his pocket and started the truck.

The drive out of the park took forever and by the time Beau arrived at the hospital, a crowd had gathered in the emergency room. He waved Duke down. "How's Sierra?"

"She's got some bruising where the harness bit into her chest, and they're keeping her overnight for observation, but the risk of a blood clot is minimal. She was lucky, Beau. The doctor said he's seen people die after being suspended in the air thirty minutes or less."

"Does Jordan know?"

"Yeah. Dad's on his way over here with her. If you want any privacy with Sierra, you'd better talk to her now." Duke pointed to the curtained-off cubical at the end of the corridor.

Beau walked down the hall, and cleared his throat before moving the curtain aside. Sierra slowly opened her eyes. When she saw him, she attempted to smile, but her effort was weak at best. He pulled a chair next to the bed and sat. They stared at each other for a long time, then tears trickled from her eyes. Beau's throat tightened as he struggled to get a grip on his emotions. After a minute he pulled the crumpled note from his pocket and handed it to Sierra. "I believe this belongs to you."

"I thought I'd lost it," she whispered, wiping her tears with the edge of the sheet.

"Why?" Beau asked.

"Why what?"

"Why are you so hell-bent on taking chances and putting yourself in danger?"

"You wouldn't understand," she said.

"Try me."

"When the doctor said I'd eventually go blind, I thought about all the things I'd dreamed of doing one day."

"So why am I not on your list?" he asked.

Her eyes widened before she dropped her gaze to her lap. "Don't, Beau."

"Don't what?"

"Don't pretend there's any future for us."

Her words sucker punched Beau. After all they'd been through together, Sierra refused to admit that what they'd shared had been more than just a good time. He had to get out of there before he exploded and said something he could never take back. Beau fled the cubical but paused in the hallway, waiting…hoping…she'd call him back.

She didn't.

Chapter 13

"Have you called Ace?" Duke asked his cousin Colt when he arrived at his aunt's house.

"Yeah. Thought he ought to see this."

Duke leaned against the grille of Colt's truck and watched his twin go head-to-head with Midnight in the corral.

"Mom saw him take a nasty fall a half hour ago and told him to quit."

"He ignored her," Duke said.

"Yeah, so she called me because—"

"Ace would have a fit."

Colt grinned. "Sheesh, hoss. You'd think *we* were twins the way you finish my thoughts."

Duke wanted to intervene but knew his brother would object. "Midnight's not tiring, is he?"

"Nope."

A horn blast caught their attention. Ace's pickup barreled into the ranch yard. When he got out of the truck, he hollered, "What's so all-fired important that I had to drive—" Ace stopped in his tracks and stared at Beau picking himself up off the ground.

"You didn't tell Ace that Beau was riding Midnight?" Duke whispered.

"Nope."

"What the hell's he doing?" Ace joined his brother and cousin.

"Mom gave Beau the go-ahead to get Midnight ready for the rodeo in South Dakota," Colt said.

"Nice of Mom to tell me," Ace grumbled.

"She said you had enough on your plate with work and Flynn getting ready to have the baby."

All three men winced when Beau stumbled on the way back to the chute and did a face-plant in the dirt. He crawled to his knees, then his feet and staggered forward.

"For God's sake, it looks like he broke his nose," Ace said. Blood dripped off Beau's chin, but he wiped it away with his shirtsleeve.

"Why's he beating himself up?" Ace directed the question to Duke.

"It's Sierra." The look in Beau's eyes when he saw Sierra dangling from the bridge would haunt Duke for a long time. He'd never seen his brother so scared. There was no doubt in Duke's mind that Beau was in love with Sierra.

"I heard about her close call," Ace said.

Duke cleared his throat. "Shook Beau up pretty bad."

"Didn't know Beau and Sierra were a couple. Then again, I'm so dang busy with my practice I don't know much about what goes on in this family anymore."

"Leah said Flynn called her after talking to Dinah, who'd run into Cheyenne at the diner, who'd heard from Jordan that Sierra had made out a bucket list and bungee jumping was on it," Colt said.

Ace stared at his brother as if he'd grown two heads. "I'm supposed to make sense out of what you just said?"

Duke clarified things. "Ever since Sierra found out she inherited her aunt's eye disease, and will probably end up blind one day, she's been participating in extreme activities like bungee jumping and drag racing."

Ace whistled low. "Let me guess, Beau's trying to stop her and she's telling him to get out of her way."

"That sums it up pretty well," Duke said.

Colt pointed to the pen. "Watch this, Ace. Midnight backs himself into position." The stallion spun then inched into the makeshift chute.

"If that don't beat all," Ace whispered.

Beau attempted to climb the rails, his boot slipping on the rungs.

"How long has he been at it?" Ace asked.

"Not sure. At least an hour, I'd guess," Colt said.

Once he'd climbed onto Midnight's back, Beau lifted the hay rake and clanged it against the metal rail. The horse bolted into the pen and Beau dropped the rake. "Midnight's hardly winded and he's still bucking high and tight," Colt said.

All three men let out a whoop when the stallion leapt into the air as he bucked. "He's a high-roller," Ace said.

Beau went flying.

"C'mon, Ace." Colt nudged his brother's arm. "Admit it. Midnight was born to rodeo."

"There's no denying the horse loves to buck." Ace shook his head. "Midnight's already in the chute and Beau hasn't even gotten to his feet."

"Beau's had enough." Duke made a move toward the pen where his twin lay spread-eagle in the dirt.

"Wait." Ace snagged his cousin's jacket.

"Beau's riding in the Miles City Rodeo this Saturday. If he keeps this up he'll be in no shape to compete," Duke said.

"I'll talk to him." Ace took two steps then stopped and pinned Colt with a glare. "You wouldn't by chance be thinking of entering Midnight in the Miles City Rodeo, would you?" Colt remained silent. "There's no sense taking a chance he'll injure himself before the Bash." When Colt remained mute, Ace grumbled and marched off.

"You're taking Midnight, aren't you?" Duke asked. "Never mind. I don't want to know."

Beau saw his older cousin heading his way. Ace didn't look pleased. Dragging his sore butt off the ground, Beau ignored the man and limped toward the chute where Midnight waited for him.

"Haven't you had enough punishment for one day?" Ace slipped through the rails of the pen and cut across the dirt.

"Butt out, Ace." Beau stepped on the lower rung and a sharp twinge shot through his ankle. He lost his balance and Ace's hand shot out to steady him.

"Come on, look at yourself. Your nose is bleeding.

You've got a split lip. You better…" Ace let his words trail off.

"I better what?"

"Stick to bulls. You suck at bronc busting."

"Think you can do better?"

"Hell, yes, I can ride better than you, but—"

"Chicken shit," Beau mumbled.

"What'd you call me?" Ace shoved Beau into the rails.

"Chicken shit!" Beau's shout propelled his brother and Colt across the drive and into the pen.

"What's going on?" Colt stepped between Beau and Ace.

"Get out of my way." Ace climbed the rails and straddled Midnight. "How do I get him to leave the chute?"

Without warning Beau clanged the rake against the rail. The noise sent Midnight into action and Ace almost got tossed on his head. He managed to keep his seat, but his hat flew off as the stallion did its best to throw his rider.

Colt and Duke hollered encouragement. Beau stood silent—glaring. Eventually Midnight decided he'd had enough and launched Ace into the air. Beau's cousin landed with a loud *oomph* but got to his feet smiling.

"Whoo-wee, Ace!" Colt hollered. "I thought you we're going to ride the buck out of Midnight."

The stallion trotted past Ace then stopped in front of Beau as if waiting for him to concede defeat. "You win." Beau patted Midnight's neck.

"I'll walk him to the barn." Ace removed the bucking strap and bareback rope from Midnight and handed them to Beau before leading the stallion away. "C'mon,

Midnight. You've earned a rubdown." Colt followed his brother, leaving Duke and Beau facing off.

"What?" Beau said when Duke watched him in silence. "Don't you have criminals to chase after?"

"I'm going to give you a pass for being a jerk. You know why?"

"I don't care why, but—" Beau spat at the ground "—you'll tell me anyway."

"You're pissed off because Sierra doesn't want anything to do with you."

"Butt out, Duke."

"Instead of beating yourself up, why don't you see if you can make nice with her?"

"And tell her what? I don't care that she's going blind?" His outburst startled Duke. "Well, I do care! I frickin' care that the woman I love—" Startled by the pronouncement, Beau lost his train of thought.

Love. Worried about Sierra's eye disease and the impact it would have on their relationship…his rodeo future…having children… Beau had refused to say the word out loud or even think it until just now. The feeling had been inside him for a while, but the fear of her waking up one day in the dark and him unable to prevent it had him running scared.

"You ever consider Sierra might not believe it's her you're in love with?" Duke asked.

"What the hell's that supposed to mean?"

"Are you sure the love you feel for Sierra isn't grounded in your need to protect her and be the one she leans on for help? You have a habit of making people depend on you, Beau. Look how long it took me to stand up to you."

"This is none of your business."

"Actually, I believe it is my business, seeing how I was a victim of your overprotectiveness most of my life."

Victim? Beau was speechless—good thing, since his brother had plenty to say.

"You've always looked out for me, Beau."

Wasn't that good?

"When Dad left me to fend for myself against the bullies on the playground, I was grateful you stood up for me."

"But…"

"You don't know when to back off." Duke shoved his hands into the pockets of his jeans. "You know what hurts the most?"

Beau waited for his brother to tell him.

"You didn't believe in me."

"What the hell are you talking about?"

"You never believed I was good enough to win on my own. You felt you had to lose to help build my self-esteem. You never gave me the chance to prove to myself, or you, or anybody for that matter, that I was good enough to beat you when you were trying your hardest."

After giving his brother's words thought, Beau said, "What does this have to do with my feelings for Sierra?"

"You smother people, Beau. You step in and take over for others when they don't want your interference."

Bullshit. Duke didn't know what the hell he was talking about.

"You don't even realize what you're doing, but you make people dependent on you, then—"

"They resent me," Beau said.

"I don't resent you, but you should have allowed me to fail or succeed on my own."

Beau didn't say a word. His brother was on a roll and he sensed this discussion was far from over.

"Not until I met Angie did I realize I was riding for all the wrong reasons. Angie gave me the strength I needed to admit that, as much as I enjoyed busting bulls, I was winning for you, Beau—not me."

Beau's chest tightened, making it tough to draw a deep breath. "I'm sorry."

"I didn't bring this up because I want an apology, but because you're headed down the same path with Sierra."

Beau's stomach bottomed out. He thought back to the times he and Sierra had been together—had he been overprotective? Smothering? If he had, couldn't she see that it had been because he cared? "Sierra's going to be blind one day. She should realize that she'll need people to help her. She can't go through this alone."

"I get it now," Duke said.

"Get what?" Beau had trouble following the conversation.

"I get why you're upset."

Normally Beau was the one to hand out advice. That he took his brother's words into account confirmed how shaken up he was over Sierra.

"You can't handle the idea that Sierra doesn't need you the way you want her to need you."

"Of course she needs me."

"Think, Beau. We grew up without a mother and Dad wasn't all that affectionate. Aside from Aunt Sarah's hugs, we weren't raised in a warm, fuzzy home."

"So?"

"My insecurities played out in my stuttering and yours played out by being overprotective of me. You wanted me to depend on you so you'd always feel needed."

His brother had gone straight for the jugular. Beau stared into the distance, trying to make sense of Duke's words. Had he unconsciously made people depend on him because of a need for love and affection?

"Remember when I told you I was quitting rodeo? You freaked out."

Beau had flown into a rage, because he'd believed Duke hadn't appreciated all the sacrifices he'd made for his brother through the years. If there was any truth to Duke's words, Beau had been upset not because his brother had quit bull riding, but because he no longer needed Beau—Duke had found Angie.

Shit. He needed a frickin' therapist.

"I don't doubt for a minute you care deeply for Sierra, Beau. Just be sure your feelings are true blue and not tied to wanting her to depend on you."

Well, hell. Did Sierra believe he was more in love with the need to rescue her than just plain love her? But he did love Sierra, and when you loved someone it was only natural that you wanted to protect them. The two went hand in hand. "Leave me alone, Duke."

His brother walked off, but stopped a few feet away. "Beau."

"What?"

"I may not need you to lose rodeos for me or beat up bullies on the playground, but I do still need you to be my brother."

Beau struggled to draw air into his pinched lungs as he watched Duke get into his truck and drive away.

"Sierra?"

Leave me be, Aunt Jordan.

"Sierra, dear? Where are you?" The sound of Jordan's low-heeled shoes clicking against the floor echoed above Sierra's head.

As was normal on a Friday night, the diner had been packed and she'd closed a half hour later than usual. Physically and emotionally exhausted, Sierra yearned for a hot soak in the tub, but halfway up the back stairs the memory of Beau's kiss in the darkened hallway had overwhelmed her and she'd given in to the tears she'd held at bay since the afternoon at the hospital when she'd hurt Beau's feelings.

"Sierra?" Before she summoned the energy to call out to her aunt, the door at the top of the stairs opened. "I know you're here somewhere."

"I'm sorry, Aunt Jordan. I just wanted time to...to—"

"To what, dear?" Her aunt descended the steps, stopping when the tip of her shoe bumped Sierra's shoulder. "Scoot over."

Sierra inched closer to the wall, making room for her aunt. She didn't want to burden Jordan with her broken heart, especially when her aunt's love life was moving along strong and steady, but Sierra felt like she'd explode if she didn't share her pain with someone.

"I'm in love with Beau, Aunt Jordan, and it hurts that we can't be together." The floodgates opened and tears dripped down her cheeks.

"Why can't you be together?"

Sierra swallowed an angry retort. Her aunt acted as if going blind was just a bump in the road, but Sierra's failing eyesight felt like a noose around her neck, slowly tightening and choking the life out of her. "I can't be with Beau because I'd be a burden to him."

And because he'd insist on doing everything for me. Instead of becoming independent, she'd become dependent on Beau and then if—when—he left her, she'd... Sierra couldn't imagine the pain.

"Are you implying then that I'm a burden to Joshua because I'm blind?"

Sierra had never heard her aunt raise her voice before. "No, I didn't mean—"

"Shame on you, Sierra. Just because you can't see, doesn't mean you can't lead a fulfilling life or that you should sit back and feel sorry for yourself as the years pass you by." Her aunt put her arm around Sierra's shoulder. "And don't you dare accuse me of oversimplifying the situation."

"But you make it sound as if it's easy to adjust to living in the dark."

"Sometimes one chooses to remember the good mostly and not so much the bad...self-preservation, I guess. But don't think for a minute that I've forgotten the hardship I faced and still do because I can't see." Her aunt brushed a thumb across Sierra's wet cheek. "I, too, cried my share of tears and experienced moments of sheer panic when I did something by myself for the first time—like riding the city bus alone."

"You've shown me that it's possible to be blind and remain independent but..."

"But what?"

"I'm scared."

"It's okay to be scared, Sierra. You wouldn't be human if you didn't fear the unknown, but that's why I'm here. And Beau will help you, too."

"I don't want to rely on Beau."

"He cares about you."

"It's because he cares that I can't be with him."

"That doesn't make sense, dear."

"Beau's a take-charge guy who jumps in and helps out without being asked."

"Some women would find that chivalrous."

"If I allow Beau to do everything for me, I won't learn how to get around on my own and then I'll become too dependent on him and one day he'll wake up and realize how exhausting it is to take care of me and he'll leave. And then where will I be…trying to manage my life after years of having someone do it for me."

"Talk to Beau. Tell him what you need and don't need from him."

If Sierra thought asking Beau to back off would be enough, she'd have said so weeks ago, but a person shouldn't have to change who they were to be with the one they loved. And that wasn't all she feared. "Beau deserves to be a father and I'm not having any children."

"Why not? You'd be a wonderful mother."

"Children are a huge responsibility and my blindness would put my children in jeopardy."

"There are no guarantees in life, Sierra, but you're the type of woman who wouldn't take chances with her children and I know you'd be extra vigilant—"

"Which could be a bad thing, too, because then I'd smother my kids and they'd grow up to hate me for it."

Good grief, with both her and Beau being overprotective parents, their children would run away at the first opportunity.

"Nothing worth having in life comes without risks."

Sierra understood that, but did she have the courage to put her heart in Beau's hands and trust that he was strong enough for both of them when the going got tough…tougher…toughest?

"Mind some company?"

Beau glanced up from the workbench in the barn where he'd been putting the final touches on the saddle for Jim Phillips. His father hovered in the doorway.

"I thought you and Jordan had a standing date on Friday nights." Beau pushed a stool forward and his father sat.

"Jordan called a little while ago and said she and Sierra are watching a movie tonight." His father studied Beau's face. "The cut on your lip looks better."

Beau appreciated that his father hadn't grilled him when he'd come into the house two days ago looking as if he'd been run over by a truck. He suspected Aunt Sarah had informed her brother about Beau's impromptu rodeo with Midnight.

"You still plan to compete tomorrow in Miles City?"

"Yep." His aches and bruises hadn't healed but he didn't care.

"You sure that's smart?"

Beau shrugged, positive it wasn't smart. But again, he just didn't give a damn.

"You know…" His father pretended interest in the

scrap of leather Beau tossed aside. "Maybe I came down a little too hard on you about Sierra."

This was a first. His father admitting he'd been wrong must be Jordan's influence. Amazing how a woman could waltz into a man's life and shake it up so violently that when the dust settled there was a whole new man standing there.

"Jordan put you up to this, didn't she?" Beau set aside his swivel knife.

"She's worried about Sierra."

"Dad, I—"

His father held up his hand. "Before you say anything…what are your intentions toward Sierra?"

"Are you asking because she and I spent the night together in a motel room?"

"No. As you pointed out earlier, that's none of my business." His father stared thoughtfully. "When you look ahead through the years, do you picture yourself with Sierra?"

After giving the question serious consideration, Beau said, "I can't imagine not having her in my life."

"Jordan's talked to me about her experience going blind."

Beau wasn't in the mood to discuss Jordan but he kept his mouth shut.

"When Jordan was diagnosed with the disease she asked her husband if he was going to divorce her."

"What did he say?"

"He'd told her that he'd married her for better or worse and wouldn't abandon her. Jordan acknowledged that he got her through several rough patches."

How many rough patches would Sierra experience,

and how long would they last? When Beau imagined being by her side, he had no idea what that entailed.

"The thing is, Jordan had been with her husband several years and they had a strong marriage before she'd been diagnosed with the disease."

"I'm not following."

"Most newlyweds have no idea what the future holds for them, which is a good thing if any marriage is to have a shot at succeeding. God forbid, if I had known how things would have turned out for me and your mother…" His voice trailed off. After a moment, he said, "You and Sierra know exactly what you're up against. If you choose to make a commitment to her and years down the road you suddenly become tired of living with a blind person and want out…that's a lot more hurtful than walking away now."

The words were difficult to hear, but Beau appreciated his father's candor.

"According to Jordan, going blind is the scariest thing in the world. For the first time in her life she had to learn to trust. Not just trust her husband when he said there was one step in front of her, not two, but she had to trust that the stranger she asked to help her in the grocery store actually handed her the can of soup she'd requested and not something different. And she had to trust the man on the corner who said the light was green and it was safe for her to cross the street."

Beau put himself in Sierra's shoes and pictured what it would be like to rely on a stranger's word. Right now, Sierra could see the sincerity in Beau's eyes, but what about ten or twenty years from now when he said "I love you" and she couldn't see the truth of the words in his expression? Sierra would have to take an incredible leap of faith if she wanted to be with him.

His father got up from the stool and patted Beau's back. "It was selfish of me to warn you away from Sierra. I didn't want anyone or anything to ruin my chances with Jordan."

"Dad?" Beau called out when his father turned to leave. "Are you afraid to be with Jordan because she's blind?"

"No. As much as I wanted to be with her years ago, we weren't right for each other then."

"But you are now?"

"Yes, we're perfect for each other now."

"Are you going to tie the knot with her?" Beau asked.

"When she's ready."

"What if she's never ready?"

"Then I'll be happy to be with Jordan any way she lets me."

His father ambled off, leaving Beau with a heavy heart and a whole lot of thinking to do.

"You sure about this?" Beau asked Colt when he stowed his gear in the backseat of Colt's Dodge.

"Yep. By the time Ace figures out we took Midnight to Miles City, it'll be too late for him to catch us." Colt gathered up the junk on the front seat—coloring books, crayons and Happy Meal toys, then tossed them into the back. "Do me a favor and double-check the latch on the trailer."

Beau inspected the lock then hopped into the truck. "We're good to go."

As Colt pulled out of the driveway his cell phone

beeped. He put the brakes on. "Better check this text in case it's Leah. Davy was running a fever last night." He looked at the message. "Shit."

"Everything okay?"

"Ace just texted 'good luck with Midnight.'"

"Doesn't surprise me. Can't pull the wool over your brother's eyes."

Colt's phone beeped again. "It's Ace. 'If Midnight gets injured you're...'"

"You're what?"

"There's a bunch of symbols and punctuation marks."

Beau grinned.

Colt lifted his foot from the brake and headed for the county road.

Sunrise was an hour away. "Any trouble loading Midnight?" Beau asked.

"Nope. The stallion practically danced his way into the trailer."

"You competing today?"

"Heck, yeah. Been looking forward to it all week."

"Need a break from married life, huh?"

"Married life is great. With Leah and the kids, there's never a dull moment."

"How's Evan?"

"He's good. Thanks for asking." Colt turned onto the highway. "He likes to Skype online so we've been doing that once a week. He's looking forward to visiting Thunder Ranch over Thanksgiving." Small talk exhausted, Colt drove in silence then swung the truck into a McDonald's on the outskirts of town and ordered two large coffees. Back on the road, he asked, "So what's up between you and Sierra?"

"Hasn't Leah gotten the latest scoop from your sister?"

"The only thing Leah mentioned after she met the girls for coffee at the diner was that Sierra seemed depressed."

When Beau remained silent, Colt said, "No comment?"

"No comment."

"Good." Colt squirmed into a comfortable position on the seat. "Now when I get home and Leah grills me on what I found out about you and Sierra, I can say 'nothing' without my face turning red."

"Why's everyone so dang interested in my love life?" Beau grumbled.

"Don't you know, cousin? No woman is happy unless all her lady friends are happy."

Exhausted from thinking about Sierra all week, Beau flipped the radio to a sports talk show.

"Okay, I can take a hint." Colt launched into a discussion about NFL teams and the drive passed quickly.

When they arrived in Miles City, Colt went off with Midnight and Beau signed in for the bull-riding event. He had time to waste before he competed, so he visited the bull pen and observed the animals for the rodeo.

He'd drawn Red Hot Chili Pepper, a brown bull with a white face. He wasn't the biggest bull in the pen but Pepper, as he was called by the cowboys, had speed and quickness on his side. Beau walked through the cowboy-ready area, then made his way toward the chutes to watch Colt compete in the saddle-bronc competition.

"Ladies and gentlemen, welcome to the Miles City Rodeo and Stock Show." When the applause died down, the announcer briefed fans on the scoring system then introduced the first contender, a cowboy from Utah who lasted five seconds before biting the dust. When Colt's name came over the sound system, Beau climbed the rails for a better view.

The gate opened and a horse named Devil's Delight barely cleared the chute before the first buck. Beau stopped breathing when Colt slipped sideways in the saddle. His cousin managed to hang on and regain his balance. Beau counted the seconds in his head, noting the bronc went into a spin at the six-second mark. The buzzer sounded and Colt held on until he found an opening and launched himself off the horse. The crowd cheered when he came to his feet. Colt waved his hat to the fans and returned to the cowboy-ready area wearing a huge grin.

"Colt Hart sure showed Devil's Delight he was the boss!" The JumboTron replayed the ride. "The judges have spoken and Hart earned an eighty-five! Hart's the man to beat this afternoon and our next rider is sure gonna give it his best shot."

Once the fans quieted, the announcer continued. "We got a special treat up next—The Midnight Express. This stallion is a descendant of Five Minutes to Midnight, a Pro Rodeo Hall of Fame bucking horse!" The crowd cheered. "The Midnight Express disappeared from the circuit for a couple of years, but thanks to the Harts of Roundup, Montana, the stallion is back doin' what he's famous for—throwin' cowboys!"

Beau made his way over to Midnight. The horse had been loaded into the chute and Colt was helping to secure the flank strap. "Midnight has won bucking horse of the year twice and made an appearance at the National Finals Rodeo five times," the announcer said.

A cowboy, who went by the nickname Tiny Joe, hopped onto Midnight's back. The stallion stamped his hoof in anticipation. Tiny Joe bobbed his head. The chute door opened and Midnight morphed into a dark mythological warrior.

The stallion's sleek black coat and muscular stature mesmerized rodeo fans. Midnight bucked high and tight with no letdown between kicks, and Tiny Joe didn't stand a chance past four seconds. The cowboy sailed headfirst through the air and a roar from the stands followed.

"What do you think?" Colt joined Beau.

"I'm thinking Midnight's going for broke at the Bash."

"Me, too." Colt's expression sobered. "You sure you're up to fighting a bull today?"

"I'll be fine." Beau brushed off his cousin's concern and walked away. An hour later the bull-riding competition began. Beau was third in the rotation, just enough time to get his thoughts in order and focus. Ignoring his sore ribs, he adjusted his protective vest. The livestock handlers loaded Pepper into the chute and the five-year-old bull stood docile. Beau wasn't fooled. Pepper had two years' experience on the circuit and was only biding his time until it was his turn to play.

"You're up, Adams."

Beau waited for his adrenaline to spike but his body remained oddly calm—not a good sign. He needed a rush of heat through his muscles to increase his strength. He scaled the rails and settled onto Red Hot

Chili Pepper. Ignoring his subdued mood, Beau took only a few seconds to secure his grip on the rope before nodding to the gateman.

The chute opened and Pepper pounced, but Beau had anticipated the move and kept his balance. Either Beau was riding out of his head or Pepper had lost some steam, because the bull's bucks felt tame in comparison to what Midnight had put him through earlier in the week. Beau rode buck after buck as if in a daze, his ears and mind numb to the cheering crowd.

The buzzer sounded, but he kept his seat, waiting for an opening to dismount. When his chance came, he jumped for safety but his hand got hung up in the rope. Pepper continued to buck and Beau tried to reach with his free hand to loosen the rope, but it was all he could do to keep himself from falling beneath the bull and being pummeled by hooves.

The bullfighters closed in, one cowboy tugging at the rope, the other trying to distract Pepper. Beau could no longer feel his hand—the rope had cut off the circulation. Pepper spun and his rear collided with the bull-fighter's horse, the impact jerking Beau's arm so hard he feared the ligaments had been torn.

Beau was running out of strength, his feet dragging against the ground. A third cowboy on horseback entered the arena and jumped into the fray. Suddenly Beau's hand broke free and his legs went out from under him. One of the bullfighters grabbed the back of Beau's jeans and hauled him away from the bucking bull then released him. Beau staggered from the arena, his arm hanging limply at his side.

"Are you all right?" Colt blocked Beau's path.

"My arm."

"C'mon, let's get you to the first-aid station."

Beau followed his cousin, feeling nauseous from the pain shooting through his injured limb. "What was my score?"

"I don't know. I didn't hear the announcer." Colt stopped at the paramedic's truck.

"Your hand got caught in the rope," the medic said. Most of the first responders watched the cowboys ride so if one of them got injured, they had some idea of what had happened.

"Might have pulled the ligaments in my shoulder," Beau said.

"While you're being looked after, I'm going to load Midnight." Colt walked off.

After an extensive examination, the medic diagnosed strained ligaments and sprained fingers. He submerged Beau's hand in a bucket of cold water and wrapped an ice pack around his shoulder, then put his arm in a sling and advised Beau to take a week or two off before riding another bull.

The ice numbed the pain but didn't prevent Sierra's face from flashing through Beau's mind. All week he'd stomped around like a bear with a sore paw because he believed Sierra hadn't cared about him the way he cared about her. But after his chat with his father last night, Beau wondered if he had jumped to the wrong conclusion.

What if Sierra kept pushing him away because she was trying to protect *him* from a future of uncertainty and challenge?

Beau was more confused than ever, except for how

he felt about Sierra. He knew without a doubt that he loved her and couldn't imagine his life without her. He recalled the fight he'd gotten into with Duke this past summer. He'd wondered how the hell his brother could walk away from rodeo when the sport had been such a big part of his life and something he'd been so good at. Now he knew.

From this day forward, nothing Beau did or would do mattered if he didn't have Sierra by his side.

Chapter 14

Saturday evening the diner sat empty. Sierra blamed it on the falling snow. Her aunt had retreated to the upstairs apartment with Joshua and the last customer had walked out thirty minutes ago.

"Susie," Sierra said, poking her head around the kitchen door. "I'm closing up early. Get your coat and scoot."

"Really?" Susie shrugged into her white ski jacket. "Thanks, Sierra."

"Text your parents that you're leaving work, okay?"

Susie pulled her phone from her coat pocket and a few seconds later said, "Done."

"The roads are slick." Sierra walked with her employee to the door. "Be careful."

After locking up and flipping the sign in the window, Sierra dimmed the lights and stared at the softly falling snow. A truck turned onto Main Street and her heart skipped a beat then resumed its normal rhythm when she noted the vehicle didn't belong to Beau. Her gaze shifted to Wright's Western Wear and Tack. The store's lighted display window illuminated Beau's custom-made saddles.

I miss you, Beau.

Almost a week had passed since her bungee-jumping disaster—six miserable days of not hearing Beau's voice or seeing his handsome face. She'd believed she'd had Beau's best interests at heart, but after speaking with her aunt, she'd begun to doubt herself.

When Joshua had arrived to eat with Jordan earlier in the evening, Sierra had been tempted to ask about Beau, but she'd chickened out. A knot formed in her chest when she thought of how happy Joshua made her aunt. Even though Sierra was glad Jordan had reconnected with her old flame, she envied her aunt.

The chances of a man happening along after Sierra had lost her eyesight were zero to none—not that it mattered. She couldn't imagine sharing her life with anyone but Beau. She was destined to remain alone. With that depressing thought in mind, she returned to the kitchen and began preparations for Sunday's menu.

Sierra had lost track of time when a knock on the back door startled her. She glanced at the clock—nine-thirty. "Who's there?"

"Beau."

Sucking in a quick breath, she fumbled with the dead bolt. Beau stood in the glow of the security light, a dusting of snow covered his hat and sheepskin jacket, which hung open because of the sling around his left arm. "You're hurt." She waved him inside and shut the door. He was such a sight for sore eyes, that it took all of Sierra's strength not to throw herself at him. "What happened?"

"Strained the ligaments in my arm. Nothing a little rest won't cure."

The deep timbre of his voice sent a warm shiver down her spine. Each night she'd gone to sleep, her thoughts drifting to Beau. Eyes closed, she'd imagined him lying next to her, whispering in her ear. Lord, she'd missed the sound of his voice.

Her gaze soaked in his face, noting his split lip. "Did you get into a fight?"

He rubbed his thumb over the healing cut. "Tangled with a bronc earlier in the week."

"I thought you rode bulls."

"I ride bulls for money and broncs for fun." He smiled but stopped short of a full grin. "I went a few rounds with Midnight. We're getting him ready to compete in South Dakota on the seventeenth." He glanced around the kitchen. "Is now a good time to talk?"

"There's still coffee left in the pot. Would you like a cup?"

"No, thanks." He laid his jacket over the chair at the bistro table and set his hat on the seat, then moved closer to Sierra. "I have a few things I need to get off my chest."

Sierra swallowed hard and braced herself.

"I realize we haven't dated all that long, but I felt—" he pressed his fist to his chest "—something right here the night I found you stranded on the road outside of Roundup. That feeling became stronger each time I saw you."

She clasped her hands together, squeezing until her fingers ached.

"The news from your eye doctor wasn't what you'd hoped for. I know you believe it's changed the course of your life, but I'm here to tell you that it doesn't have to."

Blindness most definitely changed a person's life.

"I've done a lot of thinking the past few days... mostly imagining what it would be like to be married to a blind woman. I've tried to guess how the loss of your sight would impact my life...my responsibilities at Thunder Ranch."

"Don't forget your rodeo career," she said.

"At best I've got another year or two then I'll retire my bull rope."

"And what conclusion did you come to?"

He shrugged. "The only thing I know for sure is that your going blind will affect every aspect of my day-to-day life, but how much and in what ways...only time will tell."

"That's why I—"

He pressed a finger against her lips. "Then I asked myself if I could walk away from you." His finger caressed her lower lip. "The answer was no."

Sierra's breath caught in her chest.

"In the end, it doesn't matter if my plans for the future have to be altered to accommodate your blindness, because the one thing I can't live without is you." Beau cupped her cheek. "I love you, Sierra, and I don't want to spend the rest of my days on earth without you."

Her heart melted at the warmth in Beau's brown eyes.

"Let me repeat myself." He tipped her chin, forcing

her to hold his gaze. "I love all of you, Sierra—the parts that work well and the parts that don't work so well."

Beau's heartfelt words made her eyes sting.

"I know I can come on too strong and I tend to take over and do things for people before they ask for my help. I can't promise that I won't smother you from time to time. But if you ask me to step back, I'll do my best to oblige."

Sierra fought valiantly to keep her tears from escaping.

"And if you are determined to do everything on your bucket list then I won't stand in your way, but if you'll let me, I'd like to do them with you."

"Every one?" she whispered.

"Yep. I'll even take a ballroom dancing class with you." He shrugged. "I've always wanted to learn the tango."

Sierra couldn't picture the tough bull rider light on his feet. She laughed, but the sound emerged from her throat in a strangled sob.

"Loving you is the easy part," he said. "Living with your disability will be a challenge, but I'm ready and willing and eager to fight that battle." The pad of his thumb caught a tear that dribbled down her cheek.

"No matter what the future holds for you, honey, I want to be the guy walking at your side every step of the way. If you let me...if you trust me... I'll be the light in your life when your world goes dark."

"I'm afraid," she whispered.

"Of what?"

"Of becoming too dependent on you and then one day you'll wake up and realize my blindness has stolen all the joy from your life."

"That won't happen. Because I know you, Sierra

Byrne. You're as stubborn and willful as your aunt and you won't let yourself become a burden to anyone."

Lord, how she loved Beau. She wanted to believe he spoke from the heart, but did she have the courage to take a leap of faith in herself? "You're not looking at the big picture. There are things I can't...won't do in the future."

"Like what?"

"I won't have children."

"Why not?"

Why was he making this so hard? "I won't have children, because I'd never risk the safety of my child."

"Why would our children be unsafe?"

Wasn't it obvious? "If I can't see where I'm going how will I see where my child is going?"

"You might not lose your sight for several years and I'd be there to help raise our kids. You wouldn't have to do it on your own."

"Good grief, Beau. Life will be difficult enough learning to run the diner when I'm blind, let alone care for children."

"You're overthinking this, Sierra."

"And you're oversimplifying it, Beau. You make raising children sound easy."

"And you make it sound impossible. The truth is probably somewhere in between." Beau kissed her mouth. "It's okay to be scared. I'm afraid, too, but not by your blindness, by the thought of not having you in my life."

"Beau, I—"

"Do you love me?"

Of course she did!

"I held you in my arms...made love to you...felt the

way you loved me back." He pressed the palm of her hand against his thudding heart. "I know you love me."

Sierra didn't deny it. "It's because I love you that I refuse to take something beautiful between us and have it become ugly and hurtful in the end."

"You love me, but you won't trust me with your heart."

No, it was herself she didn't trust. "Beau, I—" What was the point? She'd already stated her case.

He reached into his pocket and removed a ring. "I came tonight to pledge my love to you and ask you to marry me. I'm not a guy that runs at the first sign of trouble, Sierra. I stick." He took her hand and slid the ring over her finger. "I picked this blue diamond because the color matches your eyes."

The ring was gorgeous. Heart pounding with love she yearned to shout, *Yes, I'll marry you!*

Beau swooped in and pressed a hard, desperate kiss to her mouth. "Don't give me your answer tonight. Wear my ring and think about the next fifty years of your life. If you can envision me and you with gray hair holding hands while our rocking chairs face west, then you have your answer."

Too choked up to speak, Sierra watched Beau fetch his coat and hat and walk out the door. Her gaze dropped to the ring on her finger. Would she stand back and allow a disease to not only rob her of her sight but also her very own happy ever after?

Or…would she find the courage to accept Beau's love?

"Ladies and gentlemen, turn your attention to chute seven." The announcer's voice boomed over the sound system Saturday afternoon at the Badlands Bull Bash and Cowboy Stampede in Spearfish, South Dakota.

Beau ignored the hoopla and spoke to Colt. "You ready?"

"I'd better be or I'll disappoint our cheering section."

Beau followed Colt's gaze. Except for Dinah, who'd remained behind to safeguard the citizens of Roundup, the entire family had made the five-hour drive to the rodeo, even Flynn, whose due date was less than two weeks away.

After Colt walked over to his chute, Duke said, "Dad's still not here."

"I hope he doesn't miss Midnight's performance." Earlier that day after Beau had hit the road with Back Bender and Bushwhacker, his father had called to tell him that Jordan had forgotten something in Roundup and they'd be late to the rodeo.

"Any sign of your dad?" Ace asked.

"Nope. And he's not answering his phone," Beau said.

"You don't think they had car trouble, do you?" Austin joined the group.

Ace shook his head. "Uncle Joshua would have phoned Mom if something serious had happened."

"Up next is the final ride in the saddle-bronc competition," the announcer said. "Colt Hart from Roundup, Montana, will be ridin' King of Spades—a two-time national champion bronc!"

Ace, Duke, Austin and Beau approached the chute where Colt prepared for his ride. King of Spades had a reputation of rallying in the final seconds and throwing his rider. Duke and Ace made sure the rigging was adjusted properly while Colt played with his grip on the rope.

A few seconds later Colt signaled the gateman. The moment King of Spades entered the arena he kicked high and followed the move with a tight spin that would have thrown a seasoned cowboy into the stands. Colt held on and the crowd cheered its approval.

"He's slipping," Beau said when Colt's butt shifted sideways. *Four...five...*

"Hang on, Colt!" Ace shouted.

Six...seven...

The buzzer sounded and not a second too soon. Colt went flying over the bronc's head but managed to tuck his body and roll when he landed.

"I'll be darned! Colt Hart is the first cowboy to make it to eight this season on King of Spades!"

Colt got to his feet and saluted the crowd.

"Hart scored an eighty-seven! That's good enough for first place."

Beau glanced at his family cheering in the stands, wishing Sierra sat among them. He felt like the odd man out...all his cousins had special ladies in their lives and Beau wished Sierra was his. He'd poured his heart out to her two weeks ago, but feared he'd come up short. The only thing giving him hope was that she hadn't returned his ring.

"Rodeo fans sit back and get ready for the next event of the day—bareback ridin'!"

"Midnight's turn to shine." Duke watched Ace lead Midnight into his chute. The stallion didn't balk, as if he sensed his behavior and performance would determine his rodeo future.

When Colt returned to the cowboy-ready area, Beau congratulated Colt on his win. "You're a hard act to follow, cousin."

Duke and Austin slapped Colt on the back.

"Is this the famed Midnight?" The question arrived before the cowboy.

Beau shoved his elbow into Colt's side. "Keep your eye on Kendall. He's got a reputation for provoking horses in the chute." Beau had run into Wesley Kendall over the summer and wherever the cowboy went controversy followed.

Kendall climbed the rails and raised his arm in the air as if preparing to slap Midnight on the head. Ace's hand shot out, blocking Kendall's arm. "Watch yourself, cowboy."

"Just playin' with him." Kendall sneered. "Can't blame me for wantin' to rile him when he stands there like a docile mare."

Ace leveled a hard stare at Kendall and the cowboy walked off. "I'm watching Midnight from the stands." Ace pointed to Kendall's buddies standing nearby. "Make sure no one gets within ten feet of this chute."

"I'll check Kendall's spurs to see if the rowels turn freely," Colt said before Ace walked away.

"Rodeo fans, we've got a great group of broncs for our bareback competition!"

Midnight and Kendall were up last, and each time Kendall wandered closer to the chute, Beau and Austin blocked his path. Beau was torn between wanting Kendall to get thrown on his ass at the one-second mark and wanting him to go six or seven seconds on Midnight before being thrown, so the judges got a sense of the stallion's real talent.

"Out of my way, Adams." Kendall made a move toward the chute but Duke and Colt closed ranks with Beau and Austin, preventing Kendall from passing. A stare-down ensued. Finally Kendall backed off and waited until the announcer called his name.

"Ladies and gentlemen, the final ride in the bareback competition pairs Wesley Kendall from Sioux City, South Dakota, and The Midnight Express, the famed offspring of Five Minutes to Midnight—a Pro Rodeo Hall of Fame bucker!"

The crowd erupted in applause. After Kendall had hopped onto Midnight's back, Colt climbed the rails and reached for the cowboy's boot.

Kendall jerked his foot away. "What the hell are you doing, Hart?"

"Checking to make sure your spurs are legal." Colt spun the spur, satisfied the tips were blunt.

"Sit back and cry, Hart, 'cause this so-called famous horse your family owns is going to bite the dust." Kendall adjusted the rope around his hand then signaled the gateman.

Beau didn't know who was more surprised when Midnight shot out of the chute like a bullet—the gateman who scrambled to get out of the way or Kendall who almost lost his seat. Midnight's first buck was high and tight, interfering with Kendall's spurring rhythm. The stallion added a spin, which threw Kendall off balance at the four-second mark. The cowboy fought to stay alive, but Midnight showed no mercy. His bucks proved too powerful for Kendall and the cowboy flew off. Midnight continued to buck, adding insult to injury when he stomped on Kendall's hat. The fans came to their feet, roaring their approval.

Beau, Colt, Austin and Duke met Midnight when he was escorted from the arena. The dang stallion pranced as if he'd just won a world title. Colt whispered to the stallion and Midnight settled down, allowing Colt to walk him to the livestock area.

A few minutes later Beau's aunt, his father and Ace met them at Midnight's stall.

"He was amazing," Aunt Sarah said.

"Haven't seen a horse perform like that in years," Beau's father chimed in.

"What do you all think?" Colt asked. "Is Midnight ready to make a run for another NFR title?"

"After that performance, I agree that it would be a shame to allow his talent to go to waste," Ace said.

Colt patted Midnight's rump. "You hear that, big guy? You're going on the road next year!"

Beau tugged his father's sleeve. "Everything okay with you and Jordan?"

"Meant to get here sooner but we had to go back to town and pick up something."

"What did you forget?" Beau asked.

His father and Aunt Sarah stepped aside to reveal Sierra standing a few yards away. Beau's knees went weak when she flashed him a hesitant smile. "We'll be watching you from the stands, Beau," Duke said. "Good luck with your ride."

His family walked off, leaving him alone with Sierra. Beau's gaze dropped to her hand and his heart thudded hard at the sight of the diamond ring on her finger. He was riding in less than a half hour—no time to beat around the bush. "You're wearing my ring."

"I may not have any choice when it comes to losing my eyesight but I do have a choice who I want to spend the rest of my life with."

"You're choosing me?"

"I love you, Beau, and yes, I want to spend the rest of my life with you."

"As my wife?"

"As your wife and God willing as the mother of your children."

He grasped her hands and squeezed gently. "Once you say *I do* there's no turning back."

"I don't want to spend the rest of my life regretting that I didn't have the courage to trust in our love for one another."

Beau wrapped his arms around Sierra and for the first time in fourteen days he felt as if he could take a deep breath without his chest pinching. "You've made me the happiest man alive."

"I'll ask one more time and then I'll never ask again," she said. "Are you sure, Beau? Really sure?"

"Honey, I'm a bull rider. I live for challenges."

"But marrying me will last a lot longer than eight seconds—I hope."

"No worries, darlin'. Marriage to you is one ride I refuse to get thrown from." Beau ignored the rowdy whistles of the cowboys nearby when Sierra threw her arms around his neck and kissed him.

They pulled apart and Beau grinned. "I didn't see that comin'."

"You didn't see…and here I thought I was the one who had vision issues."

The announcer introduced the bull-riding event, and Beau said, "I've gotta head over to the chutes to watch the Thunder Ranch bulls compete."

"Beau?"

"Yeah, babe?"

"Win."

"I'm feeling pretty lucky right now." He chuckled. "Think I'll go on out there and do like you say…win." Sierra's impending blindness was all the motivation Beau needed to perform his best, not only today but next season when he went after the national title. Rodeo was a tough sport and there were no guarantees he'd remain injury-free and make it to the NFR, but it sure would be special if Sierra was able to see him ride in Vegas. He considered the grueling rodeo schedule, and being away from Sierra, and decided next year would definitely be his last run at a title.

"C'mon, I'll walk you to the stands."

Sierra's feet remained planted. "If this is going to work between us then you have to let me do things on my own."

Backing down was going to be difficult, but Beau was determined to do his best. "Okay, but I have a few conditions of my own."

"Oh?"

"The next extreme activity you engage in had better be with me—" he lowered his voice "—in our bedroom." He kissed her mouth then said, "Be careful."

She walked off but stopped suddenly and looked over her shoulder. "Don't stand there and watch me. Go on."

Stubborn gal. Beau turned away and strolled several yards before checking over his shoulder. Sierra remained in the same spot staring at him. He couldn't take his eyes off her as he kept walking…right into another cowboy.

After apologizing he glanced at Sierra, and sure enough she was laughing. She shook her head and left, making her way through the maze of cowboys and gear bags littering the ground.

Beau stopped outside Bushwhacker's chute, glad to see the bull appeared his usual calm self. Bushwhacker's good manners in the chute fooled most cowboys, leaving them unprepared when the gate opened.

"Folks, cowboy Leif Rimsky will kick off the bull-riding event. Rimsky's from Albuquerque, New Mexico, and had a good year up until July when he busted his arm. The bone's healed and Rimsky's ready to ride Bushwhacker from the Thunder Ranch in Roundup, Montana. This bull's makin' a name for himself and odds are you'll see him at the NFR in Vegas, if not this year then next."

C'mon, Bushwhacker, go out there and show 'em what you've got.

Rimsky fussed with the bull rope, then a second later the chute door opened and Bushwhacker took off, his back legs kicking before he'd even cleared the chute. The bull's muscles rippled and bunched with each powerful burst of energy. Rimsky managed to hang on until Bushwhacker twisted his hind quarters, the movement forcing Rimsky off balance. The cowboy made a futile attempt to regain his seat but in the end he went flying. The bullfighters closed in, distracting Bushwhacker who continued to entertain the crowd with his powerful kicks.

"Looks like Bushwhacker will remain undefeated this year!" The crowd cheered when the JumboTron replayed Rimsky's ride.

Once Bushwhacker was led from the arena and safely returned to the bull pen, Beau located Back Bender. The bull appeared agitated, slamming his hoof against the chute. Beau moved closer and climbed the rails, checking to make sure the rigging was properly secured. Satisfied, Beau chalked up the bull's testiness to an eagerness to rid himself of the cowboy on his back.

The gate opened and Back Bender jumped into action. He spun right then left, ending with a double kick that dislodged the rider. Back Bender continued to buck and it took the bullfighters a good thirty seconds to guide the animal out of the arena.

Happy that Midnight and the bulls had represented Thunder Ranch well, Beau put on his protective vest and headgear. He was next in the rotation and adrenaline was pumping hard through his veins.

"Ladies and gentlemen, it's been a day of hits and misses for the cowboys here at the Bash. We got one ride left and it's a doozy!"

Beau engaged in an all-out battle with his brain to remain focused and not think about how happy Sierra had made him. He'd drawn Blood Sucker, a bull from the Jeopardy Ranch in Idaho. Blood Sucker was a money bull and didn't often allow a cowboy to ride him for eight seconds.

Right now, Blood Sucker appeared none too pleased to be confined to his chute. The bull threw his side against the rails, forcing one cowboy to jump for safety before he got his foot smashed. When Beau settled on Blood Sucker's back, an image of Sierra flashed through his mind and he felt a sense of peace. Making sure his grip was secure, he relaxed his spine and leaned forward.

The gate burst open and the bull jumped into the arena with a fierce one-two kick that put a whole lotta daylight between Beau's butt and the bull. He clenched his thigh muscles against the bull's girth, which helped him regain his balance. His left arm burned with pain, the newly healed ligaments stretching and pulling against their will.

One more second, that's all he needed. Just…one… more…

The buzzer sounded and the raucous cheering encouraged Beau to hang on through another series of vicious bucks. Satisfied he'd made an impression, Beau released the rope and dove for safety. He came to his feet and applause echoed through the stands.

"Well, folks, there you have it. Tonight's winning bull ride! Beau Adams scored an eighty-six on Blood Sucker—the highest score to date on that bull. Congratulations, cowboy!"

An hour later, Beau, Duke, Ace, Colt and Austin had loaded the Thunder Ranch bulls into the stock trailer and were preparing to load Midnight when Kendall walked by and clanged his gear against the side of the trailer. The sharp noise startled Midnight and he reared. Ace moved in on one side and Colt on the other, grabbing the ropes attached to the halter. When Midnight came down, his left front leg missed the ramp and he stumbled.

"Whoa, Midnight, whoa," Colt said.

By the time the stallion settled down, Kendall was nowhere in sight.

"Don't load him." Ace crouched next to Midnight and examined the knee joint then groaned.

"What is it?" Duke asked.

"He twisted his knee. It's swelling already."

"Here." Colt handed the ropes to Duke then looked at Austin. "Post my bail if I end up in the slammer for killing Kendall."

Beau blocked Colt's path. "Leave him be. He can't avoid us forever. He'll meet up with me on the road sooner or later."

"I want to put ice on Midnight's knee before we load him." Ace stood. "Be be right back."

"Great. Just frickin' great. Midnight makes a name for himself and now this." Colt whipped off his hat and banged it against his thigh.

"Ace'll fix Midnight," Duke said.

Colt shook his head. "What if it's more than a bruised knee?"

"One day at a time, cousin," Beau stroked Midnight's neck. "Right now let's pamper this big guy and enjoy his victory."

Thunder Ranch had come out the big winner today and the future looked promising, especially for Beau now that he'd be joining the rest of the men in the family and tying the knot with the woman of his dreams.

Epilogue

Thanksgiving at Thunder Ranch was a big production. The scents of rosemary, sage and roasting turkeys filled the house. Casserole dishes lined the kitchen countertops and cooling pies sat on the windowsill. Aunt Sarah, Angie, Leah and Austin's sister, Cheyenne, hustled about the kitchen putting the finishing touches on the meal.

Beau hovered in the doorway, waiting for an opportunity to steal a piece of meat from the two birds Earl McKinley had been instructed to carve. A third bird cooked outside in the deep fryer.

"Don't even think about it, Beau," his aunt warned him. "When is Duke getting here?"

"Around three o'clock. He said to keep a plate warming in the oven." Duke had volunteered to take the day shift after Aunt Sarah had invited Austin's father,

Buddy, and Cheyenne and her twin girls to join the family. Dinah, Austin and Buddy had just left the house to go visit Midnight.

Beau wandered down the hall to investigate the shouting coming from the family room. Sierra was playing a video game with Colt's son, Evan, and by her excited voice Beau assumed she was beating the poor kid. Who would have believed his fiancée was a closet gamer?

While Leah's kids, Davy and Jill, were sprawled on the floor with Cheyenne's twins, Sadie and Sammie, engrossed in a board game, Flynn sat on the couch with her sock feet resting on the coffee table, listening to Luke read a book. Flynn's baby was due in seven days and her pinched expression conveyed how miserable and uncomfortable she was.

"Uncle Beau?" Luke said.

"What, kid?"

"Look." Luke propped the book on Flynn's huge stomach. "It stays open all by itself."

Flynn rolled her eyes.

"Hey, Flynn, where's Ace and Colt?" Beau asked.

"In the barn with Midnight."

Midnight's bruised knee was healing, the swelling almost completely gone. Since the Badlands Bull Bash, Aunt Sarah had received several calls from ranchers interested in breeding their mares with Midnight, giving the family hope that things were finally turning around for the ranch. No one had wanted to jinx Midnight's recovery by talking about the stallion competing for an NFR title next year, but Beau suspected it was on everyone's mind.

"Hey! How'd you do that?" Evan grinned at Sierra.

The kid was the spitting image of Colt but remained shy around the family.

"Watch and weep, kid." Sierra pointed the controller at the large-screen TV mounted to the wall and captured three of Evan's alien commandos. Before Sierra could gloat too much, the front door banged open and boots clomped down the hall. Colt entered the room and Jill and Davy practically tripped over themselves as they raced to their stepfather, scampering up his legs and into his arms.

"Hey, Evan, get one of these pesky bugs off me, will you?"

Evan grinned at his father's predicament. "Sorry, you're on your own. I'm about to take control of planet Zorcon."

"You and what army?" Sierra said. "Bingo! You're dead."

"Ah, man!" Evan set aside his controller and approached Colt. Jill immediately held out her arms. "Take me, Evan! Take me!"

Watching how well Colt's kids got along made Beau eager to have children with Sierra. She must have sensed his thoughts because her gaze connected with his from across the room. Each time Beau lost himself in her beautiful blue eyes, he was reminded of all the uncertainties they faced in the future. Even so, he wasn't worried. Having Sierra in his life made him appreciate each day and the small blessings that came his way.

"Beau?" Aunt Sarah called from the kitchen.

"You summoned?" he said, when he entered the room.

"I told your father not to stand so close to the turkey fryer, but he refuses to listen."

It wasn't like Aunt Sarah to be short-tempered and Beau suspected her frazzled mood had to do with Tuf not being present on a day meant for family gatherings. She had to be hurting that her youngest son continued to keep his distance from the family.

"Please go out there and say something before your father knocks the fryer over and burns down the house."

When Beau stepped onto the patio he found his father and Jordan bundled in their winter coats, hugging each other. "Hey, Dad." The cozy couple broke apart. "Aunt Sarah says you're standing too close to the fryer."

"I've been the designated turkey fryer for the past ten years. I know what I'm doing."

"She's worried one of you might get burned."

"My sister worries too much."

Jordan moved away from the fryer, tugging Joshua's coat sleeve until he followed. "Beau," Jordan spoke. "Have you and Sierra set a wedding date?"

"Not yet." If Beau had any say in the matter, they'd marry right now in a civil ceremony at Thunder Ranch, but Sierra wanted to remain engaged for a little while. He suspected she worried that he'd change his mind about marrying her, but he was a determined man and sooner or later she'd figure out he wasn't going anywhere without her. "Are you in a hurry to see us married off?"

"We were hoping you'd wed sooner rather than later," his father said.

"Why?" Beau grinned. "Do you two want to tie the knot?"

His father's expression turned pensive.

Worried he'd overstepped his bounds, Beau mumbled, "Sorry. I didn't mean to—"

Jordan held out her left hand, showing off a small diamond solitaire on her ring finger.

"You got engaged. Congratulations."

"No," his father said. "We got married."

Shocked, Beau asked, "When?"

"On the way home from South Dakota. We stayed the night in Billings while the rest of you returned to Roundup."

Jordan smiled up at Joshua. "We'd rather not tell anyone we're married until after you and Sierra tie the knot."

"Why?"

"I want all the excitement and focus to be on your wedding," Jordan said.

That might be difficult when the Harts and the Adams were procreating like rabbits. Beau was betting a new baby would be born every year for the next decade.

"As soon as you and Sierra are married, Jordan's moving into the house with me," his father said.

"Joshua and I thought you wouldn't mind living in the apartment above the diner until you and Sierra decide where you want to settle permanently."

"Sure. I guess that would be okay." Beau hadn't given any thought to where he and Sierra would live. It made sense for them to stay in town since Sierra ran the diner.

Feeling chilled from standing outside without a coat, Beau pointed to the fryer. "Watch yourself. Aunt Sarah's stressed out today."

"Every holiday is hard on her without Tuf," his father said.

When Beau entered the house all hell had broken loose. Aunt Sarah and Earl were racing around the kitchen covering the food dishes with aluminum foil.

"What happened?" Beau asked.

"It's Flynn. Her water broke. We're going to the hospital," Aunt Sarah said.

Beau rushed to the family room where Colt was helping Flynn into her coat.

"Did anyone tell Ace?" Beau asked.

"The kids ran out to the barn to get him," Colt said.

A moment later, the front door opened. "Where is she?" Ace yelled.

"I'm right here, Ace." Flynn waddled into the hall.

"It's too early," Ace insisted, his eyes pleading with his wife.

"Calm down, honey." Aunt Sarah grabbed her jacket from the hall closet. "Women have babies every day. Flynn will be fine."

"Where's my purse?" Flynn asked.

Earl retrieved the purse from the floor next to the couch in the family room and took it to his daughter.

"Thanks, Dad." She kissed his cheek. "Don't look so worried."

"What about all the food?" Beau asked when everyone put on their coats. His question startled the group and all eyes turned to Aunt Sarah.

"Earl and I will go with Flynn and Ace. The rest of you stay here and eat. We'll keep you posted from the hospital."

Ace ushered Flynn out the door, and Earl and Aunt Sarah followed. The rest of the family stood in the hallway staring at one another. The back door opened and Beau's father yelled, "The deep-fried turkey's ready!"

The pronouncement set the women in motion and the kids raced back into the family room. The men retired to the living room to pour themselves a drink and wager whether or not Flynn would have a girl or a boy.

Beau and Sierra were left standing in the hallway alone. He gathered her in his arms. "Are you ready to join this family? There's never a dull moment around here."

"You and all the chaos your family brings is exactly what I need in my life." Sierra caressed his cheek. "I love you, Beau."

He kissed Sierra, trying to convey without words how much she meant to him. When they broke apart, he said, "I'm going to need a lot more practice doing that."

"Doing what?"

"Showing you how much I love you."

This time Sierra initiated the kiss, and when it ended, she whispered, "I don't need to look into your eyes to *see* how much you love me. I feel it right here." She pressed Beau's hand to her heart, which pounded hard and steady.

"I know what I want for Christmas."

"What's that?" she asked.

"For you to set a wedding date." He nuzzled her neck.

"I might even do better than that."

"Oh?"

"If you play your cards right, Mr. Adams, you just might wake up Christmas morning in my bed."

"Now that would be a Christmas present this cowboy would never forget."

* * * * *

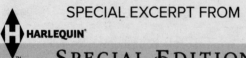
She rose from her seat of slab rock. "We'd probably better
be going. We still have one more hiking trail to cover before
we hit another set of campgrounds."

While she gathered up her partially eaten lunch, Sawyer
left his seat and walked over to the edge of the bluff.

"This is an incredible view," he said. "From this distance,
the saguaros look like green needles stuck in a sandpile."

She looked over to see the strong north wind was hitting
him in the face and molding his uniform against his muscled
body. The sight of his imposing figure etched against the
blue sky and desert valley caused her breath to hang in her
throat.

She walked over to where he stood, then took a cautious
step closer to the ledge in order to peer down at the view
directly below.

"I never get tired of it," she admitted. "There are a few
Native American ruins not far from here. We'll hike by
those before we finish our route."

A hard gust of wind suddenly whipped across the ledge and caused Vivian to sway on her feet. Sawyer swiftly caught her by the arm and pulled her back to his side.

"Careful," he warned. "I wouldn't want you to topple over the edge."

With his hand on her arm and his sturdy body shielding her from the wind, she felt very warm and protected. And for one reckless moment, she wondered how it would feel to slip her arms around his lean waist, to rise up on the tips of her toes and press her mouth to his. Would his lips taste as good as she imagined?

Shaken by the direction of her runaway thoughts, she tried to make light of the moment. "That would be awful," she agreed. "Mort would have to find you another partner."

"Yeah, and she might not be as cute as you."

With a little laugh of disbelief, she stepped away from his side. "Cute? I haven't been called that since I was in high school. I'm beginning to think you're nineteen instead of twenty-nine."

He pulled a playful frown at her. "You prefer your men to be old and somber?"

"I prefer them to keep their minds on their jobs," she said staunchly. "And you are not *my* man."

His laugh was more like a sexy promise.

"Not yet."

Don't miss
A Ranger for Christmas *by Stella Bagwell,*
available December 2018 wherever
Harlequin® Special Edition books and ebooks are sold.

www.Harlequin.com

HSEEXP1118

H HARLEQUIN®

SPECIAL EDITION

Life, Love and Family

Save **$1.00**

on the purchase of ANY
Harlequin® Special Edition book.

Available wherever books are sold,
including most bookstores, supermarkets,
drugstores and discount stores.

✂

Save $1.00

on the purchase of any Harlequin® Special Edition book.

Coupon valid until February 28, 2019.
Redeemable at participating outlets in the U.S. and Canada only.
Limit one coupon per customer.

`52616105`

`5  65373 00076 2   (8100)0 12397`

® and ™ are trademarks owned and used by the trademark owner and/or its licensee.

© 2018 Harlequin Enterprises Limited

HSECOUP04506

Looking for more satisfying love stories
with community and family at their core?

Check out **Harlequin® Special Edition**
and **Love Inspired®** books!

 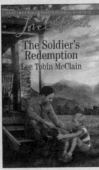

New books available every month!

CONNECT WITH US AT:

Facebook.com/groups/HarlequinConnection

 Facebook.com/HarlequinBooks

 Twitter.com/HarlequinBooks

 Instagram.com/HarlequinBooks

 Pinterest.com/HarlequinBooks

ReaderService.com

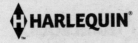

**ROMANCE WHEN
YOU NEED IT**

HFGENRE2018

Love Harlequin romance?

DISCOVER.

Be the first to find out about promotions, news and exclusive content!

Facebook.com/HarlequinBooks

Twitter.com/HarlequinBooks

Instagram.com/HarlequinBooks

Pinterest.com/HarlequinBooks

ReaderService.com

EXPLORE.

Sign up for the Harlequin e-newsletter and download a free book from any series at **TryHarlequin.com.**

CONNECT.

Join our Harlequin community to share your thoughts and connect with other romance readers!
Facebook.com/groups/HarlequinConnection

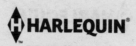

HARLEQUIN®

**ROMANCE WHEN
YOU NEED IT**

HSOCIAL2018